THE WRAITH KING

JULIETTE CROSS

For Jessen

ACKNOWLEDGMENTS

Deep gratitude goes to my beta readers for this project—
Cherie Lord, Malia Kramer, and Marielle Brown. And a special
thank you to Crystal Cook and Jessen Judice whose insight went
above and beyond in helping Goll and Una's story come to life.
Thank you all so much.

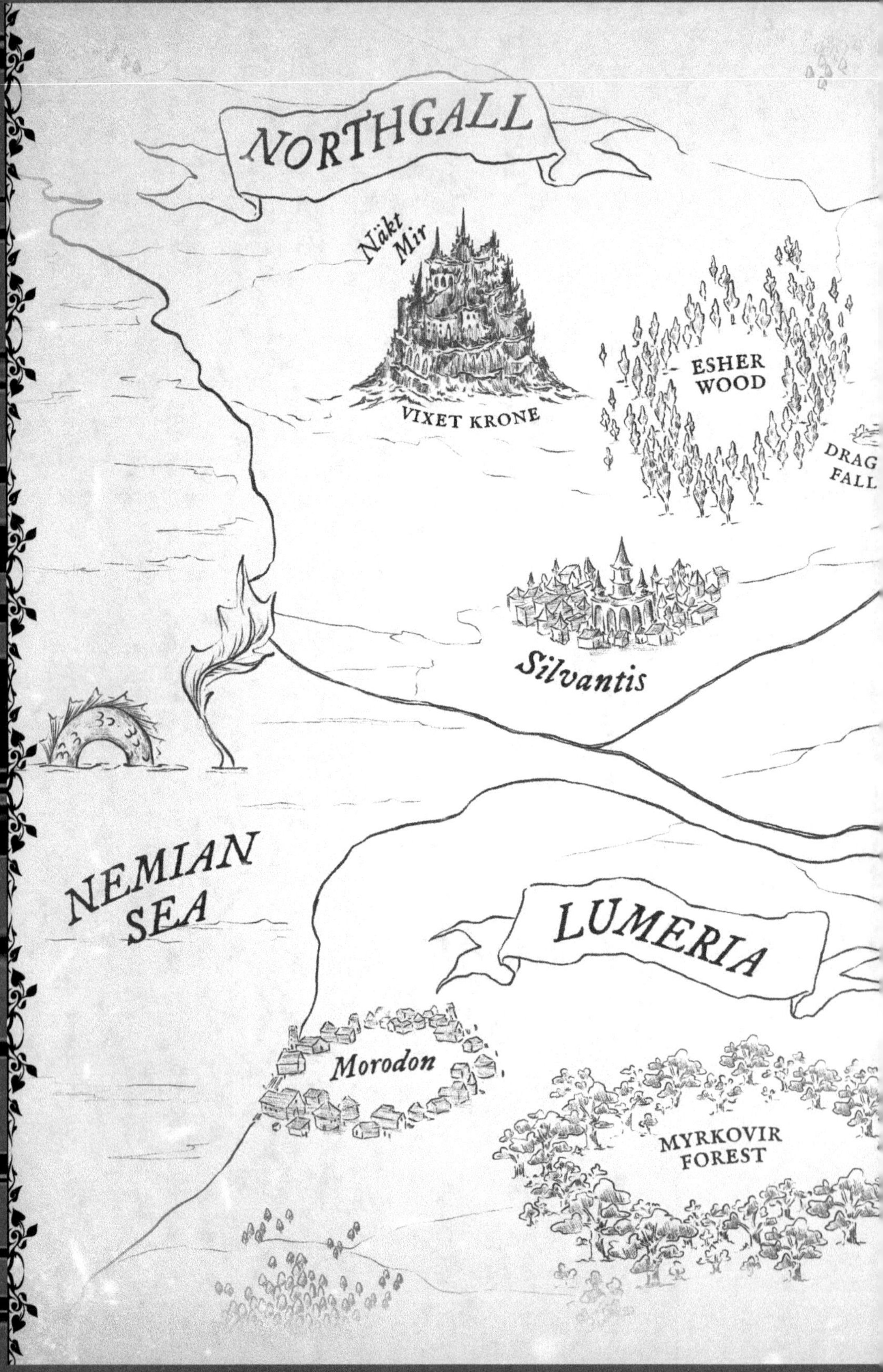

NORTHGALL
Näkt Mir
VIXET KRONE
ESHER WOOD
DRAG FALL
Silvantis
NEMIAN SEA
LUMERIA
Morodon
MYRKOVIR FOREST

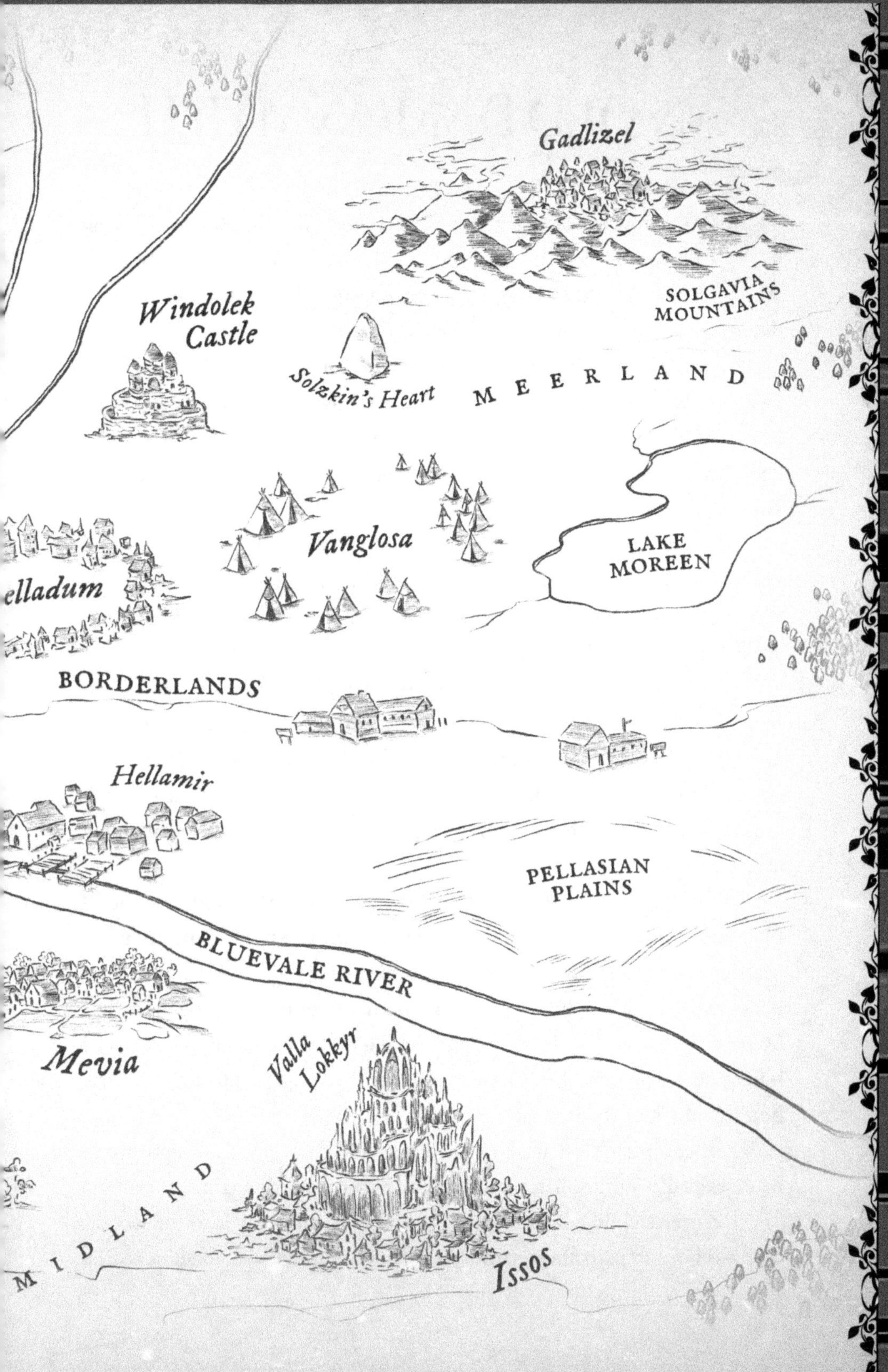

Gadlizel
SOLGAVIA MOUNTAINS
Windolek Castle
Solzkin's Heart
MEERLAND
Vanglosa
LAKE MOREEN
elladum
BORDERLANDS
Hellamir
PELLASIAN PLAINS
BLUEVALE RIVER
Mevia
Valla Lokkyr
MIDLAND
Issos

AN OLD DEMON MYTH

Näkt, the god of night, once saw a beautiful fae maiden picking flowers under the moonlight. Her name was Zarrah, and he fell instantly in love. He knelt before her, promised his eternal devotion, and offered his hand. She took it.

He flew her into the night sky and showed her the wondrous heavens, the deep black, and the expanse of the world as he saw it. She loved him back. In the meadow where he first saw her, she made a soft bed of moonflowers, night phlox, and primrose. Every night, he returned and loved her there.

When Zarrah became pregnant, she wanted time to commune with her unborn child, to pay tribute to the goddess of the wood for a blessing. She traveled to the woodlands she'd once called home, promising Näkt she'd return before their babe was born. He waited for her.

While Zarrah was away, the moon goddess Lumera saw Näkt bathing in a steaming pool and desired him greatly. She wanted a fine lover to make her beauty shine brighter. But Näkt denied her. That night, she covered the moon with clouds and seduced him in the dark in the guise as his Zarrah. She brought him to pleasure many times until he fell asleep in exhaustion.

That same night, Zarrah returned home, full with child. She found Näkt and Lumera naked and entwined beneath the moonlight upon the meadow bed she'd made. Her heart broke. Her pain was so great, she burst and splintered into glistening shards, freeing her baby from her body in that moment of agony. Zarrah then cast the broken pieces of her body and spirit into the heavens to always remind Näkt of the beauty he'd forsaken, of the love he'd lost.

In complete despair, Näkt fled into the dark sky, wanting only to be close to Zarrah's spirit, never to return to the earth again.

Zarrah's child, a girl, fully grown at birth, ran away into the woods. She was born in pain and sorrow, her spirit consumed with loneliness. She was also the daughter of night and sought the darkness to comfort her. So, she found the deepest cave and hid herself from the world. Then she wept.

It was Vix, the god of the earth, who heard her faint cries. Through the stones of his mountain home, her sadness called to him. He found her deep underground, where he cradled her in his arms, then carried her to his hearth and home in the earth, whispering words of compassion and kindness.

The first day, she would not stop weeping, so he rocked her in his arms and let her grieve. The second day, he offered her water in his large cupped palm, and she drank it. On the third day, he offered her bread from his hand, and she ate it.

"What is your name?" he asked her.

"Mizrah," she answered. Her name was a word in an ancient tongue that meant both misery and vengeance.

Vix smiled. "It is a strong name for a strong spirit."

Mizrah stopped weeping. On the fourth day, and every day thereafter, she fell more deeply in love with Vix. He devoted his life to her, warming her dark soul. Together, they begat many children—the demons of fire, earth, shadow, and beast, spreading their magick into the world.

Many, many years later, Vix held Mizrah on her deathbed, for she was not immortal. As she neared death, he cradled her close and carried her to his dragon. Upon dragon back, with her in his arms, they flew into the starry night so that she might be close to her mother and her father. There, he whispered a promise as her spirit left this world.

"One day, my love, Lumera will pay for her betrayal. Her people will not shine so bright. Her descendants will fall, and ours will rise. Then will enter your reign…the era of night."

And so this story has been told to the dark fae children,
to the generations of night, as they wait for their turn to rule the world.

PROLOGUE

Una

rip. Drip. Drip.

D I shuddered as a stinging wave of pain sharpened beneath my shoulder blades where my wings had been cut from my body. Curled into a ball on my side, I pressed my cheek to the dank stone floor and shivered. I bit my lip to keep quiet. I didn't want to bring them back.

A trickle of blood trailed from the open wounds in my back, down the sides of my ribcage to the dungeon floor. They'd torn open the back of my gown, the tattered remnants covering only parts of my body.

It didn't matter. I didn't care. Only the pain mattered at the moment—and trying to survive.

I huffed out a shaky breath. The only light came from the flickering of a single torch near the arched entrance to this cell block. Whenever the shadows disappeared and the cell grew brighter, that meant one of them was coming for me. That's why I dreaded the rhythmic bootsteps of one of my jailers and clung to the shadowy dark.

My body shook with another ripple of pain, a numbing sensation beginning to overtake me. Min said that happened when one was close to death. The spirit left the body a little at a time.

I'd been put in this cage and dragged out so many times by those foul creatures. Tongueless and earless, horned and clawed, they followed someone's orders to poke and prod me with demon-forged weapons, their dark magick piercing through my skin, tearing at my core.

I'd never see home again. I was going to die here. Soon.

A sob ripped from my throat. I sniffed and stifled it, tears slipping down my face.

"Shh, shhh, *basta met*. Shhh."

It was the hag in the cell next to mine. She'd kept to the shadows since I'd been in this infernal hell. She shuffled closer across the stone floor now, while my own agony kept me still. She reached her hand through the bars and brushed my filthy hair away from my face.

"*Sorka, lillet.*" She spoke in demon tongue, brushing my hair and whispering softly. "*Ora est miyett, lillet.*"

"I don't understand." My voice cracked, my throat raw from screaming.

Finally, I turned my head so that I could see the occupant of the cell next door for the first time. She was nothing but skin and bones. Her dark hair hung limply around a withered face. But her eyes shone with a hue I didn't expect—the deepest shade of purple.

My gaze skimmed along her shoulders and found no wings. Hers might've been cut off like mine, though she had no horns either. Her pointed ears were small and delicate, not tall and pronounced like most dark fae.

But why would she be speaking in demon tongue?

She held a clay cup through the bars. When I reached a hand up to take the cup, a sharp pain twinged from the wounds in my back.

"Ah!" I cried out and shrank into myself.

"Shhh." She lifted my head and urged me to drink. I did. The filthy water was gritty with soil and smelled foul, but it was heavenly to my parched throat. I slurped it down, gagging only once before swallowing the rest.

She nudged me to lay down and continued to pet my hair, pushing the tangled mess away from my face.

Her small act of kindness and gentle words sparked a wave of grief mixed with gratitude. "Thank you," I croaked softly, wishing I could use my magick to bless her with a healing balm.

Once again, I closed my eyes and willed my goddess-given magick to come to me, to give me the healing power I so desperately needed.

But not a spark. No distant hum of buzzing energy in my blood. Nothing. It was gone.

I lay still, mourning the loss of my most precious gifts—my fae power to heal and my beautiful wings.

That seemed the purpose of those foul creatures—ripping magick from every light fae they found as punishment for merely existing. Hatred and a sick kind of satisfaction had reeked from their hollow eyes as they'd tortured me.

The hag's sibilant whisper shimmered like an ethereal ghost in the dark with words that trembled along a hum of power. Magick?

I thought she was a hag, a creature bereft of any meaningful power. But what I felt vibrating between the bars separating us was significant. More than a spark, it was potent and strong.

Then I heard something shatter.

I peered through the bars where she held up a sharp piece of the clay cup. She pressed it into her wrist and sliced into her skin, all the time whispering indecipherable words.

"No. Don't," I argued, though my protest was faint and weak, my body exhausted and my mind listless.

She dragged the jagged piece of clay up her arm, still speaking in that foreign language, then slipped both her arms through the bars. While holding my hair back with a gentle but firm press to the top of my head, she dipped her fingers in her own blood and began tracing something on my forehead.

Dark fae often cast charms over someone with demon runes, spelling them with magick and demon sign.

Perhaps it was the fact that they'd taken everything from me and killed whatever will I had left to live, but I couldn't fight her while she whispered in the dark and cast her spell with her own blood.

"*Ora est kel ohira. Ora est kel näkt los. Ora est meheem.*"

Then I felt it. Her magick. It vibrated and pulsed through my blood, giving me new vigor. It was powerful and jarring, pulling a whimper from my throat. Her hands shook as she continued going over and over the signs on my forehead with trembling fingers.

"*Ora est kel ohira. Ora est kel näkt los. Ora est meheem.*"

She gasped and collapsed to the dungeon floor. I lifted up onto my elbow and crawled closer. "Old one?"

She didn't answer. I looked around for the bucket of water she'd fed me from.

"Let me help you."

Shaky fingers touched my chin, guiding my face to look at her. The dim flicker of torch-flame darkened the hollows of her eyes and cheeks. Even though life had been unkind to her, especially now near the end, I could see she'd once been lovely, her dark purple eyes glittering with goodness.

"I'm sorry," I added, holding her hand with one of mine, feeling utterly useless without my own healing magick. "I wish I could help."

Her mouth tipped up in a feeble smile before she spoke in my language. "You are the destiny. You are the dark lady." Her dialect was perfect Issosian. "You are for him."

As her eyes grew glassy and her spirit left her body, I knew those were the words she'd been repeating over and over in demon tongue.

"*No.*" I closed my eyes and gripped her lifeless hand, tears pouring yet again. But for once, they weren't for me or what I'd lost, but for this poor, sweet fae of my homeland who'd died in the dark, whispering nonsense and trying to care for a stranger.

Then my gut clenched. The sound of bootsteps drew near as the cell grew brighter.

They are coming.

Goll

The wights were hungry tonight. Desperate groans rumbled louder than their normal low murmur and hissing. Their skeletal fingers clawed at the stone wall of their pit, making that grating *click–click* sound.

Sometimes, it felt like the sound actually penetrated my skull and scraped me on the inside, driving me slowly insane.

I looked away from the pit, wishing my vision wasn't so clear, even in the near pitch-black of the dungeon beneath Näkt Mir. Pushing to my feet, I then wandered to the left of my cage. The chain attached to my right ankle clattered as I dragged the heavy links across the stone floor.

The chain served no purpose but to add a layer of humiliation to my imprisonment. The warded iron bars were the true barrier holding me within this confined space in the heart of my father's guarded keep.

My father, the Demon King of Northgall, held court a few stories above this wasteland of death and bones. His courtiers, the most appalling sycophants adorned in leather, lace, and malevolence danced to his every tune somewhere above me in his throne room of obsidian and glass.

He kept me, his only son, as his prized prisoner in the deepest, darkest pit of his realm. No one cared. No one would come for me.

My mother would have had my father not beheaded her then cut out her heart for committing adultery when I was ten.

Mother was the only one who would've faced my father's wrath to try to free me from this cage. She was the only one who could keep his paranoia in check. Before he so brutally murdered her, of course.

Ever since Father's treasured oracle Vayla envisioned that I would one day usurp him and take his crown, I have been kept in this filthy, maddening hell. The only reason he let me live is because Vayla warned that if he killed me, or even gave the order, then he'd pay with his life.

I wondered what he'd done to Vayla for her prophetic vision of his demise. He'd have not taken kindly to such news.

So here I was. Living. Breathing. Counting the agonizing days.

Father might think I have accepted my fate to waste away in this cell for eternity, going insane with monotony and isolation, but he was wrong.

Leaping upward, I grasped two bars along the top of my cage and began my routine, pulling my weight up then lowering in a slow, even pace. I focused on the tempo of my heartbeat, the flex of my muscles, and the mild pain that reminded me I was alive.

My complexion had faded to a pale ashen gray rather than the deeper shade of a healthy wraith fae. But as long as I was breathing, there was a sliver of hope that I would get out of here.

The warded bars blocked my magick, but I felt it sizzling under my skin, itching to be used, whispering through my blood. During the past fortnight, I'd felt a sudden quickening of powerful energy through my veins. The melodic refrain told me my time was almost here.

I lifted myself repeatedly, finally reaching the point where I'd pushed past the pain when suddenly there was the clang of the iron door opening at the top of the stairs.

Feeding time.

The wights erupted into ravening groans, knowing what that sound meant. The bone-keepers were hauling some poor mortal down to their doom.

Gaunt arms with exposed bone and fingers covered in pasty gray skin reached up toward the platform suspended high over the pit. The black-stained hook where they'd lower the victim dangled freely, waiting for fresh meat.

I realized long ago that my father housed me here next to his pit of foul wights, his army of bone soldiers who obeyed only him, for a reason. Putting me within sight where he'd feed victims to his death horde would eat away at my sanity.

The two hulking bone-keepers were clad in leather tunics, their ears severed. Their tongues were as well. My father spoke to his guards through mind alone and kept them deaf and mute to any order but his own. They wouldn't hear the anguish and despairing cries of their captives, only the demonic voice of their king.

I was glad the gods hadn't bestowed on me the gift of neklia, to raise and use the dead as my army. But I'd been given the remarkable power of a zephilim, able to wield feyfire with a single word. Not that it did me any good behind these wards.

The bone-keepers hauled a sack between them with the wights' dinner struggling inside. My pointed ears pricked at the muffled sound, for it was…feminine.

Scowling, I leaped toward the bars, gripping them tightly. They'd never fed a female to the wights. The victims thrown into the pit were alleged traitors to my father, wraith fae who'd wronged him or light fae captured near the border. But never once a female, not even a magickless hag, not even they were fed to the wights.

"Let me go," came the soft cry within the canvas sack as one of the guards set it on the platform above the pit.

My gut clenched at the desperate plea, but nothing prepared me for what happened when they pulled the sack open and she fell to the platform floor.

A guttural groan trembled up my throat at the shimmering light filling the room, haloed around the beautiful creature—battered and bruised—whose slender arms were now held tightly by the foul bone-keepers. When she twisted to try to get away, I saw an open gash on her back through her torn gown. Her wings had been ripped from her body. My grip tightened on the bars.

Her skin was as smooth and white as the marble carved from the northernmost mountains of Solgavia. Her white hair was soiled and dirty, strands falling loose around her fear-brightened face. Her gossamer gown was tattered and torn.

A delicate light fae female. She was young, just a girl. An innocent. My gut clenched at the cruelty of it.

When she turned her angelic face down toward the pit, dawning horror washed over her expression.

"*No!*" The first word I'd spoken since my imprisonment scraped raw and true out of my throat.

My magick replied with a fervent ripple through my body, bashing against the wards of the cage, relishing the spark to life.

The bone-keepers forced her onto the hook dangling above the platform and tied her to it with tattered ropes. Rather than fight them, she grasped hold of the hook, as if this instrument might be her savior.

Frantically, she kept glancing from the guards to the pit below. One of the bone-keepers pressed a lever, and her slow descent began. She cried out in alarm, the sound piercing through my flesh and bones, snaking through my body like an invading viper. An ethereal whip lashed at me to act. *Now.*

"No," I repeated, burning with rage, feeding it to my magick, allowing the power that lived within my royal blood to burst forth in torrents. The magick listened and relished the aggressive fury, devouring the darkness that lived inside me, kept bound for far too long.

A dark fae's power was a sentient, dominant force that craved to be free. And mine burst from within.

My muscles bulged as I poured my power into the iron, breaking the chains with surprising ease. It was as if the wards were never a barrier for me at all. I'd only needed a catalyst strong enough to set me free.

My gaze riveted on the frightened faeling, her slender arms clinging helplessly to the hook lowering her to her death.

Just as the lower edge of the hook reached the frantic hands of the hissing and groaning wights, I roared with rage.

An explosion of red light sliced through the gloom as the wards broke, and then the iron bars bent to my will with frightening ease. I leaped through the opening of the bars and bounded toward the pit.

She cried out as wights pulled at her tattered gown, clawing at her bare legs. Her mouth opened in a soundless scream, while I roared yet again.

Charging across the dungeon, I swiped my hand out at the creatures that were reaching for the hook to try and pull her down. Feyfire poured from my body. A wave of euphoric pleasure washed over me as the flames incinerated a dozen wights into dust. The dark victory filled me with an ecstasy I'd never known before.

The girl looked up from the hook where she clung, her clear violet gaze full of desperation and fear. I soared over the pit and onto the hook, swinging us like a pendulum.

I breathed a word and disintegrated the ropes binding her, then hauled her into my arms. She gasped but didn't struggle as I walked on top of the groaning piles of wights trying to pull us down. My steel-heeled boots cracked craniums and arm bones as I used the wights as stepping-stones to lift us out of the pit.

All the while, I gripped her closely against my chest, careful not to scrape her silken skin with my claws. I bounded up and over the wights, back onto the gritty stone floor of the dungeon. Her slender arms clung tightly around my neck.

Before the two bone-keepers realized what was happening, I whispered, "*Etheline,*" and waved my hand.

Flame leaped from my fingers in a red stream, incinerating them into dust. Power poured through my body, like a forgotten river that found its way back through a dormant valley.

It was sublime.

Following the shadowy passages I hadn't seen in decades, I hurried down the deserted hallways winding away from the castle. The girl shivered in my arms, her teeth chattering. Hoisting her higher and trying to avoid the wounds in her back, I held her close and slipped through the shadows quietly, knowing the best way out.

An odd sense of rightness swept over me. In defiance of my father, I was going to escape his pit of death. And I was bringing one of his poor tortured creatures with me.

The scrape of boots on stone from around the next bend of the darkened corridor made me freeze. The fae girl sucked in a breath then went quiet, sensing the danger. Quickly, I spun back the other way. There was a small alcove not far from the main cell block where I'd been kept. I'd seen bone-keepers walk in and out of it for decades.

I ducked inside the alcove, finding a small cell without bars, tables piled with all manner of sharp instruments. Some of them still stained with the dark red blood of light fae.

"Don't look," I whispered close to her ear. I didn't need her screaming at the sight of blood and giving us away.

She tucked her face against my shoulder, while I pressed my back to the wall beside the entrance. The footsteps drew closer.

I set the girl down. She went quietly onto her bare feet then I nudged her into the far corner, away from the entrance. Snatching a particularly sharp and short blade from the table, I pressed close to the entrance, out of sight.

The boots pounded closer, a single set of them. As soon as a hulking frame passed the entrance to the alcove, I leaped from the shadows, gripped his horn and jerked his head to the side, then easily sliced through his throat. He was so surprised, he barely fought me. By the time he did, it was too late. I sliced a second time, so deep that I partly decapitated him. He fell with a weighty *thunk*.

He wore a heavy fur cloak, apparently one of the guards who either roamed the woods to seek out more victims for the dungeon or who watched the closest exit of the keep. He might've even been the one to capture the moon fae girl inside the alcove.

Growling, I straddled the glassy-eyed guard, his blue blood leaking onto the cobblestone. Then I cut the lacing clasps of the cloak near his throat and pulled, shoving his giant body with my boot so he rolled off of it. I tucked the blade into the waist of my loose-fitting trousers.

When I stepped back into the alcove, I heard nothing at all. For a moment, I thought the girl had run away in fear.

"Fae girl?" I asked dumbly, not knowing what to call her.

I sensed movement from the other corner farther away, then she stepped out of the shadows, still shivering, her eyes on the bleeding guard behind me.

I held out the cloak. "I know it smells foul, but you'll freeze to death once we get outside."

From the scent of snow on the cloak, I knew it was winter. She stepped quickly toward me and allowed me to wrap it around her, the hem falling to her ankles.

"I'll carry you." I pointed at her bare feet. "You have no shoes and will slow us down."

She merely nodded, pulling the dirty fur cloak tighter to her body. I scooped her up, stepped over the dead guard and stalked swiftly back toward the exit of the keep.

She said nothing, still shivering in my arms. The long corridor leading toward the exit was empty. Likely because I'd killed the guard meant to patrol this area.

As we came into the final passageway, I heard the slowly marching steps of a guard near the back of the keep. I knew there was an exit nearby, because I'd been morbidly fascinated with the dungeon when I was a little wraithling, exploring where I shouldn't.

I followed my instincts now, peering down the long passageway where it ended. Between two flickering torches on the wall a stone staircase spiraled upward.

That was it, the exit.

I kept to the shadows. I was about to set her on her feet so I could grab the knife in my waistband to kill the approaching guard, but the guard walked right past the stairwell and kept going, never even glancing our way. When the footsteps receded altogether, I hurried across the corridor and up the spiral stairs.

The fae girl was light in my arms as I continued upward. Halfway there, I stopped to listen. I heard no one above or below, so I rushed up the final spiral and onto a landing where there was an iron door.

I set her down, cursing myself, for there was likely a key. But when I gripped the latch and pushed, it swung open easily. Cold wind gusted inward. The girl gasped but still said nothing.

One probably only needed a key to enter from the outside. At the moment, I didn't care. All I knew was that freedom awaited us. Without a word, I swept her back into my arms and marched out into the snow, tiny flakes falling from the gray sky, and hurried toward Esher Wood.

I carried the faeling at a brisk pace into the snow-dusted forest of esher trees. For a while, there was only the sound of my heavy boots crunching in the snow and the light wind knocking naked limbs together in the boughs above us.

As we wound farther into the woods, I lamented that it was deep winter. The esher trees, bare of their blue leaves, resembled gray-trunked ghosts standing solemn as we passed and offering little cover.

"Thank you," came the soft voice of the fae in my arms, husky from her ordeal in the dungeon.

Frowning, I replied, "Don't thank me yet," I answered in high fae, having learned it from a young age since it was the common tongue across the kingdoms. "We have a way to go."

And I wasn't sure where to take her.

Her injuries were severe. We wouldn't make it to the Borderlands for days if I had to carry her. But who could I trust in the closest city of Silvantis? My one true friend was Keffa and he'd been taken prisoner by my father at the same time as I had.

I needed a place to hide myself while I planned what to do next. There was the baker Ogalvet who lived on the edge of Silvantis. He never seemed to be a fan of my father. He'd likely help me and find a way to get the girl back to her people.

"My name is Una," she said, voice quivering.

I kept my eyes on the trail, glancing back over my shoulder to be sure we weren't being followed, not in the mood for conversation. I thanked the gods that it was snowing, covering our tracks as we went.

"You're a wraith fae."

I continued on, ignoring her.

"Why were you in that dungeon?"

I didn't owe this girl anything, least of all the truth that cut me so deeply.

But she was a puzzle, piquing my curiosity. Had the guards found her at the Borderlands and abducted her?

"How did the bone-keepers capture a young, moon fae female like you?" I asked.

She lifted her head, her gaze riveted to my face. She stared with open fascination, but no fear.

"I was caught near Dragul Falls."

I stopped suddenly, scowling down at her. "What in all the hells were you doing so close to the palace?"

Her violet eyes widened, but her gaze remained steady and calm. "I was looking for something."

"Something so important it was worth losing your life?" I snapped.

"Yes," she answered coolly.

"Alone?"

She dipped her chin in a stiff nod.

I shook my head on a sigh. "Stupid girl."

She turned her face toward the path.

Now in the afternoon light, I noted what I had first thought was a bloody cut on her forehead was actually demon runes. They were smeared and illegible, written in blood beneath her hair. I wondered what kind of horrific spell the bone-keepers might've been commanded to put there. She didn't seem to be suffering in any way other than her physical injuries. The spell must not have worked.

She whimpered when my splayed hand on her lower back slid upward. I shifted her gently, higher in my arms, keeping my hand around her slim waist to avoid her wounds.

I walked on in silence, carrying her deeper into the woods, no sound but my heavy footsteps crunching in the snow.

"They didn't know," she murmured softly.

"What are you talking about?"

"My family. They didn't know I left, so it wasn't like they let me go off alone."

"But you did it anyway."

"It was *important*," she emphasized with a bit of steel in her soft voice that drew my gaze to her scowling face.

I huffed, wanting to laugh at her foolishness. "And look where that got you, faeling."

Distracted for a fleeting second, I didn't hear the whistle of the arrow until it was too late.

It struck the left side of my chest, painfully close to my heart, the force of it jerking my body backward. She screamed, falling to her knees beside me, the filthy cloak slipping from her shoulders.

"Let go of her, you fucking wraith bastard," came the deep voice of a male.

Just as I pushed myself up, the arrow still jutting from my chest, a fair-haired male fae in sapphire and gold regalia grabbed Una around the waist and flew backward, his white wings shimmering in the gloom. He carried her several feet away, swirling snow into the air.

Growling, I shifted up, only to be pierced by arrows twice more in the right thigh and hip.

"Stop it, Baelynn! You're hurting him!"

The male fae held her back with both arms, his rage furiously aimed at me as a guard of at least twelve fae males uniformed in blue and gold armor appeared out of the shadows. A royal guard of Issos.

"Hurting him?" The one called Baelynn shouted, now holding Una by the shoulders and inspecting her with a fearsome expression. He visibly flinched when he saw her wings were gone. "We must get you home, sister," he hissed quietly.

Sister? My mind reeled. She was the royal princess of Issos, Tiarrialuna, the only daughter of Connall Hartstone, High King of Lumeria. I knew this because it was drilled into me by my father to know our enemies and know them well.

"Not before you help *him*," she yelled. Tears streaked down her face as she tried to free herself from her brother's grip. Tears for me?

A strange charge rippled through my flesh as I knelt in the snow, pulling the arrows from my body, one by one.

"He captured you, Una. What are you saying?"

"He *freed* me, Baelynn. I would have died without him."

The fae prince looked over her shoulder at me, still scowling. The animosity radiating from him and his guard was a palpable whip in the air. Six of his guards had arrows nocked and aimed at me. I could've incinerated them all, but I held still. Some instinct whispering from the place where my magick lived kept me calm and immobile.

"Go home, girl," I told her, still on my knees. "You don't belong here."

Una stared at where I'd been hit, blue blood trickling down my chest.

"Your brother's little arrows cannot hurt me," I sneered, disdain falling from my lips.

Though I'd never met the prince, and currently our kingdoms were at a truce, he was my enemy. It was fortunate he did not know my identity.

"Come, Una," he said, giving her no choice as he urged her toward the fae guard, closing in.

One of them with dark blue wings and black hair stepped forward with a gold cloak and draped it over her shoulders. He gripped her shoulders and whispered softly, "You are safe now."

She nodded, as if she knew him well and welcomed his comfort.

The small exchange tore a hole open inside of me, one that wanted to devour and maim and crush. My lips curled back, revealing my fangs, which the black-haired fae noticed.

She turned toward me, a wisp of white hair escaping the hood of her cloak.

The fae guard fell in around her to form a shield. Then her brother lifted her into his arms, his wide wings beating hard as he lifted off into the sky. The rest followed, rising fast and hard.

That was how they'd come so far into our territory without being seen. And surely how the princess had dropped out of the sky into Northgall. Only something had happened and she'd been captured.

I watched her leave. The falling snow and billowing clouds swallowed them, blurring their figures, but I caught a flash of violet as she looked back over her brother's shoulder.

Then they were gone.

Rising to my feet, my wounds a mere ache with no pain, a new flame burned white-hot around my heart. This flame was for my father.

I smiled, a twisted sort of joy burning through my soul. He'd put me in that infernal gorge of hell, expecting me to rot and waste away into death. But his spiteful brutality was not strong enough to kill me.

For whatever reason, the god Vix gave me the strength to break my father's wards and fulfill a prophecy he tried to prevent. Now more than ever, I knew my rightful path.

A soft voice and fair eyes flickered across my mind. I blinked it away.

Peering over my shoulder, I eyed the pinnacles of Näkt Mir jutting toward the winter sky, then I turned back toward the woods and walked on. Vayla was right. My path was resolute and sure—to take my father's throne.

CHAPTER 1

Five Years Later

Una

"How long has it been since he's spoken?" The burly wood fae stood opposite me, his son's bed between us.

"Three or four weeks." He stared down helplessly at his sleeping son who couldn't be more than ten years old. "My sister watches him by day when I'm at the mill." He gestured outside.

His house was on the outskirts of Issos where his mill was situated on the river. He wasn't a wealthy man, but he earned a good wage and employed others in the trade of grinding grain for the bakers of Issos.

"My sister gave him a sleeping draught before she left so he might get some proper rest." He looked again at the boy. "I do what I can, but I need to work. I need the coin to care for him."

I took a seat in the chair beside the boy's bed and held out my hand to Min, my handmaiden and dearest friend who came with me everywhere. Frowning, she handed me the healing orb.

"You don't need to explain yourself to me, sir," I told him.

He rubbed a hand through his tousled hair, his pointed ears tipped red like his cheeks, emotion coloring his face.

"I don't know how to help him," he whispered with anguish.

"We don't have a cure," I told him honestly, taking the luminous white healing orb in its iron cage from Min and set it in its holder on the table beside the boy's head. "But we've found ways to ease the pain and extend life."

Her green wings quivered at her back, something she did when nervous. Min was my lady in waiting, but also my closest friend. She didn't like leaving the palace, even heavily guarded as we were. But I simply couldn't remain holed up when news came that yet another light fae was in the throes of the Parviana Plague. My own father was in his sick bed and had not spoken for the past seven months.

I gave Min a smile of reassurance then turned to the miller. "This healing orb will help with the pain." As it had for my father the past year.

"I can't thank you enough, my lady." The miller clasped his hands together in earnest. "I can't pay much, but—"

"No need for payment," I told him. "We are all suffering while this plague sickens our loved ones." I turned back to look at the boy, brushing his bangs away from his forehead. "It's my duty to help those I can."

When I entered this one-room home, a family table for eating and two beds against the back wall for sleeping, I knew this was a humble man with little means. And I didn't care if my brother complained that I gave away valuable resources needed for soldiers in the battlefields. He could wage my father's war against the dark fae abroad while I battled this plague taking root in homes across our land.

I didn't fear catching the sickness from touching the boy. I'd been at my father's bedside ever since the plague had put him there.

"What's his name?" I cupped his cheek to find it unnaturally cold, as expected.

"Aven."

For the thousandth time, I wished I had my healing magick so that I might help him. Or at least try.

I gently lifted one of his eyelids with the pad of my finger. His green iris was ringed white, the tell-tale sign of the plague taking root. The disease now moved faster through the body than it did when my father first caught it almost two years ago. Others had caught it and died within a year. Papa still lived, though barely.

"Does Aven want to be a miller like you when he grows up?"

His father chuckled. "No. He wants to be a mason."

I patted the boy's shoulder and smiled at his father. "We always need strong builders in Issos."

"Aye," he said, his voice cracking as he stared helplessly at his frail son.

No doubt he worried that Aven wouldn't live to become a man.

"I can't thank you enough, my lady."

"I'll send someone from the palace to check on him as I can't leave very often." I stood, offering him what compassion and reassurance I could. "Hopefully, we'll have a cure soon."

That old bitter reminder that I'd once been close to finding the cure stung me hard. I'd also nearly died for it.

"I hope so too, my lady. If there is anything I—"

The wooden door to the home burst open, wood splintering. I jumped back, startled. Then my blood ran cold. Bending their horned heads and emerging into the small room were three gray-skinned wraith fae with weapons. Min screamed.

Aven's father grabbed a poker by the hearth and lunged for the first one. A giant of a beast, he grabbed the poker and jerked the miller closer, slicing a blade across his throat before dropping him to the ground.

"No!" I cried, grabbing Min's hand and glancing toward the door for my guards, my heart beating in my throat.

We'd come with twenty Issosian guards, and I hadn't heard one sound of a skirmish outside.

"Now then, princess." The killer who'd just killed Aven's father spoke in demon tongue, which I knew well. He wiped the bloodied flat of his blade on his hide trousers. "Your guards won't be coming to the rescue."

He was horrifying to behold. His four thick horns almost scraped the beams of the ceiling. His fangs protruded from his mouth. His bare arms, visible from wearing only a black vest, rippled with muscle as he flexed the clawed hand not holding the weapon.

While I'd thought the miller a large strong wood fae, he seemed a child next to this creature. Now, the poor man was dead on the floor. I glanced at Aven then back to the killer, dread speeding my pulse.

His sharp blade was curved and as long as my leg, nearly touching the floor at his other side while he examined me with a sinister grin.

I couldn't even mourn Aven's father as my mind raced to find a path to escape.

One of the other three who'd entered the home, still standing near the entrance, pointed a dagger dripping with blood at me. "How do you know it's her for certain?"

The killer stepped toward me. Min clung to my side, whimpering.

"Look at her," he said, his voice a menacing rumble. "No other moon fae female with a face like that and wings the color of night exists in all the kingdoms."

Deep fear burrowed into my bones. He was definitely here for me.

"Then grab her," said the one with the bloody dagger. "Need to move before we've got trouble."

"No!" screamed Min.

The biggest one grabbed my arm and jerked me hard. I cried out as he pushed Min aside.

Min fluttered her wings and flew at him, going for his eyes with her nails.

"No, Min, don't!" I screamed.

The killer turned and shoved his long blade straight through her stomach with frightening ease. My knees buckled and bile rose up my throat as he jerked his blade free, and my dearest friend crumpled to the floor. I didn't make a sound as she stared up, mouth agape with shock, the light in her eyes fading.

"Min!" I reached for her, but the wraith fae still gripping my arm dragged me out into the night.

I stared back in horror at Min's small body on the wood floor, a pool of crimson spreading wide on her blue tunic, her eyes glassy. Aven slept on while the healing orb beamed bright. I prayed to the goddess he wouldn't wake up alone to find his dead father and poor Min.

Finally, my own will to survive snatched me out of my stupor. I beat at the beast's arm while trying to yank free. When he hauled me closer, I slapped him across his cruel face with all my strength. His head snapped to the side, and my hand stung.

One of his comrades chuckled. I waited for the killer to kill me, too, like he had my sweet Min. Instead, he let go of my arm and seized me by the hair, arching my neck and bending my head back. I bit my lip to keep from whimpering at the pain.

He sneered in my face, his orange eyes feral and mean. "Best save the foreplay for your new master, sweetling."

"Let's get moving, Erlik," called one of the others.

"True enough." His fanged grin sent prickles along my skin. "King Xakiel is anxious to meet you."

I froze at his words, my chest tightening with cold dread.

He let my hair go and snatched both my wrists, quickly binding them together with a rope he had on his belt. Someone else instantly gagged me with a rope from behind, binding it so tight that a lock of my hair pulled painfully at my scalp.

I couldn't breathe, sucking in gulps of air through my teeth around the rope, the cord biting into the corners of my mouth. I was struggling uselessly s I tried to calm my panting breaths and grasp what was happening.

A quick glance told me there were seven of them, and they'd killed all of the king's guard who'd escorted us here, their bodies bleeding in the road. They were deep in our territory with only a few warriors. A covert operation—to abduct *me*.

Another wraith fae warrior walked out of the shadows from the side of the house leading a giant Pellasian stallion. The fae had blood-red eyes and four horns like the one called Erlik, but there were thick silver bands at the base of his horns. I knew that meant he was high ranking.

"Time is wasting," he said gruffly, mounting his stallion. "Hand her up and let's go."

They moved faster at his command. He was their leader.

The others who had entered the home were all mounted now.

When the cruel one, Erlik, lifted me roughly up to their leader, I knew my fate was sealed. All I could do was kick and writhe, trying my hardest to free myself. My wings didn't even flutter, useless as they were.

"That's enough," said the leader, hauling his hand back and swinging it hard toward my face.

I woke to being jostled roughly. I was hanging face-down across a saddle. A hand pressed to my back kept me in place.

I could see nothing but the ground speeding by in the dark, listening to the pounding of hooves and the snuffs of the winded beast carrying me. My head pounded. Whether from being upside down so long or being knocked unconscious, I wasn't sure.

After what felt like forever, the horses slowed, and the sound of hooves clacking on wood echoed around me. Rushing water gurgled nearby. We were crossing a bridge.

One of the wraith fae said something I couldn't hear. Then the voice of their leader above me growled fiercely, "Not another fucking word until we're at the Borderlands."

The horse lurched into a gallop on solid ground. I tensed my body against the jarring pace.

The Borderlands. I'd flown over them once before when I had wings that worked. When I'd foolishly flown into Northgall territory to try to find the cure for the plague to help my people.

I always wondered what had happened to that wraith fae male with the unusual eyes who'd saved me. He was noble born for certain, and I wondered what crime he'd committed to be put down in the dungeon.

Despite my protests, my father demanded recompense for the brutality I'd suffered. King Xakiel's response was to attack our northern border. It was the beginning of this long war that seemed to never end.

When my father became too sick to command his armies, Baelynn took control with ease and vigor. He'd managed to keep the fighting far away from our palace, Valla Lokkyr, and our capital city of Issos in Lumeria. I'd never felt unsafe traveling within Issos, not even to the outskirts as I had tonight. There had been no signs of the enemy anywhere close to our capital.

I still always traveled with a full guard, but that hadn't mattered against this small band of wraith warriors. They'd come with stealth by night into our city to take the daughter of the King of Issos. They must've kept vigilant watch on the palace, awaiting the perfect opportunity. And I'd given it to them.

I would become a bargaining chip to end this war. To force my brother to surrender.

My mind trailed back to Min—the way she always made me laugh and spoke with kindness to everyone. And they'd killed her so cruelly. Tears finally slipped free—for my friend and myself, for Aven and his father. For my people.

The cost of war had already starved many since food and weapon resources were sent to the front. Perhaps this was for the best. That I should sacrifice my life in order to end this war. Still, the fear of it burrowed deeply. I didn't want to die, and certainly not by the hands of my ruthless enemy.

The horses slowed, and torchlight appeared up ahead. No one spoke as our mounts trotted into an enclosure, my stomach roiling with nausea. We came to a stop. A hand gripped the back of my cloak roughly and tossed me backwards to the ground. I fell with a jolt onto a thin bed of hay, my hip jarring hard, my hands and mouth still bound.

"Get her hidden and guard her. Geylan, go get the stableman to feed the horses. Then fetch something from the tavern to tide us over. We'll eat and rest briefly then be off again. No telling how long it will be before the palace guard sends reinforcements."

"Aye," snapped one of them, marching out the open stable door.

Erlik hauled me to my feet. I stumbled, but he didn't slow down, shoving me into a small, empty stall. "Watch her," he growled to one of the other warriors as he slammed the gate closed.

I slid to the ground, pressed my back against the wooden wall, and curled my knees up, winding my bound wrists around them. Shivering from nausea and fear and shock, I kept quiet and listened.

The Borderlands separated Northgall from Lumeria, the dark and light fae territories. There were taverns and inns along this barren region between the two kingdoms where both light and dark fae traveled. They obviously kept me hidden in case there happened to be any of my own kind about.

My captors wandered close by inside the stables. I heard another voice that sounded much younger speaking demon tongue and then some horses being led away. It must've been the stable boy.

"This'll be the end then," said the one I recognized as Erlik.

"If King Connall knows what's good for him," said the deeper voice of the leader.

"Will King Xakiel give her back when he's done with her, you think?"

"He plans to send pieces of her to her father, one at a time until Connall surrenders Lumeria," said their leader. "We know our sire's appetites. He'll spoil her thoroughly for the marriage bed first. They may not want what's left of her once they finally sign the accord."

There was a round of laughter. Acid churned in my belly. I closed my eyes and bit down on the rope in my mouth, wishing I couldn't hear them heartlessly laughing about my sad fate. Knowing the king's plans for me made it worse.

If I could get hold of a weapon, I could kill myself first. Then they couldn't bargain for my freedom. Then my brother wouldn't be forced to surrender and our people crushed beneath the brutality of Northgall.

I focused on calming my breaths, barely listening as someone returned with food and they ate loudly. After a time, I heard the door to my stall opening, jolting me to attention.

"What the fuck are you doing, Geylan?" asked Erlik.

"Giving her food," he answered, apparently the lowest in hierarchy among them.

"No food," said the leader. "She'll vomit it up on the ride. Just water."

"If she tries to scream, hit her," added Erlik.

My gut tightened as the younger warrior entered with a hide flask. He was no less intimidating in appearance, towering over me as he entered. I remained still as he knelt on one knee and set the flask on the hay.

"Lean forward," he said, pointing to the rope in my mouth. "And don't scream when I remove it."

I held his gaze as I eased forward, allowing him to loosen the rope. I whimpered with relief when I could close my mouth, the tender skin had been rubbed raw.

"Here." He lifted the flask to my mouth.

I drank until I spluttered and coughed.

He sat back on his heel. "Easy. Take a breath."

He didn't smile, but there was sympathy in his yellow eyes when he looked at me. That was unexpected. I knew he didn't feel so sorry for me he'd help me escape, but maybe...

"Another sip?" He raised the flask.

I nodded, noting that he wore many blades in different sheaths around his waist and across his chest. There was a slender one tucked into the front of his wide belt.

When he helped me drink, he was still too far away for me to reach it. After the third sip, he asked, "Enough?"

I nodded again. He set the flask down and leaned closer to retie the gag. I eased forward, pretending to help him reach. It was just enough to allow me the distraction and space I needed. Slowly, I reached up—wrists still bound—and slipped the small dagger free.

"What are you--?" He leaned back, frowning down at his belt.

Gripping tight with both hands and sending a prayer to the goddess, I thrust the blade toward my throat.

"No!" He swiftly closed his clawed hand around my fisted fingers, stopping me as the blade's tip scraped my skin.

I huffed in distress, my gag back in place, tears pricking as I begged him with my eyes to let me do it.

"What happened?" came the leader's voice from the open doorway.

Geylan averted his gaze from mine, pulling the dagger from my hands and standing. "She tried to hurt herself, my lord."

The leader crouched down beside me, pinching my chin and turning my gaze so I was forced to look into his crimson eyes. He examined me intently.

"Yes," he seemed to mumble to himself. "You would do it, wouldn't you?"

I said nothing. Not that I could with the coarse rope back in my mouth.

"No, my lady." His voice was hard and cold, a merciless whip. "You'll pay for starting this war. And before we send your pretty corpse back to your family in Issos, you'll end it."

CHAPTER 2

Goll

The wind rattled the door and windows as the snowstorm howled outside. We sat around Ogalvet's dining table where I'd been studying the map of my father's troop movements. The hearth burned brightly, heating the room despite the blizzard sitting over Silvantis.

Soryn pointed his finger to the map. "They're gathering here on the south side of Belladum."

"How many?" I asked, referring to the allies we'd collected in the city closest to Silvantis.

Pullo crossed his arms. "Three hundred. Maybe four."

"That's not many," said Ogalvet, setting two bowls of hog stew onto the table.

"It's enough to take the palace," I assured them. "With the hundred we have here."

It had been more difficult to gather allies so close to the castle. We had to be cautious. Many here feared my father's punishment should they be caught for treason. That fear overrode their hatred for him. I knew that their fear would only help me in the end. When my father was dead, I'd instantly gain their allegiance.

"And what of his *entire* army?" asked Soryn, scowling at the map.

"Goll only needs to take the palace. The rest will fall in line," said Dalya, still wearing her priestess cloak, the hood over her delicate, curved horns.

"She's the seer," said Pullo with a shrug. "She should know."

Soryn grunted. "Pardon my skepticism, my lady. But I don't fucking trust seers. I trust the facts. And those are that Xakiel has a force of one thousand protecting the castle of Näkt Mir. And an army of tens of thousands scattered at the southern border making its way across Lumeria. As it stands, it will still be two to one in taking the castle. And all of that depends on having a plan for a surprise attack to kill the bastard." He turned his red-eyed gaze on me. "Which we still don't have. Let's not forget the hundreds of wights beneath the castle, and why are you fucking smiling?"

I chuckled. "Because the pieces are falling into place, Soryn. I appreciate your candor and your skepticism. It keeps me grounded. But we have what we need."

I'd planted my own soldiers within his army who'd been spreading discontent for this long war that kept them from their families and homes. Not to mention those who'd died in battle, burned in pyres on foreign soil. I only needed the right moment to kill my father. I was certain I could turn the tide in my favor. And then I would need to end this war swiftly.

"He's right, though," said Dalya. "You need a perfect plan to take Xakiel by surprise. Or you won't get to him."

"His wights," I acknowledged.

If my father felt any threat to his life, he'd summon his army of wights to protect him. But if I killed him by surprise, then his wights would die with him, giving us the upper hand to take the castle and the throne. And those who weren't so loyal to my father would fall to their knees and pledge fealty to me.

"Look, our primary goal is—"

The door opened with a flurry of snow followed by a small, cloaked figure who pushed it shut. The hood fell back, and Hava sneezed.

"Hava?" I ushered her toward a stool beside the fire. Her black, leathery wings shivered where they protruded through her cloak. "Why have you come?"

Hava was my mole within Näkt Mir. We met only rarely in Silvantis to keep suspicion low.

But she'd left on a night like this. Even with her ability to fly— granted by her half-blood gift on her father's side—it would've been a treacherous trip in this blizzard.

She smiled even while her pointed teeth were chattering. "I bring news. *Big* news."

"Here, sweetheart," said Ogalvet, handing her a steaming bowl of stew.

"I am not hungry, Ogalvet."

"It'll warm your hands. Set it on your lap, keep your palms around the bowl."

"So smart, you are." She beamed a smile at him.

"What news?" I asked, now leaning my shoulder against the mantel.

Pullo, Soryn, and Dalya had also corralled closer.

"I know where the king's elite guard went."

"Where?" I snapped.

We knew they'd been sent on a covert mission. My own scouts had lost track of them near Hellamir, a light fae town on the Bluevale River.

"They went far into Lumeria, into Issos itself, to capture a prisoner."

My entire body went rigid. I knew before I asked, "Who did they go to capture?"

"Princess Una, King Connall's daughter."

"And did they?" asked Dalya earnestly.

"Yes," said Hava, her excitement dampened now by pity. "They will use her to force her father to surrender."

No one said a word for a long moment, realizing my father had done the impossible. This may very well bring about the end of the war and bring Northgall into power.

Soryn who broke the silence first. "It would've taken immense stealth to go into Issos and capture the princess."

"It did," added Hava, no longer shivering. "They killed a farmer and his family outside the city on a hill with a perfect view of the comings and goings of the palace. When they saw a large royal guard following a carriage leaving Valla Lokkyr, they followed, expecting it to be her, or possibly someone important who might help them get to her. The guard and carriage went all the way near the outside of the city."

"It was her, wasn't it?" I asked.

Hava nodded. "She was bringing a healing orb to a sick boy, a villager."

"Why would she risk her neck so stupidly?" asked Soryn.

No one bothered to answer. The princess had been foolish once before. Seems the outcome was the same. She'd become a prisoner of Näkt Mir for a second time. However, this time, my father had orchestrated it, knowing the power a prisoner of her importance might have on the war.

"They're holding her in the dungeon, I presume." I turned my attention to the fire, trying to stop the erratic buzzing in my blood at this news.

"Not the dungeon."

"Where are they keeping her?" asked Dalya.

"Under guard and lock and key. In the concubine quarters."

"What?" I asked on a hushed breath. A white-hot stirring of my magick burned in my veins.

Soryn stood next to me, crossing his arms. "Are you telling us that King Xakiel has made the virgin Princess of Issos his new whore?"

"Not yet." Hava stood and handed the untouched bowl of stew back to Ogalvet and faced me. "The king has been meeting with his warriors near the front. He'd planned to join them on their push toward Issos, but he halted orders to move forward and returned to Northgall when he heard news that his secret mission had worked."

"She's just a child," I grated through my teeth.

Hava frowned. "She is a woman grown."

When I'd taken her from the dungeon of Näkt Mir, she'd been only a slip of a female youth.

"Has he arrived yet back at Näkt Mir?" I asked, my magick humming for action.

"Word is he's expected tonight. He plans to have Princess Una presented at his court to him tomorrow morning."

"Poor princess," murmured Dalya behind me. "She must be terrified."

"That's not all," added Hava. "It's said that he plans to cut off her wings and send them back to her father with his first demand for surrender." She pulled her hood back over her head and small horns, adding quietly, "Then he'll do other things…and cut off other parts."

"No need to say anymore," growled Soryn. "We know exactly what Xakiel is capable of."

"How do you know all this?" asked Pullo.

Hava lifted her pointed chin higher. "I'm a good spy."

Dalya quickly added, "And now we know that he plans to use the princess to finally gain the kingdom of Lumeria under his rule."

"No," I said so coolly while my body burned, my magick smoldering hotter. "Tomorrow morning, we're going into Näkt Mir and take her first. Then *we* will use her to gain the allegiance of both Northgall and Lumeria."

All eyes swiveled to me in silence.

"It's time for me to take my throne."

CHAPTER 3

Una

The room was warm, but I still shivered. Sometime in the night, the blizzard had died. And with it, an impending doom settled over me. I had hardly slept since I'd been imprisoned in this room several days ago.

In the fireplace, they burned blue coal—a heat source quarried in their mountains. It gave off a pale luminescent blue light. It should've given me comfort, reminding me of the moonlit temple in my home of Valla Lokkyr. It did not. There was a solemn coldness to the light, casting its hue across the luxurious chamber.

When a servant had brought warm tea at dawn, she'd ordered me to change into the gown I now wore since I'd be presented at court today. Someone had crudely cut openings for my wings in the back since the gown was apparently made for a wingless dark fae.

Though the single window in this room was boarded shut, I could see through the cracks. The gray skies brightened as the morning waned.

The first few days here, I'd remained in the practical blue gown I'd been captured in. It was soiled with drops of blood from Min and filth from the journey. I'd allowed myself those days to mourn and grieve what I'd lost, but I also understood that being presented at court would mean that I'd face my people's greatest enemy—King Xakiel, the Demon King of Northgall.

I had to shed my mourning shroud to face him. The dress I'd been given to wear wasn't obscene in any way, other than the fact that it was pearlescent white. I wasn't a fool. I understood what was happening. It was the color of innocence and purity and moon fae royalty.

King Xakiel wanted me dressed in pristine white, like the moon fae princess I was, to show his court he had captured the one who'd started the war in the first place. It was my capture and torture that had compelled my father to act so many years ago.

Here I was again in this hellish place, now a tool in the Demon King's quest to force my people to surrender. But I wouldn't go to him defeated and terrified. I'd swallow my fear and behave according to my station, no matter what he planned to do to me.

Still, I bit my lip, worrying over what Baelynn must be going through, not knowing where I was and fearing the worst. At least my father was bedridden and barely lucid. Small blessings for his illness now.

The bolt on the outside of the door clicked, and the door opened. A tall wraith fae wearing the black cloak of the guards stepped inside. He wasn't one of the wraith fae who'd abducted me. Thankfully, I hadn't seen anyone but maidservants since I'd been here. This warrior wore the black hood up over the horns that curled back along his head.

"Princess Una," he said with gravity. "Come with us."

I wondered briefly if this would be the march to my death, my pulse thumping in my throat. As I promised myself, I held my head high and walked straight-backed through the open door. There were three others, all hooded, waiting to escort me. One of them stepped beside me on my left—taller than the others—but he didn't look at me or say a word.

The other one who'd opened my chamber door took his place on my right and moved forward. We made our solemn march through the black-walled castle.

After my capture, I'd become morbidly fascinated with the dark fae and their royal castle Näkt Mir. It was built on top of Vixet Krone, the former volcano that was the center of their realm. The castle's walls were carved from volcanic glass. The last time I was here in the dank, ghastly dungeon, I imagined that the upper palace must've been a dark, depressing place.

I was wrong.

The torchlight glittered and sparkled on the walls. There were ornate tapestries, silvery rugs, beautiful carvings and sculptures depicting their god Vix, kings, and lovely maidens at every turn. I found it more disheartening that the royal palace was filled with dark beauty and sophistication. For if that were so, how could their king be so heartless and cruel? The king I was about to finally meet.

I focused on my breathing, trying to remain calm as the guards marched me through two open double doors into a high-domed room. It was circular with tall pillars and lovely architecture, but it was the audience that held me riveted.

The guards around me stopped in the middle beneath the high dome. Surrounding us in a wide circle was obviously his court. Beyond a fleeting glance to discover they were ornately dressed and bejeweled as the noble four-horned wraith fae would be, I kept my gaze forward.

Standing in two rows at attention and facing each other all the way to the throne were the king's elite guard, Kel Klyss. The Culled was what the wraith king's guard was called in our language. They were carefully selected and bound to their king through some sort of mysterious dark rite none of the scholars I'd asked could tell me.

The Kel Klyss were indeed all that my books had described. These dark fae didn't look like the deformed creatures who'd held me in captivity so many years ago. They appeared much worse—fearsome, formidable, and cunning.

They were covered in black, steel armor that formed to their seven-foot-plus frames. The traditional wraith fae weapon—a curved sword forged here in their homeland—was strapped to their sides, hanging down the length of their thick thighs, the sharpened tip reaching past their knees.

Most of the warriors had two horns, but a few had four—all of them curving backward around their heads—with silver guards around the base of each horn, like rings on a finger. For decoration or for strength to use their horns as weapons in battle, I wasn't sure.

Their dark hair was worn loose except for one who'd shaved the sides, leaving a long, braided tail down his back. Some wore gold jewelry woven into smaller braids along their temples. Gold was as revered everywhere as the black steel mined in Northgall.

Their skin was varying shades of gray, some pale as storm clouds, others as dark as the slate quarried out of Vixet Krone. Their eyes ranged in hues of yellow, orange, and red, though not one pair had landed on me.

Though their clawed hands hung loosely at their sides and their closed mouths hid their canine teeth, there was no mistaking we were in the presence of powerful dark fae. Demon magick hummed thick in the air.

All dark fae were descended of the demon god Vix and appeared in various likenesses of him. Just as the light fae bore the likeness of our gods of the heavens and the sea. It was one thing to be told of them, to see portraits and sketches, but it was another to see them in the flesh.

Movement at the head of the room in a dome of shadow caught my gaze. Then the creature who stepped down from his throne stole my breath. I bit the inside of my cheek to keep from making any noise at all, for the sight of their king struck me with terrible fear.

He was a behemoth, dressed in black hide trousers, and that was all. His forehead and chest were covered in runes, like most wraith fae nobles. Only he had more. His four black horns curled over his skull then swept up to sharp points, the two larger ones with wide bands of gold at the base. The smaller horns were encased entirely in gold, serving as his crown.

But his appearance wasn't what frightened me most. It was the sinister grin he wore and his expression of malicious intent as he stalked closer. The courtiers whispered. King Xakiel's boots echoed in the chamber as he walked down the tunnel of his wraith warriors.

A jolt of magick hummed from my left. I glanced at the guard, but his head remained bowed in deference to his approaching king.

The Demon King lived up to all my horrifying expectations as he came to a stop before me. His ice-blue eyes with pupils slit like a serpent's raked me with calculating interest. I wondered why his were different than most wraith fae, recalling that I'd seen similar eyes before.

"Welcome to Näkt Mir, Princess Tiarrialuna."

He didn't bow his head in any semblance of propriety. So neither did I. And I wasn't about to be ingratiating for this greeting when everyone in this room knew that I'd been dragged here by force after his warriors murdered my dearest friend and an innocent Issosian.

"Have you sent terms to Issos yet?" I asked.

His smile widened, revealing his sharp canines.

"A woman with spirit. You'll need it."

Some courtiers tittered. Acid burned in my belly that they found this vile display so entertaining.

"Have you?" I asked more forcefully.

Not only did I want my brother to know that I was at least alive, but I needed to know how long my torture would last this time in Näkt Mir.

The king's smile vanished. "Careful, Princess."

"That is why I'm here, am I not?" I asked, ignoring his warning. "To force Issos to surrender?"

He tilted his head, examining me as if I was an enticing curiosity.

"Of course, it is," he admitted evenly, then added with bite, "my lady."

More laughter circled the room from our audience, except from the warriors who remained alert, poised, and silent.

I gulped hard when the king took a step closer, forcing me to crane my neck to meet his gaze.

"But perhaps I won't give terms at all for your return." His gaze trailed down my throat and lower. "Perhaps I'll still march on Issos, crush your brother's armies, behead your father, and keep you as my own personal war prize."

He stared into my eyes with cold intent. It was a miracle I was able to keep myself upright.

"If you submit and serve me well," he began suggestively, "I may even let you go back to Issos."

He lifted his arms and turned toward the courtiers. "What do you say, lords and ladies of Northgall?"

The sudden uproar of shouted approval and applause made me flinch, my knees going weak.

"How long should the princess serve me to pay for her father's mistake in starting this war?"

A male wraith fae somewhere behind me called out, "The war has lasted almost five years, my king."

"Ah, so it has." He turned his fierce attention back on me, stepping close.

I dropped my gaze to the stone floor, my courage flagging.

"You will stay in my keeping," he declared roughly. "You will serve me obediently for five years. And then I'll consider whether you deserve to return to your home. It's much better than my alternative plans. I was going to send you back to your father in pieces. Starting with these lovely black wings."

He caressed my left wing over my shoulder. I flinched but remained in place. He chuckled.

"We'll start," he growled fiercely, "with you dropping to your knees and thanking your new king for his mercy."

Light laughter echoed through the hall, while my entire body trembled with both fear and rage. Strangely, it was his last demand that sparked a hot flame in my heart.

It wasn't the threat of abuse or violation of my body that had ignited fresh anger inside me, but the demand that I should kneel before him like his slave and actually *thank* him for it.

I lifted my gaze, voice quivering as I replied, "I will *never* kneel at your feet. You are *not* my king."

His lips curled back in a sneer as he reached for me. Suddenly, a hand shot out from the guard on my left. With a forceful shove, the guard pushed King Xakiel who stumbled back and stared in shock at his warrior.

The guard removed his hood, then raised his long, curved sword gripped in both hands.

I gasped, recognizing his face at once. He stepped between me and the king who finally found his voice.

"Gollaya."

"Hello, Father." His deep timbre was steady and sure and deadly. "Vayla was right."

Then he swung his sword with swift precision and force, slicing through the throat of King Xakiel. Blue blood sprayed, and courtiers screamed, but I stood there in shock, watching the king's head topple to the stone floor.

CHAPTER 4

Goll

Magick crackled around me in a halo of power. I knew in that moment as I stared down at my father's severed head—his kingly eyes wide and glassy—that I was meant to take this throne. The gods sanctioned it with a surge of magick, giving me my rightful inheritance and my place as king.

But first, I must destroy my father's devoted warriors.

The four men I'd planted in the room had already swung their swords and killed half of my father's Culled. The courtiers were running for the door, but Soryn had done his job on the outside, killing the guards and bolting the door shut.

With ease that almost shocked me, I called up my magick. My bloody blade in one hand, I raised the other toward my father's second, Erlik, the one who I hated the most, who had personally thrown me into my cell below Näkt Mir years ago.

He was swinging his sword down on one of my allies.

"*Etheline*," I whispered.

Fire surged from my palm like an arrow of flame across the room, hitting Erlik before his sword hit his target. He instantly burst into flame then fell to the floor in a pile of blackened bones and ash.

I did the same to the last of his Kel Klyss still standing and fighting, disintegrating the rest of my father's blood-bound and most faithful guard.

All that was left were the whimpering, crying courtiers, including the council members who held great power in their influence with our people.

I re-sheathed my long sword while my men surrounded me. I avoided even looking at the princess. Not yet.

Stepping over my father's corpse, I bent and took hold of one of his horns and lifted his head in the air. One of the females in my father's court fainted.

"I am Gollaya Verbane, son of Xakiel, rightful heir to the throne of Northgall," I proclaimed in a clear voice. "Pledge fealty now and you will be spared."

There was no hesitation, not even from the council members. Instantly, they fell to their knees. Dropping my father's head to my side, I marveled at how light it was in my hand, as if the weight of the king's head should be greater. It was rather enlightening to find that in death, he was of very little consequence.

"Open the door, Pullo," I commanded.

He rushed for the door and knocked four times swiftly then twice more with drawn out pauses, letting Soryn know that we'd accomplished our task.

Soryn pushed the door open and marched inside with a dozen of my warriors, all of their blades smeared with blue blood. Like my own. Deep satisfaction burrowed deep. After all of these years, I'd done it.

Soryns' gaze flicked to my father's body on the floor behind me, then to my hand. His mouth quirked with the faintest of smiles, then savage determination hardened his expression once more.

"The gate is blocked and guarded. My king."

I arched a brow at him. I wasn't king yet.

"Keep the courtiers locked in here."

"What about her?" He nodded to the princess behind me.

Finally, I looked at her. By the gods, she was radiant. *A woman grown*, Hava had said. That didn't proclaim nearly enough about the light fae female standing tall and proud before me, surrounded by her enemies.

She pressed herself back against a column and watched me with surprising calm, her gaze glancing from my father's headless corpse back to me. I stepped forward, unable to keep myself in place, lured by some deeper force. Her eyes widened, her focus dropped to my hand. I'd nearly forgotten.

Turning, I held out the head to Soryn. "Take care of this. I'll handle the princess."

He took the head by one of its horns.

"Then we sweep the dungeon," I added. "Drakmir will guard the forest for any guards trying to escape that way."

With a stiff nod, Soryn called into the corridor. A dozen more of my armed allies entered.

"Knock out Councilman Kellock," I whispered to Soryn. "He's a nekliam."

I doubted he was stupid enough to stand up against me now that my father was dead and I was first in line to the throne, but I wouldn't take any chances. A nekliam could reanimate any nearby corpses and command them to do his bidding, just as my father had. Seeing as there were quite a few on the floor of the throne room, it was best to knock him unconscious now to be safe.

With that, I dropped my sword and swiveled back toward the princess, watching with interest as her poise vanished when I stalked closer to her in three long strides.

Gods, I wasn't prepared for how fucking beautiful she'd become. Her wide violet eyes searched mine, her throat working nervously as she swallowed. Before she could open her mouth and say a word, I bent, scooped her over my shoulder, and strode for the door.

She instantly started struggling, whimpering "no" as she clawed ineffectively at my black armor.

"Pullo! Tierzel!" I called. "With me."

"Yes, Sire," they bellowed in unison, their bootsteps echoing behind me.

"Put me down," she cried, clawing uselessly at my armor.

Rather than head upstairs, I strode directly toward the door tucked inconspicuously below the staircase and opened it.

"Wait here," I told Pullo and Tierzel at the door.

The parlor was exactly as I remembered it. Small and windowless. A wall of books on one side with a giant black marble desk that my father never sat at. On the other side was a fireplace, currently cold and empty, in front of a comfortable set of chairs.

I heaved the princess back off my shoulder and plopped her in the chair. She swung at my face as I stood straight, but I caught her thin wrists.

Her pale skin was mottled pink, flushing her chest, neck, and cheeks. But she didn't say anything now. There was no need.

She'd fallen out of my father's captivity and into mine. I held her delicate wrists in my large grasp, realizing how utterly weak and helpless she actually was. I gave her a firm squeeze to remind her.

Then I leaned closer so that she could see it in my eyes. I owned her now. I shook my head and spoke one, weighty word.

"No."

She flinched, blinking quickly, forcing whatever tears had sprung back to their well. She clenched her jaw and glared at me with all the hatred in her heart.

Good. That would help her.

Straightening, I released her and marched out of the room. When I shut the door behind me, I spun to Pullo.

"Guard this door with your life. *No one* gets in. Do you understand me?"

Pullo clamped his jaw tight. He wanted to join the fight. I knew that he did, but he was one of my best warriors and someone I trusted.

I clamped my clawed hand on his shoulder, giving him a shake. "Tell me you understand your command, Pullo. Do not leave this door."

"We won't," said Tierzel, the only man closer to Pullo than me.

"With our lives," added Pullo.

I gave them a nod of approval and stormed toward the stairwell leading into the dungeon. Another party of warriors waited for me then followed in step behind me.

As we descended deeper into the underground, the noise of fighting grew distant and muffled. The labyrinth of corridors and cells that made up the dungeon was rather vast. When we came out onto the main floor, there was no one there.

"Seems the bone-keepers are already on the run," I said, unsheathing my black steel dagger at my waist. "Find and kill them all."

My father's dungeon guards were ensorcelled by a blood spell to obey only him. Now that he was dead, they'd fall into madness and become nothing more than mindless killing creatures. They had to be put down.

The warriors swept out in all directions in stealthy silence.

I descended another winding stone staircase into the part of the dungeon where I'd been held captive, where I hoped I might find an old friend still alive. It was a faint hope of mine since my own escape. I'd thought Keffa had been executed by my father, but Hava had been able to discover that as of a few months ago, he'd survived. It was another reason I had felt the urgency to act soon to take my father's throne.

But now, fear dug deep. What if I'd waited too long? Or what if Hava's source had been wrong and he'd been dead for years?

As I stepped out of the staircase into the lower dungeon, a blade swiped toward my head. I dodged and jabbed my dagger upward, embedding it through the bottom of the guard's chin, straight up into his skull with a crunch. Withdrawing the dagger, the guard fell dead to the floor. I wiped the flat of my blade on my trousers and moved on.

I made my way quietly down a familiar corridor and came out where the pit of wights were held for my father, awaiting to be called upon if he needed them. He'd been winning the war against Lumeria and had only used them on occasion when going against larger armies of the light fae. It was probable he planned to use them when he invaded Issos, a target his army had close in their sights.

But when I invaded Issos, I wouldn't use an army of wights. Nor would I use my power over flame. I had another plan altogether.

When I approached the deep pit where I'd listened to the wights groan and shriek and tap their skeletal fingers along the walls for years, all was silent. I hadn't expected to be overwhelmed with such a deep satisfaction at seeing the pile of bones and skulls unmoving in the pit.

Complete silence. I stared across the pit at the cell where I'd been kept, where my father had put me and warded the bars to keep me in. Then I smiled at the bent bars that I'd forced open when my magick had returned to me in an avalanche when I'd seen a small moon fae girl being tossed into the pit.

She'd been the catalyst for my magick to surge and return to me. And her capture again had been the spark to set my plan in motion to finally kill my father. Refusing to contemplate that for long, I continued down another corridor leading off of the pit.

At the very end, I sensed life. A faint stirring like someone sliding a bare foot on the stone floor drew me deeper. No torches burned here. Holding my blade in one hand, I lifted a torch from its holder on the sconce on the wall and whispered, "*Etheline.*" A flame instantly ignited the blue coal set at the tip.

Nothing but stillness in the cell before me. I thought the sound must have been my imagination until I finally reached the barred doors and stirred my blue flame higher, burning brighter and casting flickering light into the dank chamber.

On the floor, there sat a skeleton on one side, the wrist still bound in chains to the wall, the two-horned skull of its unfortunate owner had rolled away from the body as the flesh rotted away. But on the other side of the cell, there was movement.

The wraith fae raised an arm, covered in tattered, soiled clothing, squinting at the light. One of his horns was broken and one of his eyes had been gouged out, a large scar trailed over the puckered flesh of his socket and down his face.

"Keffa?" My voice was hoarse with emotion as I wondered if the thin, pale gray fae peering up at me with one orange eye could possibly be my former mentor and dearest friend from so long ago.

"By the gods," came his deep raspy voice, "is that you, my boy?"

"It's me, Keffa," I answered, joy and desperate relief making me move quickly.

I set the torch in the sconce beside the door and found the keys on the opposite wall. I quickly unlocked the door and pushed open the heavy, creaking panel. He hadn't moved from the floor as I approached, extending his hand for me to help him up.

I hauled him carefully to his feet, finally recognizing the proud lines of my friend's face. His features had sharpened from starvation during his incarceration. I expected to be scorned for having taken so long, for leaving him to rot in this dismal hell. I even expected madness to shine back at me from the depths of his one good eye. What I did not expect was the wide smile as he gripped both my shoulders or the words he spoke.

"You did it, didn't you? You killed him."

"I did, Keffa. Your Vayla was right."

His eye slipped closed. "Then she did not die in vain."

"No, my friend. She did not."

He opened his eye, and it seemed to shine even brighter here in the dark, reminding me of the intelligent fae who'd taught me so much in my youth.

His expression was tight and grave, his voice gruff as he said, "Then let us begin the work undone. Let's put you on your throne, Gollaya."

CHAPTER 5

Una

I paced the bedchamber I'd been put in days ago. Gollaya had tossed me in that small parlor and left me there with two guards outside the door, I hadn't seen him since. For some time, I heard the echoing yells of fighting in the palace halls, the marching of feet, calls of orders by one wraith fae to another, then eventually silence.

I'm not sure how long I stayed in that dark parlor, but I'd drifted off in a chair, awoken by the door unlatching and the bright streak of light through the opening door.

The wraith fae with two horns, his head shaved on the sides with a long, braided tail down his back stepped inside. Pullo was his name.

"Follow me, my lady."

For a moment, I was shocked with how respectfully he'd spoken to me. I worried what would become of me now. Gollaya obviously had staged a coup to kill his father and to take the crown himself.

Gollaya.

A shiver trembled down my body. I'd never known that the young wraith fae who'd saved me from certain death in that dungeon had been the lost son of our enemy, King Xakiel. The Prince of Northgall had saved me from that dungeon. Back then, I'd thought he must be a high noble, related to the wraith fae royal family. His unusual eyes told me as much. But I never knew he was the lost prince.

Baelynn had told me there had been rumors that King Xakiel had killed his only son and heir for some unknown reason, while ambassadors had reported there were tales that he'd fled the palace and was still alive somewhere.

It had never mattered because our sole enemy had been King Xakiel for these past five years of war. The war my father started when I'd returned home battered and bruised, my luminescent white wings cut off.

My wings fluttered at my back at the memory. When they had grown back, I'd believed it a miracle of the gods. Lumera was shining her divine light upon me. But as they unfurled—at first the deepest purple giving way to black as they dried and stretched bigger—I knew I'd been cursed. Besides being the shade of the palace where I'd been tortured, they were useless. I could not fly.

And here I was again, a prisoner in the infamous Black Palace of Näkt Mir.

At least I wasn't being held in a dank pit. I wasn't quite sure where I was, but the room Pullo led me to was certainly a space most likely meant for an honored guest.

The chamber door was made of blue-gray wood with gold filigree painted around the edges. The black obsidian walls of the corridors extended into this room as they apparently did through the entire palace.

Along one entire wall, a giant tapestry hung. It was filled with sprites and nymphs and bursting with flora, all in lovely shades of green, gray, and blue. There was a female skald fae—one of the sea fae who lived in the luxurious blue waters of Morodon—sunbathing nude on a rock. Her beautiful green hair hung over her porcelain skin and down the rock into the water. Her webbed feet dangled in the transparent water, one of her webbed hands rested on her rounded belly, the other arm bent beneath her head.

In the water, a male skald fae watched her, his entire body and half of his face hidden beneath the surface. Only his dark, expressive eyes and his blue hair curtaining sharp cheekbones could be seen. He worshipped her with that gaze. I thought it a strange tapestry for a dark fae bedchamber, though it was beyond lovely.

A giant four-poster bed, double the size of my own in Issos, was draped in a pale blue counterpane. The rest of the room was furnished in rich blue velvet chaise lounges and chairs, carpets sewn with threads of silver and gold, giant black iron candelabras, a beautiful golden dressing screen in one corner, and a golden tub peeking from behind a semi-transparent screen covered in white muslin.

The crown of the room was a white marble mantle with a flourishing, feminine design framing a fireplace I could literally walk into had there not been a crackling fire kept burning a bright blue flame for me since I'd been put here.

I stepped toward the fire now to warm my hands, trying to grab hold of my emotions.

This was not at all what I expected when Pullo and the other one called Tierzel had escorted me here. While grateful not to be housed in the damp, fetid dungeon of my first visit to Näkt Mir, I hadn't expected this. I wondered how long before I knew what my fate would be. I was well aware that I was a valuable prisoner.

Of course, I hadn't seen my host since I was put here—assuming Gollaya was now in charge. No one would tell me anything.

I still couldn't reconcile that the young-looking fae who'd saved me from that dungeon was the lost heir of King Xakiel. And that he'd cut off his own father's head. Bile rose up my throat with the memory of it. Not that I mourned the king. He'd been battling and killing my people for years now. And it was obvious he'd had foul plans for me. Perhaps, Gollaya would be more open to a treaty and an end to this war.

I remembered the brightness of his eyes as he sliced through his father. It seemed more than revenge or wrath that lit his face. It was more like joy that had flickered across his expression.

I shivered and walked to the boarded window where, yet again, I could at least see through the crack to the outside. There had been comings and goings of troops of wraith fae on horseback the past few days. I'd been brought food and water by quiet, solemn soldiers who said nothing at all to me as they came and went.

When I asked the one called Pullo how long I'd be kept prisoner here, he seemed surprised I spoke their language. That was probably because I spoke it so well. When I'd returned home, I'd worked earnestly to learn and even practice it with one of our ambassadors who frequently had to travel to Northgall.

Perhaps the gods knew all along that I'd be brought back here. But for how long this time?

A soft knock came at the door, then it opened. Frowning, for no one had ever knocked before, I stepped closer to the hearth, watching as a dark fae female entered carrying several folded garments in her hands. She was unlike any fae I'd ever seen before.

She was tiny, by far the smallest dark fae I'd met. Her skin was dark gray, her two slender horns curled prettily back over fine black hair that was cut short and close to her dainty head, little wisps hanging over her forehead. Her pointed ears stuck up rather long, out of proportion with her delicate features. She also had black leathery wings stretching tall from her back, but thin and elegant.

Even petite, she had a fine hourglass figure with a tiny waist. She was dressed in black form-fitting trousers with a red overskirt and a black top that formed to her breasts and ribs, all with ornamental silver stitching. Her clothes appeared more like what a warrior might wear to a formal ceremony, the craftsmanship absolutely magnificent.

But the most wondrous thing about her was her beautiful, wide red eyes with dark, long lashes and her bright smile with tiny fangs. She visibly vibrated with excitement.

"Hello, Princess," she said in demon tongue. "Can you understand me?"

I nodded.

"Pullo said you could speak our language. How wonderful, for I never learned high fae myself. I am Havallah. I have the great honor of being your lady's maid here at Näkt Mir. You will have others to tend to you." She gestured behind her where several wraith fae females entered the room, none of them with wings, their eyes downcast in supplication, hands clasping buckets of steaming water. "But I will tend to your daily personal needs."

Another handmaiden walked in with a covered tray. Havallah pointed her toward the fireplace, and the female glided over to set it on a table.

I glanced toward the door, expecting a soldier to enter behind them, or even Gollaya, but the door closed and I heard the familiar click of it being locked from the outside.

"It is a pleasure to meet you, Havallah." I could keep my good manners, even if I was obviously still a prisoner.

Her eyes grew impossibly wider, then she laughed, a sweet, infectious sound as she hurried closer to me. "You may call me Hava, if you like. My friends call me Hava. I am so, so, so very happy to finally meet you."

Hava made a *tsking* sound and snapped her fingers. The other handmaidens instantly hurried toward the dressing screen and the golden tub behind it. For such a pleasant, small fae female, she seemed to carry weight in this palace.

"Let's get you into a nice hot bath, shall we?"

A bath. A luxury I didn't realize how badly I wanted until now.

She took my hand and led me behind the dressing screen. I found her familiarity endearing, rather than alarming. It reminded me of Min. I blinked away the tears that quickly stung my eyes. I still hadn't mourned my dear friend properly.

"Hava," I asked as I turned and let her unlace the dress from the back while the handmaidens poured their buckets of water and added spiced and floral-scented oils that smelled heavenly. "You are not from here, are you?"

"No, no." She smiled sweetly. "I am from Gadlizael, the shadow fae kingdom."

"You don't look like the shadow fae my brother described. Except for the wings." I'd never even met an ambassador of their kind, since they avoided us altogether. The shadow fae lived far outside Lumeria in the Solgavia Mountains. "I'm sorry. Is it rude of me to say so?"

"Not at all."

She was working on the buttons of my sleeves now and helped to remove the dress I'd been wearing since the king had been beheaded a few days ago. There were dried dark spots of his blood on the white fabric. I didn't mind since it reminded me that what I'd seen had actually happened, and that our enemy, the Demon King of Northgall, was actually dead.

"My father was a wraith fae," Hava continued. "That's where I get my gray skin. The wings I got from my mother who was a shadow fae. But apparently, there is naiad blood in our ancestry as well. That's why I'm so small."

Naiads, nymphs, and sprites all shared a common ancestry to the lesser water goddess Beatha. Legends claimed she was small in stature but mighty in the magick she wielded over nature.

Hava helped me out of my shift and lifted a silver silken robe for me to slip my arms into while we waited for the handmaidens to finish preparing the bath and setting out cloths and more oils.

"I think you're lovely, Hava," I told her truthfully. "And very kind."

Her eyes and mouth widened into pure joy. "It means so much to me to hear you say that, my mistress. Plus, I'm a zypher. I inherited the power of feyfire from my father. That's another reason I believe my king assigned me to you. I can protect you if needed."

My pulse tripped faster at her mention of her *king*. "He assigned you to me?"

"He did," she said proudly, then she held out a palm and whispered a word, which caused a ball of orange fire to appear in her palm. She grinned at me. "I can keep you safe."

"So, Gollaya has now been crowned King of Northgall?"

Since none of my guards had told me anything, I had no idea what had happened beyond what I'd seen in the throne room.

Hava shooed the chambermaids with buckets away. Once they'd left the room, the door closed and locked behind them, I slipped off my robe and stepped into the bath.

After I slid into the warm bath, sighing with contentment, Hava smiled. "My lord has not been crowned yet, but he will be."

She wetted a cloth and began scrubbing my shoulders and upper back.

"When will he be crowned?" I asked in earnest.

"That, I am not sure of. But he has won favor with his father's soldiers. Well, the ones he let live. Would you like me to wash your hair?"

A little overwhelmed by Hava's extreme turn of conversation, I nodded. I lowered, dipped my head back, and then sat up again.

She lathered some soap into my hair and continued on. "After what they said happened at the front, I dare say he'll be crowned any day."

"What happened at the front?" I snapped quickly.

"Oh, I'm sorry. How rude of me. I keep forgetting you are a moon fae."

I wasn't sure how she could possibly forget. I didn't look anything like her kind. She became unnaturally silent for a while as she dipped a small pitcher into the water and then poured it over my hair.

"Won't you tell me, Hava?" I implored after wiping the water from my face.

"I'm not supposed to talk too much."

"Did your sire tell you that?"

"He did. He knows I am loyal and trusts me very much." She began putting vials of oils back on a table where they were kept. "But I must tell you this," she added excitedly, holding out a large toweling for me as I stepped out of the tub.

"Tell me anything, Hava. No one has even spoken to me since I've been here."

While I patted my body dry, she fetched my robe and helped me slide into it.

"Come and sit by the fire and eat and I'll tell you how Prince Gollaya won his father's soldiers."

I followed her though I hadn't been able to eat since I'd been imprisoned here. But when Hava lifted the domed lid, revealing a tray of herbed fowl, a round of cheese, and buttery bread, I found that I was hungry.

Perhaps it was because of her company. While the guards hadn't been cruel, they certainly hadn't been overtly kind. Their wariness of me was obvious since I was the daughter of their enemy. And so, I'd been steeped in anxiety since my capture.

Now, sitting on a settee by the fire—the blue-coal burning brightly—I felt at ease for the first time.

She served me a plate from the tray of steaming food then sat back while I tucked a napkin on my lap and the plate on top of it.

"I apologize we can't go to the great hall for your meals." She frowned. "I'll have Pullo bring in a proper dining table for you."

I didn't bother asking why I couldn't eat in the great hall. I didn't want to be amongst the wraith fae.

"Thank you, Hava. Won't you eat with me?"

"Oh, no, my lady." She poured red wine into a brass goblet and handed it to me. "I am most content to just sit here with you." Then she poured another. "But I will have a drink if you don't mind."

"Of course," I encouraged her, hoping it might loosen her tongue. "Please tell me the tale you were going to tell me. About the prince."

She clasped her clawed fingers around her goblet, her red eyes glittering by the pale blue firelight.

"It was wondrous, I was told. After the prince and his allies took the palace, he rode his dragon to the war's front."

I coughed on a sip of wine. "His *dragon*?"

"Oh, yes. You didn't know?"

I shook my head, completely dumbfounded. "No."

There hadn't been a wraith king dragonrider in centuries. It was believed that the rightful kings of Northgall had dragon blood pulsing through their veins.

"According to legend," Hava added in whispered excitement, "their blue and gold eyes are a sign of their dragon ancestry. There have been many kings come and gone in his line." She added with a haughty tilt of her chin. "But Prince Gollaya is the only one in ages who has ridden a dragon. He's been riding Drakmir for many years. But he has kept him a secret in the mountain caves outside Silvantis."

For a moment, I was silent, wondering how I'd never read about this in the many books I'd read on wraithkind. But then I hadn't ever focused on their royal line. I'd never known that the one who'd saved me was their prince.

"But why?" I asked, tearing off a piece of bread and eating it. "He could've killed his father with his dragon and taken the throne any time he wanted."

"No, no, no. He could not." She shook her head, wisps of black hair hiding one eye. She tucked it behind her high, pointed ear. "In order to be considered the true king, he must face his father. He would've been contested by others if he had used his dragon to usurp the throne. It must be by his own hand."

"I see." I ate a piece of the roasted fowl. "And what happened when he flew to the front?" My gut clenched, knowing the front was in Lumeria, near my home.

"He stood high on a hill above them all and promised he would finally end this long war his father had dragged them into. He raised his father's head high above and—"

"The prince carried his father's head?" I interrupted.

"Yes, yes. He did. It was a glorious sight"—she beamed brightly—"or so I was told."

My stomach twisted at the barbarity of it, but I didn't interrupt again.

"He promised to be a better king to his people, to raise Northgall to its rightful place as ruler of all faekind and without the shedding of more of our kinsmen's blood. That was when the soldiers roared and chanted his name."

"How?" I asked, my stomach souring as I placed the goblet and napkin back on the tray. "How does he plan to win the war without more bloodshed?"

For I knew my brother, and he wouldn't simply roll over and give up our homeland to be subjugated under Northgall.

Hava dropped her gaze to her lap then gestured toward the tray. "Would you like some more wine?"

She evaded my question, which spread a sickening feeling through me. I shook my head.

"Where was he at the front?" I asked. "Where was he in Lumeria when he made this fine speech?" I couldn't help the tension hardening my voice.

She cleared her throat and stood. "I cannot tell you more, my lady."

Silence tightened between us.

"I see," I said softly, despondent. "I'd like to be alone now, Hava."

Reality sank in again. I wasn't visiting with a friend or an ally. I was still a prisoner, and I feared what the prince, the new king, planned to do with me now.

"Of course, my lady."

She gave me a comfortable sleeping gown and offered to help comb out my damp hair.

"No, Hava. Thank you for the meal and the company. I'm tired now. You may go."

Her brow pinched, and she looked sad, likely mirroring my own expression. "I understand. I'll leave you now and return in the morning with breakfast. You'll feel better after a good night's sleep."

When she was gone, I crawled into the giant bed and slid under the covers, facing the boarded window, yet another reminder that I couldn't let my guard slip and believe that I was a welcome guest here. No matter how kind Hava was or how luxurious my cell was now, I was indeed a prisoner of the new king of Northgall.

CHAPTER 6

Goll

I read the missive from Soryn in the war room my father had rarely used. In the past few days, I came to realize that my father waged this war by throwing more and more of his soldiers into one battle after another rather than wield any kind of strategy that might end it more quickly or spare any bloodshed.

After hearing firsthand some of his commands given to the officers at the front, I berated myself for not acting sooner. The toll this war had taken on our people was harrowing. So many lives lost, and yet it still wasn't over. Not officially. One step remained.

The only smart move my father made was sending his Kel Klyss on a covert mission to abduct Connall Hartstone's daughter. My gut tightened at the thought of her several stories above me in my mother's former bedchamber.

"What news from Soryn?" asked Keffa.

My old friend was recovering well. Except for the eye patch and the scar down one cheek, he looked like his old self. While he was still healing, he seemed to be gaining weight quickly and appeared vigorous and healthy. It was remarkable what the healers had managed in only a few days.

"It is time," I answered him, dropping the scroll on the table where a map of Lumeria was spread wide with campaign movements marked around Issos.

"I would like to join the soldiers at the encampment, Goll." Voice grave and solemn, he added, "Seeing as I missed all the glory, I'd at least like to celebrate with them at the end."

"You fought your own battles well enough." For many years he'd battled the darkness and loneliness and starvation in the dungeon. "I'm sorry I didn't come sooner."

He shook his head. "There will be no apologies for what Xakiel is responsible for. Leave them behind. We are embarking on a new world. Thanks to you."

I grunted and rolled up Soryn's message then tucked it with the others in a drawer in the desk.

"That will depend on Princess Tiarrialuna."

"How so?"

"Whether or not I must follow in my father's footsteps, that is. Much depends on *her*."

He grew quiet for a moment then added. "Dalya's vision. You believe she is the one mentioned, don't you?"

"I know that she is," I answered without hesitation.

Last autumn, Dalya had a powerful vision while scrying with a drop of my blood shortly after she'd pledged her fealty and service to me as my royal seer. She was a distant cousin serving as a priestess at the Temple of Silvantis, but secretly she'd been scrying for me, guiding me in my ascension to the throne.

She'd had many visions, but the one that had stayed with me the most was when she proclaimed *the female fae with the demon's mark will bring about Vix's reckoning.*

Vix's reckoning was the old legend, the promise that one day our kind would rise above and rule over all. In all the written histories of faekind, the light fae—specifically the moon fae of Issos—had dominated our world. They'd controlled the richest, most fertile lands, woodlands overfull with game, and mines of precious stones. And they'd kept their borders well-guarded to prevent trade, except when it benefited them.

Smuggling was common, especially around Hellamir. Many wood fae who lived there ignored the laws of their king that prevented trade with the dark fae of Northgall, but it was the bloody skirmishes and attacks on our fae by their soldiers that was unconscionable to me.

"My father was content to dwell here, Keffa, in this palace while he ignored the problems of our people. I will not do that. I know it is my right by birth, sanctioned by the gods, to take this crown and to rule over our land *and* Lumeria. And I will do it at all costs."

"And the princess is the key, is she."

"She is. Now, I must make her understand that."

He chuckled, his scar pulling tight on his cheek. "You think she'll accept your…invitation gratefully?"

I straightened from the desk, steeling my spine, my entire body locking tight, finally ready to go to her after Soryn's message.

"No. She'll hate me for it." I shrugged. "But she will do it all the same."

"So you will force her," he said casually. "That sounds very much like what Xakiel would have done."

"My father planned to violate her for five years and send her back in pieces to Issos. That is not my plan."

"Forcing her to be your mizrah and keeping her prisoner here isn't all that much better."

"*Keffa,*" I snapped with warning. "It must be done."

None of us knew who the *female* of Dalya's vision was, not until I laid eyes on Una in the throne room and had seen her wings. Her *black* wings. They'd grown back in the hue of my home, Näkt Mir, a palace carved into the volcanic obsidian left behind by Vixet Krone's eruption thousands of years ago. It was the color of our armor, our swords, our temples, our entire world.

She was meant to be mine, to bring about the rise of the dark fae with me at its helm. Whether she hated me for what I planned to do, for the role she must play, didn't matter. I would make it so at all costs.

We dark fae had sequestered in our separate kingdoms, eking out our lives beneath the shining beacon of Lumeria, where fertile lands of abundance and excess thrived, where their populations flourished and where magick whispered everywhere. I was not only going to open the gates to those lands, I would be their new ruler. A union with Una would strengthen my claim and keep Prince Baelynn of Issos compliant and peaceful.

But first…the princess must accept her fate.

Keffa had gone quiet, giving me that paternal expression of disapproval. I didn't fucking care.

I marched from the room, frustration firing my blood. As I ascended the first few steps of the staircase, the outer door opened behind me. I stopped to watch as Pullo marched inside with Tierzel and two other wraith fae males.

While I hadn't allowed them to leave for the front with Soryn, I did reassign two other fae on duty to guard the door of the princess so they could patrol the city.

The past several days had been precarious while we rounded up all of my father's allies. We gave them the choice to either bow and pledge fealty to me or die. So far, their decisions had been swift. Bending the knee was easy when your life was on the line. But I was aware there could still be rebellion at my ascension.

As they drew closer, I recognized the twin brothers being escorted toward me, their expressions grim and tight. I turned and awaited their approach, keeping my arms at my sides, ready to fight if that's what my cousins had in mind.

Meck and Ferryn were the only sons of my aunt, my sister's mother. They'd joined my father's forces not too long ago, so I'd heard, and had been assigned as ambassadors. Reports had told us my father had sent them north to trade with the shadow fae king to acquire more gold to fund the war.

My cousins, because of their noble blood and distant connection to King Xakiel through my mother, were the most suitable to barter a deal with the shadow fae. The shadow fae had plenty of gold in their mines deep in the Solgavia Mountains, and they coveted our black steel mined from Vixet Krone.

They'd left last spring, according to ledgers my father's scribe kept. When they reached the bottom of the steps, Pullo and Tierzel stepped to the side while both Meck and Ferryn knelt on one knee, bowing their heads.

"Greetings, cousin," said Meck, always the more talkative of the two. "We bring good tidings from the north. Prince Torvyn of Gadlizel accepted the offer of black steel. We return with payment in gold…for you."

I didn't bother asking why they negotiated with the prince and not the king. There were rumors that Prince Torvyn's father had gone mad. That conversation could wait for another time.

"For *me*?" I questioned sharply. "My father commanded you to take this mission. As I'm sure you know by now, he is dead. And while I can assume that your return with gold owed to Näkt Mir is a sign of your allegiance to the crown of Northgall, I cannot accept your loyalty until it is actually given. To *me*."

Meck lifted his gaze to mine while Ferryn kept his on the stone floor. I hadn't seen either of them for years. They'd grown to be fine looking warriors.

They had no father, and my aunt left Silvantis to raise them in Belladum. My mother had always felt sad for her sister who was forced to raise her two sons on her own. I thought my aunt had always envied my mother, who had wanted for nothing as my father's mizrah. That is, until he accused her of adultery and murdered her.

"I, Meck Vulsgar, pledge my life and loyalty to the rightful heir of Northgall, Gollaya Verbane." He withdrew his short dagger at his belt and cut his palm, his offering and promise by blood. "May our god Vix hear my sincerity and truth." He fisted his palm, letting blood drip to the stone, then pressed it over his heart in a salute to me.

I descended the steps, eyeing Ferryn, who finally met my gaze. They both had unusually pale-yellow eyes, the same as my aunt and my mother.

Ferryn pulled out his dagger and cut his palm, tightening his fist and pounding it to his chest. "I, Ferryn Vulsgar, pledge my life and loyalty to the rightful heir of Northgall." His expression was intense and tight. "To Gollaya Verbane."

Our relationship had never been close or comfortable. When they were young boys and I was an adolescent, I'd play swords with them in the yard at Windolek, where I spent summers with my mother. I believed they admired me then, even if there may have been a touch of envy there.

But as they grew older, my aunt stopped visiting, then my mother was killed by my own father and I hadn't seen them since.

Until now.

It was no wonder they both wore tense expressions. Though we shared blood, we didn't know each other anymore. And I could reject their pledges of fealty since they served as ambassadors to my father, an honored position in his central court. I could kill them for it, just as I had killed my father's inner circle in the throne room. My father would certainly execute them if he were in this position.

But I was determined not to rule as he had done.

"You will both serve me as your new king, but not as my ambassadors."

Meck pursed his brow, and Ferryn clenched his jaw, still on one knee, their bleeding fists over their hearts.

"You will join my Kel Klyss. That is the only way you may serve me."

Their tight expressions instantly softened to surprise.

"Keffa will guide you in your trial. If you endure it and survive, then you will have your rightful place in my Kel Klyss as my kin."

Meck swallowed hard. "Thank you, my lord."

Ferryn was speechless, the brothers sharing a brief smile.

"When?" asked Meck.

"Now." Then I turned to Pullo. "Prepare them for the rite. Their trial begins at once. I'll speak to Keffa to oversee their trial and send word to Dalya at the Temple."

"Yes, sire."

Then I turned back toward my war room on a heavy sigh. It seemed my visit to the princess would have to wait.

CHAPTER 7

Una

"Thank you, Hava."

She set the stack of histories of Northgall on the table next to the hearth. I'd asked for reading material to help pass the time.

"Can I get you anything else?" she asked, noting my somber mood.

It had been at least a fortnight since I'd been taken to the throne room and then locked into this room.

"I'd love to know what my fate is to be. Is this my life now?" I asked with a touch of bitterness. "Sitting in a luxurious apartment, bathing and eating and sleeping?"

Hava glanced at the two chambermaids who were changing the linens on my bed. "I cannot say what is to happen."

I walked to the boarded window, crossed my arms, and peered through the sliver to see what little of the gray sky I could. "You might at least un-board the windows. I can't fly away."

They'd figured out I couldn't fly since I'd not once tried to use them to escape. When Hava asked me outright last week, I confessed the truth. There didn't seem any point in lying about it.

"They don't want you to…harm yourself, my lady."

I turned, ready to tell her that I wasn't about to take my life. I could endure quite a bit of pain and still survive, as my torture in the very dungeons beneath me as a young girl attested.

But suddenly, the echo of someone approaching in the corridor drew louder and closer. Someone moving swiftly and with purpose. We both watched the door.

There was a murmur from the guards, and the door unlocked. Then he entered, the prince himself.

My chest constricted, and my knees quivered as I blew out a shallow breath, hardly daring to move. He was *not* the wraith fae male I remembered who carried me out of the dungeon beneath this palace. Not at all.

Striding to the center of the room was the tall, armor-clad figure of King Gollaya, his black-fur cape billowing behind him, his gaze solely on me. He was taller than most of his kind, his chest broad, and he appeared far more intimidating than any I'd encountered. That included the loathsome ones who'd abducted me.

I wasn't sure if it was the black steel armor plates jutting at his shoulders or the curved short-sword at his waist or the intensity of his stare, but he was wreathed in power and potency that pushed oppressively against me.

His four horns still bore no rings of gold. Not crowned king yet, it seemed.

He bore more demon runes etched in his forehead than back then. He'd only had two small symbols above each brow when I'd first met him. Now, there was a line of black demon sign curling up his brow and disappearing into his hairline.

I knew these markings were burned into their skin by their god Vix upon rites of passage. I wondered what had pleased his god to put so many signs upon him.

His sleek black hair hung loosely well past his shoulders and down his back, no braids or ornamentation of any kind. His skin was darker than when I met him the first time, a deep, luminous shade like the shadows on the moon.

And his eyes. *Goddess save me.* Glacier-blue with a serpentine pupil ringed in gold. They'd fascinated me when I'd first seen them, when I looked on him as my savior. But now, he was the new tyrant of Northgall. My new master. I clenched my teeth as he marched closer.

He was breathtakingly and unaccountably beautiful.

He stopped in front of me, his gaze roaming my face, neck, body and wings—lingering especially on my wings—with undisguised interest. I remained perfectly still, refusing to squirm under his perusal.

"Leave us," he snapped, his deep voice emotionless.

Goll's attention never left me, his expression remained cold and hard, but his fiery gaze was not. Breathing became rather difficult. I couldn't look away either, my chest rising and falling more quickly.

Hava and the chambermaids immediately hurried from the room, the door closing with a sharp click.

Then we were alone.

Breathing out a slow exhale, I tilted my face up to meet his gaze.

I was not afraid of him when he'd carried me out of that dungeon, but the male standing before me wasn't him. This was the heir to Northgall who'd decapitated his father and burned his guard to ashes with a whispered word and potent magick. He was the new ruler of Northgall and appeared every inch the conquering Demon King.

"You have changed," I said, breaking the palpable silence.

"So have you." His silver-blue gaze strolled slowly down my body then back up, lingering yet again on my wings. The tiniest quirk of his mouth tipped up on one side. "Black."

"What?"

He stood a few feet away, his hands clasped behind him like a gentleman. It was disturbing, considering the last time I saw him he carried his father's head in his hands. "I had heard that the Princess of Issos's wings had grown back, but I didn't know they were black. Until I saw you again."

Plenty of courtiers had whispered about the dark marks behind my back, even though Baelynn did his best to shut them up. Still, it wasn't a secret.

"You are the first light fae to have black wings, are you not?" He quirked a brow, his tone telling me he knew the truth already.

"According to the histories, yes."

I'd know. I'd searched every book in our possession and then sent emissaries to seek out knowledge from the scholars of Mevia and Morodon.

Those blue dragon eyes continued to trail over my face with piercing scrutiny.

"Is that why you wanted a moment alone?" I asked haughtily. "To discuss the unique color of my wings?"

His gaze snapped to mine. No hint of a smile. "I want to present my terms of surrender directly to you since you are the one who will fulfill them."

"Surrender?" I frowned. "Of Issos?"

"Of Issos," he stated calmly. "And all of Lumeria."

I huffed out a shocked breath. "Is this why I'm still prisoner here? To be your pawn in a trade to my brother for peace?"

"There will be no trade, Una."

I frowned at him using my shortened name so intimately. I swallowed hard, his burning gaze tracking the movement down my throat before returning back to meet mine.

"What are you terms of surrender?" I asked, my voice low and trembling, betraying me. "To be your concubine?"

That was what his father intended though Xakiel had plans to kill my family as well.

He took a confident step closer, his hands still clasped behind his back. His scent enveloped me—snow and wind and the musk of a wild animal. His dragon.

Though he towered over me, I held my chin high, refusing to break from his intimidating stare.

"You will not be my concubine." He tilted his head, watching me intently. "You will be the mother of my heir."

I blinked several times, my pulse quickening. "What?" I whispered.

"You are the highest born light fae female of all the kingdoms. The magick of your bloodline is the strongest and most potent. Combined with my bloodline, our child, my heir, will be the most powerful wraith fae ever born. And our alliance will unite our kingdoms. Under *my* rule."

I focused on breathing and not fainting at the shock of what he was declaring to me, demanding of me.

"There is only one problem, my lord. I have no magick." None that was of use anyway. More like a curse than a gift. "It was all stripped away *five* years ago in Näkt Mir."

His smile was feral as he dipped his head lower. "No lies between us, Princess."

"It's true," I snapped. Though not entirely.

He smirked. "I'm aware you can no longer fly."

I flinched. Though it was a cold hard fact, no one dared ever say it aloud. The wraith king spilled my hard reality like it was nothing at all, water pouring out of a pitcher.

"That doesn't matter," he continued casually. "Whatever you believe you have lost does not change your bloodline. It remains the same. Do you accept the terms?"

I blinked in astonishment, anger vibrating through me. "The terms to give you an heir in exchange for my entire kingdom?" I asked, incredulous.

"I will rule Lumeria as I will Northgall, with fairness and care for its people. As long as you adhere to your end of the bargain."

I stared in utter shock. He wasn't jesting. He wanted my compliance and apparently my womb in exchange for the safety and prosperity of my people.

"What becomes of me after I give you an heir?" I stammered in complete disbelief. "And what if it is female?"

"The firstborn healthy child you give to me will be my heir. Male or female."

I couldn't help the scoff that escaped past my lips. "A female wraith queen? I thought your kind had no queens." For the histories of dark fae had all verified there never had been one.

His smirk widened. "We do not co-rule with any other, that is true. But if my firstborn is a daughter, then I will teach her to rule as a proper wraith fae monarch."

"Firstborn? Are you expecting more than one child from me?"

One shoulder lifted in a casual shrug, which was not disarming in the least. "You may enjoy my company in your bed and decide to give me more."

I gasped and stepped back, clenching my fists at my sides so I wouldn't haul back and punch him in the face.

He laughed. Actually laughed. And the sound was irritatingly pleasant. I *hated* him.

Exhaling a hard breath, I stated clearly, "I will not want one moment more in your bed than what is legally required. It's bad enough you're forcing me into this."

"I'm not forcing anything at all." His amused demeanor vanished. "You are welcome to refuse."

"And if I refuse, you will continue your war, burn the whole city of Issos to the ground, I presume?"

He lifted that same shoulder in a casual shrug again.

Holding onto my control by a bare thread, I then asked, "What becomes of me once I've served my purpose and given you an heir?"

His voice had morphed into the colder timbre I'd heard him use with his father the second before he beheaded him.

"I'll keep you here in this luxurious apartment in the palace of Näkt Mir, which befits your station. Or there is another castle to the north of Silvantis. Windolek Castle is small but comfortable. Farther away." His eyes softened for only a second, then they were hard again. "You may live there, far from me, if that is your wish. Or you may return to Issos if you prefer."

"And leave my child behind?"

"My heir will not be leaving Northgall, but you are welcome to do as you please after you've done your duty."

Flaming ire shot up my spine. *Done my duty.* Spread my legs for the murdering wraith king and give him a piece of my body. My soul, too.

Flames of heat licked up my neck into my cheeks. Yet again, he noticed with that all-too-knowing gaze.

"You will not separate me from my own child," I finally managed to say. Near panting now, I was furious and terrified he'd send me away from a child I didn't even have yet.

He hardly seemed to be affected by this entire conversation at all, and that alone made me angrier.

"As you wish. You may stay in Northgall."

"If it will save my people of Lumeria"—I licked my lips, my mouth gone dry—"I will accept."

A transformation came over his face, slow and subtle, an expression of surprise. Perhaps he expected more tears and wailing and nonsense. I wasn't that kind of woman. I would never refuse an offer to save my people, not even at the expense of my own life. My own will.

But this could all be a trick. There was no path now set before me that didn't lead to ruin and pain and heartache. I had to find out if it was true that he had Issos under siege. There were high walls and gates around the city. It had never been breached before.

Since the moment of my captivity, I hadn't once thought of Gael. But, of course, now I did.

"I am betrothed," I added quietly.

He narrowed his gaze, his expression hard. "You are no longer betrothed."

Papa had arranged my betrothal to Gael, our noble families a good alliance for Lumeria. We were to be bound in the Moon Temple in Valla Lokyr when the war was over. I respected Gael but had no love for him. Still, the sting of betrayal at breaking our betrothal without a word to him cut deeply. But my kingdom mattered more.

"Don't bother crying over whatever light fae your father chose for you."

"I'm not crying," I snapped with defiance, though I was still trembling with emotion.

He unclasped his hands, veined and claw-tipped, now hanging loosely at his sides. He stepped closer, well into my personal space. I moved back, suddenly afraid of the look in his dragon eyes.

"Tell me, Tiarrialuna Elzabethanine Hartstone," he crooned softly, as if to calm a wild animal, but speaking my full name only made my heart speed faster.

He continued forward. "Have you kept your promise to your goddess and kept yourself virtuous?"

My spine hit the tapestry against the wall. I flattened my palms against it, holding myself steady.

He eased forward, though his movements were deliberate, not casual. "I'll know if you lie to me."

Only a few inches separated us.

"Why would that matter if I'm only to be a vessel for your heir?"

"It won't matter in that regard. But it will matter to *me*."

I couldn't understand the sudden fury dancing across his face, the possessive madness in his eyes.

"I'm a maiden," I snapped, a heated blush filling my cheeks.

He examined me closely and then seemed to finally believe me. But he wasn't done.

"How many times did he touch you?" he asked silkily. "Your betrothed."

"What?" was all I could manage to breathe out in shock and panic.

One of his clawed hands threaded into my hair and cupped the back of my head, holding me captive. Then I felt his other hand on my thigh, his fingers inching up the fabric of my gown.

"Tell me how many times he touched you, Una." My name lingered on his lips like a velvet caress.

"He—he didn't."

"He did." The material of my dress and chemise were bunched between us, the pads of his fingers trailing from the outside of my bare thigh toward the inside. "How many times?"

The inner slit of his iris burned a brighter gold within the blue as I panted and clutched onto his armored forearm. "Please, Gollaya."

"Tell me." Leaning his head close to my ear, he whispered, "I believe that you're a maid, Una, but I will know how many times that blue-winged fuck touched your body." His fingers brushed closer to my bare sex.

I gasped and rose onto my toes, horrified at the sudden rush of heat in my lower belly and the realization that I was equally frightened and aroused.

"If he touched you here, I'll have to kill him," he whispered with velvety softness, all while he inched closer to my quim.

"*No.* He didn't touch me there."

He froze and eased his head back to meet my gaze. "Where?"

"He—" I cleared my throat, my focus still on the long, thick fingers now wrapped around my inner thigh with a possessive grip. "He kissed me once and…" I glanced away.

He released the back of my head and gripped my chin, guiding my gaze back to him. His other hand remained wrapped around my thigh. "And?"

I huffed out a breath, embarrassed to have to admit something I'd barely been able to confess to Min in the privacy of my bedchamber. It had been after a feast, and he'd cornered me in the corridor after he drank too much wine.

"And he touched my breast. But I told him that wasn't proper, and he stopped instantly."

Perhaps not instantly, but near enough. I firmed my jaw. Goll tilted his head, still measuring me for truthfulness, it seemed.

"Two times. That's all. I swear." I still couldn't figure out why this mattered or why he cared, but I needed to end this awful conversation.

Finally, his mouth eased into a bewitching smile. "Good."

With one last gentle squeeze of my thigh, he removed his hand from between my legs and dropped my chemise and gown back into place. He even brushed out a wrinkle that caught on my hip. I pushed his hand away, trying to regain some sense of control while my cheeks flushed with heat and embarrassment.

He seemed amused as he took a decided step back while I went about brushing out wrinkles that were no longer there, calming myself after what he'd just done. Or almost did. My heart still raced with what I was afraid to admit was *want*.

Then something dawned on me. "How did you know Gael had blue wings?"

He didn't answer me, of course, simply arched his brow. His arrogance and aggressive familiarity had slid under my skin and spiked my own anger.

"So I'm simply to hand myself over and do your will when I haven't heard one word of my brother? For all he knows, I'm dead, not that it matters to you. And how do I know you actually have Issos surrounded and can command such a thing of me?" I scoffed bitterly. "Perhaps you are lying to keep me compliant as your prisoner here. I could just as easily kill myself and prevent you from siring a child on me. My brother's army could still defeat you."

He stared at me in silence, his expression completely unreadable. Then he gave a stiff nod. "Come with me, Una." Then he turned and walked for the door. "If you don't follow now, I'll have to carry you."

He opened the door and kept walking. I huffed in frustration and followed him.

CHAPTER 8

Goll

Hearing her swift steps behind me, I smiled to myself. For the first time since I'd severed my father's head, I began to feel like the rightful king. Perhaps it was gaining Una's agreement to be my mizrah that was the final piece to the puzzle in settling my mind. I wasn't sure. All I knew was this elation of rightness as I led her up the steps to the floor above and opened the door to the wide outer terrace.

I stepped out, the sky dark now, the full moon rising. How fortuitous that Una's goddess should offer such a full and bright omen tonight. My soldiers had done a fine job in removing the spiked parapet here as I'd ordered.

Drakmir purred at the sight of me, the giant dragon barely discernible in the dark. His silver-blue eyes glowed by the moonlight as he lifted his head.

I stopped and glanced back. Una had frozen.

"Goddess above," she muttered, easing closer behind me, the edge of her wing grazing my wrist.

I stared down, stunned still at the softness of her before returning my attention to Drakmir. "He won't hurt you. He's gentle as a lamb."

"I'll bet he eats lambs." Her voice quavered.

"He does, in fact. Actually, he prefers goats. Lambs aren't much of a mouthful." I held out my hand, wondering if she'd take it.

I'd been more than harsh to her thus far, and she had no reason to trust me. But I still craved her faith in me.

"There is no reason to fear him, princess. You've faced bigger threats before and shown little fear in the face of it."

I remembered the way she'd challenged my father and his contemptible behavior right before I killed him.

She snapped her gaze to mine, anger still bright on her face. "I've been terrified from the moment your father's brutes killed my handmaiden and abducted me."

I blinked in surprise that she'd even admit that to me. She didn't guard herself against me as I had imagined she would. I'd expected a pampered princess, defiant and wholly resistant. I'd expected tears and wailing and protestations before finally accepting her fate. After years of being groomed into her royal position, a haughty facade was the very least I anticipated from her.

I took a step forward and curled my outstretched fingers, beckoning more gently. "Come."

Whether she was simply following her survival instincts to seek my protection or my softened voice gave her courage, she hesitantly took my hand, her gaze moving to Drakmir, as she let me guide her closer. Drakmir slowly lifted his head where he'd been lazily resting it on the terrace. He snuffed the air at the unfamiliar scent beside me.

"*Gloyen*, Drak. *Asha styen*," I said in a soothing, calm voice as we approached. "*Asha styen*."

His nostrils flared as he curved his neck lower to sniff the air. Una tightened her hold on my hand, and a jolt of awareness pulled my attention back to her.

"Have you ever seen a dragon?"

"No. They do not fly near Issos." She stepped closer beside me, her eyes on Drakmir.

"The myth about dragons that they only attack when they sense fear is sheer nonsense," I told her.

"Is it?" she asked shakily as I lifted her hand in mine and stretched her arm toward Drakmir's snout.

"Dragons aren't simple animals, beasts who react with predatory instincts." I placed her palm on the flat space between Drakmir's nostrils upon his smooth black scales, my palm covering the back of her hand. "They are magickal creatures, not mindless monsters."

She exhaled on a sigh, easing closer to stroke him. Drakmir's eyes closed to half-mast, a low purr vibrating in his chest. "When do they attack? When their master tells them to?" Her gaze flicked to me, and she stopped petting him.

"Dragons have no masters."

"Then what are you to him?" Those violet eyes I'd seen in my dreams thousands of nights held me captive.

I'd never forgotten her, the young fae girl who I'd saved from death by my father's wights. And yet it had never occurred to me that she would grow into such a stunning beauty. Her eyes, still a luminous violet, were no longer those of a girl but of a woman who'd known hardship and pain.

Drakmir nudged her on the shoulder. She jumped back, fixated on him with the tiniest of smiles. My dragon wanted more of her petting. I understood the craving.

"*Shaleem*, Drak."

He groaned and settled into a crouch, his tail knocking some of the balustrade's stonework over the side. I didn't care. This was now his devoted perch when he wasn't wandering the skies or the woodlands. He tended to favor the Esher Wood behind the palace.

I didn't even think to get her cloak. I unhooked mine made, from a Meer-wolf pelt, and wrapped it around her shoulders.

Glancing up to the night sky, I noted, "At least there's no snow. But it'll be cold up there."

"We're *flying*?" Her shaken voice made Drak snuff.

"There is something I must show you."

I nudged her toward his side and climbed up the rope ladder connected to the saddle, then held down my hand. "Climb up to me."

She frowned but didn't protest, then hauled herself up until I could reach her. Once in my grip, I pulled her up and settled her crossways onto my lap, careful of her wings. Humming at the satisfaction of having her in my grasp, I shifted her body till she fit perfectly within the bracket of my arms and thighs.

For a brief moment, I remembered the softness of her skin on her inner thigh then banned the memory instantly from my thoughts. I couldn't fantasize about what I couldn't have just yet. Not until the mizrah ceremony in my palace. Not until she bathed in the black lake. My gut clenched, a single thread of dread at the thought of it.

"How do I hold on?" she asked, glancing over the edge nervously.

"You can hold onto me if you like."

That earned me a fierce look. *Mmm.* I wanted more of that.

"Hold onto the pommel here." I placed her hand on the pommel closest to her. There were two, one on either side of the saddle. "You'll need trousers to fly astride, then you can hold onto both." I buckled the harness around both our waists, tightening the strap. "But don't worry, my mizrah," I crooned into her ear as I wrapped an arm tightly around her waist, one hand on her outer thigh. "I won't let you go."

She looked away, but she asked softly, "What does mizrah mean?"

I smiled, ignoring that conversation for now, and then shouted to Drakmir, "*Hyvellin!*"

Drak beat his wings and shoved off the terrace, shooting us up into the sky. Her weight fell into me on the upward slant. She gasped but didn't scream, both her hands white-knuckling the pommel. Drak flew at an angle toward the night sky, Lumera's round moon seeming closer as we ascended. We were far above Näkt Mir, but her eyes were still on the stars.

"Well done," I praised, my mouth close to her ear as I tightened my hold on her upper thigh and ribcage. "No fear on your first flight. I'm impressed."

"It's so beautiful," she breathed out, the roaring wind nearly stealing her words.

"*Gasta met*, Drak!"

He instantly turned and circled south. I showed him through our mental link where to go. By horseback, the ride would take days. But on dragonback, we'd be there before the moon had reached its peak in the night sky.

I remained quiet, catching glances of Una's enthralled expression as she observed the world from above. Drak flew higher until we were above the clouds.

Una gasped. I couldn't suppress a small smile at trying to see from her eyes. The gray clouds stretched out like a soft blanket, the moonglow silvering the sky like an ethereal dream.

For the moment, I soaked in this feeling of contentment, my mizrah in my arms, the kingdoms almost mine, the old promise given by my god Vix finally coming true. But as Drak descended, I steeled myself for what was about to come.

We lowered out of the clouds and closer to the ground, passing over the glittering Bluevale River. She tensed, knowing exactly where we were now.

"Sweet goddess," she murmured as we passed over the fields beyond Issos, where thousands of wraith fae gathered outside the walls.

Then we crossed over the walls of the royal city, she saw there were thousands more in the streets below. Blue coal-fire torches filled the streets. Pale moonlight illuminated her vast city, the white bricks of the castle an architectural beauty.

I couldn't see her expression, but I heard her heart beat faster with my heightened hearing and felt her breathing quicken beneath my arm.

Drak dove low as we drew closer. Her white hair shimmered in the moonlight like her pale skin. My stomach tightened with the need to touch its softness, to trail my fingers through its length, to wrap it around my fist.

My soldiers were chanting my name below Valla Lokkyr. The repeated, deep reverberation echoed up to us.

"Goll! Goll! Goll!"

The fact that my army had chosen my name for their mantra was a positive sign, indeed. All of my father's army had fallen swiftly in line, seemingly eager to follow me, their new king. While I was yet uncrowned, they chanted my name as their leader of this victory.

But there was one step yet to take, and we were about to take it. The wraith fae and now the light fae of Lumeria must understand that I ruled with an iron fist. It was the only way to assure obedience and dissuade rebellion.

I tried not to tighten my hold on Una's arm as she was far more delicate than in my dreams, but I needed this tangible proof that I truly had her. I stole a sidelong glance. She kept her chin high and her wings straight. Her *black* wings.

Son of Vix. She was made for me. Refashioned after that fateful day with the mark that told the world where she belonged. At least, according to Dalya. And very few knew my soul seer Dalya's vision. I'd been waiting for the sign, and there it was, sprouting from her back.

She would indeed give me the heir I deserved, that my people deserved. To right the old wrongs. And the kingdoms would be united under *my* rule as was foretold.

I ordered Drak to land on the bridge leading to the eastern tower, the one closest to the great hall at the top of Valla Lokyr, where Soryn would be waiting.

He beat his wings as we lowered and landed with a thud. I eased off behind her first then lifted my arms up to help her down. My gut instantly clenched at the glassiness of her eyes. Now she understood. She had no choice.

Deklam, one of my lieutenants, approached with a dozen of his infantrymen behind him. They'd been looking for me. After pulling Una down and setting her beside me, I turned.

"Sire." Deklam thumped his chest with his fist in obeisance and bowed his head. "We are stationed throughout Issos. Soryn and Prince Baelynn await you in the great hall."

Una flinched in my grasp and made a sound of protest, but I ignored her.

I took hold of Una's hand to guide her at my side to the throne room of her former home.

She was tense and quiet. Too quiet.

"Do not worry, Princess. I have no plans to harm your brother." I glanced at her fearful expression. "Or you," I added.

She didn't answer as we passed through the white corridors of Valla Lokyr, my wraith fae on guard at every turn.

When she finally spoke, her voice had a detached, dreamlike quality. "I do not know what is in store for me now. All I know is that my life is no longer my own."

I would like to have argued against her belief, but I would not lie to her. She was right. Her life was no longer her own. Fate did indeed have a certain future orchestrated with her as its primal center, its glorious star. And for that future to come to pass, she must be mine.

And I was about to ensure that once and for all.

CHAPTER 9
Una

As we approached the doors of our great hall, I pulled my hand free of Gollaya's. I wouldn't be dragged into my own goddess's temple by him. I would walk with my head held high when I faced my brother. I wouldn't have Baelynn see me with fear in my eyes or being hauled like baggage into our home.

As the two wraith fae guards opened the doors, I soaked in the splendor of the Moon Temple, a place that had always brought me solace and peace.

The glass dome of the great hall above us cast a pool of moonlight onto the center of the white marble floor. Within that moonlit circle were inlaid, painted tiles, a mosaic in the likeness of our Goddess Lumera's face—high brow, sculpted jaw, eloquent nose, soft mouth, intelligent eyes.

Stone pillars carved in the shapes of her handmaidens wreathed the wide chamber, their arms reaching up to hold up the ceiling of this hallowed room that served as both a receiving chamber and a temple to honor our most sacred goddess.

At the head of the room were two thrones on a dais, one for Baelynn and I to greet ambassadors and visitors as we had together since our father had become bedridden.

For hundreds of years, the royals of Issos have received foreign ambassadors and nobility of every great house across Lumeria to Skeldos. But never in all the histories I've read had there been a dark fae king and his army standing within these walls.

The room was lined on both sides by Gollaya's Culled, his elite guard. The one striding quickly for us was the one he called Soryn, apparently his second in command. He had four horns, the bases of each encased in decorative silver. His bare wrists were sheathed in silver guards also, decorated in some kind of pattern. His eyes were deep red, and his face was handsome, though his dark scowl was set on me before he looked at his king.

He called loudly in demon tongue, "*Veksal Gollaya il Näkt Mir et Northgall.*"

The other warriors bellowed in unison, "Goll!"

As Soryn moved closer, I saw my brother held on the other side by two wraith fae. "Una!"

Without hesitation, I ran across the room toward him. Goll must've given the guards a signal behind me for they let him go. Baelynn met me halfway and pulled me into a tight embrace.

"Are you alright?" he whispered, voice trembling.

"Yes, yes," I assured him, pulling back so that I could look at him.

There was a purple bruise coloring one cheek, below his eye. "You're not," I snapped.

"I'm fine." He gripped my shoulders. "You are truly unharmed?"

I nodded. He bent his head closer to me.

"Don't worry," he whispered. "I've read the treaty his drawn up. I won't sign it. I won't allow him to take you back there."

Studying his face—both fury and fear mingling in his expression—I managed to smile, trying to ease his distress. He had no idea that Gollaya wouldn't allow it. I was certain of that.

I glanced over his shoulder to see there had been a number of the Issosian Royal Guard, hands cuffed in iron and seated on the floor to one side. They must've taken the palace mere hours before. Gael was one of the Issosians also cuffed and held against the wall. His furious gaze bore into mine.

I shook my head at him, willing him to understand there was no other way.

"You're just in time, Sire," said Soryn behind us where Gollaya stood, surveying the room and watching me. "It took us three days rather than one to breach the walls and secure the city. I'd hoped to have things more settled when you arrived."

"Your messenger arrived just today," Gollaya told him. "Seems everything is well in hand."

"Except that we don't have enough prison cells to contain them all."

"That won't be necessary," said Gollaya. He and his lieutenant strode across the room toward me and my brother.

Baelynn instinctively stiffened. I knew that he was about to do something foolish to protect me, as if he could, but I placed a hand on his shoulder.

"Baelynn." When his gaze snapped to mine, I said, "I know the terms of the treaty."

And now I knew that Gollaya hadn't bluffed. Not at all.

I turned to face Gollaya. "I fully accept the terms."

"No," grated Baelynn. "You *can't*, Una."

Gollaya completely ignored him and held out his hand to Soryn. His second placed a scroll in his king's palm who then handed it to me.

I unscrolled the parchment and swiftly read the accord, noting that he'd laid out the terms clearly in demon tongue. His oath to provide protection and peace to the people of Lumeria would continue, only if I remained in Northgall until I bore an heir. Our child would be raised to be the next monarch of both Lumeria and Northgall.

Finished reading, I exhaled a slow breath then marched to the steps of the throne dais and to the tall table which usually held refreshments when we were at court. When I turned, it was to find all eyes staring at me in wonder.

"Unless you plan for me to sign this in my own blood," I said to Gollaya, "I'll need a quill and ink."

Soryn snapped at one of the soldiers, but I watched as Gollaya strode steadily across the room and up the steps, his mouth quirked in an annoying smile. He stopped before me and lifted his hand, brushing his fingertips under my upturned chin, his claws lightly scraping my skin. I managed not to shiver though the light caress was unexpectedly enticing.

"Such a smart female. I knew the gods would choose one like you for me, Una."

I bristled at his arrogance, but somehow found myself blushing at the odd compliment.

A wraith fae walked up the steps and set a quill and inkwell on the tall table at my side then left the dais. I dipped the quill and signed my full name without much flourish then handed the quill to Gollaya.

I refused to look at him, knowing he likely wore that same smug smile. I looked at my brother.

"Baelynn."

He stood there, his complexion pale. He shook his head.

"Baelynn. This is the way. I'll be alright." I managed to sound confident and convincing. For him.

We stared and I pleaded to him without saying another word. Finally, he cursed under his breath and marched up the steps. He jerked the quill from Gollaya and stared down at the document for several minutes. Finally, he signed it, dropped the quill, and then spun to face Gollaya, stepping close.

"If you harm her, treaty or not, I'll come to Northgall and kill you."

"Baelynn, please." I grabbed his arm, trying to push him back, afraid he was going to get himself hurt.

"I'd expect nothing less," said Goll, calm and steady.

I looked up at him, "Can you and I have a word in private now?"

Without waiting for an answer, I let go of Baelynn and quickly descended the stone steps, crossed the floor, and exited into the corridor. The guards there didn't stop me, but simply watched as I crossed to a vestibule where there was a cushioned bench seat against the wall.

I used to sit here and look out at our kingdom, at our beautiful city. Now, there was nothing but blue torchlight and the faint chant of Goll's name. They were still reciting his name in that deep, haunting mantra. He may have only recently taken over his father's army, but it was obvious they worshipped him now.

I heard him step into the corridor and draw closer. I also heard the guards leaving their post, assuming he sent them away. At least he was being respectful enough to adhere to my wishes. I didn't want witnesses for this conversation.

"I've signed your accord. And I will…give you what you want." I turned to look up at him, his expression an frustratingly unreadable mask again. "But I have a demand of my own."

He blinked slowly then asked, "What is it you require, Una?"

"To be bound here in the Moon Temple."

For the first time since we'd arrived, he conjured a casual pose, crossing his arms and cocking one knee out while leaning his weight on the other leg. "We don't believe in marriage, Princess."

"But I do."

"Whether we are or aren't *bound*, our union is not a marriage as you see it. You will not become my queen with your sacred words. You will be my bedmate until I fill your belly with my child. That is all."

His words sank heavily like a cold stone in my stomach. Whatever small respect I felt minutes before for him was completely gone now. I would be a vessel, his brood mare.

"I understand," I replied with equal coldness, "but if I leave Valla Lokkyr into your keeping and bear a child, I will be considered a pariah to my people—ruined, regardless that I'm giving up my life to save theirs. Unless we hold the sacred moon-binding ceremony before we go."

He stared, his mask vanishing, giving way to anger. But he said nothing, as if my request was ridiculous.

"I will not be the wraith king's whore," I stated bitingly, "at least not in the eyes of my own people."

The wraith fae would know what I was to their king. And Baelynn would never publicize or likely tell anyone what was stated in the accord we both just signed to save our entire kingdom. If I was bound here, everyone would assume it was a proper union to keep the peace. That's the very least I could hope for in this unholy alliance.

"I'm giving up my entire life. All I ask for myself is that you suffer through a short ceremony. If it means nothing to you, then why refuse me?"

He clenched his jaw, looking over my head at the moonlight spilling through the window, then he exhaled a heavy breath. "Fine.

If it will keep you compliant." He uncrossed his arms and turned to stalk in long strides toward the closed double doors.

"And may I see my father before we go?"

He stopped and turned. I wasn't surprised he'd already been aware of my father's illness. For he barely even blinked before snapping, "Go see him now." He motioned for the guards to go with me. "I'll tell your brother to get whatever priest is needed for this ceremony. But it is all to be done in less than an hour. Hurry."

And those were the lovely words spoken to me by my soon-to-be husband.

I rushed down the corridor with my wraith fae guard on my heels to my father's bedchamber.

CHAPTER 10

Una

"Papa," I whispered as I settled on the side of his bed. The guards gave me privacy and waited outside. "It's Una, Papa." I took his hand in mine. "I've come to say goodbye."

The low, steady chant of the wraith fae outside reverberated through the thick palace walls. They seemed to be waiting for his return on his dragon.

Surprisingly, Papa opened his eyes and looked at me. I blinked back the stinging tears. His irises were full white now, only the tiniest sliver of dark purple rimming the outer ring. He'd lost his ability to speak seven months ago. He'd been bed-ridden for well over a year.

But sometimes, his whitened gaze held the lucid intelligence he had before the sickness had begun to slowly take his life thirteen years ago. Like now. The way he looked at me, I knew he heard me.

A luminous healing orb vibrated, hovering over the foot of his bed and casting a golden hue throughout the room. The healers kept a charged orb—called a moon chalice—radiating out life-saving magick that fed into my father day and night. It was all that was keeping him alive. Sometimes, I wondered if he wanted us to just let him go.

Not for the first time, I wished I'd been able to create an orb for him myself. But that magick was long gone from me. I fluttered the wings at my back, reminding myself that I'd at least gotten one thing back that had been taken from me. Not that they were of much use.

"Papa, I'm going away for a while."

The tiniest crease formed between his brows. He didn't like it when I was gone. He probably hadn't realized that I'd already been gone for many weeks.

I remembered how he'd scolded me as I lay in my sickbed when Baelynn had brought me back from Northgall five years ago. When he demanded I tell him why I'd gone, he'd become even angrier with me. I'd risked my life to find a cure for all of those falling ill with the Parviana Plague, this sickness that had crippled so many of the moon fae. And now, he was dying with it.

Parviana was the name of the first moon fae girl who fell ill with it. Nothing and no one had been able to stop the illness from taking her life.

"I know you hate it when I go away, but it won't be for long," I lied, knowing this was goodbye.

Näkt Mir was far from Issos, and I had no idea when or if I would ever return.

I squeezed my father's hand. "I'll be back, Papa. I promise."

At least, I'd try. As soon as the wraith king let me, I would come back.

Papa blinked heavily. I sniffed and wiped the tear that slipped down my cheek. "Yes. I love you, too. So dearly." I leaned over and kissed his cheek.

He closed his eyes and fell back into his slumber.

I left my father asleep and marched directly for my chamber with my two wraith fae guards in tow. When I reached my bedroom, I turned to them.

"I'm packing my clothes. Please allow me some privacy."

They frowned at me for a moment then the one seemingly in charge nodded and they remained at the door.

I took very little time packing as many gowns and chemises as I could into my traveling trunk. I included my gold necklace of the moon's crescent. Glancing at the open door to be sure they weren't watching, I then pulled my bound journal from beneath the bed where I kept it.

I'd gathered prophecies from all three kinds of oracles—soul seers who could attach to one person and foretell their destinies, god seers who heard and spoke the will of the gods, and world seers who prophesied the fate of fae kind. But it was the visions that pertained to the plague that had kept me vigilant in my search. And I'd found them all. All three.

I grabbed a folded chemise on the bed and hurriedly wrapped it around the journal full of the prophecies I'd collected. Then I stuffed it at the bottom of the trunk.

Finished, I strolled back to the doorway, facing the senior guard.

"My trunk is ready. Please ensure it makes the journey safely as that is all of my homeland I'll have for a long time."

The wraith guard simply nodded. "It will be done, my lady."

Now it was time for me to marry Gollaya Verbane.

The glass dome of the great hall above us cast a pool of moonlight onto the center of the white marble floor. I stood inside Lumera's glow beneath the glass dome next to the priest. But my gaze was on my brother near the throne dais whispering vehemently to Gael, now uncuffed as he argued with Baelynn.

Everyone had been removed from the chamber except for Baelynn and Gael. Goll and his second strode toward us from the hall doorway, both wearing stern expressions. I don't know what any of them had to argue or be cross about. I was the one on the sacrificial altar.

When they reached me, I asked, "Why is he staying?" I nodded toward the dais.

Because forcing Gael to watch me marry another man would be torture. While I held no love for Gael, I'd been committed to him and prepared to marry him for most of my adult life. And I was aware he had deep affection for me though it mattered little now. Still, I didn't think it kind to force him to watch it.

"The priest said we must each have witnesses." Goll's voice had gone hard. The conquering warrior king now stood on the altar with me.

"My brother should be enough."

"No," he answered quickly. "His second will remain as witness too." Goll's steely gaze slid to Gael.

My heart beat faster, for Goll knew that was my former betrothed.

Then my brother was crossing the hall with Gael behind him toward the temple stone, which is what we called the sacred circle where I now stood. He took his place behind me. I met Gael's gaze, flinching at the fury burning there.

Of course this was difficult for him, but not nearly as difficult as it was for me. He had no right to argue with my brother over what I'm positive were his losses as my betrothed. I would be losing much more.

Goll took his place facing me within the temple stone, Soryn stood behind him and scowled. He didn't like me, that was certain.

The priest who'd been standing quietly outside the circle, stepped beside me and Goll. He began speaking of the importance of binding in heart, body, and soul, but before he'd gotten two sentences out, Goll raised a hand, stopping his speech.

"Let's get to the meat of it, priest. My men below are getting restless, and I'd rather not keep them waiting too long before they decide to go against my orders and pillage anyway."

My mouth dropped open. "They'd pillage the city when we've surrendered?"

Goll turned his intense gaze on me, those eyes always sending an electric shock through me. "Until I leave this palace *with you*, the bargain isn't set. Delays make soldiers restless and might give them the impression there's trouble." He arched a brow. "My men love trouble."

Clenching my jaw, I said through gritted teeth, "Please hurry, Elder Lelwyn."

"Yes, Elder Lelwyn," Goll said mockingly. "Make haste, shall we?"

For the first time, his second behind him smirked, his red eyes narrowing with amusement, making me more angry.

"Yes, yes, of course." Elder Lelwyn was a kind, old fae who'd served our house for many years. He'd even joined my parents in their own moon-binding ceremony. He jumped quickly *to the meat of it*, as Goll had suggested.

"Clasp your hands and press your forearms together for the binding words."

I held both my arms up, bent at the elbow. Goll just looked at me, his gaze roving my upturned arms.

"Take my hands and do as I do," I whispered.

Goll stepped forward and lifted his arms. The immensity of him, especially covered in thick, black-steel armor, seemed almost ridiculous at this moment. I was used to prettily dressed fae males in silk and brocade with perfumed hair and smooth hands. Goll was completely the opposite.

His calloused palms pressed to mine, then he curled his long fingers through mine, reminding me where those fingers had recently been. His claws touched the back of my hand, but they didn't pierce the skin. His eyes blazed with that familiar fire I'd seen when he first walked into my bedchamber back at Näkt Mir.

I gulped hard as Elder Lelwyn asked us both to repeat after him. But when I began to speak, Goll said nothing. He just watched me with unnerving intensity as I recited the sacred words.

"My king," said Elder Lelwyn, "you must repeat after me. You say the vows at the same time."

"I'm aware of your custom, priest," said Goll, his eyes on me, "but the princess will be reciting her vows for her own peace of mind. I don't need them."

"I see, well, I see that…hmmm. I'm not sure that—"

Baelynn stepped forward and placed a hand on the priest's elbow. "It's fine, Elder Lelwyn. We will recognize the ceremony's validity regardless. Won't we?"

The poor elder stared wide-eyed in his white robe at my brother, never having been put in this situation. He'd be performing his own magick on this ceremony for the binding. A priest's magick was considered sacred for the binding magick it held.

"I'm not sure the binding will take if both don't speak the words."

The vows in a moon-binding were part of a spell that wove with the priest's god-given magick to bind us. The bond wouldn't hold, of course, since we were not a proper match, but the ceremony would be recognized by all of Lumeria, branding me as that pitiful fae princess, bound to the wraith king. At least, I would not be renounced a whore, and that's all that mattered to me at the moment.

"That might be for the best," I said, still clasped in Goll's grip.

"I see." Elder Lelwyn cleared his throat. "Then repeat after me, Princess." He began to recite the vows.

"I bequeath to you my loyalty, my fidelity, and my love." I frowned at the falseness pouring from my own mouth as Elder Lelwyn went on. I repeated, "My trust and my companionship till our years are long and our days are done." I swallowed hard then repeated, "I give you the…"

I stumbled at the next part.

"You must repeat it," said Elder Lelwyn.

Goll smiled, a predatory gleam in his dragon eyes. He squeezed our clasped hands and leaned closer, his blue eyes glinting in the moonlight. "Yes, I want to hear this last part from your lips, Princess," he whispered intimately, his gaze dropping to my mouth.

Taking a deep breath, I repeated what the priest had said, "I give you the fruit of our coupling with an open heart, vowing to treasure any children who come of this consecrated union. I vow to hold sacred this binding, sanctified by the blessed Goddess Lumera beneath her divine light."

Elder Lelwyn said the last sentence again. Then I repeated it.

"I give my whole self, body and soul, into your care and keeping. For as long as the moon shines and magick reigns."

Goll grinned so wide I could finally see his pointed canines. Rather than repulse me, my heart raced with excitement. How could that possibly be?

Then Elder Lelwyn's magick began to burn along our clasped wrists, our hands and fingers, sliding in a tendril of silvery-white light. It wound tighter around our wrists, creating a band of light tethering us together. Goll stiffened, sensing the ropes of light fae magick sizzling around us and along our skin.

For the first time since he'd entered this chamber, I smiled. I liked seeing Goll confused and uncomfortable.

"It won't hurt you. Or taint you, my king," I said mockingly.

His scowl deepened. "I know that. Light fae magick can't hurt me."

"Not the almighty, fierce wraith king?"

His scowl softened, and a wicked light flickered in those blue-gold depths. "That's right, Princess."

Elder Lelwyn clapped his hands once, the shimmering strings of magick entwining our clasped hands and wrists fading. But they left behind a raised bracelet of flesh around my wrist, where the priest's magick had burned brightest. I wondered if there would be traces beneath Goll's armor.

"By the Divine Goddess Lumera, you are bound as one," proclaimed Elder Lelwyn. "There now. All done, my king."

But Goll didn't immediately let me go. His intense gaze moved from my eyes to my wrist. He was likely wondering how long I'd have this mark and if he bore one as well. He released my hands, but when I stepped back, he wrapped a hand around my forearm and kept me from stepping away.

"You said only two times." He searched my face. "Isn't that right, Una?"

My brow pursed as I tried to figure out what he was talking about. "Two times?"

He held me tight but also gently, his finger at my chin sliding up my jaw, his thumb trailing behind to caress my cheek before he let me go.

With agile swiftness, he stepped around me in two long strides and grasped Gael by the throat. I gasped and covered my mouth, watching in horror.

When Baelynn went for his dagger, Goll's second stepped forward. "Don't bother, prince. King Goll will have his due."

Goll pinned Gael to the closest column. Gael's face flushed red as he clawed at Goll's hand fruitlessly, his face contorted in fury, his wings beating helplessly. A deep, guttural growl rumbled in the room, raising the hairs on the back of my neck. When Goll leaned forward, Gael's expression subsided to fear.

Suddenly, Goll released his throat, only to grab his right wrist and press the back of Gael's hand to the stone pillar.

"You're right-handed, are you not, my lord?" Goll asked mockingly as he slung his short-sword high.

"What are you doing!" yelled Gael. "Stop, no! Don't! Please!"

I sucked in a horrified gasp, unable to look away as Goll sliced through the air and cut through flesh and bone, his blade clinking against stone. Gael screamed as blood sprayed crimson, two of his fingers rolling across the white marble floor. Elder Lelwyn fainted.

"Sacred goddess," I murmured, nausea rising in my stomach.

Goll re-sheathed his short sword and strode toward me, his face lit with the raw brutality of the king he was known to be, his cheek sprayed in Gael's blood.

While Baelynn tried to help Gael, who'd fallen to the floor writhing and screaming in pain, I stood in horror as my new husband stalked closer.

"*Why* did you do that?"

"It was necessary," he proclaimed, taking my uninjured wrist in his giant hand and leading me toward the exit.

"No! It was *not*. It was monstrous." I tried to jerk my wrist free.

He turned suddenly, pulling me close, his face inches from mine. "This news will be spread everywhere. If they think me monstrous, so be it. But all will know the consequences to anyone who dares touch what is mine. That goes for my land, my property, and *you.*"

I shook my head, unable to understand why he felt the need to be so barbaric.

"You desecrated the temple," I whispered, actually afraid of the fiery-eyed demon staring down at me.

"She's your goddess. Not mine. Now let's be gone from this place before Issos learns the true meaning of a wraith fae pillaging." Then he turned toward the door, dragging me along. "Come."

I glanced over my shoulder to see one of the guards hefting my trunk onto one shoulder like it weighed nothing, the rest of the wraith fae falling in line behind us.

Baelynn still knelt beside Gael on the blood-spattered floor, having wrapped his hand in a kerchief. My brother's gaze found mine, full of aching pain and regret, then he mouthed the words *I'm sorry* before he disappeared from view and I was hauled away by my new master.

CHAPTER 11

Goll

We'd conquered Lumeria. The war was over. And I had my mizrah at my side, the high fae Princess of Issos. The knot in my gut loosened. Actually, she was currently in my arms as we flew on Drakmir to the encampment. As we lowered over the Bluevale River, Una stiffened.

"We aren't returning to Näkt Mir?"

"We will in the morning. Tonight, we camp with my soldiers."

We had much to celebrate, and as their king, I must assure them all that I was one of them, that I was a king to be trusted, to follow.

"Is it safe for me?" she asked.

The tremble of fear in her voice fired anger in my blood. I didn't like that. I had to remember that she'd been abducted, her handmaiden and fellow Issosian killed before she was dragged to Northgall by my father's men. The faint bruise I'd noticed on her left cheek told me she hadn't been treated gently. That was why I'd taken so much satisfaction in incinerating Erlik and my father's second in the throne room. One of them had been responsible for that.

Clenching my jaw, I studied her profile while the frigid wind gusted around us. "Hear me," I commanded. "You will not be treated as my father would have. You are to be the mother of my heir. You will not be harmed in any way."

"Will I not?" she arched a brow.

"You believe I plan to hurt you?"

She didn't answer, keeping her gaze on the river below, a silvery serpent cutting across the land.

I scoffed, gripping her chin, and forced her to look at me. "Who do you think is going to harm you?"

She blinked nervously, a blush filling her cheeks as she averted her gaze.

"Ah." I chuckled. "I suppose there will be some pain the first time. But you agreed to the terms."

"I know what I agreed to. I know my *duty.*" Her words were laced with more ice than was in all of Northgall.

"You never know." I let her chin go and whispered in her ear. "You may enjoy it."

"Never."

That had me outright laughing. She turned a surprised expression on me right as Drakmir dove for the encampment. She clutched the pommel tighter while I held onto her for the landing. Drak's landings were always rough. Probably because of his adolescent isolation, he never learned from dragonkind. He was rougher and more savage due to that early separation from his family.

"*Gloyen*, Drak," I crooned, praising him for flying us so well. I patted him roughly then climbed down first.

I didn't even have to tell Una to come to me. She was ready to get off my dragon, hurrying down the rope ladder. Grasping her around the waist, I eased her to the ground. Her breath hitched when I set her close to me.

Her hands clutched mine, she ordered in that royal air of hers, "You can let go now."

"Best get used to my touch," I told her before I stepped back.

We'd landed right outside the encampment. Drakmir stalked toward the trees, preferring to sleep there since there were no caves to be found nearby. Hundreds of tents dotted along the Bluevale River with some soldiers left behind tending to work, preparing for our return.

As we drew closer to my tent, Ogalvet stepped from the large fire he'd been tending. "Sire?" His yellow-eyed gaze slid to the woman trailing me, his fanged mouth hanging open in awe.

I stopped and gripped her hand, drawing her closer. "The army will be returning within the hour, Ogalvet. Can you prepare a plate and bring it to my tent for the princess?"

"Of course, Sire." He planted his fist over his heart and bowed his head, horns forward in obedience.

"Thank you. Tell Keffa we've arrived and send Meck and Ferryn to guard my tent."

"Right away, Sire."

I'd had to wait for my kinsmen to complete the trial of the Kel Klyss before I finally met with Una. I'd brought all them and Keffa on Drakmir to the encampment, having received the message that Soryn had breached the city walls of Issos and would have it under control within a few days.

Dalya had assured me they both endured the trial with the strength of true wraith fae warriors. Ferryn had suffered the most, she reported, though he'd never asked to leave the site.

The trial required being chained in the lower caves of Vixet Krone beneath Näkt Mir where the spirits of Northgall whispered and roamed. Meck and Ferryn were given a single drop of water from Näkt Lykenzel, the black lake deep underground. The sacred water invited the spirits to visit them. If they withstood the visitations all night, they could join my elite guard.

The test wasn't one of physical strength, but mental. And whether they were devoted to me enough to take hours and hours of psychological torture. For the ghosts who dwelled in the heart of Vixet Krone weren't all benevolent. They could fill any trespasser with the pain and loss and grief they carried into the afterlife. The trial to be one of my elite warriors was a true test of loyalty.

Of course, Una's test would be more dangerous by far. But I wouldn't think of that yet.

Meck and Ferryn's first assignment was to be my mizrah's personal guard. I wasn't so arrogant to believe she welcomed her new fate. She might try to escape. And if she didn't try to flee, there was always the chance that a hidden enemy might do her harm to get to me. She wasn't entirely wrong that her life may be in danger. The threat just wasn't from me.

I tugged her along, noticing two of fae males carrying chopped wood for the campfires and the old smithy sharpening swords outside his tent. All three froze like stone as I led Una back to my tent. I ushered her inside, a knot tightening in my chest at the thought of all of their eyes on her.

Of course, they would stare. I knew this. Not only was she foreign and different, but she was the light-fae Princess of the highest court in all of the realms. And she was undeniably, jarringly lovely.

When I ushered her inside, she exhaled a breath, closed her eyes and crossed her arms. She was obviously relieved. Perhaps it was better for her too to stay away from all those prying eyes. I couldn't avoid it forever, but I could give her a moment's privacy to catch her breath.

"Make yourself comfortable. Ogalvet will bring you food soon," I told her.

She nodded, finally opening her eyes and taking a look around. There wasn't much to see besides a store of weapons and a small trunk of clothes. There was a fire dome, now cold, at the center of the room. A standing lantern had been lit, awaiting my return, casting a blue glow in the small chamber.

Stepping toward the fire dome, I opened the grate and whispered, "*Etheline.*" Flames leaped to life on the coals.

She held her palms out to the grate, relief softening her face. My chest eased at the sight but tightened again when her gaze finally landed on the wide bed of furs. She recoiled and gulped hard, her disgust for our marriage bed blatant.

"Do not fear," I told her, my irritation obvious in my voice. "We will consummate our union in Silvantis, not here." Not in Lumeria.

She nodded, looking down at the raised markings on the tops of her hands where the priest's magick had left traces behind.

"Are you pleased we did your moon-binding?" I asked her curiously.

It galled me to do anything beneath Lumera's light, but I wasn't going to argue with her once she'd agreed to the terms. It irritated me to no end that I'd have done anything for her to agree.

"It will save my reputation since the rest of me will be lost." She clasped her hands demurely and looked up at me with the haughtiness of an Issosian royal, gathering her shield around her. "Maybe I'll be lucky. Maybe I'll become pregnant after the first time and I'll never have to suffer you in my bed again."

I wondered if the gods blessed me or hated me by giving me this feisty harpy of a moon fae. For the way I wanted her was frightening, humiliating, and all-consuming. While she despised me. As she should. She would hate me more after the Rite of Servium.

Over the years of war, word had come to me by my spies how beautiful the Princess of Issos had grown, how remarkably elegant in speech and manner, how regal in her bearing, how enchanting her violet gaze. But I'd never been able to picture anything but the young girl I'd taken from the dungeons. Nothing had prepared me for the reality of her.

Now, here we were. She was by all accounts already mine. And she loathed the very sight of me. The gods could often be cruel, but Vix had put her in my path for a reason, so I could use her to gain control of Lumeria. And I would use her however I wanted. It was my right after all her people had done to mine, after all the bloodshed and heartache.

When I stepped closer to her, she didn't budge. I liked it when she stood her ground, a steady warmth burning low in my core.

"Best not get ahead of yourself, Princess."

"Of course not," she said sarcastically.

"And just to be clear, until you give birth to my heir, you will not go anywhere without my permission."

She arched a brow in defiance. "Are you afraid I'll seduce one of your soldiers?"

"Hardly. But I am concerned a rival amongst them might take advantage and put a babe in your belly before I can in order to make my men doubt my right as their king."

She frowned. "Your people worship you."

She was still so naive, my little princess.

"By all appearances." I stepped toward the entrance and held open the flap, needing to get away from her. "But appearances can be deceiving, my mizrah." Then I stormed out into the cold, a more welcome companion for the night.

CHAPTER 12

Una

I heard them long before they began to march into camp. The heavy tread of the cavalry sounded like a long roll of thunder that might never end.

Standing at the tent flap, I peeked through, watching the first of them approach the edge of the encampment. It was easy to make out Goll's second in command—Soryn was what he'd called him. He stood even taller than the other cavalry on the back of the largest horse I'd ever seen. They rode Pellasians, a sturdy and hardy breed from Hellamir, a northern province of Lumeria.

I wondered how they'd managed to steal so many of the prized herd of the light fae who lived right on the borderlands of Northgall. No ambassador of Hellamir had come to seek help from us in Issos. Or perhaps they had, and Baelynn simply hadn't passed that information along. It wasn't as if I had been privy to all of the military maneuverings or the many disappointments as King Xakiel began to invade our lands.

I winced, thinking of Baelynn, wondering how he would manage without me. I'd heard Goll and Soryn talk as we walked through the corridors to Drakmir on the east bridge. My brother was to remain essentially under guard as steward of our kingdom. No—no longer our kingdom. It was all Goll's now. I blinked away the harsh loss and focused on the new arrivals.

It made sense that they would want Pellasians. Only steeds standing twelve-feet tall with hooves as round as dinner plates could carry the weight of the wraith fae.

Goll stepped into view close to Soryn, who swung off his horse. There was another I hadn't met yet standing next to Goll. He had a broken horn.

Smaller soldiers, probably adolescent warriors in training, came forward to take the mounts to a makeshift pen on the open plain.

Curious, I pushed open the flap to get a better look.

"Do you need something, Mizrah?"

A pale gray wraith fae with four horns curling backward and many runes painted on his forehead looked down at me with bright yellow eyes and a determined expression. He wore his hair with multiple small braids at the temples that were pulled back in a queue to hang loosely with his long black hair.

"No. I was simply curious about the horses. How did you acquire so many of our Pellasians?" I gestured over his shoulder the soldiers dismounting and entering camp.

He frowned then looked where I pointed. Glancing around, I hadn't noticed a second wraith fae standing to the left of the tent opening. He matched the other one in appearance and demeanor. So much so that I was fairly sure they were twins. The second one stared at me with open wonder and interest.

"Mizrah," said the one in front of me, "we bargain regularly with horsemasters in Hellamir."

Frowning, I protested, "But trade is illegal with Northgall. That would be against the laws of Issos." The old laws, rather.

The wraith fae smiled, and I noted he was rather handsome.

"That does not mean they won't take our money anyway."

"I…" I didn't know what to say to that. Perhaps I was naïve in thinking no Issosian would dare barter with the enemy. It seemed there was much I didn't know about the world, about my own people.

"Please, Mizrah. Wait inside."

"I apologize," I told my polite guard. "I do not know your name."

He dipped his horns forward in a bow of his head. "I am Meck, Mizrah. At your service. And this is my brother, Ferryn."

I nodded a bow at him and then his brother who still hadn't spoken, but he watched and listened intently.

"At *my* service?" I asked. "Or simply at the king's service to keep me quiet and placated?"

The pale skin on his neck and jaw darkened slightly with a flush of purple. He was blushing.

"Ah," I said. "That's what I thought."

"Our role is to keep you safe, Mizrah. And content."

"Why do you call me 'Mizrah'?" I asked. "Isn't she one of your lesser goddesses?"

Goll had called me that earlier tonight, and he hadn't explained why.

Meck's yellow eyes widened slightly. But it was his brother Ferryn who stepped closer and replied, "She isn't a lesser goddess. She wasn't a goddess at all. She was a mortal fae."

"Truly?"

He nodded, blinking his eyes curiously at me. "You do not know the tales of Mizrah, the mate of Vix?"

"One of his concubines, you mean."

He blinked those unique eyes at me again. "Vix, our chief god, had only one companion. Her name was Mizrah."

"What?"

I was quite confused. I'd studied dark fae culture for many years, and all the accounts of Mizrah was that she was the earth god's chief concubine, giving him four sons, the demons of earth, fire, beast, and shadow. The wraith fae were descended from the fire demon. The shadow fae mostly dwelled in the east. And the beast fae were said to be a cursed race, part animal and fae. I could find nothing at all on the earth fae. As if they never existed.

But Vix was a promiscuous god, well-known for his sexual prowess and manipulative escapades.

"You must be mistaken," I told Ferryn. "The tales of Vix are some of the most entertaining, if a bit diabolical. I remember the one where he disguised himself as a water serpent and tricked a pool of wood nymphs to ride on his back. He then carried them to a lone island and forced them all to copulate with him as the toll to return back to the mainland."

Meck's brow shot up, stretching his runes into his hairline. "That"—he shook his head—"is not a tale of our god Vix."

Confused, I asked, "You've never heard that one?"

"That is a fable," Ferryn declared emphatically. He did some sort of sign with his hand, touching his forehead, his chin, and then his chest, then stretched his long fingers toward the ground, palm up. He looked back at me. I took his ritual as a religious gesture to his god Vix. "The reason we call you Mizrah is because that is your title. It is what we call the king's chosen female to bear his heir."

"I see." I swallowed hard against the bitter gall trying to rise up my throat. Yet again the reminder that I'm no more than a sold sow, waiting to be mounted and bred.

"I don't think you do, my mizrah." Ferryn frowned.

Loud laughter suddenly bellowed through the trees and someone played a flute of some sort.

Meck opened the tent flap, "Please, Mizrah. It would be better if you stayed in your tent. There will be celebrating now."

I walked through the opening while he held the flap aside. He glanced past me to the untouched tray of food on the bed. "Is the meal not to your liking?"

It was prepared rather plainly compared to what I was used to. Roast eskel with the starchy purple vegetable, delly root. Though I enjoyed venison very much and was used to eating delly root since it was prevalent in Lumeria, I was more accustomed to spicy sauces and caramelized onions and sugared vegetables. But even if the meal had been prepared by the best cooks of Issos, I could not have eaten.

"I'm not hungry," I stated simply.

"You must eat, Mizrah. And rest."

I simply nodded, knowing I'd never sleep tonight. He smiled and let the flap fall shut. While the laughter and music continued, I realized how truly alone I was.

CHAPTER 13

Una

I'd tried to sleep and failed. Once I was changed into my nightdress and covered in my green velvet robe, I'd been pacing the room, trying to wear myself out.

The coals had burned down, but there was still an ethereal blue glow barely lighting the room. It should've been soothing, but there was simply no way to calm my nerves.

I'd taken off my velvet robe so that I could climb into bed, only to realize my chemise revealed my body quite clearly. I then slipped my robe back on and slid beneath the white Meer-wolf fur atop King Goll's bed.

As soon as I laid my head on a down-stuffed pillow, my senses were assaulted with the heady scent of Goll beneath these covers, on this pillow. I pulled another pillow from the pile, but they all smelled like him.

Eyes squeezed shut, I attempted to block out his distinct scent that seemed to wrap around me as tightly as the furs. My mind went directly to our ride into the night sky, his entire body surrounding me, his arms holding me against his hard chest, between his thick thighs.

"Ugh," I protested to no one, throwing off the fur because now I was sweating. "I can't sleep in this robe."

I rose, tore off the robe, and tossed it over the closed trunk. That's when I first heard a new sound among the drunken revelry outside. Feminine laughter.

"What in all the heavens?"

I crept to the tent flap and opened it the tiniest bit. From here, I could clearly see one of the many campfires the wraith fae caroused around. I recognized one or two from the Culled sitting around the fire as well as Soryn. And upon their laps were light fae women!

It couldn't be!

But there was no mistaking their opalescent wings shining by the firelight, almost as brightly as the wraiths' silver-ornamented horns. It was the women's scantily clad dresses, dipping low at their breasts and slitting high upon their thighs that told me where they'd come from.

I was no fool. There were many brothels in Issos these women could've come from, but I'd never in all my life thought they'd betray their own people and sell their bodies to our enemies. The enemy who'd just beaten us in the war.

My heart skittered faster as I searched the firelight for Goll, wondering what woman would catch his eye for the night's celebration. He'd told me we wouldn't consummate our union here, so he must be finding his own wench to celebrate with tonight.

He wasn't amongst them. My gaze stopped on Soryn, who had a buxom dark-haired fae in his lap. He was telling a story I couldn't hear to the others when the prostitute turned and straddled him, kissing him on his neck. He stopped what he was saying, drank down his tankard of ale, dropped it to the ground, and stood with his hands cupping her bottom. The wraith fae laughed and cheered as he stalked away and into a nearby tent.

I stepped back from the opening, not wanting to see Goll if he was with one of those women. This felt like jealousy, but that was absurd. We didn't have a real relationship. I didn't even *know* him. But even so, by all the gods, he could have some decency and not sleep with another woman the night of our moon-binding.

Storming back to the bed, I crawled underneath and pulled the top fur up to my chin, staring at the tent's door, wishing he'd return so I could tell him what I really thought of him.

"I hate him," I hissed into the air, blinking back the stinging tears of my laughable and humiliating state.

To be forced into sexual servitude to produce his heir and used whenever he saw fit while he paraded around as master of the world, sleeping with whomever he liked. My blood simmered beneath my skin, rage covering me in a sheen of sweat.

No, there was no way I would sleep tonight.

I must've dozed, but something woke me. Not the sound of wild laughter and carousing, but the opposite. It was quiet except for the sound of a beautiful male voice singing.

Unable to help myself, I donned my robe and slippers then opened the tent flap. Meck and Ferryn were still right there on duty, not saying a word as I stepped outside and listened.

"Who is that?" I asked.

"I don't know, Mizrah," answered Meck. "The celebrations have mostly died down."

"Can I get a closer look then?" I gestured toward the firelight not far away.

Meck and Ferryn shared a look but it was Ferryn who said, "Yes, my lady. Follow me. We can move close enough for you to see."

The woods were steeped in shadow, the few circles of campfire giving off the only light. They'd used wood rather than coal outside, it appeared.

I stepped closer to the voice that had lured me from my tent, easing quietly to the circle of wraith fae who sat enraptured at the song.

The wraith fae with a broken horn was singing. Goddess save me, what an unearthly beautiful sound coming from his mouth. It was a strange juxtaposition. For this male had been the most hideously scarred of all the wraith fae I'd seen here, and the only one with a broken horn. He was ugly in appearance, and yet his voice was heavenly. Like the goddess had bestowed on him a special gift to make up for his scars.

But the goddess wouldn't bless a wraith fae. It would have to be Vix or one of the wraith gods. I found myself pondering this strange trail of thought while soaking in his words in demon tongue, trying to decipher the story he wove into song.

We stopped well outside the circle of warriors around the fire but still close enough to see and hear better. I noted none of the light fae prostitutes were in this campfire circle.

Leaning close to Ferryn, I asked, "He sings about home, yes?"

He nodded, glancing down at me. "This is a favorite of the wraith fae. Keffa is what's called a skyldenbard."

"What's that?" I didn't recognize the demon word.

"Our song-master. Keffa was once revered across all of Northgall as one of the best."

"Once?"

"He's been in prison for many years by King Xakiel. But Gollaya set him free." Ferryn's brow creased as he watched the singer. "Though I'd never heard him sing myself, he's legendary according to the fae here."

"Bards are important to wraiths?" I asked, rather surprised at this.

Meck seemed amused as he answered, "Of course, they're important. Keffa has a way of singing that speaks directly to the heart." He paused, watching Keffa thoughtfully. "His song is like when magick comes, filling you with that blinding euphoria."

I'd not considered my new magick very special. It didn't feel the same as before. But there were moments, like when I soared into the clouds behind a hawk's eyes, that the magick burned brightly through my veins. That was when I remembered what it was like to be a powerful light fae.

"Don't you need a song for your heart, Mizrah?" asked Ferryn.

It was an innocent question, his gaze calculating like he truly wondered at the answer.

"I suppose you're right. We all need one."

Keffa's voice rolled softer and deeper with a melancholy timbre as he continued in demon tongue, singing of a son lost to war and a mother still standing at the door awaiting his unlikely return.

Tears pricked my eyes at the thought. I'd only ever seen King Xakiel, and then Gollaya and his army as the enemy, giant monsters who needed to be annihilated. And yet, the soldiers probably had no more right or will to deny the call of their king than the Lumerians did when my father, and then Baelynn, had called them to action.

There were mothers, wives, and sisters who'd lost on both sides. War was the true villain, the real enemy. And one I was able to defeat by giving myself, my life, to the wraith king. In that moment while Keffa sang a lovely song of his homeland, I determined to make the best of this new life. It wasn't what I would've chosen for myself, but it prevented the greatest of evils from killing more light fae. As well as the dark. I was coming to realize they weren't quite as different from us as I'd always believed.

My neck prickled with awareness, drawing my attention across the fire to my right. Goll leaned against a tree, half concealed in the shadows, his arms crossed, his eyes on me. They glowed more gold by the firelight. As always, he didn't look away when caught watching me. No. He looked his fill as if it was his right.

Who was I fooling? It was his right. He could do whatever he wanted to me. If I protested, he might return me to Issos and pick up his sword again against my people.

Why was I not furious at this? At the way he'd trapped me into this unwanted new path, into *his* path. The only anger I felt right now was at myself. I couldn't tear my gaze from him, and I couldn't cut him with a disdainful rejection.

No, instead, I soaked in his gaze, basking in the icy fire burning a trail down my body and slowly back up. His face was a mask of stony indifference, but those eyes devoured me, one small, greedy bite at a time.

A roar of cheers and thumping of fists to chests—wraith fae applause—jerked my attention back to Keffa. The bard bowed his head in thanks.

"More!" yelled Pullo, the younger Culled warrior with a broad smile. "Another, Keffa!" He nudged the young Culled warrior Tierzel who'd guarded me back in Northgall. A shy fellow.

Others chimed in, urging him to give them another song. He raised a hand to quiet them and sang in a livelier tempo a song that told of boyhood friends growing into strong warriors. I smiled as Pullo and Tierzel clapped to the tune, smiling with joy.

When I was finally brave enough, I looked back to the shadow to find Goll. But he was gone.

CHAPTER 14

Goll

"One more, Sire!" Lykel called, carrying another brimming tankard to me.

"No more." I gestured that I was done as I stood from the wooden bench they'd erected around their fire out here on the eastern side of the encampment.

A chorus of disappointments joined Lykel, my general of the foot soldiers, as he said, "Just one more." His red eyes were glassy with drink, his long braid coming apart from a night of carousing with his friends.

Two of the cavalry played flutes while a few others danced with the women they'd acquired in Issos on their way out of the city.

I'd given Soryn the order to ensure the soldiers took care not to hurt them. Light fae were delicate-boned, their bodies easily broken by our larger ones. I'd even handed over the coin to pay handsomely for the ladies' company tonight, enough that they could hire coaches from the next village to return to Issos. The last thing I needed as I gained control of each province was the working women who held the ears of many spreading rumors of our brutish ways.

I wanted the people of Lumeria to fall into line easily under their new king. So I wouldn't give them any reason to defy me, not even the mistreatment or underpayment of Issosian prostitutes.

"Lykel"—I raised my voice loud enough for the others to hear as I lay a heavy hand on his shoulder—"if I did *one more* with every round of soldiers in this encampment tonight, I'd never wake up to return to Silvantis." I eyed the crowd of fae whose faces lit on the mention of home. "And don't we all want a swift journey to Silvantis?"

A cheer went up around this final group I'd visited for the last several hours.

"For those journeying to different parts of Lumeria tomorrow, know that I hold you in the highest regard." While some would return home, many would begin our occupation all over Lumeria. I must ensure the light fae understood who now ruled them. "Enjoy yourselves tonight. You've earned it."

The flute player stopped playing. The fire crackled as I turned my gaze around the small group. "We would not have won this war without each and every one of you. Good sleep, warriors."

With another eruption of cheers, the flute player started up with a swift, lively tune. I then made my escape back into the shadows. I'd stopped at every fire circle tonight, staying longer with the soldiers than with my Culled and the front cavalrymen.

The front line deserved more of my attention. They'd been fighting for my father for years, and only recently for me. I wanted them all to understand how much I appreciated their valor, their honor, their spilled blood, and their loyalty. I needed to tell them myself. Something my father had never done.

Dalya's last vision had left me unsteady. While I knew I was on the right path, that Una was my path, there was the addendum to her vision that kept me awake at night.

Two sides of the same coin. Demon-fae. One true, one not. Beware the raven's back, for he seeks your place…in all things.

Like a lot of Dalya's visions, it was shrouded in mysterious, nonsense verse. But what I gathered more than anything was that I had an enemy in my ranks. Somewhere. Either here among my soldiers or back at Silvantis. Or possibly farther abroad. Perhaps he would be a problem as I took control of Lumeria.

Because of a lurking enemy, I wanted to ensure these fae here all knew their importance to me. They'd all be rewarded justly with coin and provisions when we returned home. Some would be awarded lands for their long and valiant service, something else my father never would have done. Though it was still a dangerous idea, I wanted my people to know that I was *not* him.

Perhaps in Silvantis, the enemy would be clearer.

Weaving among the tents, the sound of revelry and fucking could be heard from every one of them. Heaving a sigh, I made my way back to my own tent, eager yet not so eager. I'd be forced to lie next to the woman I'd been having too many fantasies about.

Word of Princess Una growing into the most beautiful woman had heightened my curiosity about the girl I carried out of the dungeons long ago. But nothing prepared me for the woman herself.

Vix's blood. She was fucking otherworldly in her beauty, more lovely than Lumera herself. I was sure of it. And a thousand times more alluring.

Black wings. They'd regrown—I'd known that—but somehow, I'd never been told the color. And then to behold them, all the lovelier in contrast to her pearl-white skin. It took every ounce of willpower not to claim her back in Näkt Mir.

Patience, I thought as I rounded toward my tent, noting Meck and Ferryn still stalwart on guard.

I would not take her in haste, but only after all the Silvantian rites had been completed. My blood burned every time I looked at her.

Not long now.

"Meck. Ferryn."

They saluted me, fists to chests, heads and horns bowed. "Sire," they said in unison.

"All quiet here?"

"Yes, Sire," said Meck. "All is well."

"You two can join the others and celebrate."

Ferryn frowned. "Won't you need a guard through the night?"

"I can defend myself and my—" I glanced at the tent entrance and cleared my throat. "I can handle protecting the mizrah tonight. You deserve to enjoy the celebration."

"Thank you, Sire," said Meck with a dip of his head.

Ferryn did the same, and then they turned and walked toward the closest campfire.

I entered the tent, the coal still burning blue, warming the small space. But my gaze went directly to the shape of the woman beneath the furs and the sudden spike in her heart rate. Her breathing quickened, a soft huff in the quiet tent.

Removing my belt with the sword and scabbard, I set it on my side of the bed. "Couldn't sleep, Mizrah?"

She remained still for a moment, perhaps wondering if she should pretend to be asleep.

"I know you're awake. You might as well speak to me."

She bolted upright, twisting her torso to face me, her clear violet eyes more vibrant by the light of the volcanic coal. "Why should I speak to you?"

"You're angry," I noted casually, unfastening my armor.

"Of course I am, you imbecile."

Very angry. I forced myself not to smile.

"Tell me what's on your mind, Una." I hefted the giant piece of shoulder and chest plate armor over my head and dropped it to the floor. Then I went to work on the thigh plates that were fastened into my pants with leather lacing.

"You brought harlots from Issos to celebrate your victory," she spat venomously.

"I could hardly bring them from anywhere else. We needed many to serve the soldiers who wanted to partake. Issos is the closest city to accommodate our needs."

"How could you force prostitutes to…to do their work after you just conquered their city," she accused rather than questioned.

It had not missed me that her fury had her chest rising and falling swiftly, pressing her full breasts against the thin fabric of her nightdress. I tried not to let my gaze linger too long, instead focusing on her ire as I continued undressing.

"I am aware that you're a sheltered maiden and are perhaps *un*aware of a male's needs, but the brothels could've refused our coin. They did not. They welcomed it and sent word to several bawdy houses along your lower Issosian district, who in turn showed up in our encampment by the carriage-load just in time for our celebration." I began unlacing the top vee of my black linen shirt.

"I'm not *unaware* of a male's needs. I'm not ignorant." Her gaze dropped to the fur covering her lap.

"I see. But you've never experienced the fire of battle blood, have you?"

Her eyes rounded, finding my gaze again, giving me a near-painful look of innocence. I reached over my shoulder and pulled my black linen shirt over my head, trying not to snag it on my horns lest Havallah chastise me for ruining another shirt. I dropped it beside the bed with my armor. Her eyes widened further then I went on.

"Battle blood builds up, pumps a man into a fury of unspent energy and emotions following a vigorous fight. Oftentimes, they can cry out their victory, hack their enemy up a little more to release that energy. But on a night like tonight, when they recently won the battle on the plains outside Issos, only to capture the city and restrain their energy for hours upon hours while they awaited word of our final victory, that the peace treaty was signed…" I huffed out a breath as I shoved off my boots and began working the lacings of my trousers. "Let me tell you, princess. They needed to either spill blood or their cum."

She flinched and I found some perverse thrill in her discomfort. The haughty princess needed to be reminded that she was in the hands of the barbarians she proclaimed us to be.

"I opted for brothels over blood," I added casually.

"What are you doing?" Her wide-eyed gaze was on my trousers. My cock twitched beneath the fabric.

"It isn't customary for me to sleep in my clothes," I said softly.

"You should keep…some clothes on." Her voice had ticked up, laced with nervousness.

I had one hand gripping the flap of my trousers, the other I dropped to my side. "Wraith fae males do not wear all the pretty underthings and excess clothes as Lumerians, Una. As you most certainly have noted, we are much less civilized." With that, I shoved my trousers down, my half-hard cock bobbing between my legs.

She gasped and squeezed her eyes closed, then promptly fell to the bed, facing the other direction. I smiled at her modesty even while I couldn't help but give myself a half-hearted stroke. I certainly appeared to be the vile monster she thought me to be now.

With a frustrated sigh, I jerked my hand away and scrubbed it down my face. I lifted the furs and fell onto my back, clasping my hands behind my head and closing my eyes to focus on leveling my breathing. This was going to be very difficult.

"I don't care what you do with other women," she snapped with bitterness, still facing the opposite wall, "but do not sleep with any while we are trying to create a child. Sexual promiscuity can spread diseases and…it's—it's humiliating to me." She whispered the last part, seemingly embarrassed that she'd even confessed it aloud.

I turned my head toward her, noting the silky softness of her hair flowing over the pillow and fur. What I wouldn't do to caress those beautiful tresses, press their silkiness to my face and lips, inhale her sweetness.

"You do not want me to fuck other women while you and I are?" I asked, using coarse language to try to remind myself there would be no soft thoughts or tender words between us. I couldn't get lost in asinine thoughts about caressing her hair.

She stiffened. "Whatever you did with whomever tonight, let it be the last time until…until I've conceived and can leave your bed."

Her back was a straight line, her shoulders stiff. She thought I'd fucked my own harlot tonight while I'd left her here alone on her first night away from Issos. And it…bothered her. It bothered me.

Still, I couldn't get wrapped up in concern over her feelings. She was here to beget my heir and give me the alliance needed so I could ensure complete control over Lumeria. That was all.

I could've let her believe I'd been enjoying the pleasure of a woman all night. I could've even lied and told her I'd fucked several and would have as many fae whores ride my cock as I liked. But instead, I found myself mesmerized and worried by that hard line of her back to me.

So instead, I admitted something to which I hadn't ever planned. "There will be no women in my bed while you are in it."

Her shoulders rounded forward ever so slightly. Then I added more quietly, "There was no other woman tonight."

That straight line softened, curving with the sinuous slope of her beautiful womanly form. Her body relaxed, pressing sweetly into the bed. Her soft huff of relief loosened something inside me and agitated me.

Forcing my gaze away, I looked up at the slanted slope of the tent roof, then threw my arm over my eyes. Defiantly, I added with bite, "Get some rest, Una. You will need to perform that duty soon enough."

I ignored the immediate tension I sensed from her, and I refused to look at her to see if that soft curve had stiffened again. I fought against any urge to soften for the woman who I'd saved and whose family launched a war against my people.

In all my recent dreams and fantasies of this woman, I never thought that I'd yearn for more than her body, the child she'd bear me, and her royal alliance. But now—against my will—there was a small coal of my own, smoldering in the dark recesses of my blackened heart, longing to be ignited. To burn hot and bright.

CHAPTER 15

Una

A bellowing horn sounded from the palace parapet in the distance. It had been nearly two weeks since the night in the encampment, and since Goll had delivered me back to the palace before returning without a single word to me.

I suppose I understood why he thought it important to make the journey on horseback to Silvantis, the capital city of Northgall. It was a way to show his loyal soldiers and his people he was one of them.

But he wasn't. He was not a common soldier or simply a wraith fae warrior. He was set apart as one of their royal line, touched by dragonblood.

From where I stood on the steps of the Temple of Vix, I saw Drakmir circle the palace spires. He'd been circling it ever since I'd been returned to it, no longer keeping his king company on the road. I wondered if Goll had ordered Drakmir to watch over me or if perhaps my own strange magick was calling to him. When I first touched him, I tried to reach out with the power that had replaced my healer's magick, but he seemed to block me from entering his mind. No other winged beings had done that before. But a dragon was a highly intelligent creature.

Hava stood next to me on the top terrace of the temple. There was a semi-circle of steps leading to the wide, white-stoned terrace and entrance to the temple—a sharp contrast to the temple made of the same black obsidian as the palace. The priestesses stood quietly on the semicircle of steps, facing the street.

"They'll be coming right up that road any minute," Hava whispered to me, pointing to the main street funneling into the city from the south.

She didn't need to tell me. I could hear them. The clopping of hooves on stone and the cheers from the wraith fae filling the streets of Silvantis told me of the approach of their king and his returning army.

To my left stood the two-story black marble statue of their mighty god, the four-horned Vix, riding his dragon named Silvantis. The namesake of the city. Vix held his sword aloft, swinging it wide as if in battle, their fierce defender and most sacred god.

The noise and cheers grew louder. Then they entered the wide square surrounding the temple, and my breathing faltered.

Goll rode a giant of a beast—a black Pellasian stallion with a long mane. He rode at the front with his second Soryn on one side and the scarred one, Keffa, on the other. While the throng bellowed his name, his gaze found me instantly and held.

I remained still, chin held high, as he came to a stop, dismounted, and ascended the steps, walking past the high priestess and the others toward me. They all dipped a curtsy as he passed.

More cheers erupted as he came into view of the people on the streets. I waited, watching him draw nearer, but I did not curtsy. While the anger still simmered under my skin, I wasn't ready to bow to my king. But I remained poised while he looked his fill.

I wore one of my high-necked gowns due to the colder weather here. It was a deep royal blue, the color of my family crest.

Goll's mouth ticked up in that annoyingly smug smile. "Hello, Una. Have you fared well in my absence?"

"Indeed, I have. I hardly noticed you were gone."

His smile widened as he strode away from me to meet the high priestess and another priestess now standing before the statue of Vix.

The priestess next to the head held a red velvet pillow in her upturned palms. Golden cuffs set atop the pillow. Like the others, she wore a gossamer black gown with loose sleeves, her silver headdress a transparent veil over her long, black hair, her four gray horns spiraling backward in an elegant swoop.

"Welcome home, Prince Gollaya," said the high priestess.

I glanced at Hava with a frown, wondering if she had insulted Gollaya.

Hava shook her head and leaned close to whisper, "It is his proper title, but that is about to change."

She pointed back to them. Gollaya knelt before the high priestess. The crowd shushed instantly as she took the golden cuffs and turned toward the statue of Vix, raising them above her horned head. Her silver veil slipped to her shoulders as she spoke to the sky.

"By the authority of Vix whose might and power sanctifies me to bestow this crown, I call upon his sacred blessing."

She turned to face Gollaya who still knelt on one knee, his profile grave and undeniably beautiful.

"I hereby crown you, Gollaya Verbane," she slipped the cuffs onto his two larger horns, sliding them to where they fit perfectly at the base, "King of the people of Northgall, *and* the first wraith king of the people of Lumeria." The high priestess smiled as she added that title.

While the crowd erupted into roaring applause and cheers, my gut tightened and I swayed with nausea. Hava gripped my hand

and smiled up at me with sympathy. Though Hava looked nothing like my moon fae friend Min, she reminded me of her all the same. Min always knew when I needed comfort or a compassionate touch. I squeezed her hand back then let it go and faced forward as Gollaya rose, officially their newly crowned king.

He bowed his head to the high priestess then he turned to the other priestess.

"Welcome home, my king," she said, clasping her delicate hands in front of her as she dipped into a deep curtsy and held.

"Thank you, High Oracle Dalya. Rise."

She stood with all the poise of a high-born wraith fae.

"Who is she?" I asked Hava.

"That's Dalya. She's a soul-seer. She has been his seer in hiding since he returned to Silvantis a year ago. She will now be High Oracle to the king. A very important role."

"It is good to see you home and healthy, my king," she said with genuine affection and a warm smile, which she then turned to me. "Will you introduce me, Sire?" She nodded in my direction.

Goll turned and strode toward me beside her.

"Dalya of Dravencourt, High Oracle of Silvantis, this is Tiarrialuna Elzabethanine Hartstone. My mizrah."

Dalya curtsied.

I did so in return. "It is a pleasure to meet you, Oracle Dalya." I could be polite, even while my heart was breaking at the realization that Lumeria was now lost to the king, my pseudo-husband, in front of me.

"And you, Mizrah."

She seemed genuinely pleased to meet me.

"I hoped that perhaps you can be a guide to her," he said to Dalya. "As she adjusts to her new life here in Northgall."

"Of course, Sire. And when should I plan for the Rite of Servium?" Dalya asked, turning her golden gaze up to him.

"Three days."

I stiffened, not ever having heard of this rite, but sensing its importance.

Dalya blinked in surprise. "That is soon. Should we not give the princess time to acclimate, to prepare—"

"Three, Dalya," he declared sharply and a bit too familiarly when speaking to an oracle in public.

"As you wish, Sire." She bowed as Goll placed a hand at the center of my back and urged me forward beside him.

The people of Silvantis erupted again as he guided me at his side to face the crowd. I couldn't help but glance up at him, noting the pride on his face. He'd gotten what he wanted. The crown, both kingdoms, and apparently me.

As we descended the steps and he urged me toward his horse, I knew that I was merely a pawn in his plans, to secure his reign over Lumeria, and future reign through our child, his heir. But wished I was more than a means to an end, that my life was worth more to him than being his breeder.

Without even asking, he wrapped his hands around my waist from behind and lifted me to sit sideways on his saddle. I grabbed the pommel to balance myself as he hoisted himself behind me. Then he turned his steed toward the road leading to Näkt Mir.

"You could wave to the people, Una," he whispered in my ear as they cheered when we passed. "It wouldn't hurt you to be cordial to them."

"They aren't cheering for me. This is your kingdom, not mine."

He exhaled a breath of frustration, and we were quiet the rest of the way to the palace.

While the entrance to the fortress of the Palace of Black Glass was intimidating with the steep drop on either side into what was once the crater of the volcano Vixet Krone, in the distance there were lush blue-leaved trees. Esher was the name I'd discovered from Hava.

Eshers only grew in Northgall, their shiny blue leaves thick and silvery, glistening under the mid-day sun. And though the sun was currently covered by a gray pall, there was light enough to see that the esher woodland behind the palace was incredibly beautiful.

I'd been curious about them because I'd never seen white trunks with peeling bark before. And because I associated those naked white trees with my escape from this place, like sentinels guarding us as we fled Northgall, the sight of them gave me hope. I smiled.

The swift clip-clopping of horses' hooves trotting up behind us had me turning to see Soryn, Keffa with Hava riding behind him on his horse, and a number of the Culled catching up to us, including Meck and Ferryn. They fell in line as we wound the sinuous path up to another gate.

The road ahead ended where a giant gap dropped into the terrifying chasm below. Goll pulled our mount to a stop.

A crank sounded, and the black iron gate opened as a bridge slowly lowered.

A deep, loud horn bellowed from somewhere high in the palace, echoing across the keep, announcing their king's return. Goll led the others across the iron bridge. The guards saluted their king from the watch towers at the top of the gate on either side.

I had no idea what to expect from his people here in Silvantis. His warriors had treated me with nothing but respect. So far, I'd received wary, watchful gazes from the villagers.

As we wound closer to the palace, now inside the keep, the rocky obsidian gave way to vegetation. I was even surprised to see manicured shrubs and grass spreading wide around the back of the palace. Apparently, it was only the entrance that was dressed to intimidate visitors.

My gaze followed the lines of the palace, the intricate and ornate spires, sweeping lines stretching toward the sky. The windows were arched to a point with decorative designs—wraith fae, nymphs, and sprites amongst vines and trees.

The front entrance and doorway were wide enough for ten fae males to walk through side by side, and the stone steps were gray marble leading up to black doors decorated with carvings of a wraith king. No, it looked more like the statue of their god Vix in front of their temple, his dragon carved on one side of him. On the other was a beautiful fae with pointed ears. Was that his main consort, Mizrah? It must be.

I frowned, confused why they'd acknowledge her on the palace door. After all, she wasn't his queen, only the female he chose to bear his children.

Standing at the foot of the front were seven wraith fae in a long line. They were draped in robes of black, gray, and red silk, varying in design and ornamentation, but their formal attire united them as one.

There were four male and three female, all with four horns except one female, who had two. I'd never discovered why some dark fae had four and some had two, but I was determined to discover the difference and what it meant, if anything.

Goll dismounted quickly then gripped me around the waist and set me on my feet before turning quickly to his council. Then he held out his arm. Stretching my wings tall, I set my hand on his proffered arm and allowed him to guide me to the waiting robed ones.

"Welcome back, my *king*," he declared, seeming to recognize his crowned horns. The four-horned male with pale yellow eyes at the head of the line. He was striking with a full head of gray hair that hung long past his shoulders. He bowed as did all the others, pressing a fist to their chests to salute him.

"Thank you, Bozlyn." Goll held himself tall at my side, but he dipped a bow to him in greeting and then to the rest. "And thank you, everyone, for welcoming my return. May I present to you, Tiarrialuna Elzabethanine Hartstone. My mizrah."

They stared in curiosity.

"Hello," was all I managed to say, proud that I could keep my voice steady and strong.

They all dipped their heads in greeting, not in a deep bow as they had with their king, except one male who did not. He had streaks of gray hair at his temples and fierce red eyes, his top fangs longer than most of his kind. "Not officially your mizrah yet, my king."

Goll's arm stiffened beneath my fingers but outwardly he seemed calm when I glanced up at him. I heard the Culled dismounting and lining up behind us. Meck and Ferryn took a forward position to my right.

Wraith fae magick buzzed in our small circle. It was distinctly different than light fae magick which felt ethereal like a brush of gentle, summer wind. Wraith fae magick bore an undercurrent of aggression and dominance, almost like the warning lash of a whip in the air.

I held perfectly still, taking deep breaths as the tension mounted.

Goll dropped his arm, and my hand fell away as he took eerily slow steps down the line to stand directly in front of the one who'd spoken out. Goll was taller, broader, more muscular, and obviously of higher rank, but the demon fae stared back with menacing challenge as his king spoke cool words to him.

"The rites will take place in three days' time, Kellock. Officially. Until that time and thereafter, she will be treated with the respect of any mizrah."

Suddenly, I recognized him. He was one of those in the throne room when Goll killed his father.

Kellock's eyes narrowed, his face tightening as he scoffed, "An Issosian royal?"

"If the council would like to present their opposition to my decision in securing our kingdom's rightful reign over Lumeria, then bring it up at Council, Kellock." Goll stepped even closer to him, his hands clenched in fists at his sides. "But it won't fucking matter. I am your new king. And the treaty has been signed."

Kellock's gaze flicked to me, a sinister flash, but he said nothing.

The magick in the air wound tighter, sending my pulse racing. The silence only exacerbated the mounting rage emanating from Goll.

"I suggest," said Goll with chilling calm, "that you get used to the idea, as it is as good as done."

"And if I don't?" he brazenly argued.

"Then you will step down from my council."

Kellock huffed a disgusted breath, baring his teeth. "I will refuse. You cannot force me."

"But I can put your head on a pike at the front gate," snapped Goll.

A dreadful quiet swept over everyone. No one moved. Not even the horses, it seemed. The one who'd stood at the head of the line, Bozlyn, said softly, "Kellock will fall in line, sire."

Goll was locked on Kellock, who finally let his gaze drop to the stone floor. Only then did Goll take a step back. "See that he does," he growled for all to hear. "See that my wishes are obeyed, or there will be dire consequences."

Then he turned to me and held out his arm again as if he hadn't just threatened to behead his councilman.

I realized quickly that Goll ruled with an iron fist and a bloody blade. The fact made me cringe inwardly. I'd thought his men respected him, but perhaps I was wrong. Perhaps only fear made them bow so deeply and obey his every command. How many heads had he put on pikes to accomplish such a feat while I'd been imprisoned in my palace bedchamber? How many more would I have to witness in my life here in Silvantis?

While my pulse raced, I kept my features calm as he guided me up the gray marble steps and into a well-lit hall. My gaze drew up in awe at the stained-glass windows which began at the first landing of the staircase and soared upward two stories high.

The stained glass depicted the esher tree groves with sprites flying amongst its branches. Beneath the canopy of trees, a wraith king walked a solitary path. The artwork was stunningly beautiful, evoking an emotion of both wonder and sadness. The wraith king in the scene looked so similar to Goll, but it couldn't be him. This palace was built thousands of years ago. The artisan who created this piece was long gone.

"Mizrah." Goll's voice snapped me from my trance. He nodded to the fifty or so servants standing in parallel lines on opposite sides of the staircase. A few of them had leathery wings, marking them as having shadow fae blood. Goll raised his voice when he addressed them, "Everyone, this is Mizrah Una. You will see to her needs without question. Hava, bring her back to her bedchamber. She will dine with me tonight. Alone."

Then he stormed away inside the palace, his guards following him. Hava ushered me toward the wide staircase, a familiar sight as I knew I was being sent back to my prison cell, luxurious though it was.

As I mounted the steps, I found myself angry yet again. Not because of I was being treated as a captive, but because I found myself looking forward to dining alone with him. I didn't *want* to crave his company, but the damned yearning stirred hotly all the same.

CHAPTER 16

Goll

Istood on the balcony of my bedchamber, waiting for Una's arrival. I decided we would dine here until after the Rite of Servium. I wanted to be alone with her, and I didn't want to overwhelm her with court meals just yet. Those could be entertaining, depending how much wine was drunk, but I guessed that Una might find them horrifying and barbaric, knowing her kind were much more…proper.

For at least a little while, I wanted to put her at ease with my people, but more than that, I wanted her all to myself. No ones' eyes drinking in her beauty but me.

I scented Una and Hava before I saw them. Even more, I sensed Una's moon fae magick. I inhaled deeply, relishing the sweetness of it, a gentle, airy magick.

"Good evening, Sire," said Hava, stepping onto the balcony.

But it was Una who caught my attention—and kept it. *By Vix, she was beautiful.*

She wore a dark blue gown of a silky material that formed to her feminine curves, the short sleeves leaving her pale, slender arms free, the deep vee of the dress revealing her generous figure, but it was her face where I found the most pleasure in gazing.

Those otherworldly, violet eyes, her smooth, milk-white skin, her perfect mouth and the lovely line of her cheeks and jaw. She was truly breathtaking.

Hava giggled, dipped a curtsy, then left. I paid no mind. I'm sure Hava found quite a bit of amusement at my expense, but I also knew I didn't have to hide my dumbstruck behavior from her. Hava was loyal and true.

Una had been studying me as well. No telling what her thoughts were. She blinked quickly from her own trance and stepped toward the chair at the small round table where I stood.

Quickly, I maneuvered to her side and pulled out her chair. She froze, wide-eyed and surprised. Then she sat down, murmuring, "Thank you."

Gooseflesh rose on her arms. Frowning, I stepped to my chair and lifted the Meer-wolf cloak hanging over the back, then returned to her side and draped it around her shoulders. "Hava should've dressed you in a cloak." Her wings hung low, so I asked, "Will this bother your wings?"

"It's fine." She curled her fingers around the top edges of the collar and pulled the cloak tighter. "Thank you."

"The weather is turning."

Una looked out over the stone balustrade while I took my seat. "Back home, the leaves won't start changing for another month or two."

"This is the north. Like everything else here, the winters come faster and harder than in the south."

She caught my gaze, her mouth tilting up in a small smile. My chest suddenly hurt.

"That doesn't surprise me."

Two female servants stepped onto the balcony with silver-domed covered dishes. They set one in front of each of us.

"That will be all," I dismissed them. I didn't want any of the servants hovering so that they could spread gossip below stairs.

They curtsied then left quickly.

"I wasn't sure what you'd like," I admitted, "so I asked the cooks to prepare a little of everything."

We both lifted our domes. She let out a little laugh as she surveyed her plate, piled high with cuts of hog and venison, colorful roasted vegetables, sauced sweetmeats, and steamed greens—all well-seasoned, the smell of the spices rising with the steam.

"I cannot possibly eat all of this."

"As long as you eat something, I don't care how much." I cleared my throat. "Hava said you haven't eaten well lately."

A palpable silence stretched between us, awkward and uncomfortable. We'd spent little time alone so far, except that one night in the tent. And that had been filled with the anger sparking between us, and my own lust I was forced to suppress.

This was my attempt at being civil, but it seemed to not be going so well.

She lifted her fork and arched a brow at me, finally admitting freely, "I've been anxious."

It would be stupid to ask why. I knew why. She'd been torn from her home to become the mate of the enemy.

Mate. I hadn't thought of her that way. Or had I? I'd never considered her a concubine, even though a wraith king's mizrah was essentially the most important of his harem, but a part of his harem, nonetheless.

As if she could read my thoughts, she asked, "Will I be meeting your other concubines at some point?"

A trace of annoyance and even anger threaded the question. Though I wanted to smile, I kept it hidden.

"If I remember correctly, you requested that I lay with no other woman while you are my bed partner."

"I did. But I'm aware a wraith king would have concubines. I want to be sure and meet them so I can be wary of them."

"Why would you be wary of them?" This was entertaining.

She squirmed in her seat, still poking at her food, not yet tasting it. "That is obvious, Goll. I am a foreign princess, invading their home and taking the king's…attentions."

A purr rumbled in my chest without meaning to. I couldn't help the pleasure that warmed me at her concern for other women coming between us. For even though she claimed she needed to know for her own safety, it seemed that envy colored her pretty face with tense anger and frustration.

"I don't have any concubines, Mizrah."

She paused then finally met my gaze across the candlelit table, the soft glow flickering on her sweet face. "I read that all wraith kings have a harem of concubines."

"As you know, I haven't been king long. I haven't had time to assemble a proper harem."

I didn't plan on having one. She was the only one I wanted in my bed. And the *want* was killing me slowly.

Una stabbed her food again. "Oh," was all she said. "I thought perhaps even when you were in hiding you might have…lovers. Someone you might've brought to the palace."

It had been many weeks since I'd killed my father, and I certainly could've filled a harem easily enough if I was so inclined. I wasn't.

That heavy tension weighed between us again. I tried to lighten it.

"You've been reading about wraith kings?" I quirked a brow and took a bite of the juicy venison.

She dropped her gaze to her plate, still poking at the vegetables. "Eat, Una," I commanded.

She actually obeyed and took a bite of the small, orange squash that the cooks liked to roast in hog fat, salt, and sprinkles of hot spice.

Una's eyes closed as she hummed with pleasure. My cock jerked at the sound.

"Good?" I asked.

"Yes." Then she actually began eating rather than simply stabbing her food with her fork. "I've been studying your culture for a long time actually," she admitted amiably.

Another slide of warmth trickled down my body. "Indeed?"

She paused to chew and then swallow another bite, which put me at ease. "I was curious after I'd been taken here." She dabbed her mouth with a napkin. "The first time, I mean."

I sat back, my hand on the goblet of wine on the table. "Of course, you'd be curious."

She'd want to know about the fae who'd taken her prisoner, who'd tortured her near to death.

My own curiosity was piqued. "And what did you discover?"

"Many things." She smiled before taking a bite of the roasted hog.

"Like?"

"Only a wraith fae descended from the dragon line can take the throne. There was one king three millennia ago who tried to take the throne when there was no heir to the recently killed king in battle."

"Ukahaan."

"Yes! That was his name." She smiled openly, bewitching me further. "You must eat, too, Goll."

I liked when she used my name and didn't call me sire, which would keep distance between us. I shouldn't like it. I shouldn't crave the intimacy, but I did.

I sat forward and continued eating.

"Anyway," she added, "Ukahaan had failed to create an heir before he died in battle. They were at war with the shadow fae at the time, though I couldn't reason out why."

"There's always been tension between the wraith fae and shadow fae."

"Interesting. Well, you seem to know this story."

"Still, I'd like to hear you tell it," I admitted.

Pink colored her cheeks as she went on. "Another wraith fae, Tykel the Two-Horned, gained the throne for about five days before another wraith of the dragon line took it from him. And his head. Or so the story goes."

"What else did you discover?" I asked.

"A boy was found with perfect dragon eyes. Blue with a golden core." Her fork froze midway to her mouth as she stared at me across the small table, looking into very similar eyes as the boy king. "He was put on the throne."

"That was my great, great grandfather. It wasn't him who took Tykel the Two-Horned's head," I corrected. "The royal council took care of that with some of Ukahaan's former Culled."

She sipped her wine, then her gaze dropped to the table as she worried her bottom lip with those perfect, blunt teeth. I was distracted by her mouth before I realized she seemed to be holding something back.

"What is it you wish to ask?" I went back to my plate, nearly finished.

"There are many things not written down about the dark fae." She hesitated then added, "Some scholars claim to have knowledge, though I'm unsure."

"Ask me." I lifted my goblet and settled back into my chair.

"Some say that your ancestors lay with a dragon. That is how you got those eyes." Finally, she lifted her gaze to mine again, staring boldly. It stirred heat low in my belly. Lower still.

"You have seen Drakmir. Do you think it possible?"

"Well, no. Not with one like Drakmir. But not all dragons are so big."

I rolled my eyes. "You moon fae and your stories."

She laughed, the sound freezing me to the spot. It was the first time I'd seen or heard her laugh, and I didn't simply hear it. I felt it tremble through me, warming my blood further. Bewitching and beguiling.

I should beware of her. I should keep her at a distance. But the reality of my tortured state, completely dumbstruck by something so simple as her laugh, warned me that this was dangerous. Especially for a wraith king. One who must show strength and maintain a solitary, fierce front in order to hold the throne.

"Then what is the true story?" she finally asked, still smiling wide.

Resting my goblet on my knee, I leaned back into my chair and told her. "The god Vix was once imprisoned in a desert by the sun god Solzkin. Chained to a rock and forced to wither under the penetrating heat of the sun for his crime against Solzkin."

"What crime?" She set her napkin on her plate—a good portion of it gone, which eased my mind. She pulled my cloak tighter around her shoulders.

"Vix had walked past one of Solzkin's temples without paying homage or tribute. Vix rarely left his mountain home because the rest of the gods hated him so. They were always looking for a reason to punish him."

A tiny line formed between Una's brows. "I've never read this about Vix."

"What do you know of Vix?" I asked, curious.

She shrugged a shoulder, dislodging the cloak so that the delicate sweep of her collar bone and the slender curve of her neck were exposed. I swallowed hard.

"Only that he enjoyed many women and trysts. That was how he usually angered the gods in our stories."

"Of course." I scoffed. "That is how your people would see him."

She didn't comment, but her frown deepened.

"While Vix was chained to that rock, tortured without water or protection for decades, he thought for sure he would die. Even though gods never die. The pain was so great, he wished that he could. Then, one day, he spied a distant dark speck in the the blue sky. It was always clear and bright in this desert. The speck grew larger and larger until he could see the flapping of wings. It was a giant dragon."

Una's gaze lightened, her mouth quirking at the corners. She liked this story.

"The dragon was an old silverback, a king of his kind with black scales but a silver streak of mane from the head to the tip of the tail. This dragon flew down and landed with a giant roar. Vix said nothing, his throat too dry, his body too tired to even protest if the dragon planned to eat him. But that is not what happened."

Una's brows rose as she leaned forward, seemingly entranced by the story.

I smiled at her anticipation. "The dragon broke the chains with a swipe of his claws on the rock. Vix fell to his knees, gasping, desperate for water. The dragon seemed to understand. He nicked his hide and stretched the bleeding leg toward Vix. Without hesitation, the god drank the dragon's blood until he was sated. It gave him the strength to finally stand. He climbed upon the dragon's back and returned to his mountain home. The dragon was Silvantis."

"The one in the statue at the temple? And on the door carving of the palace?"

"The same one."

She sat back and shook her head in disbelief. "I cannot fathom it. A dragon recognized Vix's pain and decided to save him? When surely the dragon was hungry and thirsty himself."

"I've told you before. Dragons aren't mere beasts. They're highly intelligent. Not only that, but they have a large capacity to feel emotion. This dragon saw Vix in pain and felt sympathy and decided to save him. So Vix took him into his home deep in the mountains."

"So he kept Silvantis forever?"

"They were friends. I'd say they kept each other. I told you once that dragons have no masters."

She looked over the balcony and then up to the moonlit sky. "So you don't own Drakmir? He won't come whenever you summon him?"

"He always comes."

She tilted her head, the three braids at her temple sliding forward. "And what service did you do for Drakmir?"

"You truly believed that one of my ancestors mated with a dragon?"

"Well, not really," she admitted, a blush coloring her neck and cheeks. "But it's curious. Your eyes." She stared again.

I let her. I drank it in, relishing her intense scrutiny and obvious fascination. Whatever means I could employ so that I might ensnare her, I would. For the gods knew, she'd caught and caged my very soul.

If she begged me to leave, I wouldn't let her. If she swore to me that she'd never laugh again if I didn't release her back to her home in Issos, I'd still not let her go. If she cursed me and swore she'd take her own life, I'd bind her to her bed.

Some power beyond me—and her—had consumed my thoughts with the need to have her near me. Rapture wasn't quite right to describe it. Neither was bewitchment. It was closer to a curse.

Especially since I'd all but abducted her from her home and would soon be forcing her into my bed. Repeatedly.

The mere thought both made me hard and sickened. Every time I tried to reason that keeping her my prisoner was enough, keeping her within my palace walls would suffice, a lurking darkness whispered that she must be mine in all ways. In the most carnal ways.

There was no escape for the pretty princess. She was going to be mine.

CHAPTER 17

Una

The way Goll looked at me across the table—the candlelight glowing in his dragon eyes, the predatory glint freezing me in place—I felt frighteningly caught. My breath quickened, and I wondered what was going on in that dark fae mind of his.

They certainly thought differently than we did in Lumeria. Their chief god Vix was seen as a marauding demon and philanderer among my people. But here, he wasn't that at all. He was a strong, powerful leader who apparently cared for his mate and his people.

That had me wondering about our goddess Lumera. What they thought of her. What *he* thought.

Swallowing hard at the intensity of his stare, I broke away, catching sight of a shadow crossing the moon. Drakmir.

Standing, I stepped toward the stone balustrade and pulled his cloak tighter, wondering at the sensation of pleasure as I inhaled deeply, surrounded by his scent. I heard him move, then his heat was behind me.

A light breeze rustled through the silvery leaves under the moonlight, catching my attention. The leaves were just beginning to fall, the weather growing colder.

"We don't have trees with leaves of that color in Issos."

"As far as I know, esher trees only grow in this part of Northgall." He was so close but not touching. It felt more intimate than if we were.

"There's an old legend about how the eshers got their blue leaves." His voice was a silky rumble.

"Really?" I asked, hypnotized by this attentive, genteel side of King Goll.

From the start and specifically since we'd left Valla Lokkyr, he'd seemed either angry, indifferent, or mocking towards me. I wondered if his gentler manners were because he was now returned home, crowned and victorious. No matter the reason, I craved this side of him.

"Tell me," I beckoned.

He was quiet a moment then he said, "The story says that the first wraith king fell into deep mourning when his mizrah died in childbirth with their second child. He refused to burn her on a pyre as was tradition. Instead, he carried her alone into the woods behind Näkt Mir." He paused then continued. "His grief was so great that he sat beneath the oldest tree in the woods, slit his wrists with his dagger, and died with his mizrah in his arms. His blue blood mingled with hers and seeped into the ground, into the very roots of the forest. Thereafter, eshers bloomed blue leaves, stained from the blood and grief and love of the first wraith king and his mizrah."

Another wind gusted through the trees, more slender leaves pinwheeling down onto the forest floor as if in tribute to the story.

"It's a lovely but sad story," I said softly, "but did the wraith king truly kill himself over his mizrah? In real life, I mean." I couldn't imagine a wraith king grieving so much over a concubine.

Goll finally shifted to stand beside me, a furrowed vee between his brow. "Why would he not?"

Confused, since Goll himself had told me that a mizrah's purpose was nothing more than to bear the king's heir and would be one of many lovers to the king, I turned away. I couldn't maintain that intense stare of his, which seemed to try to glean all of my thoughts.

Instead of answering, I watched Drakmir circle lower, then spread his wings wide, soaring and landing in an open space between the palace garden and the esher woodland. The gray esher leaves on the ground curled into the air as he beat his wings on the landing.

The dragon tilted his nose up toward us, scenting the air, then he chirped in that guttural way. It sounded pleasant. I huffed a small laugh.

"What is it?" Goll was close to my left side.

"It's almost like he's saying hello."

"He is. Would you like to go down and see him?"

I looked over my shoulder, meeting Goll's questioning gaze. I thought that strange to ask. His cold mask was in place again, not the watchful hunter I saw just a moment ago across the table. Even so, there was a wariness in his expression. A vulnerability. He wanted me to get to know his dragon?

"Yes," I finally answered.

He blinked and dipped his gaze, a quirk lifting one side of his wide mouth. "This way, my mizrah."

Yet again, I winced inwardly at that moniker. I wasn't sure I'd ever get used to being called the title that essentially equaled "servant." A sexual servant.

Setting it aside, for what good was it to bemoan my new reality, I followed him through his bedchamber, wanting to slow down and marvel at the decor. From the ceiling down, the large room was draped in black and gold except the mantel, which was white marble like mine. There were intricate designs and figures carved into it, but he urged me to follow quickly.

I hesitated when he disappeared behind his dressing screen. He stepped back out of the shadows, smiling wide enough to flash his fangs.

"Frightened, Una?"

My wings flinched under the cloak. I tipped my chin up. "Of course not. Whatever harm you might've wanted to do me, you could have done at any time."

"This is true, Mizrah." His voice was low and intimate. "Come." He nodded his head for me to follow and turned away.

Behind his dressing screen, there was nothing more than a wardrobe to one side and a wall. He flattened his palm and pressed, then a door unlatched and opened inward to a dark, stone stairwell. A gust of cool air wafted into the room.

"Oh." I stepped up beside him and smiled. "Clever."

Those dragon eyes roved my face a moment too long, enough to stretch the tension between us before he stepped through the doorway first.

"Take my hand. The stairs spiral downward, and they're steep."

I took the hand he stretched out to me in the dark, and then he whispered, "*Etheline.*"

A ball of orange fire appeared in his other palm, the buzz of his magick sparking in the air. Being so close to him as he used his magick made my lips tingle. I licked my lips, wanting to taste his magick. It was so powerful I could feel it pressing against my chest as if it wanted to reach through my skin and latch onto my bones.

I yearned to have magick of that kind of my own. I did have a gift of the gods, the one that had replaced my healing magick, but I could never do something so extraordinary as breathe feyfire into the air with a whisper of a word in the dark.

I marveled that he could carry feyfire in his hand like it was nothing. He held it in front of him, lighting our passage as we stepped carefully down the stairwell till we reached the bottom.

"*Nihilin,*" he whispered, and the flame in his palm snuffed out.

He pulled me out into the moonlight, still holding my hand. I wasn't sure how I felt about that, only that I didn't want to disrupt the peace we'd struck between us.

"In one of my books, I read that feyfire has different temperatures and different effects."

He stared ahead, leading me through the garden, which was really more a grove of trees with twisted roots, dangling orange flowers, and a deeper orange fruit. Maragords. A sweet treasure. They grew in Hellamir as well, but that was as far south as the trees would take root. It wasn't the climate but something about the soil here that helped them grow better. We had the fruit imported into Issos each fall with their harvest. I suppose I wouldn't need to import the fruit now.

"It seems you finally read something in your books that was correct." His admonishment was light, almost teasing.

Heat flushed my cheeks. I kept my attention on the path through the grove toward Drakmir's humped back above the trees.

"Using feyfire is somewhat of an artform," he added softly.

"How do you mean?" I turned to him, curious.

He walked with his hands at his back, his posture straight, the moonlight gilding his black horns in silver, winking off of the golden jewelry.

"The novice user, or I should say the ones who are given a modicum of the gift of this magick, can only create natural flames that burn hot. But those who are gifted with exceptional abilities wielding feyfire can create flames that feel like no more than a whisper of wind against your skin. They can make the flames dance at will."

His voice was melodic and sonorous. I'd not yet heard him sound this way—at ease and almost tender.

"I presume you have such a power." I watched as Drakmir lifted his head from where he rested, noting our approach.

"I do."

Stopping, I turned to Goll. "Show me."

The watchful hunter had returned, the intensity of his gaze tapping on my senses. Still, I did not look away. I did not squirm but held his attention with poise.

Goll held out his palm between us and whispered a few words. A red flame filled his hand, flickering this way and that.

"Hold your hand out, face down."

"No," I instinctively snapped.

He chuckled, a deep rumbling sound that coiled tight in my belly. "Don't be afraid, Una."

Heaving a sigh, I held out my hand above his, palm down. He whispered another command in demon tongue. The red flame tripled in size, licking and swaying unnaturally until it reached my hand.

I gasped, ready to snatch my hand away, but all I felt was a light brush tickling my skin, like a feather twirling on the underside of my palm.

I laughed. "It is like its dancing." I watched the red flame tease along my fingers then wrap entirely around my hand with a gentle squeeze.

I inhaled at the pressure and the slight heat. Then he closed his fist and the flame disappeared.

"So you determine its temperature?"

"I can."

I remembered how he'd burned his enemies in the throne room after he'd beheaded his father.. My stomach dropped with a sickening thump.

"Come. Let's say hello to Drakmir." He guided me toward the giant, lounging beast. "Tell me, Drak. Have you any secret female fae lovers I should know about?"

Goll rested a hand on Drak's snout, smirking.

"Enough." I smiled. "You don't have to mock me."

The flicker of his smiling attention had my pulse racing again. "Tell me about Hava," I said, watching him pet his dragon.

"What about her? Is everything going well with her?"

"I adore Hava, but she told me she's half shadow fae. I thought wraith and shadow fae did not like each other."

"They do not," he assured me. "But that doesn't mean there aren't a few who won't choose to mate with one another, regardless of their cultural differences."

"I suppose," I admitted. After all, there were many fae of both light and dark, enjoying one another's company at the Borderlands.

And here I was mated to a dark fae king. It was simply unheard of inside the palace walls of Issos. Fae races typically stayed with their own kind.

"Hava came to me through another," he said gently, "one of my trusted military councilmen, Morgolith. He had served under my father, but he'd left under his rule to serve the shadow fae instead. Before he left, he'd heard I was in hiding and found me. He introduced me to Hava who was a servant in the palace. She pledged to serve as my spy for she saw the kind of ruler my father was and didn't approve."

"No, I wouldn't think she would. Hava is a kind fae."

Goll nodded. "He promised to return when I was king, for it wasn't as if he could help me in hiding. Everyone knew his face, and he'd be killed if my father caught him."

"Has he returned?"

"He has. Some told me not to accept him back as he'd been a traitor to the last king, but the last king had thrown me in a dungeon for decades because of a prophecy." He patted Drak, who'd done nothing but stare at us both. "Turns out the prophecy was right."

I stepped forward and reached out my hand. Drak immediately tilted his giant snout toward me. I pressed my palm along his jaw and rubbed his soft scales.

"As a child of two dark fae whose people despised one another," he continued in that soft voice that I found completely enchanting, "Hava wasn't welcome among the shadow fae. Both her parents had died, and she needed a new home. A safe place to land."

"I'm surprised Xakiel took her in."

"He took her as a servant. But I trust her as a loyal friend." He was quiet for a moment, no longer petting Drak, his gaze distant. "No one will trouble her in my palace."

"She is very endearing."

He smiled, turning his lovely expression upon me. For that was the only way to describe how he looked with a genuine, soft smile on his beautiful face. It wasn't a sardonic or lascivious one or the typical cold, hard façade he wore so often. For the first time, I felt like I was with the young fae who saved me from death, from that infernal dungeon.

"She is," he agreed, his gaze dropping to my mouth. "As are you."

A spark of fear shot through me, but I wasn't afraid of the heady desire heating his gaze. I was afraid that I liked it. A wash of shame had me glancing and stepping away, closer to Drakmir. How could I so easily open my emotions to the man who forced me to give myself to him to save my people? How could I be attracted to the king who had killed so many of my own?

As I stroked Drak quietly, the dragon lifted his head, his glowing silver-blue eyes focusing intently on mine. That's when I felt the buzz of his magick rippling into my palm and fingertips. I gasped softly, and then I was no longer there in the moonlight. His thoughts became my own as I slipped into his mind, into his memory.

I growled and snarled, the chains cutting into my throat and back leg. The three demon fae with giant black wings and thick horns laughed at me. The one with a whip lashed it in the air, snapping it across my snout. It stung painfully.

I bellowed another roar, furious and frustrated. I was in a small cave somewhere with nowhere to run, no way to escape the cruelty of these demons who imprisoned me.

The big one lifted the whip again. I bellowed another roar in rage, awaiting the pain that had lashed me for so long. Then another demon stepped into the mouth of the cave and kept walking on silent steps. This one had no wings, but he seemed familiar. His gaze met mine, and I knew. He was a brother of old.

The new demon whispered an ancient word, and flames leaped from his hands, lighting the three cruel demons afire. A burning sensation deep in my chest told me that one day, my own fire would come and one day, I would call flames to my aid just as this demon had. I was too young yet.

The fire demon ignored the screaming, burning fae and stepped toward me with hands outstretched, saying soft words that calmed me. I did not fear when he lifted a blade, for I knew he was my brother. He sliced through the air and the chains fell upon the cave floor, setting me free.

I came back to myself with a sudden surge, the whisper of magick still coursing through my blood and my mind, speeding my pulse. My wings started to flutter, a wild energy poured through me to them. For the first time since I'd lost my wings, since these new ones had grown, I felt the urge to fly.

I swallowed the lump forming in my throat.

"Una." Goll, his voice gruff, reached forward to steady me, gripping my forearm. "Are you well?"

I swooned at the intensity of the vision. I'd never traveled into a dragon's mind. I'd only been in small birds before. What had happened?

I gazed up at Drakmir, who simply stared back, rumbling a soft purr.

"I'm fine."

"Una?"

"I'm fine. But perhaps I need some rest."

Without another word, Goll led me back to the castle, up the dark stone stairwell, through his chamber and into my own. Goll whispered something to Meck, then followed me into my bedchamber.

Goll looked about the room, lingering on my open trunk where Hava had begun to unpack earlier. I'd managed to pull my oracle book out from the bottom and stash it under my bed when her back was turned.

"You have everything you need?"

"Yes."

"Then I will say goodnight."

I watched as Goll left, the door clicking closed behind him. A pang of disappointment squeezed my chest. It wasn't until his cloak started to slip from my shoulders that I realized I was still wearing it. My hand instinctively went out to the soft pelt, trailing fingers along the edge.

Drakmir's magick lingered, a warm buzz beneath my skin as I turned to the arched window, which had been unboarded. The night sky was beginning to cloud over.

My emotions spun in a whirlwind as I tried to reconcile the King Goll whose army had battled and killed my people all the way to Issos to the man in my vision who'd saved an adolescent dragon from certain death. Who had also taken in a half-breed, considered an outcast, and had protected her, given her a high-ranking position in his home.

I realized with sudden and unwavering certainty that this was the true Goll, the compassionate one who hid behind a hard, brutal exterior. Or maybe that was simply what I chose to believe since there was no way out for me. Since this was my new home, no matter what I truly wanted.

I suppose time would tell who the real Goll was—the benevolent young wraith prince who'd saved me from certain death or the one who forced me to be his sex slave, the mother of his heir, without any regard to my own free will or desires.

I pulled the collar of his cloak to my face and inhaled deeply, savoring the wintry masculine scent I now knew as his.

"Tomorrow," I whispered to myself. I'd worry about all of this tomorrow and relish this small moment of peace between myself and the wraith king.

CHAPTER 18

Goll

"What do you mean? Of course she's the one."

Dalya sat across from me in my study. Her dark brows pinched together. "It is hard to tell for certain."

I scoffed impatiently. "She has the mark. Her black wings, Dalya. Surely, it is the sign of the female faeling in your vision."

She dipped her head in agreement. "That is a sign, Sire. It is simply difficult to know for certain until the prophecy is actually fulfilled."

"Then we won't know until the Rite of Servium." I tapped two clawed fingers on my wooden desk.

She clasped her slender hands in her lap. "Are you sure this is the right course, Sire?"

"I'm positive. After the ceremony, I'll get an heir off Una, a high-born heir with the purest royal bloodlines of dark and light fae. Our union will solidify my right to reign over both kingdoms."

Dalya grimaced then quickly smoothed her features. I wasn't sure why this thought disturbed her. It could be because I was forcing a female to do my bidding, become my concubine, something my father would've done.

"You were certain before, I don't understand your doubt now."

"I apologize, Sire. I do not mean to make you doubt."

"I have none at all. It's just unusual for you to second guess a vision or premonition."

She bowed her head, brow pinched.

"How is Ferryn?" I abruptly changed the subject.

Her eyes lifted and she blinked away whatever thoughts clouded her mind about my mizrah. "He is doing well."

"He hasn't needed any more healing treatments since his return, has he?"

"No, Sire," she said quickly. "He has fully recovered from the rite."

I was slightly concerned that he was suffering nightmares from his experience, thinking he may have fractured under the pressure of the rite in the cave to join my Culled. I didn't think too hard that the main reason I had wanted him to heal fully from the experience had little to do with my concern for my cousin and more to do with my fear for the Rite of Servium. My fear for Una.

"Are you sure you want to put her through the rite?" she asked, as if she knew where my thoughts were.

"You believe me cruel for doing so."

She blinked quickly in surprise. "I would never rebuke you, my king. Nor question your decisions. I am your faithful servant." She dipped her gaze to her lap in submission.

Heaving a sigh, I leaned back in my giant wingback chair. "Dalya. You are not simply my High Oracle. You are also one of my oldest friends. You helped me rise to power. Do not fear that I will punish you for being truthful with me."

She kept her gaze on her lap, but another frown pinched her brow before she finally met my gaze, her bright golden eyes filled with emotion.

"Every mizrah of this kingdom before her has willingly taken the Rites of Servium. But Una Hartstone is being forced to. She may not live through it, sire. Are you prepared to risk her life?"

That knot that had been slowly twisting since we'd arrived at the palace tightened that much more. "She will not die."

"She could."

"Not if she is the one you saw in your vision, Dalya." I leaned forward, lacing my fingers tightly on the desk before me. I kept tight control on my temper, for I felt it burning hotter. "I realize you have doubts. But I do not. She is meant to be at my side and help me raise Northgall, the leader of the dark fae, above all other realms. It is our time to rule the world, and Una is key in making that happen. She is *mine* and will be my mizrah."

By the end, my voice was gruff with aggression. I heard her, but she was wrong. I was sure of it. I'd only ever been surer of one thing—to slay my father and take his kingdom from him, to guide us into a brighter future.

Una would not die in the waters of Näkt Lykenzel. If she survived bathing in the black pool beneath the palace, then she was indeed fated to be mine. I must have faith in the signs and the prophecy and the gods. No matter Dalya's doubts. This was a truth I felt bone-deep.

Dalya dipped her head in obedience yet again. "Does she know what will happen during the Rite of Servium?"

"I thought it would be best coming from you."

"I see."

"Shall we have a divination before we go to her?" I opened my drawer, reaching for the small dagger I typically used when Dalya scried my future. She always needed blood to open her oracle gift.

"Not today, Sire. I think it best I go to your mizrah and speak to her."

It had been many weeks since her last divination, the last one right before Hava appeared that night and told me that the princess was my father's new prisoner. But Dalya was right; I didn't need a new prophecy right now, not as urgently as Una must know what is to come in two nights' time.

"She is in the garden now," I said. "Will you prepare her for what will happen? What is expected of her?"

She stood with me and bowed her head. "Of course, Sire."

Heaving a breath, I walked Dalya to the garden. This exchange between Dalya and Una might very well send my mizrah into a terror and hatred of me that could not be undone.

CHAPTER 19

Una

"They're too sweet." Hava scrunched her cute face into one of disgust, then spit out the bite of maragord.

I laughed, nearly dropping my basket of ripe maragords the two of us had collected together.

"We treasure these in Issos," I said. "They're so hard to get, and only once a year do we receive a shipment from the northern region of Lumeria. I suppose I can have them anytime I want now."

"No," said Hava. "The maragord grove only bears fruit this time of year. But our cooks are brilliant. They make preserves in jars that last the year." She made that disgusted face again. "I simply do not like them at all."

"You prefer savory foods?" I asked.

Her red eyes widened with excitement. "Spicy foods. Mmmm. The cooks are preparing a rare feast with the eskel and tusked boar from the recent hunt. The feast we will have for the court following the Rite of Servium."

I knew what that was, but not what would happen. "Can you tell me about the rite?"

"That is what Dalya is here for," came the baritone voice behind me.

I turned suddenly, finding King Goll standing next to the maragord tree we'd just picked from, Dalya at his side. Their dark coloring and deep, moon-gray skin made them look like a perfect royal couple, like they belonged together.

The intrusive thought churned acid in my belly. Goll took a step closer to me, asking in a low voice, "Are you well, Mizrah?"

It reminded me of last night and all the feelings I'd had as I fell asleep with his cloak tucked in the bed with me. I'd been disgusted by myself this morning, folding the cloak by the door and had asked Hava to return it to him.

"Yes." I looked past his shoulder to the High Oracle, her keen gaze on the two of us. "I would very much like to speak with Oracle Dalya about the rite."

He stepped away. "I will see you at dinner." He gave a look to Hava, who instantly dipped her head and left. Goll looked back at me, his expression inscrutable, no telling what he was thinking. Then he simply walked away.

When I turned to Dalya, she seemed to be waiting for me to say something first. It was a polite mannerism given to the host in Issos. I suppose this was my home, not hers, so I gestured down the path.

"There is a quiet place to sit and talk just beyond the grove."

She nodded and fell in step next to me as I led the way. I'd only been here two days and one night, yet this grove was right below my window. I'd studied it from my bedchamber, and had spent the better part of today wandering its paths with Hava.

Where the grove ended, there was a manicured walkway with tall, thin evergreen trees lining either side. Up ahead, the tall evergreens surrounded a gray stone courtyard. At its center was a statue of a fae female, her pointed ears prominent, her stare into the distance beguiling, her gown pressed to her body as if she stood facing an unseen wind. Since she had no webbed feet or hands and no wings, I knew she must be a wood fae.

"This is Vix's Mizrah, is she not?" I asked, though I was sure she must be.

"Yes. The third wraith king of Northgall, Eerlion, had this statue commissioned for our god Vix's mate, but he used his own mizrah as the model."

"She is lovely."

"She is."

Stepping closer, I noted a small iron plaque. "There is an inscription." It was in demon tongue.

"Vix is here," I read. *"He guards and keeps the realm of his demon kin. He gives the king the right to rule and gives him his beloved, fruitful treasure.* And then in quotes, it says, '*I choose you.*'"

"Your translation is perfect." Dalya smiled.

"Thank you."

"I've spent many meditations with my priestesses in the palace gardens, but those are also ceremonial words."

"Why do you meditate here?" I wondered aloud. In Issos, the priests and priestesses remained in their white temple for prayer and meditation.

"To the wraith fae, this place where Näkt Mir sits is the most sacred and hallowed of grounds. The palace itself was built from the volcanic rock left behind from our revered god Vix. When his mizrah died and he had laid her to rest, his grief caused the eruption of Vixet Krone thousands of years ago."

I'd read something somewhat similar, but it was Vix's anger that had caused the eruption. And it burned anyone who was too close, the fires of his wrath roasting them alive. But now, I wondered at the stories that had been written down and transcribed, then taught to me and all other Issosians. There was a discrepancy somewhere. I simply wasn't sure if it was more on our end or the dark faes.

"Everyone keeps calling me 'mizrah.' But I am not that title yet. One of the councilman said as much."

Dalya stared at me with her lovely golden eyes. "He has chosen you. It is the king's right, guided by the gods, to choose his mizrah."

"Guided by the gods." I huffed a laugh, taking a seat on the bench in front of the iron statue. "This has nothing to do with destiny. This was the king's chosen ending to the war, to show Issos how powerful he is."

Dalya took her seat next to me, angling toward me, her hands demurely clasped in her lap. "Simply because you were taken as a war prize to be his mizrah does not negate that it could also be fated by the gods."

I blinked at her, but her expression gave nothing away. "Do you believe that?"

"I believe…it is possible. But not certain."

"Does Goll believe that?"

When she flinched, I realized I'd used his first name, not his proper title or *Sire* or *my liege* or *my king*. I simply preferred to think of him as Goll, the man who'd saved me. The young prince who showed me compassion and kindness once.

"King Goll does believe that you are destined to be his mizrah." Her gaze swept up to my wings.

I fidgeted with my cloak's tasseled drawstrings which dangled in my lap.

"What will happen during this Rite of Servium? *Servium* means selection, correct?"

She turned her attention back to the statue. "Yes. It also means *to serve*. It is the king's right to choose his mizrah during the selection."

"I am aware of that." The sardonic words slipped through my lips.

She looked back at me. "It is a privilege to be chosen as our king's mizrah."

"It was not a privilege to be taken from my home, to be forced to be his—" I could not finish the sentence.

"To be forced to be *his*," she stated without an addendum. "He will guard and protect you above all others. He will keep you safe above his own life. He will serve you as you serve *him* by begetting his heir."

My brow pinched and I stared at Dalya in confusion. "Is this how all kings treated their mizrahs? I read that King Goll's father murdered his mizrah, Goll's own mother. Xakiel did the opposite of protecting her."

She actually smiled. "King Goll is not his father. He takes his oaths seriously."

A breeze blew through the trees, rustling the leaves, drawing my attention back to the grove. The weather was turning toward winter.

"I was told by one of my scholars in Issos that wraith fae do not believe in marriage the way we moon fae do. Is this ceremony similar to a moon binding? A union between two fae?"

"Many wraith fae complete the Rite of Servium, but they take mates, not a mizrah as the king does."

"But a mate implies there is only the two of them. I will simply be his chief concubine. He will take others once his child is born," I added bitterly.

She did not reply, did not say that I was wrong. I was not a fool to think that even the noblemen of Issos did not take lovers behind their wives' backs. Wraith fae simply did it out in the open.

"Some wraith males choose only one mate," she added quietly.

I held her golden gaze. "But not a king."

Her smile was somewhat sad when she added, "He will always keep you safe."

But he would not be faithful to me once I was with child. Why I was so obsessed with this thought, I had no idea. I should be overjoyed I'd be forced to be his bedmate for only a short time. Yet a thickness built in my chest, making it difficult to breathe.

I inhaled deeply. "Tell me what will happen at this ceremony."

"Before the ceremony, my priestesses and I will take you below the palace."

I flinched and jerked my head toward her.

"No." She shook her head. "Not to the dungeon. Not to that part of the palace. Deeper below, there is a cave left behind by the god Vix. There is a lake called Näkt Lykenzel. It is god-touched. Every mizrah must bathe in this lake the night of the ceremony. It is where the dead speak to the living." She paused, looking down at her hands. "Mizrahs are sometimes given visions by the gods. If the gods deem them unsuitable to be the king's mizrah, she may suffer."

"How do you mean?"

"Some have been given painful visions that damage the female fae. Some have never come back up alive."

I stared in shock for a moment. "You are telling me I could die?" My voice rose with a sudden spike of anxiety.

"King Goll is certain that you are meant to be his. He claims this will not happen to you."

"I suppose if King Goll says it, then it's all fine." I crossed my arms to stop the tremble of dread as I stared up at the statue. "What then? If I survive my bath in the lake."

"We will take you back to your bedchamber and paint your body in the sacred symbols. Then you will be taken to the throne room where the king and his court await."

"Painted?" I asked, unsure what she meant.

"Your entire body. From your neck down so all can see your demon sign and that you are healthy to bear his child. In that state, you will walk a circle through the court for all to see. Then you will take your place, kneeling within the circle beneath his throne. He will light feyfire to surround you, a symbol of his protection, then he will say the ceremonial words of the Servium. He will then take you within that circle. And bite you."

By now, I was trembling, trying to imagine how I'd possibly be able to walk and parade through his court naked, so that what? They could all inspect my body to be sure I was worthy to carry a wraith fae royal child? The humiliation of it. Then my attention snagged on to the last part.

"Are you saying that he will consummate the union in the throne room in front of"—I swallowed hard—"in front of everyone?"

"It is common of wraith kings. It is a way to show everyone that he has chosen her and that no one has the right to bed her but him. That it is his seed that plants the child and no other. It is tradition."

It was *barbaric*.

My stomach rolled with nausea. All words stuck in my throat, I couldn't even question for what purpose he would bite me. "Excuse me." I jolted to my feet and walked swiftly away.

"Do not fear, Mizrah," she called after me. "It is an honor he bestows upon you."

I half-laughed at her parting words, swallowing hard against the thickness in my throat, the tears pricking my eyes, and the bitterness in my heart.

Ferryn stood not too far away, waiting for me. He was assigned to me today. His frown deepened when he saw my distress, scowling past my shoulder at Dalya.

"Are you well, Mizrah?"

I swept past him. "No. I am not."

He quickly stepped in line beside me. "Should I summon the king?"

"Why would you summon *him?*" I asked, dumbfounded as I hurried toward the back entrance of the castle. "He cannot help me. He is the cause of my distress."

Ferryn remained quiet, following close behind me into the palace and up the back stairwell, as if there was some way for him to protect me against the emotions now spinning me into a wild panic. I bit my lip to keep from making a noise, but the tears came, nonetheless.

"Mizrah, please let me help you," he said with deep sincerity. He had once seemed colder than his twin Meck. Now, his kindness somehow made me cry harder.

I stumbled on a step and inhaled deeply, the tears coming hot and fast now.

"Please, Mizrah." He offered an arm.

I took it and let him lead me up the staircase, leaning my weight against him so I wouldn't crumble in a heap on the stairs. "I can't do this," I whispered to myself.

"You can," Ferryn encouraged me, continuing to carry most of my weight up the steps. "You are the mizrah our kingdom has been waiting for, my mistress. Beside the king, you will lead Northgall into a new era of strength and prosperity and beauty."

His words of encouragement only made me sadder. I didn't feel like this person he described. How was that to be me?

I stumbled again, my eyes blurry from tears.

"It's all right." He helped me with a gentle arm around my waist. "I've got you."

Once at my bedchamber, he opened the door and then stepped back respectfully, bowing his head.

"I will be out here if you need anything at all."

"Thank you, Ferryn."

Then I closed the door, tumbled into my bed, and wept till I fell asleep.

I awoke to Hava stoking the fire that had gone out in the grate. It was late afternoon by the color of the sky.

For a moment, I blinked awake, simply soaking in the beauty of my bedchamber, then I remembered. My heart sank with dread.

"Time to wake up, my mistress," said Hava, bustling over to the wardrobe where she'd put away my dresses. "You must get changed for dinner."

Sitting up, I said, "I'm not going."

Hava turned her surprised red eyes on me. "Are you sick?"

I huffed a laugh. *Sick to my soul*, I thought. But I shook my head. "No, Hava. I'm not dining with *him*."

She paused, watching me carefully. "You are angry with him?"

"Very," I snapped, standing and striding to the window, feeling sluggish and tired and sad. I pushed open the glass pane, needing the fresh air.

I'd never wished for the use of my wings more in all my life, desperate to leap from this window and fly far away. Tears pricked the backs of my eyes.

"My king will not like it if you refuse to dine with him," said Hava quietly, closer behind me now.

My sadness evaporated like a whiff of smoke, pure fury taking its place. I whirled. "Really? The king will be *upset*?" My voice rose. "Gods forbid!"

"Mistress, is there something I can do to—?"

She didn't get to finish her sentence because Goll slammed the door open so hard it hit the wall behind it. His dark gaze went to me then circled the room in an instant. He was obviously looking to find some danger, the reason he apparently heard my raised voice.

I crossed my arms and glared daggers at him. When he realized the danger wasn't a threat against me but rather coming *from* me, he commanded quietly, "Leave, Hava."

She half flew, half ran out of the room, pulling the door closed behind her.

Goll said nothing at first, simply stared, taking in my fuming anger. Then he strode to the middle of the room, closer to where I remained with my back to the window.

"This is about your visit with Dalya," he stated.

I swallowed hard, trying to regain control of my temper before I spoke, but it was no use.

"This is about the fact that you expect me to go through some sort of wraith fae ritual that could *kill* me."

He didn't flinch. Not at all. Like this news was nothing to him. Like my life meant nothing.

"You will not die," he said so calmly it only made me angrier.

"You don't know that," I hissed.

"I do."

"Because you're *king*?" I practically screamed. "You know everything? You're willing to bet my life on it. You care so little about me that you'd let me die to get what *you* want." I trembled in rage. "Why didn't you just stab me through in Valla Lokkyr and be done with it?"

His cool demeanor slipped as he closed the distance in three long, steady strides. I remained rigid and unmoving. He didn't reach for me, thank the gods.

"Do you think I would risk your life after saving it years ago?"

"I have no idea." I turned away from him and went to the window where the strong breeze blew cold across my face. I gripped the stone sill, relishing the cold on my fingers. "I don't even know who you are," I whispered more to myself. "All I know is what is expected of me. That in order to fulfill the treaty I've agreed to and keep peace in Lumeria, I must bathe in a cursed lake below this castle that might make me go insane or kill me. And *if* the gods let me survive," I blew out a disgusted breath, "I have to parade naked in front of your entire court and willingly..."

I couldn't say the last aloud. It was difficult to imagine and even more so to say what I would be forced to do. I couldn't even fathom where I'd find the strength to go through with this, if I even lived through the first part of the rite.

I sensed him approach me slowly. When he gripped my shoulders, I flinched. He dropped his hold but kept his body close, a warm, impenetrable wall at my back.

When he spoke, it was that deep, gentle rumble. "I understand that you are frightened. And that you don't understand the importance of the rite."

I wanted to whirl around and yell some more or even better, beat him, but apparently my spirit was deflated. I was exhausted.

"But hear me, Una."

There was a plea in his voice, a desperate tenor I'd never before heard him use.

"I know that this is the path the gods have set before you." He paused then added, "And me."

"Your gods or mine?" I asked, still facing the window, inhaling deeply of the cool air as the sky deepened to purple.

"Both," he answered quickly. And with certainty. "You will bathe in Näkt Lykenzel, and you will not go mad. Nor will you die." His voice was both commanding and gentle. "You will complete the Rite of Servium and become my mizrah as the gods decreed."

Finally, I turned, frowning. "The gods decreed that I would be coerced to leave my home and become *your* concubine? The gods must hate me."

I was aware of the repulsive lilt in my voice, but could he honestly believe I'd rejoice in such a declaration?

A deep furrow creased his brow. "It is their will."

"How do you know?"

"Dalya has foreseen it."

"That it would be me? The gods gave my name?"

His dragon eyes glowed a piercing blue. "The gods never tell us names. You know that. But I am sure of it. You'll have to trust me."

I arched a brow, my mouth quirking into a cynical smile, "Trust *you?*"

His cold gaze finally broke with some vulnerability. I'd actually managed to hurt him, it seemed. It didn't have quite the satisfying effect on me as I'd thought it would.

Just as quickly, the softness vanished behind the austere mask I was accustomed to. The dragon was back, looking down at me with an unreadable expression.

Then he asked, "Are you telling me that you've decided not to go through with it? You've decided to break the treaty?"

I scoffed. "You bastard. You know I won't." Narrowing my gaze, I lifted my chin. "I will go through with your Rite of Servium. I do not break my vows."

My mind flitted to the moon-binding in Valla Lokkyr. I'd already promised myself to this wraith king. And though he dismissed that ceremony as inconsequential, I'd as good as given my heart and soul to him, body too, the night we left Issos.

"Very well," he said coolly. "Then get some rest, Mizrah. You'll need it."

He turned and left quietly, but the silence screamed with tension after he left. Tomorrow, I'd either die in the bowels of this palace in a black lake. Or I'd survive and become the king's official concubine, his vessel to use and toss aside when he was done. At the moment, I wasn't quite sure what was worse.

CHAPTER 20

Una

I sat upon the chaise facing the crackling fire, readying for the rite, for my possible death. Beneath the black velvet ceremonial cloak, I wore a sleeveless, black silk chemise—the meager garment I could be wearing when I took my last breath.

Since my visit with Dalya yesterday, I had not left my bedchamber. Hava had not insisted I meet the king for dinner, and he had not returned to my bedchamber even once.

For a while, I was furious he would drag me back to Näkt Mir to be humiliated in this barbaric rite to become his—no, I could no longer equate being his mizrah to being his whore.

But in my mind, it wasn't too far off. He might deem my womb important and therefore protect me until I gave him the child he so desired, but then what would happen to me in this unholy land where public fornication and biting were celebratory acts? Would I still be allowed Meck and Ferryn as guards when he cut me loose or sent me to live in a nearby tower?

"Mistress," Hava asked. She knelt at my feet and took my hand, her brow pinching with a frown. "Your hands are cold." Then she began warming my hand beneath her tiny ones, rubbing to stimulate circulation. "King Goll has asked to speak with you before the priestesses come to take you to Näkt Lykenzel."

"No," I said curtly. "Tell the king I will see him in the throne room at the Rite of Servium."

She dipped her head while warming my other hand then placed them both in my lap. Her nearness was comforting. I knew that even our short time as friends, she truly cared for me and I for her. She was my only true companion here. I would carry that feeling in my heart—I was loved and I was a strong royal princess of the Issosian line—as I marched into their ceremony, hoping I'd survive.

She stepped to the table by the fire where I'd left my meal uneaten and returned to my side.

"Here," she whispered, though there was no one there to overhear her. "Drink this." She held out a chalice of Mevian wine. "I took it from the kitchens when the cooks weren't looking. They're too busy with the feast anyway. Drink it, Una."

I took the chalice and gladly gulped down half the glass. "The feast they'll be having in honor of their king taking his mizrah, I presume."

"Yes," she agreed quietly. "There is to be dancing and entertainment. Everyone will celebrate when you become the king's mizrah."

"I'm glad there are some who will benefit from the occasion," I said bitterly.

She pet the back of my hair. She had spent hours plaiting tiny braids all along the front and twisting them in a unique style so that it was all completely bound tightly from my forehead and past my ears. The back was also twisted and plaited in multiple ways until I had one long rope down my back that brushed my buttocks. She said it was the ceremonial way for every mate or mizrah at her ceremony.

Hava pulled me to my feet, or rather I let her as she was so much smaller than me. She flitted around me, smoothing out my cloak.

"What of other mating rituals?" I asked. "The union ritual between two mates of dark fae? Do they also have a Rite of Servium?"

"Oh, yes. It is done in a much smaller ceremony and less formal than the wraith king's, of course. And there is no trial in Näkt Lykenzel."

"Of course," I added bitterly. "And do the wraith fae males take their women in front of everyone?"

Her brow pursed, her red eyes contemplative as she fiddled with my braid, placing it over the front of my shoulder. "No. They've likely mated many times before their ceremony anyway. That part is done behind closed doors." She smiled gently. I could not return it. "But they do bite them. It is a sign of public claiming. That is the end of the ceremony, and it is time to rejoice. To feast."

"Why does a king…?" I couldn't say it.

Hava knew what I wanted to know anyway.

She spoke softly. "A king taking his female before his entire court is more than a symbol. It's showing everyone that his seed already lives inside of her. It keeps any wraith fae competitors from trying to take what is his. If she is a worthy vessel for his heir, a high born like you, then they all must know he has claimed you for his own."

He'd said something similar to me in the tent that night. About rivals.

"But the wraith fae seem so devoted, dedicated to him. His Culled would kill anyone who dared to attack him or…" I paused, realizing I thoroughly believed this. "Or his mizrah."

She nodded adamantly. "This is true. But King Goll had to execute and expel many since he killed his father. There were many who had faithfully followed King Xakiel, who quickly switched allegiance at his death. King Goll showed some of them mercy, allowing them to prove their loyalty. They have, but there is always a chance a usurper wants his place."

A soft knock came to the door. Hava and I turned to see Dalya enter, covered in a black velvet robe similar to mine. She wore a lacy black veil that draped over her horns and hair, and swept down to cover half of her face, only her lips visible

She curtsied reverently. "It is time, Mizrah."

From beyond the door, I heard whispered chanting and smelled burning, spiced incense. I walked to stand in front of Dalya. "I am ready."

She lifted her gaze, a look of both awe and adoration on her face. "You are," she agreed, examining my expression. "Pardon me," she said as she stepped close and pulled my mantel's hood over my head. "Follow me, Mizrah."

She went into the shadowed corridor. I followed. On either side of my bedchamber were two lines of ten wraith fae priestesses, all robed in black, singing a soft chant. I only caught the words *ancient,* *binding,* and *home.* The two at the front held lanterns with burning blue coal, which cast an eerie light in the hall. The two priestesses second in the lines held a gold chain attached to a ball where the burning incense billowed out, filling the air with a smoky haze.

Dalya stopped just ahead of the front priestesses holding the blue coal lanterns so that I fell in line between them. The chanting stopped. I took note that my guards were no longer in the corridor as they usually were. Neither was King Goll. No one but the priestesses was anywhere to be seen. When I looked back into my bedchamber, Hava was gone as well.

Then we all walked together, the priestesses singing softly in demon tongue, the melodious sound hypnotizing as I was guided down the corridor and the staircase.

Below stairs, there was yet again no soul in sight. It was as if the palace were deserted.

Dalya guided us through the open double doors and along a path away from the esher woodland and the maragord grove. It was the stone path that brought us through the great iron gates. But rather than walk across the bridge, she continued on the path to the right where it circled downward.

The chill wind pushed my cloak against my body, the clouds wispy over the moon above. I breathed a prayer to Lumera, that she would be with me this night, that she would protect me.

As we descended in a winding path down below the castle, the stone cold beneath my slippered feet, I did not look at the steep drop-offs on either side. Rather, I focused on the singing prayers of the priestesses, their soothing melody brought me comfort.

I found myself muttering a prayer to Vix as well, the smoky incense billowing around me as I walked on. Vix wasn't a god we revered in Lumeria, but he was the god of this land. This was his sacred space. Surely, he would listen to a moon fae who found herself thrust into the world of his dark fae children.

"Bless my spirit," I whispered to myself. To Vix. "Keep my body and mind whole and safe, my lord."

A buzz of warmth pooled in my belly. It felt almost like magick, a strange and ethereal touch of knowing, of power, and warmth.

Dalya led us into a cave opening, both sides lit by torches of feyfire. The flames danced slowly, unnaturally, a welcome light guiding us into the dark. The priestesses stopped chanting at once.

The paved path disappeared into a trail of black sand that led deeper into the cavern. The sound of dripping water and the soft shuffle of our feet was all I could hear as we wound our way around a corner.

Then I saw it, surrounded by torches—Näkt Lykenzel, the black lake where I would either seal my fate as mizrah to King Goll. Or where I would die.

Dalya stopped at the edge. We all halted behind her. When she turned to face me, I instantly unhooked my cloak and removed it. When I would've dropped it to the ground, a priestess quickly took it from me. My wings sprang free, Hava wisely cut openings for them to slip through the ceremonial chemise.

I stepped around Dalya to look down into the dark abyss. The pool of water didn't seem menacing in any way. One side of it was a steep cavern wall, water sluicing down into the pool. Strangely, steam rose from the surface.

"It is a heated pool," I muttered, grateful for that at least. My last dip into icy waters in Silvantis had led to me being captured, tortured, and stripped of my goddess-given magick.

"Yes," Dalya confirmed softly. "There are deep pockets and hot springs below this sacred place that still warm the waters here."

Even so, I shivered in my gossamer shift, gooseflesh prickling my skin. I stood straight and tall. "Let us begin."

Dalya raised her arms and hands wide. "Vix give us guidance, bless this female, accept her into your beloved embrace."

With her arms opened to the cavern ceiling, she stepped into the black pool. The priestesses followed behind her in their parallel lines, stopping when the water reached their thighs.

On instinct, I walked forward, my body wanting to be in the water. The warmth of it surrounded my ankles, my legs, my belly and buttocks as I stepped past Dalya and the line of priestesses.

"Stop there, Mizrah."

I did.

"Now, fall back into the water. We will catch you and pull you up after you submerge."

Either dead or alive, I thought to myself.

Finding that I was extraordinarily calm at a time like this, I didn't hesitate. Closing my eyes, I fell backward. Slender arms and hands caught me beneath my head, shoulders, hips and legs, as the warm water enveloped my entire body. My long braid of hair and wings drifted downward. I held my breath when my entire head went under.

At first, nothing. Then…blinding flashes of memory. Not all my own.

The hag whispered in the dank dungeon, her cold, skeletal fingers tracing runes in blood on my forehead. "Ora est kel ohira. Ora est kel näkt los. Ora est meheem." Then her eyes lit with a burning light, something that hadn't happened in the dungeon but seemed more real now than the memory. Then she spoke in perfect Issosian in a monotone chant, "You are the destiny. You are the dark lady. You are for him."

A flash of pain, then a different vision. Not a memory. Only voices in a dimly lit room. I couldn't see anyone, only hear them, their voices intimately close. A single candle burned in the corner of a small bedchamber. A female whispered, "Two sides of the same coin. Demon-fae. One true, one not. Beware the raven's back… It's you, isn't it?" A male replied, "You know it is me. You've always known. Don't pretend I'm not destined to take it all from him." Then the voices faded, still whispering vehemently.

Then there came a vision of three sprites flying in a circle and singing, "A dark fae lady with secrets to see. A dark fae lady, lady…" They giggled and flew away into the shadows, their figures swirling into mist.

Out of the vapor stepped a menacing and dominant King Goll, his dragon eyes burning with blue-fire. "That is correct, Princess. You are my mizrah." His aggression vanished, and in its wake only pain etched his face and desperate longing. "Mine," he whispered, reaching out to me before vanishing into smoke.

Then my entire body was wracked with agony, burning from the inside as yet another vision came tumbling into my mind with jagged force. This one held weight and gravity, more than any other before. A four-horned wraith fae—no, something more, something bigger, greater— flew on dragon back, the moon shining behind him. In his arms was a female wood fae, her black hair streaked with gray lifting in the wind as the dragon soared in the night sky. Then the man, the god—he was certainly a god—cupped the cheek of the sleeping woman in his arms. "Rest now, my love. It will all come to pass as it should. My vengeance for you will be justice, and it will turn the world right again."

There was the sound of a dragon's flapping wings then the vision vanished into the gray clouds of the night sky.

I choked and spluttered the water clogging my throat and mouth. Dalya's wide eyes stared down at me as she held my head above water.

"Vix," I croaked, my voice raspy. "It was Vix." Then I slipped into darkness.

CHAPTER 21

Goll

I *must not hurt her.*

Watching from the shadows beyond Näkt Lykenzel, I'd tried to stay away, trusting in my instinct that she would be well. That she was the one.

I'd watched as she boldly marched to the edge of the black pool and slipped right in. As if death had no hold on her at all.

Gods above, she was so fucking beautiful. So brave.

I'd read every book and listened to every scholar on the accounts of mizrahs bathing in the black pool. Four had died, and one had gone mad. The kings hadn't chosen wisely. Vix had punished the females and the kings for their arrogance, for not listening to his guidance.

Una was mine. She was *always* meant to be mine. It was a fact, not a feeling or notion begot by my own superiority. Hell, what king would choose this path if they weren't guided by fate? She was the daughter of our greatest enemy. And yet, I'd never felt the compulsion to claim and possess any woman, any creature at all, as I did her.

My gut tightened as Dalya lowered her into the water. My instinct was to run to her, to take her into my arms. But I couldn't.

This trial must be true. To ensure that our gods bless this royal union. The Rite of Servium must take place. For my people to accept and understand that it doesn't matter she was born a moon fae. She is mine now. And so she will be theirs.

One of her slender arms thrashed out of the water, but her head was still submerged. She was having a vision, for certain. A thread of calm wound around my heart. Then her entire body shook, and a white foot lifted out of the water. She gasped.

I could stand it no longer. I marched from the shadows right as Dalya lifted her head. Una coughed the water from her mouth then said hoarsely, "Vix. It was Vix."

Her body went limp in the arms of the priestesses right as I reached the edge of the pool and waded in. Several of the females gasped.

"My king!" shouted Dalya. "You must not be here. No one must be present at the bathing but myself and the priestesses. You must go."

I was already nudging them aside and pulling Una's limp weight into my arms. They let go easily so that I could hoist her close to my chest, her head lolling against my shoulder, her warm breath against my skin.

"I am king, High Oracle." I held Una tighter against me, the anxiety unwinding. "I can change the rules." I turned as I barked over my shoulder, "And no one will tell me I cannot hold my mizrah."

Carrying her from the cave, I marched up the winding path and through the empty palace. On this night, every single servant, courtier, or Culled must be in the throne room as witnesses, awaiting the gods' decision to see if their mizrah had been chosen.

Normally, the king would be waiting, too, but I couldn't let her go through that entirely alone. I'd prayed to Vix from the moment I saw the blue-coal lanterns approach in the distance.

I carried her through the empty corridors and into her bedchamber, then lay her down on the bed. Her eyes twitched, but she was still unconscious. Finding my Meer-wolf cloak hanging over the chaise, I quickly draped it over her body. There was nothing warmer.

Dalya entered the chamber quietly as I rubbed the fur over her arms, wanting the circulation to return quickly, needing to see her eyes open, needing to see her well.

"My liege," Dalya chastised softly. "Please go and let us prepare her. We have an herbal tea to warm her and wake her gently. But you must go."

This time, I didn't argue, but I took one more moment to gaze upon her lovely face. I traced the pad of one finger along her hairline and cheekbone, noting the wet braid.

"Be sure to dry her hair as best you can."

"The blue-coal will do the trick."

Four priestesses carried in the warming lanterns and placed them near her head on either side of the bed.

I couldn't stop caressing the silky softness of her cheek, her jaw, recognizing the delicacy of my mizrah.

I must not hurt her. I must not hurt her.

"Goll," Dalya pleaded quietly.

I stood and stepped back, finally turning to Dalya. "Be gentle with her."

"Of course, my king."

Then I stormed from the room to ready myself for the next part of the ceremony. The part I both yearned for and dreaded the most. If she didn't hate me before, she would soon enough.

CHAPTER 22

Una

Somehow, I was no longer afraid. I didn't tremble at all, even as I stood right outside the giant double doors to the throne room, listening to a rhythmic beat of drums and the lowly chanted name "Goll" like they did outside of my palace at Issos.

No, that was no longer my palace. This was.

Dalya paused at my side as I looked at the black obsidian door, carved with wraith kings of old. Even in stone relief carvings—sitting upon a throne, wielding a curved sword, standing beside a dragon— the images portrayed strength and power like I'd never known.

Beyond this door sat a living, breathing king upon his throne who was going to be my one and only mate. For I knew I would take no other, even after I beget his child and he cast me aside. I'd made a vow beneath Lumera's light and, to me, that was binding for life.

"Go through when you're ready," Dalya whispered. "Or"—she hesitated—"if this isn't what you want, you can choose not to walk through that door. You can go back to your room and change. I can help you."

There was such sincerity in her voice as she told me she'd help me run away. I turned my head to look at her. She held me in her golden eyes. I was shocked she'd offer such a thing, that she'd betray Goll. For surely, he'd see that as a betrayal.

Was it for my sake or her own? Or her kingdom's? What would happen if an Issosian moon fae begat the heir to Northgall?

I wasn't sure of her motives, but I was certain of something else entirely that struck me to the bone as I told her, "This is where I belong."

Her expression tightened with concern. She lowered her gaze as she curtsied, then slipped off down a side corridor. She'd told me she could not enter through the front entrance; only the mizrah entered here on this night. When I stepped through the door, it was my acceptance of the people of Northgall and a promise of devotion to the wraith king. Dalya had told me to be sure before I walked through, for there would be no turning back.

When I'd woken in my bed with Vix's final vision repeating in my head, I was certain of everything. A *god* had given me his memory, his will, his blessing through that strange vision.

"I am certain," I whispered to myself.

Even as I'd stood naked in my bedchamber, my feet planted wide so that the priestesses could cover my body from neck to feet with shimmering gold paint then use dragon-mane quills to paint black demon sign around my breasts where I would feed the king's child, around my stomach where the babe would swell, down my legs and arms so that I might carry the babe with strength, I did not fear or flinch at what was coming.

The beating of a drum and the chant continued as I readied to push open the door. My long braid brushed my buttocks.

The god's words whispered back to me. *It will turn the world right again.*

I was somehow a part of that. I could help turn the world right again by walking through this door. We'd been plagued by sickness and war for so many years. But that final vision spoke directly to my soul. That was my purpose. This was my destiny.

I straightened my wings and my spine. I braced my hands on the handles of both doors and pushed them inward, opening both wide. The drums and chanting silenced at once.

At the front of the long oval hall, Gollaya sat upon a giant throne, a dragon carved into the black stone.

Goddess above. He looked magnificent.

He wore nothing but a leather skirt that ended above his knees. Without his armor, he looked more powerful, not less. Most might appear vulnerable in such a bare state. He did not. With the gold jewelry decorating his horns, the gold cuffs on his wrists, the demon runes burned into his chest and prominent forehead, his broad, muscular body could only belong to the most virile of kings.

His ice-blue eyes flared bright, but he kept his clawed hands on the arms of his throne, his fingers curling at the ends as if he were striving to keep himself in place.

The sounding of one drum began to beat, a slow, steady tempo for a march. That's when I finally tore my gaze from Goll to the room. The courtiers—male and female wraith fae, all in their regular garb, not half nude like Goll or fully bare like me—stood in a wide circle several fae deep.

My heart tripped faster. There were easily two hundred present. Maybe more. Gathering my courage, I stepped out to the beat of the drum, walking along the back of the circle as Dalya had instructed. No one made a sound as I kept my chin up, my back straight, my wings high and made the walk of the mizrah, presenting myself to the wraith fae royal court, awaiting their acceptance as their mizrah.

I skimmed over the royal council, not wanting to see the disapproval in their eyes, seeking the Culled in the crowd. My heart burst with relief when I found Keffa, his gaze on my face only, his smile genuine and proud. Soryn beside him still looked grave as always, but he gave me a nod of approval, which sent an unexpected spark of happiness to my soul. I needed their approval. I *wanted* it. It was a strange discovery.

"Mizrah," said Pullo, the younger one with the shaved sides of his head and the braid down the center of his back. His smile was wide when he said again, "Mizrah."

Then Tierzel at his side joined in, chanting with him as I continued my march around the room to the beat of the single drum. Then two more after that.

My gaze landed on Meck and Ferryn. They, too, kept their eyes above my shoulders. They were male, and I'm sure they looked as well as every person in the room. But when I met their eyes, they were fixed solely on mine.

Meck smiled wide. But Ferryn frowned, a look of concern on his face, likely from the last time I saw him when he'd practically had to carry me to my room. But then he bowed, dipping his horns low in reverence.

Then more joined in. "Mizrah. Mizrah. Mizrah." It was a low chant, slowly gaining strength.

My gaze found Hava closer to the throne near other servants of the palace. I blinked away the emotion as they chanted "Mizrah," the acknowledgment that I was accepted by the people of Silvantis, by Northgall itself. Tears streamed down Hava's heart-shaped face.

I came to the throne but did not turn to face Goll as Dalya had instructed. I must walk the full circuit of the room before presenting myself to him. I passed Dalya on the far side of the throne, her eyes shining with emotion, a sincere smile on her face. She was complex, but I felt it to my bones that she was genuinely happy in this moment. For me or for Goll or for her people, I wasn't sure.

As I rounded the other side, my gaze landed on some of the royal council, most of them chanting. But not all. The gray-haired elder Bozlyn chanted my name, his gaze respectfully on the ground. But the other elder, Kellock, did not. His eyes bore into mine, his jaw clenched, his disapproval blazing clear and bright.

Yet no one paid him any mind. Everyone else chanted my new title over and over again as I continued to close the circle. Their expressions were lit with an array of emotions—happiness, excitement, indifference, even confusion. Some appeared puzzled that a moon fae princess was indeed about to become their king's mizrah. But Kellock was the only one defiantly disapproving of me that I could see.

Ignoring him, I completed the circle back to the entrance of the throne room. The chanting and drumbeat continued as I turned to face Goll, then increased in tempo, growing louder, as I walked down the center of the room. A line of black chalk encircled a large white velvet pillow, demon runes scrawled the perimeter of the circle.

Slowly, I lowered to kneel upon the center of the white cushion, staying upright on my knees, my arms at my sides, my chin held high as I stared at Goll.

The chanting and drums ceased at once. No sound at all, not even a whisper as Goll drank me in, still sitting tall upon his throne. He was the embodiment of power, his magick already humming in the air, encircling me where I knelt before him.

Then he stood and took slow, steady strides toward me. He stopped before me, reaching down and cupping the bottom of my chin. He held my gaze for an eternal moment. Then another, time stretching while he lingered over my face with intense longing. The sliver of golden fire around his serpentine pupil glowed brighter than

I'd ever seen, the ice-blue of his eyes an otherworldly blaze. I was hypnotized, caught in the eyes of my king.

Yes, *my* king. I was more certain than ever now.

When he spoke, his voice rumbled loud and deep for all to hear. "Vix is here within these walls of Vixet Krone. He guards and keeps the realm of his demon kin." Still cupping my chin, he swept his thumb along my jawline, his intense stare burning hungrily. "He gives the king the right to rule. He gives him his beloved, fruitful treasure." His voice softened when he repeated, "My treasure." Then his voice boomed loud again, "I choose Tiarrialuna Elzabethanine Hartstone, daughter of the moon fae of Issos." Then softer again, his words only for me, emotion swelling in his eyes, "I choose you, Una."

My pulse pounded in my throat, filling my entire body with wild sensations of excitement, elation, and dread at the public act to come, I smiled shakily up at him, ready and willing.

He let go of my chin as he took a step back and raised his arms at his sides, palms up, his biceps flexing. "*Etheline!*"

Feyfire ignited in his palms then leaped to the stone floor and wound around the perimeter of our small circle, enclosing us within. The flames licked higher and higher as the roar of the crowd rose in the domed throne room.

When there was a wall of flame high above the figures barely discernible on the other side, Goll stepped toward me. He gripped me by the upper arms and lifted me to my feet, his expression hard and feral but his eyes shone with urgent concern. He pulled me against his body, and I gripped his bare waist.

"I choose you, Una," he repeated as he lowered his head.

My fingers curled against his skin, unaware somehow that he would kiss me, that he'd want to kiss me. My mind had been filled with the act of copulation in front of everyone, I'd not expected him to want to kiss me.

But when his lips brushed gently against mine, a flare of need burned hot through my veins. He coaxed my mouth apart, his lips warm, enticing a small noise from my throat. When I opened wider, he slanted his mouth to mine, his tongue sweeping inside.

My mind suddenly felt light, my entire being wrapped in this kiss, this luxurious warmth spreading through me. His arms slid around my back and waist, pressing and holding me close, dipping his head low to reach me.

I stroked my tongue into his mouth, sliding against his fangs, eliciting a groan from him. It rumbled in his chest, teasing my bare breasts, my nipples tight and aching. I whimpered when he released my mouth to kiss and nip down my neck.

Then I remembered.

I stiffened, wondering if this is when he'd bite me, afraid of the pain. Instead, his mouth coasted lower as he bent to brush his lips across one breast, smearing the demon sign and sucking at the taut peak. I moaned, the pleasure coiling hot and wet between my legs.

Then he scooped me off my feet and lay me flat on my back on the cushion, bringing me back to awareness of where I was and what was about to happen in the throne room. I looked toward the wall of towering flames, noticing the shapes of the shouting wraith fae, their drums beating loudly again. They weren't even recognizable on the other side, but they were still there in the room. Discomfort stiffened my limbs.

"Una," Goll beckoned.

I turned my attention back to him, a pained expression darkened his eyes. He lowered his mouth—dusted with gold—to mine again, sweeping me away with yet another devouring kiss, his lips firming over mine. He nipped my lower lip with his fangs, stinging with a small prick. He licked the metallic drop from my lip and groaned, yet again, kissing his way down my throat.

This time, I thrust my breast up for him, eagerly wanting that sensation of pleasure again. He licked and circled with his tongue then sucked the tip, which had me gripping his two larger horns to hold him there.

Another rumbling growl vibrated from his chest, which was pressed to my torso. He opened my left thigh, his grip firm but not painful. I couldn't help noting the claws of two fingers of his right hand were filed blunt. I quickly realized why when he slid that hand up my thigh and caressed my quim through the folds.

My head fell back to the cushion as he lingered on one breast and stroked a finger over the tight nub at the apex of my sex. My mouth fell open on a gasp. I'd touched myself for pleasure before. Of course, I had. But no one else ever had. The sensation of having this giant dark fae, the wraith king, hovering over me, sucking my breast and stroking me *there* sent a thread of hot desire throughout my body.

I squirmed beneath his touch, rocking up for more. He stopped tending to my breast, lifting his head to look at me, his fingers still slowly circling, igniting, stirring a maddening flame inside me.

I'd thought his gaze was feral before, but now, it was downright savage, locked on mine. He slid an arm beneath my shoulder to grip the back of my nape, cradling it actually, the tips of his clawed hand sinking into my braided hair.

"Show me," he whispered. "Show me what little joy I can bring to you, my mizrah."

His words were strange and distant, and yet I felt them singing to my bones as he slid the tips of those two fingers to my entrance and pumped shallow strokes before returning to the sensitive bud, slick and warm, pressing and circling with relentless urgency.

I panted, still gripping his horns, squeezing them as I rocked my pelvis up into his questing fingers. A startled cry erupted as my climax spun higher and higher, so fast that I had to bite my lip to keep from crying out.

"Show me," he commanded. Begged.

I kept his gaze as he circled and flicked my clit with increasing speed until I was soaring with a hard climax, my body jerking as I dropped my head back. His mouth was on my breast, sucking fiercely, causing more spasms to ripple. He covered my mound with the flat of his palm, sliding those two blunt-tipped fingers inside me just a little.

My sex squeezed and pulsed around the tips as he continued to lave my breast while I came down from my glorious high. As I did, my surroundings came back to me quickly. The high flames still blocked out the courtiers, nothing but blurry shadows on the other side—all still present, voices overlapping, rising above the drums.

Some chanted Goll's name. Some chanted "Mizrah." Yet another voice shouted, "Show us, my liege!" And another something similar with a boisterous laugh.

I stiffened, realizing we were still on public display, even if they couldn't see us. Goll was hiding us with his feyfire.

He slid up my torso, caging me in with his wide chest and body, his palm still cradling the back of my neck, his claws edged into my hair. I let go of his horns and gripped his shoulders.

"Not much longer," he told me before he slid those two fingers inside his mouth and sucked on them. His eyes closed briefly before he stroked them back inside me. Deeper this time, he thrust till a sharp pain made me cry out loudly and dig my nails into his skin.

Another wild clamor of noise and thumping of chests. More hearty laughter.

I realized they were celebrating their king taking my virginity. The thought stirred an altogether different emotion since I'd entered this room—shame.

This was not the way of Issosians. A couple was moon-bound beneath Lumera's guiding light. Vows were spoken, and the couple pledged their bodies in the privacy of their bedchamber.

Here, I was a spectacle, a fae woman to be claimed and owned by the king, to bear his child. A vessel for his heir, not for his heart or his love. The realization made my body go cold, even while my sex throbbed with recent pleasure and the more recent pain.

Goll saw something in my gaze that tightened his expression. He removed his fingers from my body, lifting his own higher to look between us. I felt a small trickle of warmth. He firmly wiped his bloody fingers upon the white cushion and muttered, "Fuck. Enough."

Then he scooped me into his arms and carried me toward the wall of flames. He murmured a command that I felt vibrate against the side of my ribcage pressed to his chest more than I heard him above the clamoring noise of the throne room. The flames snuffed out, filling the area with smoke as he carried me swiftly from the room.

He didn't look back or say a word as he strode through the ghostly corridors, still empty of anyone at all. I kept my face hidden, my mind reeling with worry. That wasn't right. That hadn't gone the way it was supposed to. He hadn't claimed me. Not entirely. What did that mean?

But I didn't have time to think long before I realized I was back in my bedchamber, a low fire crackling in the hearth. Goll thrust the door shut with his foot and carried me to the bed.

"Goll?" I asked, not sure what to say as he laid me on the mattress.

"Shhh." He untied his tunic and tossed it aside then he climbed in on top of me. "It'll be over soon, Una."

"Oh." He was going to finish here. I spread my legs and readied for the pain again. I was well aware there would be pain the first time. Hava had told me enough, having had lovers of her own.

But when I glanced between our bodies, most of him hidden in shadow beneath the coverlet, I could still make out the sizable length of his cock. Knowing his fingers caused pain, I wasn't sure I was ready for this. But I had to be.

"Look at me, Una."

I did, watching his ethereal gaze glow in the dark as he gripped himself and stroked the head of his cock at my entrance, grazing the tight nub that gave me so much pleasure before he pressed inside me. I widened my legs, bracing for the pain as he slid deeper.

The sting returned, not quite as sharp but close enough. I whimpered.

"You can bear it, Una." His voice was gravelly deep. "Just a little longer."

"Goll," was all I could say in response, my sex burning at his large intrusion.

His eyes slid closed as he thrust deeper and deeper until he was seated fully inside me. I panted harshly, curling my fingers into his back, my thighs wide and flattened to the mattress to take him.

"Not long," he growled, his voice tight with strain. "I promise."

Then he started to move, the painful stinging more intense now that he pumped in and out of me. Even so, there was a distant thrum of pleasure building as well. His magick sank into my skin with a tantalizing caress. His eyes opened on me again, unreadable but hot with blue flame.

I could only imagine what he saw in mine, my spirit wholly swallowed by the enormity of this moment, of giving myself to Gollaya Verbane in every way. For it was no longer simply a bodily exchange, but a passing of my soul into his keeping. I could not have allowed him to enter my body without giving him a piece of my spirit in return.

I gave it willingly, gladly. In the intensity of the pain my body felt, there was a bone-deep knowing that he was a part of me for forever now. And I was glad of it.

The magnitude of the moment, the discovery that I wanted him, that I wanted to be his mizrah and his mate, crashed through me like a dizzying maelstrom. A tear slipped from the corner of one eye into my hair.

Goll noticed and flinched, still stroking inside me.

"Fuck," he muttered looking away as he thrust deeper and faster, closing his eyes and frowning.

I clutched him harder to me as I felt the swell of his cock, the pleasure beginning to grow brighter, not overtaking the pain but getting close. On an animalistic groan, he pumped hard and deep and held, his cock pulsing as he emptied his seed.

The sensation was wildly glorious. I closed my eyes, another tear slipping free as I clung to his body pressed to mine, trembling with his climax. When his cock stopped throbbing, his rigid body loosened, both of us panting in the dark of my bedchamber.

I wasn't sure what to say, but I was desperate to hear some words of encouragement from him, that I hadn't failed in some way, for he had seemed disappointed and upset for the majority of the ceremony. And especially by the way he was looking at me now.

I opened my mouth to ask him when he withdrew from my body, his gaze glancing down between our legs. He hurried out of the bed and grabbed the tunic, retying it around his waist with quick, sharp movements.

"I'll send for Hava to tend to you." His voice was cold and unfeeling.

I sat up, pulling the sheet over my breasts, remembering that I was still covered in paint. "Goll, why are you—?"

"You don't have to worry about me forcing my attentions on you again anytime soon. I'll give your body time to heal before I return to your bed. I'll not bother you until your breeding time."

Then as he marched swiftly for the door, my heart sunk with despair.

Yes, my breeding time. Of course, that was his main concern. Even while I'd opened my soul tonight and given him more than my body, all he truly wanted from me was his heir.

When he opened the door, he stopped, but it wasn't to speak to me. There was someone right outside.

"She'll need a hot bath," he told the person.

"Yes, my liege." Hava's quiet voice. "The courtiers are concerned they did not witness the claiming."

A harsh noise then, "Whichever courtier has a fucking problem with the ceremony, they can address it directly to me. There was enough of her blood for evidence. And more on her sheets if the royal council needs more proof."

"Yes, my king," Hava agreed quickly.

"Once they're drunk and fat off the feast, they won't care anyway," he snapped before marching away.

Hava rushed in and came to me. "Mizrah, are you well?"

I curled away from her into the covers. "I need a moment, Hava," I whispered.

"Of course, Mizrah."

She set about doing things quietly. I heard her pulling the tub toward the fire, but I kept still, my eyes closed.

As much as the pain was when he entered my body, it wasn't quite as great as the pain I felt when he left it. I hadn't realized that I'd feel this way afterwards.

For a brief moment, nothing but wild elation and joy filled me at the sensation of giving my body to him. Then the sudden reversal of being engulfed with disappointment and sorrow at his neglect.

It was my own foolishness that had brought me here. His rejection did not mean that this still wasn't the right course. A fervent rightness about tonight still thrummed through me, my magick singing that we were on the right path. I had to sever my hopes for a true mating with Goll and focus on my real destiny here.

A sharp pain stung both my wrists on the underside. I gasped and jolted upright. Hava had left the room, probably to fetch hot water, so I was alone to witness the newly burned markings into my skin. They were a tiny zigzag rune I didn't know, the exact same on both wrists.

I wiped at the gold paint partially hiding them to see them better. I had no idea a moon fae could receive demon runes from the gods.

"It's never happened before," I whispered to myself, staring down at the tiny, jagged markings right over my thin veins.

Yes. I was on the right path. As Mizrah of Northgall, I would set it all right.

CHAPTER 23

Una

We walked the garden path beyond the grove, the maragord trees no longer bearing fruit, the manicured evergreens that bordered the stone path the only color beyond the slate gray of the sky. Winter would be here soon. Hava chatted amiably beside me.

It had been a fortnight since the Rite of Servium and a fortnight since I'd seen Goll. My melancholy had turned to anger, but now, it simmered defiantly in the back of my mind. His rejection had stung—more than stung—yet I had decided to focus on *my* purpose. Goll had told me countless times that the gods decreed I was to be his mizrah, but I believed the gods wanted more of me than that. I was certain.

And today, I was going to act on it.

I glanced back at Ferryn and Meck, both trailing us at a respectful distance as I marched away from the manicured garden.

"Where are you going?" asked Hava.

"I've never explored this way." Actually, I'd been this way before—many, many years ago. I wanted to see the path with my own eyes.

"There is nothing but a statue of Gozriel over there."

"Really?" That piqued my interest. "Show me, Hava."

"It is quite pretty, I suppose," she informed me, walking a little ahead and following the narrow stone path to the right, which then curved wide around the back of the castle.

"Gozriel the Watcher. So the wraith fae revere him?" I asked.

"Oh, yes. He is Vix's helper. Well, to some." She laughed as we rounded to an open courtyard, not too dissimilar from the one that had held the statue of Mizrah. "To others, he's a mischief-maker."

Upon an iron pedestal stood a bronze statue of Gozriel, the long exposure to the elements having added a layer of patina green. He stood on one leg, his leg muscles bunched, his other bent as if he were running to take flight. His wings were that of the raven that he transformed into when he roamed the world, doing Vix's bidding and guarding his realm. He had two horns and wore a fierce expression. He was eternally frozen in some intense and urgent errand for his master.

My gaze lingered on his wings, envy piercing me as it always did when I thought of my own that were of no use. Across his bare chest, he bore a string of engraved demon runes I didn't know.

"Tell me what those mean, Hava." I pointed to the statue's chest, the last rune jolting my heart into a gallop. It was similar to mine but not exactly the same. Mine had a curling tail at the end.

"Let's see now." She stepped closer. *Guardian of the dark fae. Watcher for the enemy.* And the sign that looks like a raven's wing means *bringer of bones.*"

When she came to the last rune, she glanced back at me, a look of recognition shining in her red eyes. I shook my head gently, not wanting her to mention in front of Meck and Ferryn the mark I now wore on both wrists. I tugged on my long sleeves nervously, making sure they were hidden. She seemed to understand, turning her gaze back to the statue.

"I believe the last one means *keeper of* or maybe *possessor of the gods' world.* Hmm. That doesn't make sense. I'm not sure what that last part means. My knowledge of this older demon sign is not the best." She gave me a sad shrug. We'd already discussed the sign on my wrists, which she couldn't decipher.

Meck and Ferryn had rounded behind us, standing between us and the forest of esher trees whose blue leaves were turning gray and beginning to fall. A soft wind gusted through the trees, slender gray leaves pinwheeling down and sweeping across the stone surrounding the statue of Gozriel.

Meck stepped closer first. Having apparently heard Hava, he answered, "It means *protector of the gods' heart and home.* That last sign means both *heart* and *home.*"

"What does *bringer of bones* mean? He brings death? That's not a great protector," I said lightly.

Meck laughed, his yellow eyes darker under the gray sky. "No, not death. Kind of the opposite actually. Gozriel was the first who Vix bestowed his gift of neklia upon."

I glanced at Hava who had already sidled closer to comfort me.

"Neklia," added Ferryn, stepping forward next to his brother, "is the gift of raising the dead. Vix's home in the earth gave him a distinct connection with the dead."

"I know what neklia is and what it can create." I shivered, remembering the clawing, snarling creatures. "You're talking about the wights."

Hava took my hand in both of hers and squeezed for she knew my petrifying fear of them. I held onto her.

"Yes," Ferryn confirmed. "Legend says Vix heard their souls cross over into the land of the dead, but sometimes their flesh wasn't ready to leave. So he gave the flesh and bones purpose."

"To kill innocent people?" I asked accusingly, for that was what King Xakiel had used his army for.

I trembled at the mere memory of them in that pit in the dungeon long ago.

"That was King Xakiel's way," Meck said, his expression grave. "And I'm sorry for your encounter with his wights, Mizrah."

I pressed my lips together and turned my gaze back to Gozriel's statue, embarrassed that my ordeal had spread around enough for them to know of it. "It was more than an encounter."

"Goll's father was a cruel king," added Ferryn. "Wights weren't originally made for those purposes."

"What good could an army of the dead have?" I asked, frustration and distress evident. "It is an evil gift, this neklia."

Meck flinched. "It is meant as a helper to the wraith king who wields it. To a good wraith king."

A stabbing panic gutted me still. My voice was barely above a whisper when I asked, "And Goll holds this power?" I could not, and would not, call it a gift, no matter that it was one given by their greatest god.

"No," answered Ferryn, his expression grave. "Goll was not given neklia."

"But he is a very powerful zyfer," added Meck. "The most powerful Northgall has known actually. As well as a dragon rider, which in itself is a rare gift."

Intense relief washed through my body, so overwhelming that my knees buckled. I caught myself against Hava but didn't miss the way both Meck and Ferryn stiffened, ready to leap forward to my aid.

They'd been kind and attentive guardians, even while I insulted their kind. I couldn't see any positive use for neklia. The thought of it only ignited a deep-seated fear and agonizing fury that any wraith king would wield it against their enemies. Not even their enemies, but innocents like me caught within their borders.

A memory flashed to mind of me freezing and shivering beside a small fire near Dragul Falls where a water sprite had pushed me into the icy water. Then the stomping of heavy boots coming for me through the trees and me trying to fly away, but being snatched from the air as I lifted off the ground.

Pushing that nightmare away, I straightened my wings and looked at the statue, needing a change of conversation. "Why does he have two horns? Why do some of your kind have two and some have four?" I asked.

Hava, who had two tiny, delicate horns spoke up first. "Four horns designate the highest born of the dark fae. I've heard there are even some with six."

"That's not true," snorted Ferryn. "Those are rumors the shadow fae spread to try and aggravate us. They're no better or more powerful than us."

"Some of our kind have none at all," offered Meck, his concerned gaze flicking to Hava. "And though that does designate them as having no highborn blood, they are no less than any of us."

I realized then that Meck's expression was concern for Hava, that perhaps he'd hurt her feelings since she had only two horns.

"Well, I have none," I offered with levity, "and I'm fairly certain that I'm pretty wonderful."

Hava giggled. Meck and Ferryn smiled.

"That is for certain, mistress," agreed Ferryn, his gaze flicking to my wings. "And you are one of our kind now."

I refrained from touching the new markings on my wrists beneath my sleeve and made no comment, my feelings somewhat conflicted. Yes, I was a mizrah to King Goll, but I did not yet feel like one of their kind, even with the marks of Vix upon my skin. My hidden ambition was still more aligned with my people of Lumeria and my sick father. I needed to find out if it was only Lumerians suffering from the plague.

I also needed to get to that path behind Meck and Ferryn and find out if I was right those many years ago, or if I'd lost my white wings and my healing magick in vain. The stirring desire for vindication and for the truth nearly had me marching right past them.

But I knew they wouldn't allow me to leave the palace grounds without Goll's permission. And Goddess could strike me down before I went begging him for anything. He didn't even want to see me. Fresh ire coursed through my blood.

"You know," I said, injecting fatigue in my voice, "I'm feeling a little tired. I'd like to return to my bedchamber to rest."

Since the only control I did have was over this little army of my own—all of them servants and friends and protectors at once—we immediately set out for my bedchamber.

The halls were alive with activity today, servants moving from one place to the next and many of the Culled milling about the castle corridors. I smiled to myself, knowing it wouldn't matter if all of them were guarding my door. I had a plan. I'd been thinking about it for some time, but I was finally brave enough to want to do it. I still needed Hava to agree.

As soon as my bedchamber door was closed, I whirled toward my bed and knelt on the floor.

"What do you need, Mizrah?" asked Hava, scurrying after me. "I can help you. What is that?"

I'd already pulled my thick book of oracles from beneath the bed. "Come. Sit with me. I want to show you something," I whispered.

Meck and Ferryn stood watch on the other side of the closed door. Though they likely couldn't hear through the thick door of my bedchamber, I was wary.

I settled easily on the silvery woven rug before the hearth. I loved these dark trousers with the sapphire blue overskirt that Hava had made for me. The bodice was modest but becoming with silver lacings to the top and long sleeves to my wrists.

One reason I was glad the weather was turning colder was that I could easily hide my new markings upon my wrists. Hava had urged me to show Goll at least a hundred times, but I wasn't going to him for anything. If he didn't deem it important enough to even check on my well-being after the Rite of Servium, then I needed nothing at all from him.

Sitting cross-legged, I pulled the book into my lap. Hava sat across from me, crossing her legs the same way.

"What is that?" Hava asked again, her eyes widening. "It looks important."

"It is," I assured her, then pulled one of her hands into mine and added with gravity, "What I'm going to show you are sacred visions of the oracles of Issos. Specifically, oracles devoted to the Moon Temple at Valla Lokkyr. All of the visions are from world-seers."

"But how did they let you take such an important book? Our priestesses would never let a book of visions leave the temple."

"Neither would ours," I admitted, grinning. "I scribed these myself after many visits to the temples of Issos, of Mevia, and even one our royal scribe brought back from Morodon."

Hava blinked her red eyes and grinned with wicked glee, her fanged teeth making her look even prettier. Odd, since that once would've frightened me.

"Are you going to share your secrets with me?" she asked excitedly.

"Yes. Because I need your help."

Her smile dimmed. "Will it get us in trouble?"

I couldn't lie to her. "Maybe. But look, let me show you something exciting. Proof, I believe, that the gods have placed a gift right here in Northgall." I flipped open the book to the very first vision I scribed when I was fifteen. The one that had led me here the first time. "I found this one in my father's personal library."

She gasped then whispered, "You were being sneaky?"

"Yes," I answered. "I was. And I'm still glad that I did it, because I firmly believe there is something to this."

Hava had twisted to sit beside me on my right.

"I'm sorry. I can *speak* high fae," Hava admitted shyly, frowning down at the page, "but I cannot read or write it."

"I'll read it to you. This one I found in my father's desk drawer. The parchment had been folded and creased and obviously handled over a long time. He must have read it over and over. See this name here." I pointed to the page on the right. "That is the oracle who spoke the vision. Her name was Vaylamorganalyn."

"That's quite a name," giggled Hava.

I smiled. "She was once very revered, my brother told me. A very important priestess of the Moon Temple. I don't remember her, but he said she was once High Oracle of Valla Lokkyr."

"What happened to her?" asked Hava.

"She was excommunicated by my father."

"Why?"

"For speaking this prophecy." I pointed to the book.

Hava's red eyes widened. "Gods above," she whispered. "What does it say?" She scooted closer to look over my shoulder at the words even though she couldn't understand them.

"This says, 'The Moon is round, lovely, and bright, blessing her kind, far and wide. One day soon, a new night will come and the moon will be done. Shadow, fire, and beast will reign. Moon children will fall to a plague. Only the god-touched will find the way. Only the anointed will save the day.'"

I paused, remembering the moment I discovered this vision in my father's desk. He'd not been in his office for a month, having taken ill from the beginnings of the Parviana plague.

"When I read this and asked my brother about Vaylamorganalyn, he'd told me he was just a small boy when she was excommunicated. He'd said she refused to admit that her vision was a lie. I mean, how can a vision be a lie if it's from the gods?"

"This is true," said Hava. "Why did your father want her to say it was a lie?"

"Because the whole court had heard the prophecy. And it speaks of a time when the moon fae would fall. When the Lumerian people would suffer."

Hava's brow crinkled. "And now your people have suffered."

"My father was upset that the vision predicted that the dark fae would one day become the supreme power of the realms. But I was more concerned about the plague."

"What did you do then?"

"I visited the priestess at the Moon Temple and found out that Vaylamorganalyn had left many visions in the scribe's library. So I crept in when they weren't looking and took them."

Hava's eyes rounded with excitement, and I couldn't help but smile. Back then, it *had* been thrilling, sneaking around on my own quest to find answers. But it eventually led me to Dragul Falls and the ending of my moon fae magick and wings.

"I pored through all of them and found this one that was very important." I pointed to the next page. "It says that there are three god-touched texts that can cure the land. Though she only spoke of the first text in all of her visions, it was enough to guide me here. This vision"—I tapped the page I'd read too many times to count—"it speaks of icy waters in a northern realm where streams collide and a river falls. I looked at all the maps, and it seemed the description kept pointing to Dragul Falls."

"And so you came here," Hava interrupted.

"I did. And I was caught before I could truly look for the god-touched text." I held her gaze intently. "But now I have the chance to look again. To find it this time."

Hava's expression tightened with concern. "Meck and Ferryn will never let us go there without Goll's permission."

I nodded. "I know. We'll go without them."

"Without their protection?"

"I have you for protection. You are a good zyfer, are you not?"

As if insulted, she huffed and held out a hand, whispering, "*Etheline.*" A bright orange flame shot up as tall as a sword in her palm.

Grinning, I assured her, "All we need is you for protection. Besides, it isn't far at all. I know that well enough from last time."

"You are right." She blinked thoughtfully. "It is fairly close."

"Do you think we could be there and back before dinner?" I asked.

"Yes, but how will we get around Ferryn and Meck?"

Smiling, I stood, then walked back to my bed and tucked the book into its hiding place. She was right behind me.

"Come see." I urged her to follow me behind the wardrobe screen.

Since the Rite of Servium, I'd been spending an enormous amount of time in my bedchamber, too embarrassed to leave very often in case I'd bump into a courtier and see them smirking at me.

Or worse, run into Goll and have to endure his cutting disinterest face to face.

One night after my bath, when Hava had gone to bed, I remembered that time that Goll had taken me through his bedchamber to the secret stairwell that led into the gardens. His bedchamber was right next to mine. That made me wonder about something else, and I was right. I had found it two nights ago.

"What is it?" asked Hava. "Do you need to change?"

"No." I laughed and passed by the wardrobe cabinet that held my clothes and stepped toward the wall that my bedchamber shared with Goll's. "Look at this."

I felt along the seams of the wood until I felt the tiny groove and pressed. The wall swung inward without a sound.

Hava gasped as I stepped through, peeking around to be sure he wasn't there, and then beckoned her silently to follow. She did, looking around to see that we were now in Goll's bedchamber. I pressed the paneled door closed behind us.

"There's another secret passage this way," I told her, ushering her to the door Goll had taken me through that night.

A pang of longing curled tight in my belly at the memory. He'd been so kind and attentive that night. All a ruse apparently to ease my nerves before the Rite of Servium.

I rushed across the room, glancing at the behemoth of a bed with a silken black coverlet. My heart plummeted at the thought that he slept right there every night and not once had even checked in to see me. Shaking that thought away, I pushed on the secret panel door that opened to the darkened stairwell.

"It's steep and winding, Hava. We'll need you to make some feyfire to guide us down. Then we'll be in the back of the garden."

Hava whispered and a flame ignited in her palm, illuminating her wicked grin. "Follow me," she whispered.

Then we both stepped silently along the secret staircase, making our escape out of the castle. My heart leaped with anticipation at finally returning to Dragul Falls to find what I'd sacrificed so much for on my first journey to Northgall.

CHAPTER 24

Goll

Sitting at the head of the table in the war room, unwilling to receive our unexpected guest in the throne room, I stared at the moon fae male standing at the opposite end of the table close to the door. It was an awkward place to receive foreign ambassadors, but I couldn't step foot in my throne room. The mere thought curdled like acid in my stomach.

I'd been keeping busy with my royal and military councils at this table since the Rite of Servium, so I'd summoned my guest here since I'd barely left the room for weeks. I was almost thankful to the arrogant, foolish ambassador from Issos, staring me down with an unbreakable gaze.

For the first time in a fortnight, I felt something other than hot rage or self-loathing. With the exception of those brief, illusory moments between sleep and wakefulness when I felt her sweet mouth on mine and her hot sheath as I sank into her, I'd known nothing but pure ire. Every morning, I wished I could return to those soft dreams where she wanted me, where I didn't see the tears pouring from her eyes while I fucked her.

So now, I was glad to turn my anger on someone else besides myself. I spoke low and steadily when I finally broke the silence after he'd told me his reason for coming to Northgall.

"Princess Una is well and good," I told him icily. "You may return and tell her brother so."

"Forgive me, my lord—"

"You'll address him as my liege or King Goll," snapped Keffa, standing to the fae's right. "He is not merely a lord."

The fair-haired ambassador straightened his spine, his pale-blue wings stiffening. "Forgive me, King Goll," he began again, "but I've been given explicit instructions to speak to Princess Una alone, to ensure she isn't being coerced to say what she's been told to say."

"By me," I added.

He had the wisdom to keep his mouth closed, his jaw clenching. He kept his hands clasped at his back, his stance erect and formal.

I was debating whether to stand, march across the room, and punch the man in the face or to summon Una before him now in my presence. I had no inclination to allow her to be alone with any man, least of all this dandy of an ambassador with his pretty attire and prettier face.

But the thought of her standing here now and declaring me the heinous monster she knew me to be in front of him made my blood boil and my heart clench.

Suddenly, the door opened with swift force, jarring me to my feet, my hand at the dagger at my waist. It was Pullo, his scowl fierce, as he stormed into the chamber, followed quickly by Ferryn and Meck.

"What is it?" I snapped.

Pullo passed the ambassador, sparing him a quick glance, before striding directly toward me, his long braid swinging at his back. Meck and Ferryn were right behind him, each falling to one knee when they reached me, heads bowed as if awaiting punishment.

"What?" I growled.

Pullo reached me and whispered close to my ear, too low for the ambassador to hear, "She's gone."

My vision hazed with sheer panic at those two words.

"We're looking everywhere in the palace and gardens, but we can't find her."

My gaze snapped to the ambassador, his expression curious and grim. Did he know? Was that why he'd actually come? To help the princess escape and bring her back home? It made no sense.

And yet, surely, she hated me enough to leave me. Had she somehow gotten word to them? In all this time I'd been avoiding her, had she managed to get a message to her kind?

Pullo took a large step away from me, bowing his head. I could feel my magick brimming with fury, electrifying the air around me.

"Keffa. Take the ambassador and hold him in a chamber without windows. I don't want him flying away."

The ambassador spoke with indignation, "You are going to imprison me?"

"Keffa. *Now*," I barked, my voice echoing off the black stone walls.

He quickly guided the ambassador from the room, shutting the door behind him, leaving me alone with Pullo, Meck, and Ferryn.

"Explain," I demanded, cold rage chilling my blood.

"Sire," Meck began, looking up at me, "she took a walk in the gardens this morning with Hava then returned to her bedchamber with her. We never left the door. When a maidservant brought a platter for luncheon as she has been since the Mizrah's arrival, she returned from the room with the platter in her hand and asked where the mizrah was."

Ferryn finally met my gaze as well. "We immediately searched the room and found no one. We never left our posts, King Goll. I swear we did not."

I stormed across the room, the three of them right behind me. As we crossed into the corridor, Soryn strode up to me, panting after apparently running to the war room.

"We've caught her scent as well as Hava's. They took the trail heading east through Esher Wood. The Culled are mounting horses now."

That trail ended at the river where she could follow it directly south and across the border into Lumeria. Then back to her home of Issos.

I'd thought I'd known fury before, but nothing had prepared me for the living fire burning through my veins now, searing me from the inside out.

"Soryn, you lead the Culled to get them."

His scowl deepened. "You're not going?"

"Oh, I'm going," I growled. "Havallah will be alone shortly." If they were indeed alone and not being helped by some other Issosian ambassador. "Bring her back. I'll take care of my mizrah."

Without another word, I whirled toward the palace kitchens, the closest exit to the back gardens. Closing off my fury for the moment, but letting my urgency ring clear, I reached out to Drakmir telepathically. *We must ride, brother. Be ready.*

Everyone stepped out of my way as I stormed down the corridor, through the kitchens, and out the door. Drakmir rumbled a growl, waiting for me in the clearing beyond the maragord grove where he rested when he wasn't wandering the skies or hunting across Meerland.

Keeping our mind-to-mind connection open, I showed him where we needed to go while I launched up his shoulder and into the saddle.

"Fly, Drak!"

Instantly, we were airborne, soaring toward Esher Wood and the eastern trail. Soryn and the entirety of my Culled pounded their way on horseback from the stables from the right of the palace, but my focus was on the trail.

I did not believe she would do this. Even after the Rite of Servium, I didn't think she would hate me so much that she'd try to return to her homeland. She knew that if she broke her vows, I could punish her people. I still had garrisons occupying all of Lumeria. I could slaughter them all with the power of feyfire living inside me.

Especially now, stirring with the hot emotion of bitterness and betrayal that she would do this to me. That she would leave me.

The fury twisted into a spire of pain that nearly choked me. Cold wind gusted against my chest. A rumble of thunder vibrated in the distance, mirroring the storm growing inside me. For a moment, I closed my eyes and let the sensation of flight cool my burning blood. It barely worked, and the fire stoked anew when Drak purred a low growl.

There they were, walking along the trail, almost to the river. Drak knew where I wanted to go. He dove for the well-worn path and banked with beating wings to slow his descent in front of them, then landed to block their path.

Una and Hava jumped in surprise. Hava's eyes widened in fear. As they should. Una, however, looked furious, which only burned me hotter.

As soon as Drak's feet were on the trail, his girth and tail breaking branches reaching toward the path, I climbed down, leaped to the ground in seconds, and strode straight for Una. That was when her expression widened with trepidation. Whatever she saw in my eyes had her taking large steps backward, her black wings fluttering helplessly.

"Yes, Una. Go on." A predatory thrill slipped through my blood, pumping my heart faster. "*Run.*"

As if the survival instincts built inside her could do nothing else, she did. My body hummed with magick and desire, hardening every part of me at the sight of her fleeing into the woods as fast as she could go.

Then I was after her, letting the maelstrom of emotions I'd been having since the night of the Servium to twist and fly, spurring me on to catch my prey and bring her back to me, back in my embrace where she belonged. The feral desire to bear her down in the grass and fuck her senseless hazed my vision with dark need, to make her understand she could never leave me, to make her know she belonged *to me*.

She was fast even without the use of her wings, her long legs eating up the forest ground as she dodged around one tree and then the next, her feet crunched on the fallen leaves, her breaths grower louder, her white hair flying behind her. She made a whimpering sound in her throat as I inched closer and closer, a similar sound to the one she made when she writhed and came beneath me in the throne room.

By now, I was furious and fucking rock hard when I took the last step to close the distance and wrap both my arms around her waist. Her wings pinned between us, hanging down toward the ground, she kicked with her legs and struggled against me.

"Let me go, Goll! Stop this!"

Her writhing body and hypnotic scent only amplified the inferno building inside me. I planted my feet and buried my mouth in her loose hair close to her ear. "You dared to leave me? My mizrah? The one the gods chose for me. You swore an oath, *Una*."

"I wasn't leaving you," she panted.

"Just taking a leisurely stroll to the river where you might catch a passing ferryman who could take you straight into Lumeria, I suppose."

"What? No." She jerked and struggled again, obviously feeling my hardness pressing into the cleft of her ass. If I wasn't so furious with Hava, I'd want to thank her for sewing these trousers for her mistress.

With a quick movement, I whirled her around and tossed her over my shoulder then marched back toward the trail.

"Not this again," she grumbled. "*Goll!* I wasn't leaving."

I scoffed, not dignifying that with an answer.

"You can put me down. I won't run."

"Fucking right, you won't. Not ever again." I was going to make sure of it.

She beat on my back with her fists. It only made me harder. "I wasn't leaving you, you imbecile."

"Right." I retraced our steps back to the path with increasing speed. "You crept secretly out of the palace without your guard because you wanted to simply walk in the woods all alone with your handmaiden."

"I was going to Dragul Falls."

"Why?" I snapped, rounding a tree that put us on a wider game trail. We were almost back to the eastern path where I'd found her.

She didn't answer. Her silence made me angrier than her hot words. I stopped at a thick-trunked esher tree and flipped her upright, setting her on her feet. She staggered back, her palms bracing on the wide trunk. I crowded her close, sinking both fists into her unbearably soft hair, cradling her skull with my knuckles.

Pressing my body fully against hers, I tilted up her face so that I could see those beautiful eyes, wide and accusing. "Do you think you can so easily break your vows to me?" I hissed, my mouth close to hers. "Did you think I'd simply let you go?"

Her hands came off the trunk and wrapped around my forearms, her rounded nails digging into the thick fabric of my winter shirt.

"I was seeking something I did once when I was fifteen. I didn't find it before I was taken into Näkt Mir's dungeon and tortured near to death," she spat angrily. "I thought I could find it now that I was within my rights to be in this territory."

I couldn't process what it was that she sought so many years ago and still sought, my mind spinning with other questions.

"Why didn't you simply come to me? Ask me? I would've taken you."

Now it was her turn to scoff, a slender brow arching with mockery. "When might I have spoken to you? I haven't seen you in *weeks*." She was furious, her face burning with rage. At me.

"You got what you wanted," she said more softly, hurt rather than anger lilting her words. "Then you disappeared. I suppose it is the way of all men. Or is it only kings who use their women then cast them aside? Have you found someone new already, my liege?"

The mockery was back in her voice, but it was mixed with sharp, sorrowful pain. I flinched. I had done that. I had caused that look of bitter sadness.

My fists tightened in her hair, cradling the base of her skull. "I have done nothing every day but wish for you to be in my presence. I wanted to summon you day and night, then I would force myself not to," I grated out through clenched teeth. "Do you want to know why?"

She said nothing, her dark lashes growing wet as she blinked quickly, emotion welling in her eyes.

"Because I was afraid of what I'd do to you if I got you alone again. I know how badly you despise me for forcing you into this union. And I saw the pain and grief on your face when I fucked you. But Vix save me," I growled, holding her ethereal gaze, "none of that matters when you're near me. All I want to do is bury myself deep and get lost in the oblivion of your body. When you're near, I care about nothing but wanting that soul-shaking sensation again of being so deep inside you. This craving is pure madness," I whispered against her lips and closed my eyes.

She said not a word, letting me brush my lips against hers and that sliver of a taste sped my pulse. I nipped her bottom lip with my fang. She gasped, opening her mouth. I took advantage and slanted mine against hers, sinking into her sweetness.

I groaned at the heady sensation of kissing her again. She didn't protest so I went deeper, stroking my tongue inside. She whimpered and tilted her head back farther, letting me taste her sweetness. I ground my hard cock at the juncture of her thighs, causing her to make that little moan in the back of her throat.

Did she want this, too? Impossible.

I drank in the pleasure of her silken mouth, fighting the desire to strip her here and take her on the forest floor. Gods, she was divine.

Then the sound of pounding hooves nearby snapped me from my trance. She stared, her expression unreadable as I eased back. Slowly, I unclenched my fists from her hair then gripped her wrist and tugged her to follow. Thankfully, she did not fight me.

We came out onto the path right as the Culled were surrounding Hava, who hadn't moved since we'd left. Drak lifted his head when he sensed me. I didn't speak to Soryn or Keffa as I rounded to Drak's side and lifted Una by the waist.

"Climb up," I ordered, but she was already pulling herself up by the loops in the leather strap that wrapped his girth. I climbed up after her and slid behind where she straddled the saddle.

"Drak," I barked.

He turned from the circle of horses and took a few steps along the trail then lifted off into the air. We rose above the snaking river and Dragul Falls before turning back toward Näkt Mir.

As dark clouds billowed closer, my attention snagged on a streak of lightning between us and the palace. I was calculating if we would make it before the rain caught us. It would be an ice storm, no doubt, pouring out of the north. Then something else caught my attention and held it hard—the distinct scent of feminine arousal.

I tightened my arm around her waist and pressed my mouth to the skin of her neck. She uttered that delicious whimpering sound and arched into my embrace, her ass pressing into the crotch of my pants.

"You cannot ever leave me," I murmured, remembering the stark, horrifying fear I felt the moment Pullo had said she was gone. I grazed my mouth along the side of her slender throat, licking and tasting her sweet essence.

Her hands came back to my thighs, clinching and holding tight as she bent her head so that I might kiss her neck more easily. I trailed my open palm down her corseted top to the lacings of her trousers and slowly slipped the lacings free, opening the flap.

"You can never leave," I murmured again, a madman on repeat.

"I won't," she said breathily, squirming as I slid my hand into the opening of her trousers.

I trailed my fingers over her thatch of hair, parting the slick folds beneath, stroking gently. She gusted out a whimper.

I mounded her breast with my other hand. "Never, Una," I commanded.

Her hands clenched on my legs. "I won't," she repeated, her eyes slipping closed as I kissed and licked her silken skin.

I stroked a slow circle around her tight bud, relishing the heady sounds of her heavy breathing and her hips slowly rocking back against me.

A sharp crash of thunder made her jolt in my arms, pulling us both away from the dizzy arousal simmering between us and the dangerous storm spiraling closer. But I wasn't having it. I needed her right fucking now.

"Hold on," I yelled over the sudden rush of wind and first drops of icy rain.

She gasped as I slipped my hand from her open trousers and held her tight around the waist, connecting to Drak's mind, telling him where we needed to go.

He roared and instantly banked a sharp right, cutting across a sheet of freezing rain as a streak of purple lightning lit the sky.

Una screamed and pressed back against me, her hands still clenching my thighs. A primal satisfaction sank into me when she sought my protection, even in this small way. I wrapped both arms around her and cradled her in the curve of my body.

"I've got you," I promised her.

Drakmir beat his wings then spread them wide, letting them soar toward the rocky outcropping leftover by the eruption of Vixet Krone thousands of years ago. These low mountains that circled the back of Silvantis had no name, but they served to shelter many a beast. Specifically, the cave where Drak now landed had been our favorite escape when we were out hunting together or in the early years I was in hiding.

The mouth of the cave was wide enough for Drak to curl and rest out of the weather, but I'd added a few small comforts for myself deeper in the narrower part of the small cavern. The rain and wind still pelted us hard at the entrance as I helped Una down without slipping and falling.

"This way." I urged her to follow me deeper inside then ignited a ball of feyfire in my palm.

Drak heaved a growling sigh as he curled at the entrance, blocking out most of the crashing storm with his giant body. He settled in a ball, tucking his long neck and head around him, his tail curling inward.

After finding the thatched bedding still there, I made sure no other creature had decided to make this cave home while I'd been away. As always, the smell of dragon kept it clean and untouched by wild animals. Pulling out the lantern with the blue coal, I lit it. Instantly, it's dry warmth filled the cavern. I snuffed out the feyfire in my palm and set the lantern on the cavern floor near the bedding.

Unhooking my Meer-wolf cloak, I spread it out over the bedding, fur facing up, then I finally turned to look at Una.

Her face sparkled with a few drops of rain, her hair damp but not wet through, though it was mussed wildly by the wind. She was the most stunning creature I'd ever seen.

"Una," I called to her, bringing her attention back to me since her gaze had been wandering the cave. "Take off all of your clothes."

CHAPTER 25

Una

My entire body hummed with desire. It made no sense whatsoever. Goll had chased me through the woods, behaved like a barbarian and carted me away, and all I wanted was more of his touch, more of his hands, and his tongue, and his growling voice.

It was madness. He was right. This feeling defied sense and sanity. It was driven by a desperate, trembling need. And something else altogether that I couldn't identify or explain. So when he commanded me to take off all of my clothes, there was only one thing I wanted to do.

But my pause had caused him to arch a brow, his dragon eyes glowing in the semi-dark. "Take them off," he repeated calmly. "Or I'll tear them off."

A shiver of anticipation prickled along my skin. I unbuckled the belt holding my overskirt around my waist and tossed it aside then unlaced and shoved off my boots. I then went about efficiently removing the rest of my clothes. My trousers were already unlaced, so those were easily removed.

I took my time unhooking and untying the laces of my corset, thankful Hava had put them in the front so that I could do it myself. I was glad not to miss the expression transforming Goll's face from one of desire to one of unwavering, feral hunger.

My own fingers trembled as I finally unhooked the corset and slipped it off then lifted the short hip-length chemise over my head.

Then I stood before him completely nude. Yet again.

Except this time, there were no marching drums or raucous audience, or even the barrier of gold paint and black runes on my skin. Except there were actually. I twisted my inner wrists to face away from him, not yet ready to discuss what that meant. I wanted his full attention, and I seemed to have it.

His breathing was labored as he drank in the sight of me. Slowly, he unbuckled the belt and dagger at his waist.

He didn't wear full armor today. He hadn't since we returned to Näkt Mir. He wore simple clothing. Today, he wore a long-sleeved black shirt and pants made of soft leather, darkened to charcoal, a shade darker than his skin.

By the time he'd shed his last bit of clothing, the blue coal had heated the cavern while the sizzle of lightning and rumbling thunder continued to roll and beat violently down on Northgall. Drak slumbered, blocking out the storm. Here, our little world was toasty warm and colored in hues of blue and gray, the light dipping over his beautifully muscled form and his long, thick erection.

When his hand went to his length and he gave it a long, slow stroke, I gulped hard. My mouth was dry, but my pussy was wet. He inhaled deep, his chest puffing out and his eyes closing as he smelled the air. When he opened his gaze on me again, it was the dragon who looked back.

"Get on your knees."

I paused for only a second before I stepped onto the Meer wolf fur and knelt. He walked a slow circle behind me then lowered to his own knees. But when he touched me, his hands weren't where I thought they'd be.

He swept my hair over one shoulder, and then his fingers gently trailed the skin where my wings jutted from beneath my shoulder blades. He traced with tender slides of his fingers, easing his body closer to mine. The heat of him was a wall at my back, yet for a few moments all he touched was where my wings sprouted from my body.

"I know you believe these are useless, that they can carry you nowhere. But you are so wrong, Una." His lips touched the curve of my shoulder. I trembled as he slid his hands to my hips and his mouth up my nape. "These wings carried you to me." His grip tightened as he whispered against my skin. "Where you belong." Then his voice darkened. "Lean forward."

I knew what he wanted and what he planned to do. I'd seen a Pellasian stallion mount a mare before. And gods above, the image of him doing the same to me had warmth pooling quickly between my legs. I fell forward onto my hands.

His palm skated up my spine, between my wings to the base of my neck. "Lower," he commanded.

I bent my elbows, but he continued to press and guide me until my cheek was against the fur, my breathing quick and unsteady. Then he slid his hands to my hips as he shifted back.

Confused, for I'd expected to feel him pressing at my entrance, I jolted when I felt his warm mouth on my pussy. "Ah!"

He gripped my thighs, sliding his thumbs to open my folds, and groaned as he lapped at me. "Slick and wet for me, Una." He suckled my clitoris on a groan. "You're dripping." Another flick that made me jump and whimper. "Your body doesn't seem to hate me even if you do."

I curled my fingers into the fur, reeling too high from pleasure to feel ashamed of what he was doing to me, acknowledging that he was right. I might be furious with him, but I didn't hate him. Not anymore.

I couldn't understand the truth of it, so I let my body go, let myself experience the pleasure. He moaned and licked me intimately, his tongue sliding inside me, his lips closing on my clitoris where he sucked me hard.

That wondrous sensation of arousal spiraled higher, dragging incomprehensible noises from my throat. "Goll," I whimpered as my climax tore through my body, melting me with pleasure.

He growled deep in his throat, that familiar sizzle of his magick stroking over my skin. I tried squirming away, but he held my thighs and drank deep from me.

Then his mouth was trailing up my spine, between my wings where he purred against my skin, his magick sparking a tingly fire along my body.

He planted one clawed hand next to my head, and his face dipped low as he gripped my hip tight, "You were meant for me." Then pressed his cock inside me on a deep, savage groan.

I breathed through the tight sensation, panting with pleasure. Only the pleasure this time. There was a brief moment of discomfort when he seated himself fully, but it lasted only seconds before there was nothing but ecstasy.

He pumped with long glides in and out of my body. "You are *my* mizrah," he breathed into my hair, his forehead pressed to my shoulder.

His words felt as desperate as his body, stroking and stretching me, trying to communicate some indefinable message that he wasn't able to articulate clearly enough. He grunted in frustration then wrapped his arms around my waist and chest and sat back on his haunches, bringing me upright with him. I cried out at the jolting sensation of sitting fully on his cock, digging my nails into his forearms to hold on.

He reached one arm across my chest to the opposite shoulder, holding my back tightly to his front. He slipped his other hand between our legs and stroked with the pads of two fingers, the ones still filed short, and massaged my sensitive sex where he entered me.

He didn't move, simply held me pressed tight against him, inside me, his mouth at my neck as he gently spread the slick from my sex through my quim and around his cock.

"I'll never let you go." His fingers worked me while he remained buried deep, unmoving. "Do you understand?"

It was a king's command, a promise. It was no use to tell him yet again that I hadn't been trying to leave him. He wanted it abundantly clear that I was *his* and would always be so.

I brushed my palms up his forearms, arousal tightening where he speared inside me. If he was giving commands, I could demand a promise of my own.

"Vow to me," I whispered, turning my head to find his glowing gaze by the blue-coal, "that I will always be your mizrah." I nuzzled my nose alongside his, our breaths mingling. "Your one and only female. Even after I give you your heir."

I'd seen all manner of expressions on Goll's face. His was a beautiful face to study, and I'd given in to that guilty pleasure more times than I'd care to admit.

But this visage I gazed upon now—both soft and sharp, gentle and violent, adoring and savage—this was the face of the man who'd stolen a piece of my soul the night he carried me, bleeding and terrified, out of the dungeon of Näkt Mir. He was also the king who demanded my submission in all ways to save my people.

How could my heart long for both the tyrant of Northgall and the young prince who'd saved me? Perhaps it was because his dominance wasn't a barbaric whip. It was a seductive promise of protection and devotion that was as hard and impenetrable as the obsidian walls of Vixet Krone. He was my fortress, and I wanted his promise that he would always be so.

"Vow to me," I whispered against his mouth before I licked his bottom lip.

His arm at my shoulder slid to my throat as he raised partway on his knees, grinding slowly and deep. His grip at my throat was gentle but firm as he brushed his mouth against mine.

"I swear upon Vix himself, I will keep only one mate—my mizrah. For as long as I draw breath, there will only be you." He held me tighter, eyes slipping closed as he whispered, "Only you."

That was all I needed to hear to fall farther, the farthest, into his keeping. No matter that his vow said nothing of love or the pretty promises of a moon binding, it was enough for me. More than that, it was enough for my heart, for I felt it beating faster and harder for him, devoted solely to him.

The submission of my heart and soul to Gollaya Verbane felt as right and as true as the stars.

"Yes," I murmured, rocking my hips in rhythm with his own.

He groaned and began to pump in and out with deeper strokes, his mouth sliding to my shoulder. "Yes," he agreed. "You are *mine*." Then he sank his fangs into my skin.

I jerked at the sudden pain, which somehow rolled into more intense pleasure, my sex squeezing his cock as he thrust deeper. I curled one hand into his hair, finding one horn, holding him there while he claimed me the way he was supposed to—as a mate, not his whore.

He thrusted hard and deep, his fingers circling the sensitive bud between my legs. He licked at the bite then brushed his lips up to my ear. "You are so fucking beautiful, Una." He pounded me harder, still holding me upright in his strong grip, his body curling around me. "You are," he paused, his cock swelling inside me, "everything."

Then he groaned and held himself deep, his seed pulsing inside me. The throb of his cock within me and his attentive fingers sent me careening toward a second climax.

"Yes, my mizrah. Come on your king's cock."

I wasn't exactly proud of the fact that my body always wanted to obey Goll. But in that moment, coming as he commanded sent my spirit into heady oblivion.

He growled into my ear, squeezing my throat and stroking my quim, grinding deep as he continued to fill me up with his seed. My body welcomed it, welcomed him. His dominance. His aggression. All of him.

I'm not sure how much later, for I felt suspended in that place of ecstasy, he lay me gently down on the fur and pulled from my body. I was so tired, overcome with the anxiety and emotions of the day— of the past weeks, if I were truthful. My eyes slipped closed while the rumble of thunder drifted farther away.

I felt him curl around me and a blanket of some kind drape over us. He pulled me closer into the curve of his body, lifting my head to settle on his bicep. I hummed a wistful sigh, my mind already drifting.

"Sleep, Una," he coaxed in a soft whisper as he cradled me close.

His warm body cocooning mine and the sound of the distant storm and the sensation of feeling safe sent me straight to sleep.

CHAPTER 26

Goll

I did not sleep. I could not. For the first time since I'd broken out of my father's dungeon, since I'd slain him and taken his throne, since I'd defended my people and battled against the moon fae, I finally had what I wanted right here in my arms.

No. I could not sleep through this profound emotion suffusing my mind and spirit. I didn't want to miss a moment of this feeling lost in dreams that could not compare to reality. I couldn't remember ever feeling this before. Supreme, undaunted joy.

I'd felt triumphant, satisfied, and even content at my achievements since I'd rallied allies in secret and then killed my father to take his throne. But never this. Never unbridled happiness.

I stared down at her, so lovely and still, blissfully asleep in my arms. I frowned at the bite mark on her shoulder. I hadn't been able to stop myself, even though I knew it would be painful. She likely thought me a monster because of it. I'd apologize later, but I wasn't sorry. I wanted everyone to see that I'd marked her as a proper mizrah should be. There would be no question now whether the Princess of Issos was truly my mizrah.

There should have been no question after the Servium, but I'd seen the side glances from courtiers, heard the whispers that I never went to her bedchamber, that it was a formal arrangement for political purposes and no other reason.

Now she wore my bite and soon she would bear the roundness of my child. Even so, none of that satisfied me as much as this right here. Us, alone.

She roused and mumbled something in her sleep. I smiled. Awake, she was the most formidable woman I knew. Asleep, she seemed sweet and fragile, a precious treasure I wanted to protect and keep all to myself.

Soon, we'd have to return to the palace. Soryn and Keffa were likely scouting the perimeter, searching for us. They knew I wouldn't stay out in the storm, especially not with Una. But I had no desire to face the world just yet. I pulled her closer, relishing her soft, warm body.

Glancing over at the small table I'd built for rudimentary cooking when I came here, I wondered if I had any rations stored in my satchel still on Drakmir. Likely nothing worthy of feeding my mate.

Son of Vix. My mate. I squeezed my arm around her waist, still savoring the warmth of her beneath the wool blanket I was glad I had packed on Drakmir.

Finally, her eyes blinked open, bright by the blue-coal still burning. I should've given her time to gain her bearings after what we'd experienced together, given her a moment to collect her emotions, but I was too ravenous for her thoughts. I'd been ruminating on her the whole time she rested, the storm long past now.

"What were you seeking at Dragul Falls?"

She blinked rapidly, turning her body to peer up at me. She didn't try to put space between us. For that, I was grateful.

She trailed her fingers through my curtain of black hair spilling onto her chest. "I was looking for a text. One that is god-touched."

Frowning, I asked, "How do you know one is there? What is it for?"

She moved her hand to my chest and traced the runes etched into my skin by my gods. I couldn't prevent the low groan at her sweet touch.

Her mouth quirked up on one side while she continued to explore my skin, and I attempted to focus on the conversation. "When I came here before…" Her eyes lifted to mine, the gravity of what she was confessing catching my full attention. "I was trying to find this text that was prophesied by our oracle to be there, one that I was sure would help against the plague."

"You were seeking a cure for your father?" The pieces finally fell into place, what she would've risked her life for so many years ago.

"Actually, my father hadn't fallen ill with it yet. But so many of our people have." She heaved a sigh, her breath brushing my bare skin, bringing me back to awareness of her intimate embrace. "And now he is dying from it."

"An Issosian oracle said it was here, so close to Silvantis?"

She nodded. "I can show you."

"How?"

That mischievous smile returned. "I brought the book with me. I'd hoped that I could look again since I'd be so close. Maybe the gods wanted me to find it."

"By sending you to me?"

She turned those violet eyes down, away from me. I touched her chin, tilting her gaze up. She finally met mine again.

"The gods did send you to me," I informed her. "Vix would not have allowed you to live after bathing in Näkt Lykenzel if you were not."

Fire returned to her gaze. "What if I'd died? You could've been wrong."

"Did you believe you would die?"

She hesitated, then finally, "No."

"Neither did I. There was fear, I admit, but I've always known. Since the moment I saw your wings in the throne room as you stood up to my father." I quirked a smile at that memory. "I think even before then. When I saw you in the dungeon being lowered on that hook—"

When she shivered, I stopped, pulling her tighter against me, brushing my hand up and down her spine. She rested her forehead against my chest, trailing a delicate hand to my waist.

"I apologize. I didn't mean to remind you of that day."

There was a lengthy moment where I wondered if I'd hurt her by reminding her. But then her reply baffled me.

"When I returned home, I was horrified at what I'd risked, at what I'd lost. I still mourn the magick I had and my white wings. But I also felt there must be purpose in it. I've always felt it could not be for nothing. And you're right." She lifted her gaze to mine again. "I am meant to stand beside you. Perhaps it is to discover and cure this plague. Or something else. Something greater. But I know down to my bones that I am where the gods want me to be. It seems so strange, an Issosian princess and a wraith king." She huffed a laugh. "But I know it's true."

A growl rumbled in my chest as I swept my mouth across hers. "It is true. It is right." Then something caught my attention as she ran her hand down my arm.

"Una." I took hold of her hand and raised her wrist closer so that I could examine the demon rune etched into her skin. My chest warmed, a proud knowing at the sight of it, while my heart raced with excitement. "You were given this on the night of Servium." I knew it instinctively.

"It's on the other wrist, too." She wriggled to lay more on her back and showed me. "What does it mean?"

"Hava didn't tell you?"

"She didn't know. And I didn't want to ask you."

I wouldn't question why, for that was already clear. I'd ignored her and neglected her like a fucking fool. I would never do it again.

"This is another sign, a marking by Vix."

"I know that," she said with confidence and a bit of annoyance that made my mouth twitch. "But what does the sign *mean*?"

"Runes are tricky, sometimes having multiple meanings. And they are possessive by nature, reflecting the one who wields them."

I brushed the pad of my thumb over the black-etched mark with a crisscross line and a curved tip on one stroke, like a curling ribbon. She shivered beneath my touch.

"This is the symbol for hearth and home." I examined her closely, watching her brow dent with concentration as she stared at the mark on the wrist I still gently held. "Does that upset you?"

"Of course not."

"The gods have decided that you are home here in Silvantis." I didn't need to add that it was once the place of her nightmares. Perhaps still was. "With me."

She gazed up at me, a defiant fire burning in those ethereal eyes. "It could also mean I am *your* hearth, your home. And you belong to me."

Her boldness stirred my arousal. I wasn't prepared to leave this quiet paradise we'd created together.

"Oh, Una," I purred against the thin skin of her wrist. Her pulse quickened against my lips. "Of that, there is no doubt."

I kissed her long and deep till I smelled her arousal warm the air and I could do nothing but shift my body between her legs and slide inside her again, taking her slowly, gently. I watched her intently, savoring her subtle smile and the crease of her brow as she came.

When we were sated a second time, I remained inside her, hovering over her, breathing her air, not wanting to return to the palace, but knowing we must.

Her expression seemed to mirror my emotions. Then she said, "Can't we just stay here?" She combed her fingers through my hair.

It was more than I could've ever dreamed, that she'd want me like this. Like I wanted her. I pressed my forehead to hers. "We will have many more moments like this, Una."

"You promise?"

Rather than giving her words, I kissed her lovely mouth, her luxurious sweetness arousing me yet again. But I wouldn't allow my desire to demand more of her. When I felt my cock hardening inside her, I pulled out of her body, cherishing her small sound of anguish at our parting.

I retrieved the flask of water from my satchel, wet a cloth and warmed it near the blue-coal, then I wiped her clean and helped her dress. As I knelt at her feet and laced her boot, her hand on my shoulder, she laughed softly.

"What is it?" I asked, switching to her other boot.

"It's interesting. I never thought to see you, King Gollaya, kneeling at my feet."

I finished lacing her boot and looked up at her. "Interesting. I feel like I've always been here."

She bit her lip as I stood before her, frowning a little at my quick admission.

I'd not felt this sweet vulnerability since before my mother died. I hadn't thought I'd ever seek it out for myself, this tender connection. It was an intimacy I had intended to live without. Until Una.

I stole one more moment kissing my mizrah, knowing full well that this was what Vix had felt for the first Mizrah—he would have had one, and only one, mate. I felt more confident, a deeper power, a bonding closer to one woman rather than having none at all with many women. This feeling filled me with a newfound strength I couldn't describe. Like a secret only we could know.

It was rather terrifying, bewildering, and euphoric at once. While the reasonable side of me knew the dangers of a king allowing such emotions into his heart, the fae who longed for this intimate union didn't much care.

Therein lay the danger. I could easily forget myself and my duties in the arms of Una. But it wouldn't stop me from devoting all I had to her in the hopes that it would be enough.

"Come." I took her hand and led her toward Drak.

He roused when he heard us crossing the cavern floor. After a low grumble, he uncurled, allowing the night air to rush in at his back. Una stepped close to his muzzle and petted him along the jaw.

After I fetched the satchel, having folded the blanket and packed it inside, I looped my fur cloak back around my neck. The scent of sex, of her, had me groaning inwardly. I wanted to rewind time to that moment Una moaned with pleasure when I first entered her.

After the Rite of Servium, it wasn't a privilege I thought I'd ever experience again. I'd expected every coupling to be her *enduring* me and her burden, her face turned away with tears in her eyes.

I smiled at her crooning and whispering softly to Drak, his half-lidded gaze showing he was enjoying her attention.

"Before long, he'll no longer be my dragon, but yours," I teased her, helping her up into the saddle.

"You told me that no one could own a dragon." She smirked over her shoulder at me as I settled behind her.

"True. However, they do have their favorites."

Dragons have no masters. Yet, I was a dragon demon, a brother in blood, and I knew then and there that I was owned—body and soul.

Una gripped the two pommels and I held onto her as Drak leaped over the edge of the cliff and beat his wings toward Näkt Mir. Night had stretched its arms over Silvantis, a half-moon peering from behind billowy clouds. The storm had left a glistening sheet of ice over the land, glittering like stars in the dark.

"You know," she said softly, turning her head so that I could hear, "Drak has let me see into his memories."

Puzzled, I asked, "What do you mean?"

"When I told you that I had no magick, that wasn't entirely true."

"I'm aware. I can sense magick living inside of you. Even while you denied it. Are you saying that you have a telepathic link with Drak?" My heart raced wildly, for I had the same connection.

"It isn't exactly telepathic. I'm able to see through the eyes of winged creatures. It only ever happened with birds before. Back in Issos. I tried once when you first introduced me to Drak, but he wouldn't let me connect."

"But he has since that time," I confirmed.

"Yes."

Fascinating.

Then she said no more as we glided over Esher Wood, the starless night deepening the landscape in shadow.

"You won't tell me what you saw?"

"I saw you," she answered after a moment. "I saw you saving him when he was an adolescent dragon."

"Mm." I remembered that day. "Some fucking shadow fae dragon slavers had him chained in a cave. I was on a hunt in Meerland when I heard him. They were torturing him for entertainment."

She stiffened in my arms. "Do the shadow fae always do that sort of thing?"

I held her more tightly as Drak banked left toward the palace, lowering out of the clouds. "No. To be honest, they didn't seem right. They didn't seem well." Shadow fae were a peculiar race, but they weren't innately cruel. No race was. Something was wrong with those fae. "After that, Drak followed me back home to Silvantis. I let it become his home."

"And eventually he let you ride him." She spread a palm over Drak's hide next to the saddle. "I read there has been no dragon rider for over a hundred years."

"That's true. The last was Verek, the blue-eyed boy who became king, the one you mentioned to me once. But he managed to befriend a full-grown dragon on his first boar hunt."

Drak glided closer to Näkt Mir, the black spires reaching toward the heavens.

"This is a wondrous gift you have, Una," I said close to her ear. "It's extraordinary."

"I don't see how. All I can do is fly with birds and, apparently, dragons." She sighed. "I think sometimes it was a gift from Lumera since I can no longer fly with my own wings. She has given me a gift to allow me to still feel that sensation."

"It could be from Lumera." My gaze lingered on her dark wings hanging low between us. "Or it could be from Vix."

She huffed a laugh. "Why would a god I don't worship give me a gift?"

"The gods exist, whether we worship them or not. They have their own designs for our destinies, and they'll do as they wish, regardless of whether or not we acknowledge them." My mind strayed back to the reason she'd left the palace. "Will you show me your book of visions?"

She turned her head to catch my gaze, her expression soft and open. "Of course, I will. I want to show you. I want you to help me."

She'd never looked at me with so much trust. It tore something open inside my chest. It felt like a blessing, a precious gift. But this one wasn't from the gods. It was from my mizrah, my mate.

I brushed a kiss on her temple. "But first, you have a visitor and then you must eat."

"A visitor?"

"An ambassador from Issos."

Her muscles stiffened yet again. "Is something wrong in Issos?"

"No. I believe your brother wants proof that I haven't fed you to my dragon."

She chuckled and leaned harder against me as Drak descended toward the back of the palace gardens. "Drak would sooner eat you before he'd eat me."

"Undoubtedly."

Then we braced for the landing, and I prepared to give her time alone with that fancy fae in my palace.

CHAPTER 27

Una

"Is my father well, Athelyn?" I asked upon entering the windowless parlor where the Issosian ambassador was being kept under guard.

Goll and I had returned shortly before dawn. I'd taken a bath and assured Hava, who wouldn't stop fussing over me, that I was perfectly fine. Hava had thought Goll had taken me away to beat me. But when she saw the bite mark when I undressed for my bath, she only smiled, glad he wasn't too rough in his *punishment*.

He hadn't been too rough. Quite the opposite. He had handled me in the most wonderful way.

Hava had spread a soothing, minty oil on the bite wound, promising it would heal but leave a scar as the king undoubtedly wanted. I should've been appalled, but the thought only made me smile as well. She helped me get cleaned and presentable for the ambassador.

But Athelyn wasn't an ambassador. He had been the leader of the Issosian Guard. He bore the looks of an Issosian-born, the long white hair and violet eyes. His wings were pale blue, tall and strong at his back.

"Your father is much the same," he said with sympathy. "Perhaps a little weaker than when you left."

I swallowed hard at that. What he wasn't saying was that my father would die soon. There was no doubt of it.

"Why have you come? What is wrong? You're not one of my brother's ambassadors."

His expression tightened with even more sympathy as he took a step toward me then glanced at the door. Though we'd been left alone, he knew that Goll and Keffa were standing on the other side. Goll agreed to give us privacy, but he'd said he'd be waiting for me while giving a death-glare to Athelyn.

"I am now his second," Athelyn said. "And he trusted this errand with no one else."

"What errand?"

He glanced at the door again before he stepped closer and whispered, "Are you truly well? Are they—is he—treating you as an Issosian princess should be?"

I nearly laughed. I knew definitively that no Issosian princess had ever been stolen away on dragon back, dragged into a cave, and been pounded into pleasure by a wraith king. By *her* wraith king.

"Yes," I answered honestly with a sincere smile. "I am very well."

Athelyn frowned. "Are you sure?"

I did laugh then. "Yes." Then something occurred to me. "If you're Baelynn's second, what happened to Gael?"

Gael had been my brother's second since the moment we became co-stewards of the kingdom, since Baelynn had been forced to take over the army when our father became too ill to manage it himself.

Athelyn clenched his jaw, his mouth a grim line. "Gael has resigned his station at Issos. He has returned to his home estate in Mevia to lead the House of Ryleen."

Stunned, I stated, "You mean he has abandoned my brother when he needs him most. Because of me."

Athelyn, ever the proper diplomatic Issosian, did not reply. He didn't need to.

"Were his injuries…?" I asked, unsure what to say of them.

"He recovered. The palace healer managed to stop the bleeding and mend the wounds." He flinched, likely when he saw my face go pale at the memory of that day. "I apologize, Princess."

"No need."

Gael may not have deserved the injuries for the reasons Goll chopped off his fingers, but his abandonment of my brother burned a new bitterness in me for the man who might have once been my husband. I couldn't imagine it now. I couldn't imagine giving myself to any other but Goll.

"It is no longer princess, Athelyn. My title is mizrah now."

He blinked, surprise widening his gaze. "You are their queen?" he asked in a hushed whisper.

I smiled, a little sadness welling in my heart. Like so many Issosians, he thought a wraith king's first concubine was a queen. But that was not her role. Still, I cherished what I'd become to Goll and what he'd become to me.

What happened in that cave had changed us both. We weren't merely creatures of flesh. I wasn't simply a brood mare, and he wasn't only a tyrannical ruler driven to sire an heir. We were bound now beyond words and titles. The cool sting of the bite at my shoulder reminded me of who I truly was, making me more certain of my place in Goll's world.

"How is Baelynn?" I asked softly.

Remorse swept through me, thinking of my brother's stricken face as I was taken from the Moon Temple. That look of horror and regret and shame while he watched me being dragged away had burned itself in my mind. I'd avoided thinking of Baelynn as much as I could since I was so absorbed in adapting to my new reality, navigating my new life.

"He is well," Athelyn answered, but there was a grim set to his mouth. "He worries about you daily."

I pressed a palm to my heart. For so long, Baelynn and I had depended on each other. Our mother had died when I was very young. When Papa fell ill, we'd relied heavily on one another for guidance and comfort and solace.

I noticed Athelyn had averted his gaze to the floor. Something was wrong.

"What aren't you telling me?"

His eyes widened. "Pardon me?"

"There's something you aren't telling me, Athelyn. I demand to know."

His training as a servant to the royal family seemed to click into place as he heaved out a sigh. "Your brother is showing the first signs of Parviana."

My stomach fell like a heavy stone as I sucked in a breath. "No." I shook my head. "Please tell me no."

He clenched his jaw then added, "He is still able to do all the things he could before. It's very early yet."

In my father's early stage of the disease, he would simply freeze in the middle of doing something and forget why he was even in the room. For Baelynn, ever the in-control master of himself, that alone would be a nightmare.

I had to find the god-touched texts. And fast. I couldn't allow my brother to succumb to this awful plague like my father. For even though Athelyn didn't say it, I knew my father was not long for this world.

Clearing my throat, I straightened and said, "Please assure Baelynn that all is truly well. Tell him that I am sure my path is guided by the gods here." Though I wasn't sure it was our Goddess Lumera anymore.

Athelyn breathed out a genuine sigh of relief. "I will gladly bring him such news. It will make him very happy to hear this."

At least I could put his mind at ease while I searched for a cure to save him, and hopefully Father and all the afflicted.

"And how is the rebuilding going?" I asked, knowing that would be a monumental task.

"Better than we could've imagined. Of course"—he chuckled—"the wraith fae are brawnier than our lot, and that actually makes them much better builders."

Pursing my brow in confusion, I asked, "What do you mean the wraith fae are better builders?"

"The conscripts King Gollaya sent us."

I stood there, dumbly staring at him. Athelyn's expression shifted to amused. "You did not know that King Goll had sent us conscripts to help rebuild the burned and ravaged villages?"

King Xakiel had razed many towns and villages nearly to the ground, leaving our people destitute and barely able to survive. While Goll had come in and finished the war with his final battle on Issos, it never occurred to me that he might concern himself with the Lumerians his father had harmed in the years of war before his reign.

"No," I answered, dumbstruck. "I did not."

Athelyn donned a more serious expression, speaking as if he were giving a report at the palace.

"While King Gollaya left his garrisons at Valla Lokkyr, he left more soldiers behind for Baelynn to send across Lumeria where they were needed. He didn't just send warriors but also craftsmen to assist with the rebuilding. King Goll's ambassadors have expressed his intention that helping rebuild might mend some of the hatred between Lumeria and Northgall."

My throat was thick with emotion and hoarse when I asked, "Did King Goll say why he was giving Lumeria this boon? He'd already won the war. We'd surrendered." And he'd taken me as his prize. "He did not need to offer this assistance at all."

Athelyn clasped his hands behind him and tilted his gaze to the floor. "The ambassador from Northgall told Baelynn the king wanted a true alliance between the dark and the light fae. This could not happen by sheer force of a king's will, even if he did win the war and occupy the land. King Gollaya understood there may yet be hostility after you were taken from Issos, but his intentions were for peace between our people once and for all. The exact words conveyed to Baelynn were, 'King Gollaya does not intend to remain a tyrant like his father. He wants only to be the King of Northgall and Lumeria, and for his new, wider kingdom to thrive.'"

After a moment of absorbing his words, I cleared my throat, only able to say, "I see."

"It's a slow process, but we are making headway in the rebuilding."

"That is good to hear." I wondered at the fae I'd tied myself to, knowing there was much more to him than I'd first thought. "Come, Athelyn. Goll has planned a feast for this evening, and as our guest, you are invited."

His brow shot up curiously. "Now I am a guest? I was sure that I was a prisoner."

"In Silvantis, those can mean the same thing. But I promise you will be able to leave tomorrow after you've seen all is well for me here, and you can report back to my brother." And hopefully ease his mind.

My gut soured again at the thought of my brother becoming ill. A new sense of urgency pushed me to go to Dragul Falls. I must speak with Goll.

Athelyn nodded and followed. Though my life in Silvantis had not been easy so far, I was making my own path now with confidence. And I wanted my brother to feel safe in the fact that I'd made the right decision. That even though Lumeria had a new king—shrewd, cunning, and domineering—he was now an ally. Not an enemy.

The gods often played tricks on us mere fae but I was still sure I was walking the right path. If I could cure this plague, I would know for certain that the gods hadn't made a mistake and that my painful tragedy here at Näkt Mir hadn't been for nothing.

CHAPTER 28

Una

"Thank you," I told Meck and Ferryn who were posted outside the door of Goll's war room where they'd escorted me. After my visit with Athelyn, I'd told Goll that I needed to speak with him urgently about Dragul Falls. He'd nodded and told me to meet him here with my book.

I was about to knock, but then the door opened and Keffa stood there. "Mizrah." He dipped a shallow bow of the head. "We've been waiting for you."

We? I didn't know Goll had summoned anyone else.

When I stepped inside, I was expecting a table of maps and walls of charts, perhaps weapons decorating the room. Back in Valla Lokkyr, that is what my father's war room, and now Baelynn's, looked like. Though there was a giant map on one wall next to the long table, Goll's war room did not appear at all like my brother's.

There was a long black oak table, polished to a beautiful shine. Chairs of gray leather with brass nail-heads lining the seats surrounded the table. A white-marble mantel framed a fireplace large enough for a wraith fae to walk inside of it upright, horns and all.

Surrounding the hearth were a semi-circle of velvet-cushioned chairs and a rug of red and gold embroidery.

Standing in front of the crackling fire was Goll, his hands behind his back, his gaze on me. Soryn sat in one of the chairs as Keffa escorted me over. There were two other wraith fae. One I recognized as the white-haired councilman, Bozlyn. The kinder one who greeted me on my arrival. The other was a fierce-looking, orange-eyed wraith fae with a barrel-sized chest and a little gray in his black hair as well.

Goll stepped forward to greet me. I was surprised when he leaned down and brushed his lips against mine. "Did you sleep well?"

I arched a brow. He knew that I had since he'd slept beside me. I'd awoken to a grinning Hava in his bedchamber, chirping that the king demanded I eat a hearty breakfast.

"Yes, my king."

A low purr rumbled in his chest before he escorted me with a hand at my back toward a red-velvet chair beside Soryn. All of the males stood as I approached, so I remained standing next to the chair while Goll took care of the introductions.

"You know Soryn and Keffa, of course. This is Bozlyn, who is head of my royal council and also a member of my war council."

"I remember Bozlyn. Good to see you again, my lord."

"And you, Mizrah."

"May I present Morgolith to you?" He gestured to the fierce-looking one, who bowed.

"Oh," I said excitedly with a bright smile. "You are the one who befriended Hava."

The beefy wraith fae grinned, one of his fangs crooked. "I am, Mizrah." He bowed his head. "It is wonderful to meet you."

"And you, my lord." I knew now that all wraith fae with four horns were nobles of the dark fae and deserved the title lord rather than sir. "Hava has become a dear friend of mine."

"Indeed, I am glad to hear of it." He smiled warmly, his orange eyes crinkling. "Hava deserved a good life and a high station in the palace. And our king has given it to her."

He needn't speak of the prejudice she apparently suffered in her life with the shadow fae. I already understood she might've had similar treatment if she lived and worked in the city proper of Silvantis. But here in the palace under Goll's guidance and protection, everyone treated her with respect. It raised my esteem for Goll higher still, knowing he was the kind of king who demanded respect for everyone, no matter their origins.

"Have a seat," Goll urged softly, nudging me toward the chair.

Everyone sat except him. He stood in front of the fire again, facing me. "Now, I've caught everyone up to speed. Those here are my most trusted confidants as I had a feeling you wouldn't want this public yet. Still, we will need protection if we are going near anything that is god-touched."

I nodded in agreement, remembering it had turned into disaster when I'd gone by myself the first time. "I understand."

Then I opened my beloved book to the first prophecy I'd collected, the one I first found in my father's desk. After reading it aloud to them, I said, "This one caught my attention because of the mention of the plague."

It didn't surprise me the wraith fae shared a few looks at the rest of the vision, for it predicted a time when their people would reign higher than the light fae. It was just as the old myth had said, the one of Vix and Mizrah. Still, that wasn't my focus today.

"But this one"—I flipped to the next page—"is where I knew the first text must be at Dragul Falls." I read the second one, which was quite a bit longer, yet again mentioning a sickness in the land, "One will steal magick and one will steal the mind, one will curse the light and one the other kind."

"Madness." Morgolith's voice stopped me. When I looked up, he was scratching his chin, his expression in deep concentration.

"What of it?" asked Goll.

"When I left Gadlizel, there were rumors the king was ill of the mind. I never saw proof of it myself because when I'd heard you'd taken the throne in Silvantis, I didn't stay long enough to find out."

Goll frowned. "We hear nothing from the shadow fae, so we wouldn't know if it's true or not. Something to remember, though." He looked back at me. "Go on, Una."

I did, reading the rest where it spoke of the gods' intervention, offering fae-kind a way to balance the scales and set the world to right. Then the final description where rivers meet in the northlands and fall as one.

Soryn stood and walked to the map on the other side of the room. "That certainly sounds like Dragul Falls," he admitted soberly. "I can't see where else it might be."

"That's what I'd thought," I said, Goll's attention on me.

"And this oracle," Goll began, a heaviness in his voice, "is he or she still there in Issos? Can we speak to them?"

I shook my head. "No. She was excommunicated by my father years ago."

Goll's eyes widened with shock.

"I know," I added, realizing he must be surprised my father would do such a thing. "He didn't want any more prophecies about the downfall of the moon fae, it seemed."

"What was her name?" he asked with serious urgency.

I hadn't told him the oracle was female. "Vaylamorganalyn."

"Vayla," Keffa whispered, standing beside Goll and staring at me with a mixture of shock and sorrow.

Goll turned to him and put a hand on his shoulder. It was a comforting touch I didn't understand. "Easy, friend," he whispered to Keffa.

Then I remembered. Right before Goll severed his father's head, he'd said, *Vayla was right.*

Keffa's gaze swiveled toward the fire, but he was the one who broke the tension-filled silence when he said in a gravelly voice, "You would've been just a girl when she was exiled."

Swallowing hard, my pulse tripping faster, for there was something more going on here, I said, "Yes. I was. I found these prophecies at the Moon Temple."

"And you determined to act on them all alone?" asked Goll. His voice wasn't accusing but more concerned at what I'd done as a girl of seventeen.

"I tried to get Baelynn to understand. I'd even told my father, but neither would listen. At the time, Father was concerned about the Borderlands and the increasing dark fae in the region."

I needn't explain more because it was, apparently, the beginnings of war. All it took was my own capture and torture here in Näkt Mir to put that officially into motion.

"You spoke of Vayla," I added. "Was this the same Vaylamorganalyn? Did you know her?"

Keffa remained rigid, staring into the fire. It was Bozlyn, the older wraith fae who said, "She came here to Silvantis when she was exiled from Issos. She told King Xakiel that she was god-touched with powerful magick of prophecy, a world-seer and a god-seer in one. She said she must use the gift or be damned by the gods. And the gods had sent her to Xakiel."

"So she served your father?" I asked Goll.

"She did," he told me. "She was welcomed because of her exceptional scrying abilities. And for many years she was considered the greatest oracle we've ever had in Silvantis."

"What happened?" I asked gently.

Keffa finally turned from the fire, his face a hard mask. "She had a vision that the Demon King didn't like. She told King Xakiel that one day his son and heir would usurp his throne, and he would die by his son's sword."

"Heavens," I muttered, trying to absorb the realization that the same oracle who prophesied the plague and downfall of our people also foresaw Goll's rise. I looked at him, cut in shadow against the firelight. "Then you were put into prison."

"I was. So was she."

"Fucking tyrant," growled Keffa, turning back to the mantel and bracing both hands on the white marble, his black claws out.

A new dawning bloomed in my chest, pulling me to my feet. My breathing quickened as I stared into the fire, remembering.

Drip. Drip. Drip. "Sorka lillet."

"She was there," I whispered. "She was there in the dungeon with me."

Tears sprang to my eyes and spilled down my cheeks so suddenly I gasped. It hit me like a lightning bolt.

A frenzied panic gripped me as I remembered the hag. Her quiet whisper in the dark, her bloody fingers on my forehead, her magick seeping into my flesh, her sweet spirit slipping into the afterworld.

Keffa took a step toward me, his brow furrowing deeper, tightening the scar that ran down from his missing eye. "You saw her? Spoke to her?"

I couldn't answer, tears now slipping freely down my face.

When Keffa took another step toward me, Goll stopped him with a hand on his shoulder. "Can you all step outside a moment?"

I sat back down, staring at my hands, my fingers shaking as I picked at the fringe of ivy embroidery along my overskirt hem. I vaguely recognized that everyone left, the door shutting quietly behind them. Then Goll was on his knees in front of me, wrapping his large, warm hands around mine.

"Breathe, Una. Deep breath in. And out."

I hadn't realized I was breathing so quickly, near hysterical from the sensory memory flooding my mind so fast.

"I thought she was simply an old hag. A poor Issosian who'd been caught like I was, tossed in the dungeon to rot." I sucked in a breath after a sob. "She was so kind to me." I met Goll's concerned expression. "She tried to heal me, I believe. Gave me the very last of her magick on her dying breath."

His concern transformed to an earnestness as he asked, "Did she trace runes on your forehead?"

"I didn't know what she was doing at the time. When the healer came to my bedside in Issos, there were traces of rune sign, but none of it recognizable. The healer had asked me about it, but I didn't answer. I was in shock. Then later, I didn't care to share my experience with anyone."

"When I carried you into Esher Wood"—he reached up and swiped my cheeks with his thumbs—"I saw the bloody marks, but I thought my father's jailers had done that to you. Some sort of curse."

"No." I shook my head. "It was her. Vayla. I thought she had gone mad. She said something to me in demon tongue, which I didn't know. But then she said it to me in the common tongue right before she died."

"Do you remember what she said?"

"I'll never forget it." I held his gaze as I recalled and recited exactly what Vaylamorganalyn had whispered in the dark before she died. "You are the destiny. You are the dark lady." I paused, licking my lips. "You are for him."

His eyes widened, his fingers clenched around my hands in my lap.

"I'd thought it all nonsense. But she wasn't crazy. She gave me a gift with her last breaths."

He brushed his thumbs over the back of my hands. "Vayla sent her spirit into the afterworld, but she blessed you first."

"With her magick. I know she did."

He dipped his chin in a single nod. "And her prophecy."

"She meant you," I stated confidently, not as a question. Finally understanding. "She meant that I was destined for you." My heart sank a little. "Do you think the gods are toying with us? Forcing us together?" It shattered me to think that what we had wasn't our own will but merely the gods frivolous game of fates.

Goll stood, scooped me off the chair, and then resettled in it with me on his lap. I accepted his comfort, my stomach twisted in knots, and slipped my arms around his neck.

"I believe the gods are always playing with us, manipulating us to get what they want."

My heart plummeted at his admission. "We are merely pawns?" I blinked back fresh tears.

"Look at me, Una." He lifted my chin so that I had to. "If you think the gods can force my heart to beat only for you, then you're mistaken." He took one of my hands and pressed it to his chest. "They may have guided you to my doorstep, but you're in here now. Ever-present in the soul of this wraith king. No god or fae can take you away from me now."

I pressed my face against his neck, letting his tight embrace and heartfelt words soothe my renewed grief over the old fae lady. The seer who'd gifted me with new magick before she died.

We sat like that for some time, holding one another and absorbing this new reality that the gods had forced us together, but in the end, we'd both chosen each other. What happened from here, the heavens only knew.

In the quiet, I murmured, "Keffa loved Vayla, didn't he?"

"Very much." He heaved a sigh. "She'd not given herself to him, remaining true to her vows as a priestess. But after she'd told her last prophecy, and it was obvious the king was going to arrest her, she went to him. They were found together in his bedchamber. When he fought for her, that is how he lost his eye, how his horn was broken, and he was given those scars."

Closing my eyes, I held Goll tighter, so sad for Keffa having lost his dear one, the fae woman who'd comforted me in the dark and given me the last of her magick.

Finally, I sat up. "When do we go to Dragul Falls?"

"I'll take Keffa and Soryn and leave tomorrow."

"And me," I added.

He shook his head. "There could be danger."

"But you'll be there."

"Yes," he stated firmly. "And you won't."

"Why not?" I squirmed to get off his lap, but he held me tightly.

"Anything that is god-touched can be dangerous and I won't risk you getting hurt."

I shoved off my hip the hand that was keeping me on his lap and stood. "But I discovered these prophecies and where they guide us to the texts."

"I am glad of it, so I can follow through and find them," he said in that serene manner that made me want to scream.

"They aren't meant for you to find them. They're meant for *me*."

He arched a brow in that superior way of his. "How do you know?"

Crossing my arms, I mimicked his slow and serene voice, "The same way you knew I would not die in Näkt Lykenzel and that I was marked to be your mizrah."

He clamped his jaws tight. I held his stare and waited. "Where are the other texts?" he asked.

Avoiding his gaze, I glanced down. "Farther north, I believe." I knew they were.

He scoffed and stood before me, towering over me with his height and breadth. "You're not going. You can give me the book, and I'll find them for you." Then he turned and marched for the door.

"*Goll*." I hurried after him. "You don't understand. I have to be there."

He whirled around, scowling fiercely. "Why must you?"

I shrugged. "I don't know. I just feel that I must."

"Well, I feel that you must remain out of danger. Farther north into beast and shadow fae lands? No, Una. I won't allow it."

"What could possibly happen? We'll have your Culled with us."

"Anything could happen." He glared down at me. "Dalya foresaw someone who means to take my throne. An enemy. And you want me to take my mizrah into enemy lands?"

"You are enemies with the other dark fae?"

"The beast fae, not so much. They simply don't like us and we don't like them. But we have a violent history with the shadow fae, and I've suspected for a while that the enemy Dalya warned me about might very well be among them."

I bit my lip. "Then we'll be careful."

"*No*, Una." His posture and expression told me he wasn't going to see this my way.

Calmly, I stepped around him toward the door.

"Where are you going?" he snapped.

"To prepare for the feast. If you recall, we still have a guest from Issos to entertain." I whirled at the door. "That is, if you're going to *allow* me to speak again with my countryman."

I knew referring to Athelyn as my countryman would stir his anger, but I didn't care. He may want to protect me, but he refused to even acknowledge that the gods may have a plan for me as well. It was always about what he wanted. The tyrannical wraith king.

When he did nothing but clamp his jaw tighter, I left without a word to get ready for my first feast at Näkt Mir.

CHAPTER 29

The Traitor

A roar of cheers and the beating of chests greeted Goll and Una as he escorted her into the great hall for the first time. The king had been absent from every meal since the army's return.

My sweet little spies in the servants' hall had told me the king and his soon-to-be mizrah had shared only one meal together since their return. But after the Rite of Servium, they hadn't once been in the same room. As far as anyone knew.

The ambassador from Issos trailed behind the royal couple, but I cared not. My only concern was what was happening between Goll and Una now. Their shared glance was filled with tension as I'd hoped and expected.

Yesterday, she'd escaped from the palace and had been caught fleeing into the woods toward the borders of her homeland. When the Culled caught up to them, Goll had appeared out of the woods and dragged an upset mizrah onto his dragon's back.

What I'd expected upon seeing her for the first time since that had happened was dried trails of tears, fury, and seething rage at the king for whatever punishment he'd doled out on her.

She appeared unharmed. In fact, she appeared absolutely beautiful. Radiant. As always. She was a vision, glowing like the goddess she was. But when she looked at the king, there was a tightness in her expression.

Good.

I laughed at Lykel's jest on my right while my sole focus was on the two making their way toward the dais. I was a good pretender. I clapped and applauded the king and his new mizrah as they stepped up onto the small stage, as Goll held out her chair for her, as he leaned over and whispered in her ear. She shared an unreadable look with him but did not smile.

The ambassador took a seat next to Goll, and the rest of his precious favorites surrounded him as always.

No matter. I would be sitting upon that dais soon. In the king's chair. I would hold court for my kingdom. And Una would smile at *my* whispers and blush at *my* touch.

I curled my fist under the table as I settled in to eat my meal, digging my claws into my palm, letting the pain relieve my anguish.

I'd already waited too long. I'd felt a surge of triumph when I'd discovered she was unhappy with the king and her anger for his arrogant, self-indulgent ways had only grown worse. Her unhappiness had been an encouragement, but I wanted the kingdom *now*. I wanted her *now*.

My pulse suddenly leaped as her garment shifted on her shoulder when she leaned toward him, revealing the very edge of a bite mark. Rage boiled like acid in my belly.

As always, King Goll took what he wanted. He killed King Xakiel and stole the throne when he should've died in that fucking dungeon. If he'd died there like he was supposed to, I would've ascended naturally when my lineage was known. That throne belonged to *me*.

Yesss, the Voice whispered. *She is yours to take. The throne is yours to take.*

I relished his presence. The Voice always gave me the reinforcement I needed. I stared at the black-winged royal princess. At least I wouldn't have to find a way to steal her from Lumeria. Xakiel had done that. All I needed to do now was kill the king.

"What's that face for?" asked Lykel, stuffing a bite of boar into his mouth. "Don't look so sour. That ambassador will be gone soon enough."

"Aye," I agreed, raising my ale. "I don't like their kind in our palace."

"The mizrah is their kind. Surely, you accept her." Lykel questioned me with hesitation, for it was known Goll would tolerate no defiance against Una's presence here. But that was an easy question to answer.

"Of course not," I told him honestly. "Princess Una is right where she belongs."

"Mizrah Una," he corrected. "And that she is."

I smiled and drank my ale. The drummers began playing music. Dancers draped in gossamer silk that revealed their feminine figures performed for the court, twisting and turning to the beat of the drums. Their horns were wrapped in red ribbons, trailing through the air as they leaped and twirled.

Dalya turned her gaze away, always modest when it came to lascivious displays at the feasts. I smiled to myself, remembering last night. She wasn't always modest. She would make a good concubine when I was king.

The audience watched the dancers, as did Goll and Una, whispering to one another. But I couldn't stop watching her. I tilted back against the wall behind me to fall farther into shadow, sipping my ale and planning my next steps. I only needed the right opportunity.

The ambassador stood and excused himself from the table, bowing to Goll and Una. The feast wore on while the drinking flowed. Some of the dancers began to sit in the laps of the Culled, always chosen first over anyone else.

At the end of the table where soldiers of the cavalry laughed boisterously, one of them with a raising of his tankard said, "My king! Your mizrah should give us a dance since we missed the show at the Servium!" Then he turned drunkenly to his neighbor, gripping his cock under the table. His neighbor's eyes rounded in fear, shooting up to the dais.

Suddenly, the laughter died. So did the music. Everyone froze.

"I beg forgiveness, my liege," muttered the cavalryman, his voice slurring. He realized his mistake quickly. But not soon enough.

Una remained still, her gaze on her plate, her cheeks flushed with embarrassment. Goll, however, stared at the offender, his glare nothing short of deadly.

One of the fae males at the cavalrymen's table muttered something to the offender. He quickly lurched to his feet and stumbled to kneel before the dais, bowing his head and pounding his fist against his chest in deference. "Forgive me, my king."

Goll slowly stood, no longer looking at the offender but letting his gaze sweep the entire room filled with about three hundred courtiers, councilmen and women, foot soldiers, cavalrymen, and the Culled.

"Hear me now," stated Goll in a low, lethal voice. "Let it be known now." His voice rumbled with a quiet fury. "Mizrah Una is to be respected. As the rightful vessel of my heir, she is sacred. Untouchable. *Mine.* Speak ill of her, you will regret it. Touch her, and you will die."

Then he lifted her gently with a hand under her elbow and guided her from the room. I cursed the offender, his friends guiding him to his feet. Not for his stupid, drunken slur that ruined the entire atmosphere of the feast, everyone sliding away from the tables, but because he'd taken her away from my sight.

No matter. She would be mine soon enough. And King Goll would be dead.

CHAPTER 30

Goll

"Now do you understand?" I growled as we approached our bedchambers.

"What are you talking about?" She stopped in the corridor and faced me.

"That," I pointed in the direction of the dining hall, "is why I can't take you traipsing around Northgall unprotected."

She scoffed. "Because a drunkard made a mildly obscene comment? That was nothing."

"It was not nothing." I moved close to her. "Drunk or not, the fact that he so easily let slip his disrespect means that he's not the only one thinking of you in this manner."

"He didn't mean to be disrespectful."

"Yes. I know."

Her brow pursed in confusion. "Then why are you so irate? And what does this have to do with me leaving Näkt Mir?"

"The drink loosened his tongue, and in that moment it showed me that he doesn't respect you as a wraith fae should. He doesn't see you as a true mizrah deserving of the proper regard of your station.

And if he sees you in this way then that means more most likely feel the same. More soldiers and cavalrymen sharing their thoughts with families and friends down in Silvantis, spreading rumors to their kin beyond Silvantis and farther into Northgall."

Fury raced through my blood at the thought of the rumors. I could only imagine some of the things they might be saying. *She's just his whore. A pretty piece he gained from defeating Issos. She's no wraith fae so she's not his true mizrah. Nor will their babe be a true heir.*

"It's true," she said, "I'm not one of you."

"You are *now*," I practically bellowed in the quiet of the corridor. "Una. If they don't accept you as my mizrah, then they wouldn't accept our child as heir. If I died somehow, those disbelievers might—" I broke off. I couldn't tell her what they'd do.

Traitors could and would kill our child so that he or she couldn't take their rightful place? They'd kill Una as well for good measure.

The thought chilled my blood with horrifying speed.

Una didn't ask what I refused to tell her. She simply stated calmly. "So it will take time for them to accept me."

"Exactly. And *that* is why you won't leave Näkt Mir to seek out these texts the prophecies speak of. Here you are safe. Outside these walls, the danger is far too great."

She pressed her lips together, her calm demeanor vanishing, her back and shoulders going rigid. "My people will die without this cure, Goll. My father." Her lip trembled. "My brother."

I reached out to her, but she flinched and stepped away from me. The unexpected rejection sliced like a dagger deep beneath my ribs. Then I curled my hand into a fist at my side.

"I will find the texts for you. I'll bring them back to you here."

She huffed out a frustrated breath. "You don't understand. They were meant for me to find. Not you. You might not ever find them. Then it'll be too late. All because of your stupid stubbornness."

"I won't risk it." *I won't risk you.*

"Even if it means saving hundreds, even thousands, of people in Lumeria."

"Yes, even then," I stated evenly. She narrowed her glare but then I added, "And you don't know that you're the only one who can find them."

She fluttered her black wings as if to remind me she was god-touched herself. "Yes, Goll. I do."

Then she turned and marched into her bedchamber, slamming the door behind her and firmly shutting me out.

Una

Maddening male. I punched my pillow, still trying to find a comfortable position so I could fall asleep. For the hundredth time, I threw the covers off of myself and rolled over to stare out the window, reliving my argument with Goll. Both arguments, actually.

I understood that he wanted to keep me safe, but he refused to listen to me. Some things were worth the risk. Like saving an entire people. Hava had even told me there were signs that some wraith fae in a small village near the Borderlands may have a few cases of the Parviana plague.

A soft whoosh noise came from near my wardrobe then Goll's naked silhouette passed the window and crossed the room toward me.

"Go away," I told him but he kept coming. "I don't want to talk to you."

"Good," he growled into the dark, raising gooseflesh on my skin. "I don't want to talk."

"Get out of my bedchamber," I hissed as he neared the foot of the bed.

Then he was standing there, yanking the coverlet off the bed and wrapping his long fingers around my ankles.

"I'm serious, Goll!"

Ignoring my protests, his dragon eyes glowing silver in the dark, he tightened his hold on my ankles. "So am I, Mizrah."

With a strong pull, he hauled me to the foot of the bed, my chemise riding up. He released one ankle to push the hem the rest of the way to my waist, baring my sex. Instantly, my body flared with heat and arousal while my emotions still whirled with anger.

"Goll!" I kicked out with my foot. It glanced off his shoulder.

He growled and wrapped a hand around my inner thigh, now pushing both my knees flat to the mattress.

"I told you, I don't want—" I gasped, my words sucked right out of me when his hot mouth opened on my quim.

I grunted and gripped his horns, my anger stirring me to push him away, my visceral desire telling me to hold him right there while he pleasured me.

Then his tongue was inside me and I dropped my head back to the pillow. "You don't listen," I murmured, frustrated with myself and my body's betrayal, while I rocked up against his greedy mouth that suckled me hard.

He didn't answer of course, his low purr of pleasure vibrating against my clitoris as he lapped and flicked then stroked inside me with his tongue.

"I'm mad at you," I whispered into the dark.

Then I felt a hand on my breast, fingers pinching the taut peak almost to pain.

"Ah!" I thrust up harder, rubbing my sex against his hot mouth, seeking that pinnacle I could feel mounting higher and higher. "I'm coming," I murmured, then I was.

He growled again, launching up the bed on top of me. Before my orgasm had even stopped throbbing, he thrust his cock deep.

"Goll!" I cried out, the intrusion intense and jarring. I pushed against his chest, then curled my fingernails into his flesh, wanting to hurt him but also wanting to hold on. It was infuriating.

Holding my gaze, he deftly gripped both my wrists and pressed them to the mattress above my head, holding them with one hand. Then he reached down and grabbed my thigh, bending my leg until my knee curved over his shoulder.

"I'm angry at you," I hissed though my words had less weight after the heady orgasm he'd just given me.

"I know, my sweet." His voice was low and husky, his eyes slits of silvery blue. "And I'm going to fuck it right out of you."

He pulled out to the tip and hammered back in, my breasts bounced with the force of it beneath. I wrapped my free leg around his waist, practically bent in half while he started to thrust hard and deep.

I moaned when he hit a particularly pleasurable spot inside me, furious with him and myself that this felt so good.

The slick sound of him pumping in and out of me filled the room along with my gasping whimpers and mewling moans.

He mounded my breast over the gossamer fabric of my shift with his large hand while he stroked faster then pinched my nipple with thumb and forefinger. My sex squeezed at the pleasure-pain of it.

"You feel that?" he murmured low. "You may hate me now, Una, but your cunt loves me."

I squeezed my eyes closed as my sex responded by quivering and squeezing him again. It was like my body obeyed only him and not my will.

"That's it." His raspy voice wrapped around me. "Close your eyes, my mizrah. You can still be mad at me while I fuck your sweet cunt." He pinched my nipple again, my breasts bouncing with each pounding thrust. "While your dripping honey soaks my cock."

"Unh." A second climax was building, and I couldn't understand it.

Then his mouth was against mine, brushing lightly while I panted. He changed his stroking to a slow grinding inside of me, filling me even deeper.

"Think whatever you want," he whispered against my lips, nipping me with a fang. "But this cunt is *mine*." He ground harder. "You are *mine*."

I moaned again, kissing him back, slipping my tongue inside his mouth, needing to taste him, needing more of him. He groaned into our kiss, nipping my bottom lip again when he pulled away, all the while grinding his cock deep inside me.

"Open your eyes, Una."

I did, finding the dragon staring back with feral ferocity. He moved his hand from my breast to my throat, gripping me with a gentle but firm hold.

"You understand that, don't you? You can be angry all you like, but you will *always* be mine."

I wasn't sure if his possessiveness was because his pride as king needed to stake his claim as victor over me, or if he was proving a point that my own will was lost when he had full control of my body. Either way, he was right. I was his, body and soul, it seemed. Whether I tried to pretend otherwise or not.

He tightened his hold at my throat, but not enough to restrict my breath. "Now come on my cock the way I know you want to."

Then he pumped in and out with savage slowness, dragging the pleasure out, like he knew exactly what to do to make my body respond to him.

I opened my mouth as my orgasm barreled toward its peak, my wrists still pinned, my body staked to the mattress with his cock buried inside me.

"Ahhh!" I cried out with my climax.

Goll's mouth quirked into a smug half-smile for a second. Then his own mouth dropped open in pleasure, his eyes sliding closed as he came inside me, his cock throbbing hard. He groaned as his seed emptied deep.

I should've been furious. I should've yelled and pushed him off me. He'd known I wasn't in the mood. I was steeped in my fury at him when he waltzed into my dark bedchamber and compelled my own body to betray me, seducing me heedless of my anger.

But all I could feel now was satisfaction and acceptance that this stubborn, infuriating wraith king was indeed my mate. As if the goddess heard me, I felt a tingling sensation along my hands, wrists, and forearms.

Still buried inside me, Goll released my wrists then clasped one of his hands to mine, lacing our fingers. He stared at them as I did, noting the glowing thread of the moon-binding still bright and strong as the day Elder Lelwyn tethered us under the light of Lumera.

"Yes, Gollaya," I admitted quietly while his cock still pulsed inside me. "I am yours. But you are also mine." I glanced at the glowing threads then held his shining gaze. "I won't fight you anymore." I gusted out a sad sigh. "Even though you're wrong."

He let my hand go and pulled out of my body on a grunt. I pushed the hem of my chemise down, still panting while laying on my back.

He lay beside me in silence, an arm braced over his eyes as he panted too. He seemed defeated, not triumphant.

Then he heaved out a heavy sigh. "Fine."

I lifted up onto my elbow. "What?"

"Fucking hells," he muttered then removed his arm from covering his eyes and turned his head to me. "I'll take you to Dragul Falls."

I launched my body over him and kissed his lips, grinning at his scowling face.

"Thank you." Then I kissed his lips again.

At first, he refused to respond but like I couldn't resist him, he couldn't resist me either, finally opening his mouth to kiss me deeper, his hand cradling the back of my skull. When I finally pulled back, smiling even wider now, he frowned deeper.

"But you'll listen to me, and you won't go wandering off with your handmaiden. We'll do this my way."

"Of course," I agreed, grinning wide.

"I'm serious, Una."

"I see that."

He huffed in anger and dropped his head to the pillow, pulling me tighter as I rested my head on his chest.

"Son of Vix, I must be fucking mad."

I laughed, staring out the window. Content in all ways, I finally fell asleep.

CHAPTER 31

Una

We'd dismounted from Drakmir in a meadow a ways back. The forest grew thick around the river and the brooks that sprung out from it. A familiar buzz of magick and instinct tugged me closer to the falls. It was where I'd had the magickal pull last time. And now, as we drew closer, I felt it yet again, stronger and stronger as we finally wound out of thick evergreens into the small clearing.

"Oh, no." I froze. "The sprites."

I'd hoped they'd have moved on from the falls. Sprites rarely kept to one place too long. They were nomadic creatures.

"Shove off, ya little harpies!" Soryn swatted a hand in the air at them.

Three water sprites—quite familiar ones—flitted around his head, lifting his braids, petting his horns, giggling every time he batted a hand at them.

I bit my lower lip to keep from laughing. Keffa leaned against a giant boulder, arms crossed, watching Soryn's distress and grinning like a fiend.

"Seems you've finally found some females who want your company."

"Plenty of females enjoy my company." Soryn bared his teeth and growled at the sprites, and they flew out of reach, giggling.

Goll stepped ahead of me, his boot crunching on a branch. All eyes snapped toward us, including the sprites.

I gasped as they shot through the air like arrows toward us. I raised my arms, preparing to defend myself. Last time, one had poked and pinched me, flying around my head so fast she'd made me fall into the water. Terrified I'd die from the freezing water, I hurried away into the woods with the three of them squeaking and calling me to come back. I'd intended to after I started a fire to get dry and warm, but then I was captured, and that was the end of that.

This time, none of them attacked. They circled, making cooing sounds. They were the same ones as before, I was sure of it. Their sleek blue bodies with webbed hands and long flipper-like feet were very familiar. The fins jutting from their spines were each a different color—yellow on one, purple on the second, and green on the third, matching their feathery caps of hair and bright, round eyes.

Yes, these were the same sprites, one of whom had made me fall into the freezing water in the dead of winter when I'd been here five years ago.

Their wings were less transparent than those of other sprites, smooth like their flippers since they used them to swim as well as fly.

"You're back!" the purple-haired one chirped, the one who'd pushed me into the water.

"Now is good," said the green.

"Now is right," said the yellow with a nod.

They hovered directly in front of my face, smiling.

"You remember me?"

They all laughed, a tinkling sweet sound.

"Of course," said the yellow. "You look the same."

I laughed for I looked much different to my own eyes.

"I'm a few years older."

"You are worlds older," said Yellow.

"Worlds older," chimed Green and Purple together.

Smiling, I glanced at Goll, struck by the look of confusion and wonder on his face. Soryn and Keffa wore similar expressions. I suppose it was odd for these typically antagonistic sprites to be holding a civil conversation.

"Do you know why I'm here?" I asked Yellow.

They laughed and flew in a lazy ring around my head, dancing in the air and singing merrily in unison:

"Ladies, ladies,
listen to me.
Words of wonder I
bequeath to thee.
But mark the time,
a vessel will be
a darkling fae lady
with secrets to see."

Their song made no sense. They were in the middle of singing it a second time when Purple zipped out of their circle and stopped close to my face.

"The Lady of the Wood told us, she did." Purple smiled wide, showing me her rows of sharp teeth. "I tried to show you last time, but you ran away."

Show me? I'd thought she was trying to drown me, pushing me into the water.

"No, Tikka!" Yellow arrowed right at her and slapped her on the head.

"Ow!" squealed Tikka. "No hitting, Zu." Then Tikka flew over my right shoulder, sticking out her purple tongue at Zu.

"I am the elder." Zu looked at me with haughty pride dancing in her yellow eyes. "She was *not* a lady. She was a goddess."

"Goddess of the Wood!" chirped Green.

I paused, letting that sink in, then said, "It is a pleasure to meet you, Zu, Tikka and…?" I gestured to the third.

The green-winged sprite curtsied in the air. "I am Geta. Pleasure to meet you."

I nodded, turning my attention back to Zu. "I don't understand your song. You're saying that Elska, the Goddess of the Wood, came here and left you something?"

My pulse raced wildly. Vayla was right. I smiled over at Goll. He still wore that enigmatic scowl, his arms crossed like he was aggravated. This was terrific news, so I had no idea why he, Soryn, and Keffa looked somewhat disturbed and confused.

Ignoring them for now, I turned my attention back to the sprites. "What did she leave behind?" I asked excitedly.

"Words!" squealed Tikka.

Zu raised her hand to swat Tikka again, but the purple sprite was too fast for her this time. Tikka giggled as she zipped away behind Geta.

"I am the elder," snapped Zu. "I will tell her." Addressing me, she said, "Words. She left words."

Laughing, which made Tikka and Geta giggle, too, I replied, "I don't understand."

"May I speak?" Geta asked Zu politely.

"You may," she gave permission.

"She whispered her words to the water," Geta told me sweetly, blinking her vibrant green eyes owlishly.

Then Tikka shoved her aside, snatching the air and squeezing her tiny fists in a triumphant pump. She squealed, "And we stole them!"

Zu shot a stream of icy wind from her palm. Tikka froze midair, wings and all, floating in a frozen pinwheel upside down, her eyes and mouth round in shock.

"Please be nice," I begged Zu. "I am so grateful to learn your wisdom, but Tikka is only trying to be helpful."

Tikka was floating toward the limbs of the trees when Geta touched her ankle, which seemed to melt the spell away. Tikka shook it off and flew back down to us like it happened all the time. Perhaps it did.

"She is telling you a falsehood, my lady," said Zu. "I will not allow it. We did not steal them. We scooped the words into a jar and have kept them under our protection."

"Will you show them to me?"

"Of course." Zu beamed. "We kept them safe for you."

"For me?" I asked, puzzled.

"The dark fae lady."

Geta and Tikka started singing and dancing around my head again, "*Ladies, ladies…*"

While they sang, I confessed clearly, "But I am not a dark fae lady."

All three tittered. Tikka and Geta zipped to either side of Zu in front of me, floating in the air, their wings humming as they hovered.

"You are the one we've been waiting for," assured Zu.

"Yes, yes," chimed Geta.

Tikka nodded. "Pretty dark fae lady."

"Pretty black wings," added Geta.

"You must come with us now." Zu flew slowly toward the pool of water surrounding the waterfall.

I gestured to Goll. "May I bring my king with me?"

Though they seemed harmless now, I was still a little afraid of them. Goll would protect me.

"No, no," said Zu, crossing her arms. "Kings are greedy things."

"Selfish things," added Geta.

"Mean things," chimed in Tikka.

The three flew ahead, waving for me to follow. I hesitated.

"What—?" Goll started to ask me a question, but he stopped speaking when I took his hand in mine, his gaze on our joined hands.

"Ladies!" I called to them. "May I bring…my mate?"

The three sprites gasped in unison. Tikka shot toward me. I flinched, but she went directly to my right shoulder and sniffed.

"She has a bite, Zu." Then she flew closer to Goll and sniffed his chest. "Yes, it is him."

"Well, then," Zu said, seemingly annoyed. "I suppose we have to."

"Too bad it wasn't that one." Tikka grinned and pointed to Soryn, waggling her purple eyebrows.

"Come along," shouted Zu, now at the water's edge, close to the waterfall, hovering over the water's surface.

"Sorry," I told Keffa and glanced at Soryn. "They'll only allow us to go."

Keffa nodded soberly. "We'll wait."

I kept hold of Goll's hand as we joined them at the waterfall. The three sprites dove beneath the surface.

I smiled at Goll who was still scowling. I wondered if he was thinking what I was, that I was right. He couldn't have done this without me. But then his question surprised me.

"How do you know the ancient tongue?"

I frowned. "What do you mean?"

He pulled me to a stop to face him at the water's edge. "You were speaking a language I don't even know. A very old demon dialect. I only recognized a word here and there."

Shaking my head, I said, "What are you talking about?"

"Una," he said softly. "You were speaking the oldest language of the dark fae. My tutors taught me a few words when I was a boy before I went to the Gall Guild to train as a warrior. But no one can speak it. It's a language of the gods. Some sprites and nymphs still speak it since they've been around that long. And a few gifted seers."

Zu popped her little yellow head out of the water. "You must get in."

I tapped into my magick, the thread burning bright. Magick was pulsing through me. When I listened intently to her words, I realized they weren't high fae at all. Just like Goll had said they were different than anything I'd ever heard. Or spoken. But to me, they felt like a second language. Like I'd always known them.

How can that be? A memory of whispered words and blood runes being traced on my forehead flashed to mind. Had Vayla given me not only her gift of magick but all of her knowledge, too? She must have. For when I'd encountered the sprites before my captivity, I had no idea what they were yelling and screaming as I fled into the woods. But now, I understood them as clearly as if we were speaking high fae.

The three sprites dove back into the water, but quickly resurfaced. "Come with us," shouted Zu.

I frowned, examining the waterfall. "It is behind there, right?"

"They nodded in unison."

"Can we not just walk behind the falls?"

"No." Zu shook her head, a water droplet coasting off her feathery crown. "Not behind. Only under. Come along."

Sighing, I turned to Goll, letting go of his hand to reach for the hook of my cloak.

"I suppose we have to get into the water then." I shivered, knowing how cold it would be.

Goll unhooked his own cloak, looking back toward Keffa and Soryn. "Turn around."

Soryn grinned. "We've seen her before."

Keeping my gaze down, I fumbled with the front lacings of my tunic, heat flushed into my cheeks.

"Turn. Around. Or I'll beat you both bloody." Goll's voice lowered to that scary, threatening tone.

Keffa and Soryn both laughed but did as he bid, quite quickly I noticed when I peeked up at them.

Goll moved close, blocking my body from them. "Best take off everything so we'll have dry clothes to warm us when we return."

"Yes," I agreed. "I was thinking the same."

I wasn't going to repeat my last experience here at the falls.

We undressed quickly and quietly, Goll glaring at Soryn and Keffa's backs every few moments.

When we were finished, Goll slipped in first and then held out a hand to help me in.

I shivered. "So cold," I whispered as I lowered slowly into the water.

I didn't miss his gaze flickering over my breasts, stomach, and lower, or the heated trek across my shoulders to land on the bite mark. But his voice was serious and gruff like when he gave a command to his warriors. "Stay close to me. I'm a good swimmer. I'll keep you safe."

A warmth bloomed from the pit of my belly, spreading outward. Not because I believed him, but because I felt the truth of it and a deeper emotion behind his words.

"Come along, faelings," chirped Zu, her blue skin glowing beneath the water. I smiled at her calling us "faelings," like we were children, but I suppose compared to her, we were very young indeed.

Two distinct blue glowing orbs zig-zagged around us beneath the water.

"Take a deep breath," Goll said, his confidence boosting my own.

"I wish I was a skald fae right about now." I could've used some webbed feet and hands.

"You'll be fine." His blue eyes were icier, brighter, with the reflection of the water in them. "And I'm right here beside you. I won't let anything happen to you."

I nodded, warming yet again at his words. I took a giant gulp of air then plunged beneath the freezing water.

Visibility was hazy with the splashing of the falls into the deeper part of the pool, but the glowing lights of our little guides made it easier to follow. Goll grabbed hold of my waist and gave me a fervent push beneath the torrent of the falls. I came out into a calm tunnel of water, dark on our end but greenish light up ahead.

When my lungs started to protest, I kicked and swam toward the light, never panicking with Goll at my side. A chortle of gurgling laughter drew my gaze to the purple and blue flash swimming around Goll. She had darted beneath him, near his groin, before he swatted at her in the water. She laughed that watery chortle again before zipping ahead of us.

The greenish light grew brighter, my chest began to ache with holding my breath. I surfaced with a gasp and inhaled a deep lungful of air. Goll appeared at my side, not nearly as winded. I thought we'd come out in another part of Esher Wood, but we weren't in the forest at all. We were in a large cave.

High above us, there was a round opening to the wintry forest and the gray clouds above. The cave itself bore giant stalactites hanging down from the ceiling and stalagmites stabbing upward from the floor. A steady trickle of water moved down the sides of the cave and dripped from the ceiling.

Goll slipped out of the water then reached down and pulled me up. The cave was cold, but there was a buzzing of powerful magick here, a stillness only felt where gods have been.

"It's here," I whispered to Goll, smiling despite my physical discomfort, my lips and body shivering.

Instantly, he ignited feyfire in the palm of his hand. "This won't hurt you," he promised.

Before I could ask what he meant, he whispered to the flame in his hand. It leaped into the air and spread wide into a flat sheet of flame that drifted through the air and wrapped around my shoulders like a shawl.

"Oh." I jumped, my instincts to back away from fire ingrained. But it was like a warm tickling against my skin, immediately chasing the chill away in my core. "Thank you." I smiled to Goll.

His tight expression relaxed. He gave me a nod.

"Hurry up, slow pokes!" shouted Zu, hovering halfway across the cave.

As we followed, Tikka zipped up next to me and whispered loud enough for anyone to hear, "Lucky dark lady that you get poked with that one."

She smiled her sharp-toothed smile and then darted away at Goll's growl. I bit my lip and looked over at him.

He heaved an exasperated sigh. "Fucking sprites."

"She is right, though." I glanced down at his thick manhood hanging between his legs and arched a brow.

"You keep looking at me like that, Una, and we won't make it to this godforsaken text."

"God-touched. Not godforsaken."

"We'll see," he growled as we followed Zu and the others to one side where water trickled down the cave wall.

"Here," shouted Zu excitedly. "Come, come!"

There, where the three of them flew, the cave wall jutted out. The water sluiced down the side into a shallow pool the size of a large bowl. All three sprites flew into the bowl and came out together carrying a glass vial with a cork stopper.

They carried it through the air toward me, their eyes glowing with excitement. That wasn't all that was glowing. Inside the vial, an effervescent shimmer of green brightened their faces.

"Take it," said Zu.

Glancing over at Goll, whose expression was grim, I reached out and took the vial. Nothing miraculous happened, but at closer inspection, I could see something floating inside the vial.

"Goll," I said, not believing what I was seeing, "there are actual words floating in here. But I can't read them."

They were etched in gold sparkles, swimming in the clear water of the vial.

He stepped closer, the feyfire still draped over my body lighting his face. He scowled and peered into the vial. "Old fae. Very old."

"Can you read it?"

He shook his head. "I don't know anyone who can. We've found ancient relics with this sort of writing."

"Drink!" shouted Zu.

"Drink, drink!" Tikka and Geta chimed in unison.

Yes. I was supposed to drink them. I was sure they were right. When I unstoppered the cork, a breathy whisper escaped into the tall caverns. It sounded like the word *lady*.

As I lifted the vial toward my mouth, Goll reached out and gripped my wrist, his eyes wide with concern. "Are you sure?"

A calm had swept over me the instant we'd stepped into this cave. "Yes. It will be all right."

He clamped his jaw then finally gave me a tight nod and released my wrist. With a deep breath, I put the vial to my lips and tipped my head back. I swallowed the sickeningly sweet nectar and the glowing words.

A sudden sharp vision blackened out everything else, a god vision.

A stunningly beautiful brown-haired and brown-skinned fae in a green dress walked through the woods, weeping. Not a fae. It was Elska, Goddess of the Wood. "They must mourn and remember their magick, their goodness," she whispered as she knelt at a pool of water and whispered to her reflection, "or all will perish."

Then I was back in the cave, a shot of pain streaking through my veins and stinging my wrists. My head snapped back as I gasped, the overwhelming sensation of power too big for my body filled me up. Then just as suddenly, it was gone.

"Una!" Goll reached for me, but something miraculous happened.

My wings fluttered on their own. Not simply fluttered. They beat with purpose, lifting me off the ground until my feet were at eye level with Goll. His feyfire cloak vanished as I stared down in wonder at this miracle.

I cried tears of joy, even as the effort was tiring my body quickly. "I can fly," I whispered, voice shaking.

Then it was too much, my strength exhausted from simply hovering above the floor. I lowered quickly, Goll caught me when I would've tipped over.

"I flew," I whispered to him, tears brimming my eyes.

His smile beamed with pride and something more tender. "You did, my mizrah."

I hadn't even noticed the three sprites were back to singing their song merrily, flying and dancing around us midair.

Pulling from Goll's arms, I looked down, knowing there were new words etched into my skin by the gods. "What does this new sign mean?" I asked Goll.

He looked down, but it was Tikka who zipped over and tapped my wrist. "It says *healer*," she told me delightedly, seeming to want to beat Goll to it.

"Healer?" I asked in a whisper, blinking back the tears.

Goll's hands were wrapped around my upper arms. He gave a gentle squeeze, smiling at me. Without me saying, he knew how important my healing magick had been. But I didn't feel I had that power living inside me. Not yet.

I turned to the sprites. "What do I do now? Will this magick help against the plague?" I asked Zu.

All three stopped singing, still joyful as Zu flew back to us. "Yes, when you have all of the words," she answered. "But the god words are bigger than the plague."

"I don't understand," I told her.

"You will. But you must ingest all of the texts."

"Why?" I asked. "What happens then?"

"The spell is not complete until all the words are together."

"Two more! Two more!" yelled Geta and Tikka.

I had the prophecies in my book on the other two texts, though I needed Goll's help deciphering exactly where to find one of them. The other was quite clear where to go.

"Are they all like this one?" I asked, wondering if they'd all be in pools of water.

But they went back to singing their strange song, circling higher and higher until they zipped out of the opening of the cave and left us altogether.

When I turned back to Goll, he was looking at me with an enigmatic expression. "What is it?"

He cupped my face. "How do you feel?"

Smiling, I admitted honestly, "Absolutely wonderful."

"Good." He nodded, still frowning. "I can sense magick inside you. Old magick. Like what I sense in the lower depths of Vixet Krone. Like what emanates from Näkt Lykenzel."

Blinking back to the moment I swallowed the words in the vial, the god-touched text, I told him what I'd seen in the brief vision. "It was definitely Elska. But what did she mean they must mourn and remember their magick and goodness or all will perish?"

"I don't know. It could simply mean we must end the wars between dark and light."

"But the war is over," I told him.

"That does not mean all of Lumeria or Northgall will accept this truce. This peace. There is always someone ready and willing to lead another fight." Then he heaved a sigh, taking my hand, and led me back to the pool. "The gods will give us the answers when they are ready."

"Then we must find the next text and discover what they want."

"I don't fucking like it." He stopped at the edge of the icy pool and slipped in first, reaching up to help me in. "You were in pain when you swallowed the words."

I stepped down into the water with a shiver and slipped my arms around his neck, not yet ready to take the plunge back under, needing his warmth and comfort for a moment longer.

"I was, but I think that's only normal when a fae takes in that sort of power. I feel fine now. Better than fine." My wings flickered at my back. "And for a moment, I could fly. This is right, Goll. Whatever this is. We must follow the path through to the end."

"Let's return to Näkt Mir and get you warm and fed. Then we can take a look at your book again to see exactly where the other two are."

Bracing myself for more of his foul temper, I nodded. I was absolutely certain Goll wouldn't like it.

CHAPTER 32

Una

I don't fucking like it." Goll glowered down at my book spread out on the conference table. "*Where the Meer-wolf reigns,*" he repeated the last of the prophecy.

"So we're heading into beast fae territory," said Morgolith.

Bozlyn studied the prophecy closer, the book in his lap. He sat before the fire in the war room yet again where we'd convened after Goll and I had bathed, eaten, and rested.

Interestingly, I wasn't tired. Rather, I was invigorated by the ability to fly yet again. Well, sort of. I could fly in short bursts.

"It appears the next text is written in someone's blood," advised Bozlyn. "Perhaps a Meer-wolf."

"The gods and their fucking riddles," grumbled Soryn. "Why not just tell us directly what they want? *Go here and find this.* No, we have to decipher these bloody riddles."

Goll and Soryn were both in a temper. Neither were happy about venturing into beast fae territory. Goll's foul look focused on me, and for a moment I thought he'd go back on his word and refuse to take me again. But he said not a word, stewing in his own thoughts.

"You'll have to go to their king in Vanglosa," said Morgolith. "They won't allow us to roam around their land unguarded."

Confused, I asked Goll, "They won't allow their king to go where he wants?"

There were a few sighs and shared looks. But it was Goll who said, "The dark fae are not like the light. In Issos, the royals in Valla Lokkyr ruled all of Lumeria. And while I, the wraith king, do speak for and rule the civilized world of Northgall, as well as Lumeria, the beast and shadow fae count themselves separate from us."

"I thought"—I stumbled over my words a little—"I thought the dark fae were united in this realm."

"We are not, I'm afraid." Bozlyn shook his gray-haired head before returning back to my book, flipping the pages. "Never have been."

"So will they attack us if we go onto their land?" Panic spiked at the thought of having to fight our way through beast fae land. Goll had said they were unfriendly, not truly enemies.

"No," answered Goll. "But we'll have to deal with that bastard of a beast lord."

Soryn grumbled a curse under his breath, then, "I hate that fae."

Keffa laughed. "He doesn't like us either. Best go to the armory and find a gift to bribe our passage into Meerland."

"Mizrah?" Bozlyn was frowning down at the book. "Where did this prophecy come from?"

I stood and walked over to lean over his shoulder. "Oh. That one actually was given to me personally, strangely enough."

"Given to you?" asked Goll. "You said that you'd collected them from the temple in Issos."

"Most of them, yes. But the one about the beast fae and the third text came from a scribe in Mevia."

"Where's the third text?" asked Keffa.

I brightened, happy there was no vagueness at all in that one. It told us exactly where to find the third god-touched text. "Solzkin's Heart."

"Fucking hells. Now we have to go into shadow fae lands?" Soryn looked more annoyed and grumblier than before. "They're worse than dealing with the beast fae."

"That is certain," griped Goll, glancing at me yet again like it was my fault we had to go there.

Well, I suppose it was. I simply smiled back.

Goll shook his head and turned to Morgolith. "Do you think any will be on guard as far down the mountain as Solzkin's Heart?"

"It's possible. That's well within their lands."

"Fuck," cursed Soryn.

"Language, Soryn," growled Goll, which only made me smile since he certainly didn't worry about his own coarse language in front of me. And Soryn had been cursing up a storm since he'd first heard we were heading into beast fae lands.

"But this one here…" Bozlyn looked up at me, his orange irises shining by the firelight as he pointed at the last vision I'd scribed in my book. "Where did it come from? Why did you copy it?"

I blinked down, remembering. "We had traveled to Myrkovir Forest for the Fall Solstice. Baelynn had thought it a sign of good will if we attended on my twentieth year. The war had begun to encroach farther south, and the wood fae who reside there were becoming afraid."

Keffa shifted uncomfortably near the fire. I didn't need to explain that the wood fae feared the wraith fae invading our lands.

"We passed through a village on the edge of the forest, the homes in the trees decorated with lights for the celebration. I stopped our caravan at one inn that appeared more beautiful than the others, a table of sweet squash pies there for the offering. As Baelynn, the guardsmen, and I enjoyed the pies and music, there were two wood fae sisters serving us. The inn was their father's. He talked to Baelynn, while his daughters did the serving. But I found it peculiar that one sister didn't look like a wood fae."

"How do you mean?" asked Bozlyn, his intensity more earnest as I told the story.

"She had the white hair"—I touched my own hair trailing over my shoulder— "and the violet eyes of a moon fae. But she had no wings."

"A half-breed," commented Soryn.

"Yes. Undoubtedly."

I didn't know if she'd had a different father or a mother from her sister, but the sisters seemed fond of one another of what I'd observed that day.

"As their villagers played music and danced in front of the inn," I continued, "I'd taken to rest near a large oak tree where the white-haired sister leaned and watched the merriment. Her name was Murgha," I remembered.

She was a sweet-faced, kind fae with a soft voice.

"We talked for a time about the harvest, how it had been a good year despite the rumblings of war. She told me their village was likely to leave for a while." I recalled the look of wonder come over her face as she gazed up at the moon shining through the branches of the oak trees. "Then she told me she needed to tell me something though she wasn't sure why. Her eyes went glassy, and she spouted that vision right there."

Bozlyn looked back down at the page. But it was Goll who spoke first when he commanded, "Read it, Bozlyn."

The elder wraith fae cleared his throat then read, "The world will wail for many seasons and many reasons. Sickness, rebellion, and madness will prevail. Then the dark will steal the light, setting the pale world right. The beast will catch the water maid, foiling plans the rebel laid. And the shadow will swallow the secret queen when true evil is freed. This will come to pass, or all will fall. All will fail. And the gods die with the living."

No one said a word, then Soryn huffed a breath. "Well, that sounds promising," he snarked.

Goll shifted away from the fireplace. "Look, we know the gods spout their wills and their woes all day long through oracles. Some come to fruition. Some do not. Some are important. Some are not. Right now, all I'm interested in is packing up and heading to Vanglosa so we can get what we need and then get the hell back here. Morgolith"—he turned to the barrel-chested giant—"you're coming with us. If we have to deal with any of the shadow fae, I'll need you there."

"Yes, Sire."

"Keffa and Soryn, prepare the Culled. Then everyone get some sleep. We ride out early in the morning."

They all grumbled assent and headed for the door. Goll seemed agitated. My need to console him drove me closer to him. Then the doors opened.

"Speaking of oracles," Keffa called back, stepping aside to allow Dalya to walk through the door.

"Good," said Goll more to himself. "Glad you're here," he said tightly with more formality than how he spoke to Dalya in the past.

Dalya sashayed across the room, wearing a thicker fur-lined black cloak. The weather was dipping colder. She bowed elegantly to both Goll and I.

"My king. My mizrah."

"Thank you for coming." Goll stepped closer to me, a hand sliding to my opposite hip. "We'll be journeying into Meerland, and I'll need you to come with us."

Her eyes rounded for a moment, then she glanced at me. "Meerland, Sire? For what purpose?"

"That is not your concern. We may need a healer, and I'd like you to be close at hand."

I hadn't known Dalya had the healing gift. Of course, it wasn't uncommon for oracles to have both the sight and the magick of healing. I remembered Vayla again.

"Of course, Sire. Whatever you wish."

"That is all."

"Yes, my king." Her voice seemed softer, almost timid. Then she quickly left.

"Why didn't you tell her why we're going to Meerland?" I asked.

"Because I don't want anyone knowing what we're doing. Only those who need to know."

"Like your Culled?"

He wrapped his hands around my waist, pulling my body against his, gazing intently at me. "The Culled don't need to know either. Those who just left this room are the ones I trust the most."

I toyed with a silky strand of his black hair. "I suppose we're off in the morning to Meerland then."

"The sooner we leave, the sooner we can return to Näkt Mir." He scowled. "And why are you smiling like that?"

"I've never met a beast fae. I'm excited to see a part of the world I never did as a sheltered Issosian royal."

He clenched me tighter. "I don't know if I like that you're excited to meet the beast fae."

"Are you jealous, King Gollaya?" I trailed a finger along his clenched jaw.

"Always." He dipped his mouth to my neck and kissed his way up the column. "I'm jealous of anyone and everyone who garners your attention."

Joy bubbled in my belly at his easy admission. "That's ridiculous. You're jealous of Hava?"

"Yes." More kisses to the other side. I bent my neck for him. "She has the privilege of bathing and dressing you nightly."

"You could take that job if you like."

He lifted his head, those dragon eyes blazing with desire.

When he said nothing, I added, "I believe you told me once that you were king and could do what you liked."

"I did." His hands coasted down my hips. "You would let me dismiss your handmaidens and attend to your toilette?"

I laced my fingers into his hair and curled my hands around his thicker horns, shivering at the thought of him bathing me. "Who wouldn't want a virile king as her handmaiden?"

His smile widened. "I believe it's almost time for bed now, is it not?"

"It is early afternoon." I grinned. "You have some kingly duties you must do first. I heard Keffa mention a guild master from Silvantis requesting to speak to you as we walked into the room."

"No. You misheard." He coasted a hand up my spine and twined my hair around his fist.

I laughed. "I did not."

"Keffa can handle the guild master. Let's go and get your bath."

"Goll. We haven't even eaten dinner yet."

"I prefer to eat you first. Then we'll have trays sent up."

I squeezed my thighs at the thought of that.

"Come." His nostrils flared before he stepped away. He took my hand and led me toward the door. "We'll be sleeping in tents again tomorrow night, and I want to enjoy you in our bed for as long as I can."

"I suppose I have no choice in the matter," I teased.

"Your king commands, Mizrah." He stopped at the door, cupping my cheek. I leaned into him. "Will you deny your king?" He pressed closer, his eyes fiery blue and hungry.

A thread of vulnerability whispered in his voice, his expression expectant and bracing, as if I would deny him.

Smiling, I murmured, "Never." Then we went to his bedchamber and made the best of the afternoon and the night.

I'd never tell Hava, but he was a far more attentive handmaiden than any I'd ever had.

CHAPTER 33

Goll

I couldn't describe this emotion I was experiencing as I watched Una on her pale Pellasian mare talking and laughing with Pullo who was describing how the beast fae chose to live, which was very different than the rest of the civilized world. Tierzel watched and listened from Una's other side.

When any male held Una's attention, my initial reaction was annoyance. But at the moment, I felt something entirely different. The joy on her face, the leisurely way she spoke to Pullo and Tierzel about the nomadic habits of the beast fae, and her relaxed demeanor among my warriors gave me such pleasure I hadn't realized I'd craved it.

I'd wanted this moment to come. To see this harmony of Una in my world. For she did belong here. There was no mistaking it.

She looked more natural as my mizrah than any wraith-born could have. Draped in the gray winter cloak Hava had made for her with the white Meer-wolf trim, slits cut for her wings, she guided her horse among my warriors like she was their leader, not me.

Truth be told, they were likely more devoted to her than me. If a threat came upon us, they'd defend her first, which is exactly how I'd want it. Even Soryn, who kept snapping his gaze back to check on her.

"She is making friends quickly, isn't she?" Keffa commented from next to me.

"She is."

"And the king seems content with her," Keffa noted with a touch of wistfulness. "I am happy for you."

He kept his gaze forward, but the tightness at his one good eye revealed the tension in his body. And his mind and heart.

"I am sorry I could not save her, Keffa." We rarely spoke of Vayla, but I knew that the recent revelation with Una had brought her to the forefront of his mind.

He gave a sharp shake of the head. "No reason to be sorry, Goll."

He often used my given name when we were alone or just with Soryn. He'd been a mentor to me growing up, like a kind uncle. Since my father saw me as nothing more than a nuisance as a child, I'd always find my way to the training yards where Keffa would teach me, spend time with me.

"That time has long passed," he added. "And the gods do as they will."

After I'd killed my father, rallied my allies, and freed Keffa from the dungeon cell where my father had left him to rot, we had found Vayla's corpse. I'd never imagined she'd been kept next to Una or they'd ever had an encounter. Still, it seemed prophetic that they had. Divine.

"She gave her last bit of magick to Una before she died." I'd already told him this before we left Näkt Mir and exactly what Vayla had said to Una in the dungeon. He'd deserved to know. Still, I felt the need to remind him. "What a beautiful gift that was."

He smiled then, still focused on the road ahead. "That was my Vayla. Ever giving to others. Even when they didn't deserve it. Though your mizrah did deserve it."

"Truth, Keffa."

"I am glad to know they were together in the end, and she wasn't alone when she walked into the afterworld."

We rode on in silence for a while. The sound of Una's laughter along with Hava's floating back to us when Pullo made some sort of grand gesture with his hands as he told a wild story. His best friend, Tierzel, laughed shyly next to Una. Most assuredly, Pullo was telling yet another tale about the unruly and rough beast fae she would soon meet.

Keffa chuckled at their laughter. "If my Vayla died placing those runes upon your mizrah's head, then she is indeed meant for you. Meant to unite our kingdoms."

A swelling of absolute certainty filled my body. "What of the era of night? The need for Northgall to suppress the moon fae into submission?"

I was certain that Keffa had never believed that old adage as my father had. Or not entirely. But he'd never spoken of it, even when I'd set out to defeat the moon fae in our long, brutal war.

"I believe the era of night begins with a wraith king taking a moon fae as his mizrah. As his mate." He finally turned to look at me.

I didn't deny that she was my god-given mate. I knew it down to my bones.

"It may be our time to rise, to *lead*, Gollaya. But that does not mean that we need stomp them beneath our feet as your father had planned to do."

I nodded tightly. "Agreed, old friend. With good warriors at my side, I know that we will not go astray."

Finally, he looked ahead again. "And with a female like Una at your side, you will never fall."

I couldn't agree more, but I still couldn't admit how much she meant to me. Not even to Keffa.

Perhaps it was because I'd not known this depth of emotion for another fae, not since my mother. After she died, I'd smothered any need for affection. For love. I believed that as long as I garnered the loyalty of my Kel Klyss and remained strong as their king, I would be satisfied with friendship and brotherhood.

I was wrong. My desire for Una burrowed so deep. I craved her smiles, her scent, her laughter, and yes, by the gods, her love. I knew I didn't deserve it, but selfish bastard that I am, I still wanted it.

I watched her riding astride like the wraith fae females do, her hair braided intricately into one long rope down her back, falling between her glorious wings. My heart paced faster. Simply gazing upon her made me ache with longing to have her in my arms. She was so dear to me it was terrifying.

Soryn gave a sharp whistle, halting the caravan from the front of the line. We'd passed Belladum yesterday. It was a larger settlement of wraith fae. While I knew that they would welcome me and my Culled, I'd half expected some of them to hiss or glare at the new mizrah. Though it had been five years ago and they'd rebuilt, her father had attacked and killed many in Belladum. While they'd been wary of her, there had been more smiles and words of welcome to her than anything else.

But that was my people. Not the beast fae.

Keffa and I stirred our mounts into a gallop to meet Soryn at the head of the caravan, the pointed tents of Vanglosa in the distance beyond.

When I pulled to a stop next to Soryn, he said, "They're already waiting for us."

Though we were still a few leagues away, I could see across the wide plains where several beast fae stood in a semi-circle outside their village. Some sat upon their Meer-wolves, some stood, but all of them stared directly at us.

"Of course, they are," I said. "They'd have known we crossed out of Belladum into Meerland from one of their scouts."

We never bothered sending emissaries to the beast fae if we had need for any dealings with them, which was rare. They'd only turn them away with a warning. When we'd sent word that King Connall of Issos had attacked Belladum so many years ago and we were invading in retaliation, their arrogant lord had said, 'You worry about your own, not us. If the king dares to come here, we'll kill him and all his warriors, then feed them to our wolves.'

That was the last time we'd had any communication with the lord of the beast fae.

"Slow and steady," I commanded then turned back to find Una. She was flanked by Pullo and Tierzel on one side, Ferryn and Meck on the other. Hava was now riding behind her with the rest of the Culled surrounding them. "Remain in your current positions."

Then we marched ahead as one, directly across the open plain toward Vanglosa. None of those standing and sitting upon their wolves, waiting for us, were the beast lord. But I did recognize his warrior chief, Bezaliel, as we drew closer.

He stood at the center of them, his bare arms crossed, displaying his many demon runes across his dark bronzed chest. As was their way, he wore only a skirt made of rough hide. With winter approaching, some of them wore boots and deerskin cloaks, but not Bezaliel.

He stood to his mighty height, as tall as Soryn or me, his four, spiraled horns curling back, a wider rack on his head than most. Because he wore no boots, his pelt of fur that thickened at the bottom of his legs and the tops of his clawed feet was exposed. His long tail, covered in a brown felt, the tip tufted with fur, twitched behind him with agitation. His pelt thickened along a line at the center of his abdomen, disappearing beneath his leather skirt.

"Fucking beast fae," whispered Soryn under his breath, no doubt irritated that Bezaliel refused to wear even a shirt or a cloak in these wintry temperatures. I could smell snow in the air.

"We can hear you, chief," Bezaliel called in his deep voice. He knew that Soryn was my second and leader of the Culled. "You can all stop right there."

My warriors did, but I continued to advance slowly. They wouldn't do anything to me. They knew if they tried, I could use feyfire to annihilate any threat. And though the beast fae were a wilder species, they were by no means stupid.

"We need counsel with Lord Redvyr."

When Bezaliel did not answer, his gaze roaming behind me to Una and her handmaiden, I let him take it in. He knew I wouldn't bring my mate or vulnerable females on a violent quest.

After another moment, he called back, "Haslek! Tell Lord Redvyr he has visitors requesting permission to treat with him."

The beast fae with darker skin, pelt, and tail turned and ran back into the cluster of tents of Vanglosa. From here, we could see no one else milling around the tents. Not unusual. They would've told everyone to stay inside and out of our eyesight while they determined if we were a threat.

No sound but the cold wind blowing across the open plain accompanied us while we waited. I looked back at Una, finding her examining the beast fae with wide-eyed curiosity. When she caught my attention, she smiled, excitement glowing in her violet eyes.

The messenger returned quickly enough, running directly to Bezaliel and whispering something in his ear. Bezaliel nodded and then addressed me. "The wraith king may enter with two of his guard."

"Goll," said Una, pulling my attention back to her.

She didn't need to say a word. We'd had a lengthy discussion last night in our furs at the encampment outside Belladum. She demanded to be with me when I spoke to the beast lord. If they refused our help, she insisted it was her purpose to be there to convince him to aid us.

I wasn't even sure they'd have any idea where or how to find this second text, but the vision she'd had in her book clearly stated it would be among the beast fae clans.

I nodded at her then turned back to Bezaliel, who now scowled. "I must bring my mizrah with me. And because I do, I'll need to bring more warriors."

I didn't need to add that I'd only bring her inside with ample protection. The beast fae were as protective of their females as we were.

Bezaliel's yellow eyes coasted back to Una, his expression softening with curiosity. After a moment, he said. "Six guards. Follow me. Leave the horses."

He turned and walked back into the village of Vanglosa, the other beast fae turning with him.

"Keffa, Soryn, Pullo, Morgolith, Meck, and Ferryn." I dismounted then helped Una. The others flanked us as we walked into Vanglosa.

Just like any village made of brick and stone, Vanglosa was organized into sections, separating workspaces from the residential tents toward the back of the encampment.

The blacksmith's shop was little more than a hide covering with open sides for full ventilation—a giant iron stove and anvil, metalworks dangling from hooks overhead. Next was an even larger tent with an open front revealing small iron stoves over open pits, the smell of bread and roasted meat wafted from their kitchens.

An open area between tents was set up for curing hides. At the moment, several red deer pelts were staked and spread wide on upright poles, tools left on small tables, abandoned obviously when we strangers entered their village. They were likely bulking up on furs and hides for the winter months.

While Vanglosa was their settlement most of the year, they'd be packing up soon enough for their winter farther to the southeast.

As we came closer to the center of the village where their tents were clustered closer together, I knew that we were nearing what they called the kella'mir. The home's heart. It was where all assemblies of importance took place in a beast fae community—mate unions, death pyres, birth celebrations. The beast fae were few in number compared to the wraith fae and the shadow fae, who lived wholly apart from the rest of us in the Solgavia Mountains.

While I didn't communicate often with the beast fae, I knew their population remained low. For whatever reason, they didn't multiply like other fae. Possibly the curse that had been put on them years ago that gave them a more beastly appearance and left them with only the magick of heightened, animalistic senses and strength. But every clan celebrated each new birth at their kella'mir.

And that is where the beast lord of Vanglosa was waiting as we walked into the open circle. He sat upon a dais beneath a giant oak tree. His black Meer-wolf, one of the biggest beasts of their kind I'd ever laid eyes on, lounged to his master's right.

Surrounding the dais were fifty or so beast fae males, all the fiercest of his warriors by the looks of their runes decorating their exposed skin. Behind them, there were beast fae women and children peering from around nearby tents. Some had become brave enough to move farther into the open to see who'd come into their village.

Una's hand flinched in mine, her steps slowing. I stopped and turned to her, but her gaze remained fixed and wide-eyed upon the dais.

"It's all right, Mizrah," I murmured low. "He will not hurt you."

She leaned against me and whispered, "His teeth are as long as my arm."

She exaggerated, but he was an ungodly large fae. "Trust me, sweet Una. No harm will come to you."

Her gaze finally lifted to mine. She swallowed hard.

"Do you trust me?" I asked.

"Of course," she answered easily, so fast it made my heart skip a beat.

She trusted me. It nearly felled me on the spot. I squeezed her hand tighter and tucked her close as I led us the rest of the way to the foot of the dais.

"Greetings, Lord Redvyr. We bring you tribute."

Pullo stepped around me toward the raised platform. Redvyr's giant black Meer-wolf rumbled a growl. Pullo slowed his steps and lay the fine short-sword made of black steel on the dais.

His attention wasn't on me or on the gift, however. It was on Una. I'd expected this. No wraith king had ever taken any fae other than our own kind as a mizrah or a mate.

"What an interesting visitor you bring into my home, Goll."

It didn't surprise or offend me that he refused to use my title. Though it was a fact the wraith king held power over all trade in and out of Northgall with the wider civilized world of fae, the beast and shadow fae didn't recognize my authority over Northgall. Not the lands they lived in at least. And perhaps, I didn't hold authority over them. But that didn't mean they weren't prospering from the gains I'd made for Northgall in their stead.

Even now, I could see there were bright, silky fabrics adorning some of the beast fae females. Those were silks traded between Hellamir and Belladum in the Borderlands. I'd managed to create a line of trust between us and some of the more willing captains of trade in Hellamir while in hiding, long before I'd recently ended the war.

It was also another reason that Hellamir remained untouched during the long war with Lumeria. But while the beast fae might benefit in silks and ale, or even Mevian wine, Lord Redvyr would never admit they needed us. Or wanted the help of our kind.

"This is my mizrah, Una Hartstone of Issos."

Murmurs and gasps erupted from the females behind the warriors.

Redvyr grinned, his long canines making him look more feral than fae. He stood swiftly, which had my warriors sliding swords from scabbards, blades zinging into the air.

"Easy, wraithlings," said Redvyr with raised palms, his hands large enough to wrap a fae skull and strong enough to crush it.

Soryn cursed at the insult, calling us wraithlings as if we were small children. We weren't small at all. But the fact was that beast fae were made taller, wider, thicker. They were the largest of faekind.

Redvyr marched toward the steps. His Meer-wolf stood, too, but his master raised a hand to the giant hound. It grunted and settled back onto its haunches, ever vigilant, its silver eyes watching us.

The beast lord lifted the short-sword and unsheathed the blade, noting the wide expanse and polished finish with serrated edging on one side. He grunted then slid the blade back into the scabbard and stepped down, walking toward us in long, easy strides.

I kept my body slightly in front of Una, knowing he wanted a closer look. Still, I needed to warn him so that it was clear. "The only reason I'm allowing you to come this close is because I can explode you into cinders if you make any threat against her."

Redvyr stopped a few feet in front of us, grinning yet again as he asked, "Why would I want to hurt a pretty little moon fae like her?" He crossed his arms and looked his fill, his brow pursing and his tail sliding side to side behind him in a slow, sinuous path. "Black wings," he marveled.

Una still had both her hands clutching my forearm, her body pressed to my side. The fact that she clung to me for safety eased my anxiety about having a giant beast fae standing this close. Redvyr was indeed a massive creature, bigger and wider than any of his own fae males. Or mine.

Redvyr inhaled deeply, his fanged grin widening as he winked at me. "Seems you've been busy, Goll."

I gave my head a sharp shake to warn him off that subject. Una looked up at me in confusion, but I wasn't ready to have this conversation. Redvyr chuckled, apparently getting my point.

"Seems your chief has a taste for the light fae, too," commented Soryn, thankfully dragging everyone's attention away, including Una.

I followed his gaze to Bezaliel, who was standing to one side of the dais, a wood fae female with long dark hair and a rounded belly at his side. He had his own arm possessively about her shoulders.

Redvyr's tail flicked with agitation. "Soon we'll be mounting dryads and siring twiggy trees, I imagine."

"Red," scolded Bezaliel, his arm pulling his mate closer, his frown deepening.

Redvyr huffed out a breath. "Enough niceties, Goll. Why have you come?"

"My lord." Una stepped around me, though I kept a firm grip on one side of her waist. "I have asked Goll to bring me here."

"Have you, my lady?" His expression shifted to amusement, his voice softer. "How can I be of service to the lovely new mizrah of Näkt Mir?"

Fucking hells, he was flirting with her. He liked my mizrah. How could he not?

Even worse, he was making her blush. I clamped my jaw tight, keeping my promise to Una. Last night, I'd told her Redvyr was an ornery, arrogant bastard who likely wouldn't help us. She was convinced she could get him to help us.

And by Vix, she was right. He looked as if he were about to kneel at her feet, and she hadn't said more than a few words.

She clasped her hands demurely before her in a beseeching gesture. "I apologize for us making this journey into your home without warning, but it is of dire importance that we find something very special that I know is here in your realm."

"And what might that be, my lady?"

"It is a special text of some kind. It is god-touched. It would have the lingerings of a god's magick. I know that's a cryptic description, and you're probably thinking I'm mad, but I am certain that—"

"It is here," Redvyr interrupted.

I straightened, taking in his tight expression.

Una inhaled a small gasp, her face brightening with excitement. "It's important that I find the text. Can you show us where it is?"

Redvyr turned to look at his chief, who gave a tight nod in response. Then he looked back at us, his golden eyes glimmering like a predator's at night. "Bezaliel will take you to him."

"Him?" I asked at the same time Una did.

Una then added, "No, my lord. We are looking for words written or left behind by a god or goddess on some sort of text. Not a person."

"Bezaliel," Redvyr called and waved him over rather than explain himself.

The chief was listening to his mate, who was gesturing wildly and pointing at Una. After a brief moment, he nodded, took her hand, and led her toward us.

"Take them to Grindolvek," ordered Redvyr.

"Who is Grindolvek?" I asked, stiffening with wariness.

Redvyr blinked a moment as if he had to think about his answer. It was both fascinating and worrisome. Then he finally answered. "Grindolvek is the god-touched words you're looking for."

Then he whistled to his hound, who leaped off the dais and followed him as he stalked away back into the encampment, his new blade in hand and his tail twitching behind him.

CHAPTER 34

Una

We were told to retrieve our horses but no more warriors and then follow Bezaliel. The chief warrior rode astride a gray Meer-wolf with his mate sitting in front of him, a good pace ahead of us. Our Pellasians didn't like the scent of the wolf and kept a good distance from him.

The chief kept his female protectively in the shelter of his arms, his hand spread atop her rounded belly. I smiled at the tenderness he seemed to feel for her. I also thought it interesting she was the only light fae I had seen amongst them. I wondered, did they welcome her here?

But I was also eager to finally meet her. I hadn't the chance before we began our trek across the open plain from Vanglosa to the copse of trees up ahead. Bezaliel had said there's a stream that runs through the small woodland, and that's where Grindolvek lives. Whoever that was.

Bezaliel stopped his wolf before we reached the trees. He helped his mate down, the wood fae I was sure I'd met once before, then sent his wolf trotting in a large arc around us back toward Vanglosa. The six of us stopped as well and dismounted as Bezaliel and his mate approached.

"Only one or two of your warriors can come with us into the trees," said Bezaliel. "Grindolvek is shy of strangers. He won't come out if there are too many of you. Especially warriors."

Goll turned to Soryn. "You and Keffa with me."

Meck grunted in frustration, but Goll turned to him with a smirk. "I can protect her on my own. No need to worry."

"Yes, sire," said Meck tightly. At his side, his brother also had his jaw clamped tight.

I smiled at them, giving them what reassurance I could. They'd become protective of me as my personal guards.

Pullo was beside Morgolith, glaring at the copse of trees. "We'll wait right here."

With that, we fell in line next to Bezaliel and his mate. I instantly went to her side. "I'm Una."

She turned to me, a bright smile on her face. "I know who you are. We actually met before. I'm Tessa."

"I thought we did. The Fall Solstice in Myrkovir Forest. But that was many years ago."

"Yes." She walked with a protective hand on her stomach.

"How far along are you, if you don't mind me asking?"

"Five months."

"Then you're halfway there," I offered cheerily. "What a blessing."

"We'll see if I'm halfway. I could have seven more if I follow the gestation period of the beast fae."

It was true that it took a full year for dark fae females to give birth following conception rather than ten like it was for the light fae. It had me wondering if it would be the same for me.

"I wonder," I asked, lowering my voice, "how did you come so far north from your home in Myrkovir?"

She glanced at me with hesitation, but then answered, "Our clan moved after the last Solstice celebration and settled just south of the Borderlands. Our high lord wanted to be far from the fighting."

"I see. And your sister? I remember meeting her as well." Her vision under the moonlight still burned bright after all this time.

Tessa hesitated, her gaze focused forward as she said softly, "She's still there. When I met Bezaliel, I wanted to bring her with me, but"—she shook her head—"she didn't want to come."

Recognizing the emotion radiating from her, I said, "You worry for her. You miss her."

"Very much. I understand why she wouldn't want to come and live with a beast fae clan. It's so different from how we grew up. But I couldn't leave my mate, and I worry for her living there on her own."

"But she has your father, right? The innkeeper?"

Her face tightened as she glanced at me. She didn't say anything, only gave me a sharp nod. Then Bezaliel stopped at the line of trees and turned to face us under the shade. He was truly a large fae. I nearly gasped aloud when I'd first seen Redvyr. The beast fae were molded like giants.

"Grindolvek is beast fae," he stated calmly, "no matter what he looks like."

Goll and I glanced at each other curiously.

"So that you understand, his mother went into labor here at this stream. A naiad heard her cries and helped her through the birth. Some exchange of naiad blood transferred to Grindolvek when he was born, changing him." He paused, his frown returning. "His mother died during childbirth, and the naiad who played midwife raised him. He chose to remain and live here away from Vanglosa, though we still count him as one of us."

"When was that?" I asked.

"We aren't sure," he answered gravely. "At least a thousand years ago."

"He's over a thousand years old?" I asked. The fae could live three, maybe even four hundred years, but not a thousand.

"The naiad's blood in him, I imagine." He glanced over his shoulder, then turned back to face Goll. "It would be best if only you and your mizrah go in. The other two can follow at a distance."

"You're not coming?" Goll asked.

Bezaliel pulled Tessa closer in a protective hold. "We will wait here."

His apprehension heightened the tightening tension as we drew closer to the trees.

Goll nodded to Keffa and Soryn, then took my hand as we made our way beneath the canopy of trees. The leaves had begun to turn gold and orange; our feet crunched on the fallen ones on the path. A murmuring brook drew my attention as we stepped into the cool quiet of this small woodland.

It was like an oasis of wooded beauty in the middle of the wide-open plains. Then I felt it. Gods' magick.

I squeezed Goll's hand. "Do you feel it?"

"I do."

It was strong. Like a stream of cool wind, it wound through this place, lacing it with vibrant energy. I felt as if I could breathe it in, my chest heaving from inhaling deep.

"Grindolvek," I called, having stopped before the stream.

While the trees had begun their change for the season, the thick growth of green lilies and vegetation around the water's edge remained as if it were deep summer. The clear stream had a pool deep enough I couldn't see the bottom, but then I saw something swimming beneath the surface. A shimmer of bluish-green sparkle.

It caught a ray of sunlight dappling through the trees and glittered beneath the water before it disappeared. A naiad.

I was wondering if it might've even been Grindolvek when Goll squeezed my hand and tugged me closer to his side.

I looked up to find a being standing beneath a tree that was completely covered in greenery all the way down its trunk. He'd blended in with the moss and ivy-covered tree behind him so well that it took me a moment to see him. Then he stepped to the side and the darker shadow of the woods behind him revealed him more clearly.

He had the shape of a beast fae—a giant with horns, claws, and tail. But he was green. His skin was the color of spring grass, his eyes glittering green jewels in the dark. He wore only a skirt made of some sort of brown hide that stopped above his knees. His chest and arms bore no runes of any kind.

Grindolvek stepped from the shadows and stared straight at me. What I'd thought was decorative ivy winding in his hair now appeared a part of him, molding to his temples and down his face along his hairline, trailing down his throat. He looked like a naiad or dryad where the forest had woven itself into his flesh. His expression remained placid and unthreatening, yet he walked directly until he caught sight of Goll moving in front of me.

Grindolvek stopped, glancing at Goll then back at me. "You're the one."

His voice was a soothing rasp as if he didn't use it often.

I felt the others glancing around curiously, but I gently pushed Goll to the side, saying, "He won't hurt me." Then I looked back at Grindolvek. "Yes," I told him. "I'm the one. Do you have the words that I need?"

He inhaled a sharp breath, and then all at once, his green skin lit up as if a lantern shone from inside him. Keffa made a surprised sound behind me, but all I could do was stare. In dark lettering, words swam beneath his skin, lit up by some internal light.

"Gods below," muttered Keffa.

For a moment, I couldn't speak, absorbing the fact that the words were in his blood. Grindolvek simply watched me curiously.

He stared wide-eyed, looking more like a child, even in his giant body. "I've been waiting for you. I haven't given the words to anyone else, as the Goddess of the Wood instructed."

"Elska gave you these words?" I asked, incredulous.

He nodded. "She gave them to me at birth. But she has visited my dreams. She wants you to have them, the dark fae lady with white hair. Then my burden will be gone."

Yet again, I marveled at this description. I was born moon fae, a royal of the highest realm of light fae. Yet I'd been obviously marked by the dark fae world. Apparently, it wasn't all for nothing. This was my purpose.

"I don't understand," I said. "How am I to get the words you have for me?"

"You must drink them," he said simply.

Goll growled, "She is *not* drinking your blood."

Grindolvek's otherworldly gaze drifted to Goll. "She must."

Goll turned me to face him, his scowl deep. "You cannot drink the blood of another creature like that. It could be poisoned or diseased." He shook his head with a sharp shake. "I won't allow it."

Smiling, I reached up my hand and placed my palm on his cheek, recognizing his outrage as fear for me. His stiffened posture relaxed at my touch.

"Goll, this is what the goddess wants. What the gods want. I won't disobey them." Then I tiptoed so my face was closer to his. "We must trust in them. After all, they brought us together. This can't be wrong."

"I don't like it," he growled.

"It does not matter what you like," said Grindolvek, his voice vibrating with magick.

Suddenly, I was no longer next to Goll but standing a mere foot from Grindolvek like I'd vanished in one place and appeared in another. My vision was hazed with a film of green.

Goll bellowed near the stream, "Una!" Feyfire burst to life in his open palms as he spun around, looking for me.

His voice sounded so far away, but he wasn't far across the clearing. Everything looked strange through the green filmy netting that seemed to envelop me.

Keffa and Soryn put their backs to Goll as the flash of a green-limbed creature sped past Soryn and slashed across his face then disappeared up a tree. Soryn yelled and growled upward, swiping the air and grabbing nothing.

Another flash of a naiad, this one hit Keffa in the knee as it swept past. Goll shot a blast of feyfire which hit nothing but a bush that burst into flame. A wing of water swept out of the stream dousing the burning bush.

I stepped toward them, but Grindolvek grabbed my arm. "They won't hurt them. Come with me." Then he let go of me, turned, and disappeared into the grove of trees. "This way," he called back calmly.

"Una!" cried out Goll, all while he, Soryn, and Keffa fought the extraordinarily fast and slippery naiads whose laughter echoed from the canopy. Goll shot another stream of feyfire toward the branches.

Then I saw Pullo, Meck, and Ferryn appear, blades drawn and savage expressions.

I realized the naiads had somehow made me invisible, hiding me with their magick behind this filmy shield.

Sighing, I followed Grindolvek down a narrow path that wound along the stream and into an open glade completely covered by foliage above us. Even though the trees lining the woodland were dropping leaves for autumn, those on these trees remained green and thick. It was his home, kept unnaturally fresh and cool and green as a naiad's home would be.

Against a thick trunk, there was a bed of the giant lily leaves that grew along the bank of the stream. The leaves were flattened, as it was apparently where he slept. But Grindolvek stopped in the middle of the space that was his home and sat cross-legged. I followed and did the same, facing him.

For the first time since we'd stepped into his small world, Grindolvek smiled, his fangs curved and sharp, all of his teeth serrated like a dryad or naiad.

"You are very beautiful," he said. "You are a unique creature." His gaze skimmed to my wings.

Surprised, I let out a little laugh, taking in the green hue of his skin, the jeweled glitter of his eyes. "You are as well."

"I am," he agreed without boast but with honesty, that childlike candor making me smile yet again.

Without any warning, he raised his arm, dipped his head, and sank his fangs into his forearm. He then lifted it away and held out his arm to me, now dripping blue blood, the color of dark fae blood, not green like a naiad's. Words still slipped beneath his skin like living creatures.

"How much do I need to drink?" I asked.

"That has never been told to me in my dreams," he answered frankly. "I imagine as long as the gods tell you to."

Scooting forward, I held his arm and dipped my head, opening my mouth over the wound, the metallic tang of his blood sharp on my tongue. Then a whirlwind of whispers filled my mind, and I sensed nothing at all. Only the whispers of the gods.

A blurry vision of Elska, beautiful in a green dress, long brown hair blowing in a silent wind. She stared directly at me, her eyes glittering green stars as she smiled. "The faithful shall win. The faithful shall defeat death and live such sweet lives." She held out a golden chalice to me, filled with blue blood. "The offering shall fill your soul and seal your path toward righteousness."

The blood burned its way down my throat, racing wildly through my body. I snapped away from Grindolvek's arm, screaming up to the canopy of trees. The green film vanished from my eyes and from around my body as I slipped away into darkness and pain.

CHAPTER 35

Goll

“**I**’ve brought you something to eat,” said Dalya.

My tent was dim in the light of a single lantern. I’d been sitting vigil at Una’s side. I didn’t lift my gaze at Dalya’s approach, still holding Una’s hand and willing her to wake. “I’m not hungry.”

The naiads had attacked us for half an hour then suddenly disappeared. I’d heard Una scream and followed the sound down a narrow path, finding her unconscious and alone. The sight had crippled me with fear, that I hadn’t been able to protect her.

For a moment, I’d actually wondered if Grindolvek was the one Dalya had warned me of. But when we’d brought her back to the encampment, Dalya ensured me Una was only sleeping and all her vitals were normal.

Dalya sighed then rounded to the other side of our bed of furs. She knelt next to Una and placed a hand on her heart.

“Well?” I snapped, unable to control my distemper.

“She’s still fine, my king.”

“If she was fine, she would be awake.”

"She is resting from her ordeal. She came in contact with the god-touched. That would cause anyone to lose consciousness."

"For this long?" That had been yesterday.

I'd carried her back to the encampment, assuming she would awaken by nightfall. But she hadn't. We were now well into the following morning.

"She is not harmed in any way," Dalya assured me, though it did no good. "She simply needs to rest."

I turned Una's hand in mine so that I could see the new runes the gods had etched into her skin. I trailed my finger over the delicate markings that meant *guardian* but in the female form. *Nurturer and protector* in one.

She bore the same symbols on the other wrist, the runes now encircling both. I could see now that once she ingested the final text, the runes would complete the circle around her wrist.

The markings were a blessing of the gods and a blessing to me. Lumera didn't mark the moon fae. As far as I knew, Elska had never marked the wood fae. It was Vix and Solzkin and the lesser gods of the demon fae who marked us with rites of passage.

What rite of passage was my dear Una crossing?

And the fact that her first marking had etched into her skin after I'd taken her as my mizrah, as my mate, had not slipped past me. It wasn't only these words that were sealing Una with dark fae magick. It was our union.

It was us.

I reached out and cupped her cheek, stroking her silky skin with my thumb. I needed her to come back to me or this ceaseless worrying would never go away.

"You love her." Dalya's whispered words filled the space between us.

I glanced up to find tears in her eyes, emotions of wonder and a touch of fear shining back at me. I didn't understand why Dalya would be frightened. Perhaps some vision of hers that I didn't want to hear right now. I didn't care what the gods said through her at the moment. I simply wanted Una back.

I refused to respond. When I admitted as much, it would be to Una herself first.

"I'm sure you will love the child as well."

I glanced up sharply at Dalya. She smiled.

I'd noticed the change in Una's scent before we'd left Näkt Mir. Or rather, the additional scent—a woodsy spice beneath her own summer floral aroma. Apparently, Redvyr had as well. Thankfully, he hadn't mentioned it when I shook him off at our meeting in Vanglosa.

We were now camped a short span away. Redvyr had given us permission to stay within his lands while Una recovered.

"Does she know yet?" Dalya asked.

The light fae weren't born with the same heightened senses as us. But Una might already be aware of subtle changes in her body. I'd noticed she hadn't been eating as much, and she was sleepier than usual.

"I'm not sure. I was waiting for her to tell me."

The truth of it was that I was terrified. Would Una no longer want me in her bed if she knew she was with child? I knew she cared for me, but I'd been adamant that my goal in getting her here was to bear my heir. Would she reject my attentions, my affection, my company, now that I'd put a child in her womb?

For most wraith fae, and especially for kings, the mizrah typically left the king's bed and went away to have their child. That was because many wraith kings did not bond with their mizrahs beyond making wraithlings. The thought of Una being anywhere but close to my side turned my insides to acid.

Dalya reached out to place a hand on Una's forehead. That's when I noticed some bruising on Dalya's wrist.

"What is that from?" I nodded at her arm.

She quickly pulled her hand back and tucked the sleeve longer to cover it up. "My own silly mishap. I hit it against the coal stove in my tent."

I frowned. "How—?"

Then Una mumbled something, stealing my attention back to her. Her eyes fluttered open and landed on me.

"Thank the gods," I muttered. "*Finally.*"

She smiled. "Goll." Her voice was hoarse from disuse.

I fell onto my knees and cupped her face in my hands, pressing my forehead to hers. I sensed more than heard Dalya leaving the tent.

"What's wrong?" she muttered, lifting a hand to my shoulder.

"I've been so worried," I admitted freely, my heart pounded as the relief coursed through my veins. I lifted away to look at her, to drink in her beautiful face. "How do you feel?"

She smiled brighter. "I feel amazing. There's more magick living inside me." There was pure joy in her voice.

"Yes, I can sense it," I told her, my voice shaking with emotion. With relief. "Just as I did at Dragul Falls."

She struggled to sit up.

"You need to rest." I tried to urge her back down to the bed.

"I don't want to rest."

"Una—" I pulled her into my arms and hugged her close, breathing in her lovely scent.

I couldn't tell her how afraid I was that she'd never wake, that I'd allowed her to come near to deathly harm.

She pulled me down to the bed. I gave in and spread out beside her, holding her to me, kissing the crown of her head.

"It's all right," she said soothingly, brushing her small hand along my back.

I huffed out a laugh. "Only you, Una." I kissed the crown of her pretty head again, inhaling that drugging scent that was all her own. "Only you would try to soothe me after you were the one injured."

"I'm not injured. I felt pain at first. But now, I feel wonderful."

She lifted up on top of my body, propping herself up on hands she'd placed on my shoulders, and stared down at me. She was wearing a winter nightgown, but it still revealed her beautiful figure beneath. The feyfire I'd lit in a brazier, wanting my own flame to give her warmth instead of the blue-coal, gilded her in golden light, limning the slender slope of her neck and perfectly carved face in such heartbreaking beauty that I lost my breath. My heart leaped at the sight of her, thinking of that old tale of Näkt and Lumera.

"What are you thinking right now?" she asked, her hair sliding over her shoulder to drape across my chest. Her nightgown slipped off one shoulder, revealing my bite mark.

"I was thinking of the old demon myth about the god Näkt and Zarrah and Lumera."

Her pretty brow pursed into a frown. "The one where Näkt betrayed Zarrah and slept with Lumera?"

My hands roamed to her hips, loving the feel of her warm flesh beneath my fingertips, ensuring me she was truly all right.

"No," I answered. "The one where Näkt refused the advances of Lumera. I was looking at you and wondering how in the world he had the willpower to deny her." I stroked a clawed hand through her tousled hair.

She laughed, dragging my attention back to her face. She sat up on my abdomen, her palms on my chest. "That is not how the story goes. Näkt seduced Lumera when his mate Zarrah had gone to seek a blessing for her unborn child. He fell so in love with Lumera that he kept her in the meadow bed he once shared with Zarrah. Then Zarrah returned and died of a broken heart, scattering her body into the night sky. In his shame, Näkt followed her there, betraying Lumera and leaving her broken-hearted as well."

I grinned, roaming my hands from her hips to her ribcage, then back down to rest on her hips. "Our story is different. It was Lumera who was in the wrong. Not Näkt."

"Of course not." She rolled her eyes, and I had the sudden urge to kiss her. But I felt the need to be extraordinarily gentle with her after her ordeal with Grindolvek.

She added softly, "It would never be the man's fault that he slept with two women, betrayed his mate, then betrayed his new lover and lost both of them."

I laughed, wondering whose version was more accurate. Likely, somewhere in between.

"But you know, our story ends there," she said, brow pursing like she was puzzled. "At Zarrah's death and the birth of her daughter, Mizrah. We have no tales of her." Her curiosity shone on her face. "Will you tell me the next part? Why your people revere Mizrah so much that her name has become a title for the king's…" When she paused, excitement pulsed in my blood as I wondered if she'd come to the same conclusion I recently had. Then she licked her lips and added, "The king's companion."

"Mizrah was the child Zarrah bore right before her death."

She slid down to sit on my thighs, listening, her gaze on me while she toyed with the lacings of my trousers.

Frowning, I continued. "Mizrah fled into the mountains to find solace in the night, to mourn the loss of her parents alone."

"Then what happened?" she asked, no longer toying but actually unlacing my trousers.

"Una," I warned. "You need to rest."

"And I told you," she said, reaching into the open fall of my pants and wrapping her slender fingers around my cock. "I'm not tired."

I grunted, unable to keep from rocking up into her gentle stroke.

I splayed my hands at the top of her thighs. "We shouldn't do this right now," I said, even while I slid my palms higher up her thighs, hiking the hem of her gown higher.

"What happened next?" she asked, stroking my cock which was blocking my view of her cunt.

"Vix heard Mizrah's cries and he found her alone in the mountains."

Though I could only see the seductive stroke of her hand around my girth, I slid one hand higher up her thigh. Finding her slickness with my thumb, I spread it in a soft circle around her clitoris.

She made a low moan and rocked against my slow strokes. My cock hardened at the sight and sound of her, so lush and needy. My willpower to be good and not ravish her vanished.

"Vix fell instantly in love with the maiden," I told her. "He cared for her, fed her, bathed her, held her."

I paused to lick the pad of my thumb before returning it to its purpose, her mouth falling open in silent pleasure. Reaching up with my free hand, I untied the shoulder ribbon of her gown till it fell away, revealing one pink-tipped breast. Mounding it gently, I rubbed my thumb gently around her nipple till it hardened.

"Vix made her his lover. He marked her with his bite and kept her as his mate, siring four sons on her."

She writhed sweetly on top of me, her scent hardening my cock even more, her breath coming faster at her desire rose.

"Each of their sons became the first of the dark fae." I reached up, gripped her gown with my clawed hands and ripped it apart, flinging the scrap off the bed. I wrapped my hands around her full hips. "They had the shadow fae first, then the wraith fae, then the beast, then the earth."

"What happened to the earth fae?"

"They died out long ago," I murmured, hypnotized by her delicate hand handling me with tortuous tenderness.

To my complete surprise, and delight, she lifted onto her knees, giving me a glorious view of her slick quim then she guided my tip to the entrance of her dripping cunt. "Lastly, they had the first of the wraith fae," she said on a sigh as she lowered her body over mine, impaling herself so sweetly on my cock I saw stars.

"Yes," I confirmed, planting my feet wide and gripping her hips tighter to guide her in the perfect, slow rhythm. I couldn't think straight after that.

"And then Vix decided she wasn't enough and collected more concubines," she added mockingly, even arching a brow in taunting censure as she ground her hips on top of me and splayed her hands on my chest.

"No." I lifted her hips and fucked her sweetly, her breasts bouncing with each downward stroke. "He took no other."

"No?" she questioned with that same sarcasm in her voice. Her hands coasted up to my two larger horns where she gripped and held me hard, raising her hips and meeting each of my deep thrusts.

"Fuck, Una," I growled, my eyes rolling back in my head as she held my head down and rode me exactly as hard as I wanted.

Then her voice was close, making me open my eyes. "Vix took no other because his Mizrah was enough."

She leaned in, still gripping my horns in a dominant fashion that had my cock hard as steel, swelling bigger.

"Because they were partners, mates in all ways." Her violet eyes brightened, her black wings glittering in the firelight. "Because their love would have broken into a million shards just like Zarrah. Is that not right, my king?"

"Yes, Una." I groaned miserably, so insanely aroused and enraptured I could barely form words. I thrust up inside her. "You are right—*fuck*—so right."

Then she lowered one breast to my mouth, still holding my horns, her own mouth parted as she panted, her sex soaking my cock. I needed no further encouragement and lifted my head just enough to suck on her taut nipple.

She moaned, her cunt pulsing instantly with an orgasm. I groaned, still suckling her while I pumped deep, trying to drive my emotions into her, and the words I hadn't said but felt suturing themselves into my heart and soul.

It didn't take long before I felt that familiar ecstasy shooting up my spine, locking my limbs as I speared one last time, my head falling back to the pillow as I emptied my seed inside her.

"*Gods*, Una." I grunted, still grinding and spilling inside her.

I had to force myself not to curl my claws into her soft flesh, the tips pricking her generous hips. "I needed you," I confessed only that which I had the courage to tell her at the moment.

I stared in complete bafflement at the fae female I loved.

She leaned close and pressed her elbows on either side of my head, dipping her face to give me a soft kiss. "I know," she whispered against my lips, trailing her tongue along my bottom lip. "I needed you too."

Her eyes told me she might feel the same, but both of us simply stared in wonder, the warmth of our bodies binding us closer, the threads of the moon-binding glowing by the feyfire.

When she lifted her body off of mine, I hissed at the sensation then hauled her into my arms, both of us on our sides to face each other.

We stared in silence for some time. I pushed a stray lock of her hair back off of her cheek.

"Your wraith fae customs," she started quietly, "don't seem to come from Vix. Likely from some greedy king who fancied a younger lover after he became bored with his mizrah." She shrugged, the tip of her wing on that side fluttering. "I'm well aware that not all moon fae kings were faithful to their queens, but we don't hold a tradition where infidelity is expected. It's an odd custom."

"Indeed," I agreed. "Good thing I'm a king and can change customs if I so choose."

She smiled wide, burrowing deeper into my heart. Her words were light while the meaning was not. "Your people might not like you changing customs with a mizrah they don't truly believe in."

It reminded me of the travesty at that dinner back in Näkt Mir. "You let me worry about them." Then I teased her to lighten the mood. "I can promise I'll never get bored if you continue to climb on top of me and ride my cock like that."

She laughed while playfully slapping my shoulder, her blush returning. "Goll!"

"Don't play timid. You weren't so shy a few moments ago."

Her gaze had fallen away from mine. "I was caught in the moment."

"What a moment." I pressed my lips to her forehead. "I want many more like that."

"Be a good king, and you shall have them."

"Be a good king," I repeated, chuckling at her admonishment. "I'll do my best. For you."

Then she snuggled closer, pressing her cheek upon my sternum and wrapping an arm over my waist. For a long while, we simply held one another, her fingers lazily stroking my back while I did the same beneath her wings.

It was like we were in the cave, and I rejoiced in the fact that it had not been a fleeting feeling of the moment. This binding between us was not only still there but growing and tightening like the threads of the most beautiful web.

"You know," she said sleepily, "I don't think she meant any harm, but Dalya offered to help me leave the palace the night of the Rite of Servium."

I sat up and frowned down at her. "She did?"

Una pushed me back down and put her cheek to my chest, patting me. "Like I said, I don't think she meant harm. I think she was just trying to be kind to me."

Rather than anger me, it made me sad. I heaved a sigh. "Dalya did not like that I forced you to be my mizrah. She believed I should've given you a choice."

"You did."

I chuckled. "One that didn't include me pillaging and burning Issos if you refused. She wasn't sure you were the one mentioned in a vision she had for me."

"One about me?" She lifted her head to at me.

"Yes. The one that told me my mizrah would be marked by Vix, and she would help me bring Northgall into an era of power. Of great power."

"Above the moon fae?" There was a spark of sadness in her eyes.

Clenching my jaw, I spoke with honesty, "There is more to that story about Vix and Mizrah. When she was dying, he carried her into the heavens on the back of Silvantis. He promised her that one day she would be avenged for Lumera's betrayal. Lumera's people would pay for it and the dark fae would rise to their rightful place."

"And you believe this? That I am a key to trampling down my own people?"

"I believe you are meant to stand beside me," I answered honestly. "It is not my intention to harm the moon fae. Rather, I'd like us all to live in communion and peace with one another."

For the first time, I felt this to be the truth.

"You'd defy your god?" she asked, quirking her brow.

"You've defied yours." I cupped her jaw and brushed my thumb along the lovely slant of her cheek. "You defied Lumera, coming to Northgall to be my mizrah. And I am not a king with vengeance bearing down on my heart."

No, there was only one force wrapping itself—*herself*—around my heart.

She relaxed in my arms, the tip of her mouth quirking with a smile. "That is good to know." She brushed a hand over my jaw, stroking my cheek, mirroring my touch. Then she pressed a gentle kiss to my mouth before settling her head into the crook of my neck.

I wrapped her tight against me.

"Now, if anyone should try to harm you," I said, thinking of the ending of the feast again, "my wrath would be unstoppable."

Devastation wouldn't begin to describe what I would do to anyone who dared to hurt my Una.

"Quiet now," she beckoned on a yawn. "Sleep, my king."

For once, someone was giving me orders. Because it was her, I happily obeyed.

CHAPTER 36

Goll

Later that afternoon, we dressed to go find food.

"I can smell some tasty meal that Ogalvet's cooking outside," she said, smiling brightly as I helped her into her cloak, slipping her wings through the flaps.

"He is," I smiled down at her. "I asked him to make a hearty soup for you."

"Yum." She pushed past me and outside the tent flap.

I followed. "Meck." I nodded to him. He hadn't left the tent since I'd brought her back.

"Sire." His face flushed with relief when he saw Una. "So good to see you're awake, Mizrah."

"Thank you, Meck," she said with a smile.

Then we walked arm-in-arm toward the nearest campfire.

"Rain soon?" she asked, looking up at the gray clouds covering the sky.

"Snow, I think," I answered as we stopped where Soryn, Pullo, and Hava sat with a few other fae.

A few of the Culled were out hunting, but most milled about our encampment that was situated partway between Belladum and Vanglosa.

"Una!" shouted Hava, hopping up from where she sat quite close to Keffa on a log they'd rolled near the fire. Then she literally flew over to greet her, landing clumsily and too close.

"Easy, Hava," I snapped.

"Sorry!" She stopped herself, seeming about to launch into Una's arms as she always did, and then gripped her hand instead, worry on her face. "Are you well?"

"I'm very well." She beamed, a rosy flush in her cheeks.

She was indeed fine after what I'd thought had brought her near death. I glanced around, looking for Dalya. I needed to apologize for all my growling at her through the night and into today. I'd even accused her of not doing enough to wake her.

"I feel rather glorious actually," said Una with another bright smile.

"Ogalvet!" I called over to him. He stood cooking underneath the open tent.

He nodded, not needing to hear what I wanted, and stooped over his cauldron with a bowl.

"Good to see that you're all right," said Keffa, now standing in our small circle, Soryn beside him. "Your mate was beginning to worry."

"Was he?" Una asked with a shy smile tilting her mouth.

"He even—" Keffa stopped mid-sentence.

I smelled it, too. "What is that?" I turned toward what had caught my, Soryn, and Keffa's attention. Other wraith fae also turned their heads toward the smell and sound.

Suddenly, a shout and another rose into the air from the outer edge of the encampment. We were at the center. Without a word, Keffa, Soryn, and I unsheathed our blades.

"Get behind me!" I shouted to Una. "Hava!"

She knew what I wanted and flapped her bat-like wings to shoot straight up above us. She looked beyond the tents from her height above us where we couldn't see. There was raucous yelling, snarling, and growling, and cries of fae.

"Oh, gods," said Hava.

"What is it?" I shouted impatiently.

"Meer-wolves, Sire. They're attacking!"

"How many?" I called up.

"Three!" she yelled. "No, *four*."

"What in all the fucking hells?" growled Soryn.

"Hava!" Keffa shouted up to her. "Fly to the top of that tree and stay there!" He'd pointed to the tallest tree outside the encampment.

"But, Una," whimpered Hava.

"Go!" I ordered. "Now!"

She would be one less to worry about. Keffa, Soryn, and I circled Una. Then suddenly, Meck and Ferryn were there, swords out.

"Why in all the gods' names would the beast fae send their hounds to attack us?" asked Keffa. "After they helped us only yesterday."

"I don't know," was all I managed to say, the growls and snarls drawing closer as the beasts made their way through camp.

One of the wolves howled with an eerie yip at the end, speaking to his fellow beasts. Una gasped behind me.

"Don't worry, my mizrah," I told her. "I'll turn them to dust before they get too close." I hoped that I could.

My gift of zephilim was a living kind of magick. I could wield it with infinite delicacy or like a pounding hammer. However, it was difficult to use against fast-moving targets, especially when mixed in with those I didn't want to harm. Hence, the reason we were armed and ready.

I'd hoped the beasts would round the corner of the tents one at a time. That way I could destroy them each as they attacked. Of course, my wish wouldn't be granted. And they didn't simply stalk forward. Three came barreling around the corner of the tents, one of them with a severed arm dangling from his snarling mouth. My gut clenched.

"*Etheline!*" I shouted, palm-out, sending a stream of fire from my body directly into the wolf at the forefront, a dark gray beast with black eyes.

The fire hit him and engulfed him from head to tail, but he kept coming, running wildly toward us, still snapping the air with his yellowed fangs. Now he was a weapon of fire barreling closer, a moving inferno coming straight for us.

"Get Una out of here!" I shouted back to the Culled.

I heard her make a sound of distress as one of my warriors carried her away.

"I think you just pissed it off," cried Keffa to my left.

"Something's wrong with them," I bellowed as I raised my sword.

Normal Meer-wolves didn't attack fae encampments. And they would've run in fear at the first sign of feyfire. These weren't, and one of them was literally burning to death as he galloped closer.

Then the beasts were upon us. I slashed through the air at the burning beast who wasn't even writhing in pain as he should be. Keffa and Soryn took the second, and Pullo and Meck went at the third.

I dove and swiveled out of reach as the burning hound twisted and snapped again and again, seeming to grow angrier. Why wasn't this creature dying?

Spinning, I sprinted out of the cluster of the fighting, leading it away and needing to the get the beast alone. As I expected, it chased after me, swiping it's clawed hand at my back, coming so close I felt the heat singe my neck.

"*Etheline*," I whispered to my sword as I continued to run toward the open plain, the wolf fast on my heels.

Flames burst up the black steel of my blade. With a sudden sharp turn, I thrust forward straight between the beast's eyes, the hound impaling himself on my flaming sword. I fell onto my back, the beast gurgling as he toppled onto me, his burning head upon my chest.

Through the dying flames, his glazed, yellow eyes were streaked with black striations. Like he was infected or cursed by something.

"Nihilim," I called, extinguishing the flames.

The wolf was still, his head and body smoking as I shoved my way out from under his stinking carcass.

More shouts drew my attention back to the encampment where I could now see Bezaliel, Redvyr, and two other beast fae fighting the fourth maddened wolf without weapons. Redvyr suddenly leaped onto the animal's back and slashed nonstop at his head and throat with his claws, tearing the wolf apart with his bare hands.

Then a blood-curdling scream filled the air. A feminine one that chilled my blood cold.

"*Una.*"

CHAPTER 36

Una

The terrifying hound as wide as three Pellasian horses combined had black eyes and slobber dripping from its bared fangs. It stalked closer with more caution. He'd lunged too quickly, and Ferryn had stabbed his sword into his eye. The beast had simply jumped back and pawed at his bloody, useless eye for a moment before circling to come again.

There was a sickly tang in the air around the animal. It was a disturbing ripple of negative energy, but not from disease. Or not from a natural one. Something magickal. Something evil.

Ferryn had been trying to reach the horses, to get us away from camp while Goll and the Culled killed the hounds. But the hound caught up to us first.

"Stay behind me," Ferryn ordered.

I didn't need a reminder. My entire body trembled at the sight of the slavering creature intent on killing and eating us. Without warning, the hound leaped again.

I screamed and shot straight up into the air, a tree's length off the ground. With shock, I realized I was flying. My wings had instinctively taken me high and out of danger. Ferryn hadn't noticed as he stabbed the beast before it whipped around and swiped a claw across his shoulder.

"No!" I gasped but my wings held me high.

Ferryn then lunged with his sword, slashing at the creature's throat. It yelped and circled back. Blood dripped from Ferryn's shoulder, the armor torn.

Then Goll, Soryn, Keffa, and also several beast fae ran into the fray. Goll had seen me, as had the others, before they went to help Ferryn. My wings began to tire, slowly lowering me as they finished off the maddened hound.

Goll turned and ran for me right as my feet touched the ground. He pulled me into his arms, burying his face in my neck.

"I flew, Goll."

"I know, my sweet."

That endearment warmed my heart, even more than feeling my body take flight, true flight, for the first time since my natural-born wings had taken me across Lumeria into Northgall years ago.

"The magick has given me back my gift." Joyful tears pricked my eyes.

"I'm so happy for you," he murmured, continuing to hold me for another minute before pulling away. "Are you all right?" He cupped my cheek gently.

"Yes."

With a tight nod, he said, "Come."

He kept me close as we joined the others around the carcass.

"Oh, no." I ran to Ferryn, who was holding his arm. Meck was now beside him, checking the injury on his shoulder. "You must get to Dalya," I told him.

Ferryn's expression widened with surprise as I approached and inspected the injury.

"It's fairly deep. You need healing. Quickly."

His yellow gaze was more intense than usual, his pupils dilated from the stimulus of the attack, darkening his eyes. He smiled warmly. "Do not worry about me, Mizrah. I will heal quickly from this. I've had worse."

"Don't argue with me. Meck"—I turned to his brother who was staring at Ferryn with severe concern—"take him to Dalya. She needs to work on the wound right away."

"Yes, my mizrah."

Then I turned to join Goll and the others around the felled beast. Goll pulled me by the waist into his side.

"You thought we'd sent an attack on you," Redvyr was saying.

"It had crossed my mind," admitted Goll, "which made no sense since you'd already helped us find Grindolvek."

Redvyr's face and chest was spattered with the blue blood of a wolf, his claws dripping with it. I would've recoiled if not for the fact that our fae didn't look much better. Goll had somehow remained unscathed.

Bezaliel stared at the dead Meer-wolf. "They were diseased—crazed. Meer-wolves don't attack encampments."

"Yes," I spoke up. "I could smell something was wrong with them."

"You could smell it?" asked Goll.

"Like bad magick," I tried to explain more fully. "Dark magick. It's still lingering in the air here," I noted, shivering at the feel of it. "You don't sense it too?"

There were a few questioning looks. Goll frowned and shook his head.

Redvyr's expression was grim. "We've seen some strange things of late. This is merely one of them."

"What kinds of things?" asked Keffa.

Redvyr shared a look with his chief. When he didn't answer, I asked, "Signs of madness?"

The beast lord rumbled a growl then answered, "Yes. It's usually something or someone coming down from the mountains."

"The Solgavia Mountains," clarified Soryn.

Redvyr nodded. "These creatures must've been there, come down since the weather is changing."

"Goll," I whispered. "The prophecy."

"What prophecy?" snapped Redvyr, his tail twitching. So was Bezaliel's.

Goll relayed quickly how the gods had sent a warning about madness spreading in a vision I'd found back in Issos.

Redvyr shared another look with Bezaliel, who said, "We won't be wintering that far north this year then."

"No," agreed the beast lord. "Perhaps we'll go a little farther east this year. I suggest you return to Näkt Mir, King Goll. Get your pretty mizrah back to safety and out of these wild lands."

With that, he and the other beast fae turned and stalked away.

Goll ushered me back to camp, my mind stewing. Unfortunately, there were two dead wolves in the middle of our encampment, but we couldn't leave while the injured were tended to. Not to mention Pullo reporting that two had died during the attack. There would need to be a funeral pyre for them before we moved on.

"We can't go back to Näkt Mir yet," I told Goll as soon as we were alone in our tent. "We have to go to Solzkin's Heart and find the last text."

When I thought he'd argue with me and bundle me off without listening, he surprised me yet again. "I know."

"You do?" I stepped closer and pressed my hands to his chest, needing to feel his warmth after such a harrowing ordeal.

"I won't ignore the gods, Una. They've set you on this task. It's obvious we're almost there. But we'll be cautious heading farther north to Solzkin's Heart."

"Of course. We're so close."

"I know." He trailed his clawed fingers through my hair then cupped the back of my head. "We'll find it. Then we'll head home where I can keep you safe."

He pulled me close, holding me tight. Despite the danger that seemed to be surrounding us, I felt safe in his arms.

As I walked with Hava to check on Ferryn, my thoughts were a whirlwind.

We'd burned the funeral pyres for the two fallen of the Culled at sunset. One was Pullo's quiet friend, Tierzel. It had hurt to see the usually jovial wraith fae so grim, tears shining in his eyes as we said goodbye to his dear friend.

I'd hugged him after we'd sent him to the afterlife with prayers to Vix. I remembered too well the pain and grief of losing Min so violently. Pullo welcomed my comfort and thanked me for it.

The other wraith fae I didn't know as well. But both had been loyal to Goll and kind to me over the past weeks. Their loss had cut us deeply.

Keffa sang a song about souls finding contentment in the afterworld, meeting other lost loved ones there. It had been somber, but there was another emotion wafting into the air with the lingering darkness from the wolves. Fear.

Goll had told me he'd not seen animals behave in that manner. Meer-wolves were predatory pack animals, but their primary prey was deer and wild hog. They'd only attack a fae when starving and desperate, and he'd never heard of any, not even a pack, attacking an entire encampment. There was indeed something wrong with the beasts.

Sickness, rebellion, and madness will prevail.

The plague—sickness—was already ravaging across Lumeria. This was the first touch of madness we'd seen. But if the oracles were right, and they almost always were, then we'd see more of this madness before it was all through. Not to mention a rebellion awaited. We'd just finished a long, grueling war. Who would want to stir up more trouble while Goll's warriors occupied every city and was also helping to rebuild Lumeria?

Perhaps the rebellion would be one of the shadow fae. Goll and his warriors had said enough times that the shadow fae didn't like the wraith fae. Perhaps one of their kind would go against the wraith king.

"Against Goll."

"What?" asked Hava. "What's against Goll?"

"Oh. Nothing." I pulled my cloak tighter as we wound around the tents, nodding to a group of the Culled around a campfire.

They all respectfully stood and bowed as we passed, and my heart sank a little further. We'd come out here at my insistence. Tierzel and the other Culled had died because of me. A sickening sense of guilt weighed on my heart.

Hava looped her arm with mine and kept close for warmth as we drew nearer to the last tent on the south side of the encampment. That was where we were told Meck and Ferryn were.

"I'm so happy you have your wings back," Hava said softly. "Well, you've had them back for a while, but you know what I mean."

"Yes, Hava. Me, too. Though I will say, I need to exercise them. I could barely hold myself up while Ferryn fought that wolf."

"Well, they did the trick and lifted you to safety. It's wonderful, Una."

"It is," I agreed, hugging her arm and leaning into her, wishing this strange, dreadful feeling would go away. It hadn't left since the attack. Perhaps, it was simply an aftereffect of the trauma.

"All we need is the final god-touched text, and I'm sure I'll get back the other magick I lost," I added.

"Healing magick," said Hava. "A very special kind if it will allow you to cure the plague."

That was my hope. It had me turning my thoughts to my father who, I was certain, was not long for this world. And Baelynn. My heart clenched at the thought of losing my dear brother. I simply couldn't lose him.

I had to find this last text. By the gods, I was certain I'd be able to help my people then. All people who were afflicted. Goll had said there were rumors of the sickness now touching some of the dark fae as well. I was desperate to stop it.

Goll had promised to escort me immediately to Issos and to Valla Lokkyr once we'd found the last of them. He wasn't the tyrant I'd once thought him to be. He could've refused to allow me to go back to Issos. He truly wanted peace between our people, as I did.

As we approached Meck and Ferryn's tent, we heard low voices arguing. I pulled Hava to a stop, noticing Meck and Dalya standing outside the tent. Dalya seemed distressed while Meck whispered loudly.

"That's enough. You should *go*."

I'd never heard Meck sound so angry. He always had an amiable mannerism.

"I'm trying to help," Dalya said with desperation, her eyes swimming with tears under the afternoon sun.

"You've done enough," snapped Meck with fury. "You should *leave*."

A sense of certainty swept through me; he didn't mean the tent. It seemed he wanted her to leave the encampment altogether. How strange.

"Is Ferryn not healing?" I asked, stepping forward.

They both turned sharply in surprise. I didn't want to continue to eavesdrop on what seemed a heated, private conversation, but if Ferryn's condition was worse than we thought, I needed to intervene. My innate need to heal, despite no longer having that magick, still beat strong and true deep in the heart of me.

Meck's expression shifted back to the docile wraith fae I was accustomed to. "Mizrah. It's nothing you need worry about."

I stepped forward with Hava close at my side, though I no longer held her arm. Dalya stared at the ground reverently and held her clasped hands demurely in front of her like always, though I could see they were trembling.

"Of course I'm worried. Ferryn was protecting me when he was injured. Is his wound much worse than we realized?"

I didn't want to accuse Dalya of not having a strong enough gift, but it was a fact that some were more powerful healers than others. Perhaps she didn't have enough magick to heal Ferryn.

"I've done all I can," Dalya said, then dipped a curtsy, glancing at me with something that looked like regret before walking away.

"Meck, let me see him."

A panic swallowed me that Ferryn might've been fatally wounded while trying to protect me. Meck tightened his jaw, looking as if he wanted to protest. But then he opened the flap for me and Hava to step through.

The room was shrouded in blue from the coal burning in a small stove next to the pallet of furs on the floor. As was usual for a fae healing, there were no bandages or dressings put on the wound. It needed open air to the elements while the healing magick worked on the injury.

I frowned as I knelt beside Ferryn, whose eyes were closed. The wound had sealed and seemed almost healed. Completely.

"What's your concern about the wound?" I asked Meck, confused by his exchange with Dalya. I'd expected to find a festering injury.

Meck stood on the opposite side of the bed, his jaw clenched as he stared at his brother. He didn't answer.

"He seems to be healing just fine."

Meck nodded, his gaze still on his twin brother.

Then Ferryn stirred, his yellow eyes blinking open. He smiled when he saw me. "Mizrah," he mumbled sleepily. "You came to see me."

I smiled, my hands clasped in my lap. "I had to be sure you were all right. And I wanted to thank you for protecting me."

"Always," he murmured. "It's my place to keep you safe." He lifted the arm closest to me, the opposite of the wound, and placed his hand on top of mine.

I flinched at the familiarity but realized he must be drowsy from the healing magick, which can have a drugging effect sometimes. Lifting my hand from under his, I patted it then set it beside him on the bed.

"Meck had me worried," I added lightly. "He made me think you weren't healing well, but it seems Dalya's magick is doing the trick."

He chuckled in a way that raised gooseflesh on my arms. "Dalya," he murmured, his eyes glazing a little. They seemed darker than usual, a deeper gold, not the vibrant yellow I was accustomed to.

"Mizrah," said Meck, "he needs more time to sleep and rest."

"Of course." I smiled up at Meck, who wore the amiable expression I knew so well, but there was something in his eyes that concerned me.

"Thank you, my mizrah." Ferryn's speech slurred. "I knew you'd come to me."

"Mizrah," urged Meck.

Hava was at my side, helping me to my feet. Not that I needed it. Hava seemed to want to leave, and I didn't blame her. Meck was acting strangely. Ferryn was, too, but he was under the influence of healing magick. But why was Meck speaking with such anger to Dalya? And now an urgency to make me leave.

"Good afternoon, Mizrah," said Meck, opening the flap and sounding more like himself. "And thank you for coming. We both appreciate your concern."

"Good afternoon." I left with Hava close at my side.

We moved back toward our own tents in silence until we were well away from Meck.

"What was that all about?" hissed Hava. "Why was Meck so angry at Dalya?"

"I don't know. Ferryn is healing just fine. It makes no sense."

"You should tell King Goll."

That was exactly what I did after we'd undressed and crawled under the furs together that night.

"It was just strange. Meck seemed angry with Dalya. But Ferryn's wound appeared to be healing well."

Goll coasted a warm palm up and down my spine. I lay with my head on his chest, my arm draped across his waist.

"Meck is very protective of his brother. They had no father in their lives. Not that mine was any example. But I had Keffa and others like him. Their mother, my mother's sister, moved them to Belladum after they were born here in Silvantis." He paused, seeming lost in thought, but then added, "I believe Meck is simply afraid for his brother. I owe them some extra care as their kinsmen."

I propped my chin on my hands so that I could gaze at him. His dragon eyes glowed silver in the dark of the tent. They were lovely.

"Did you know them growing up?" I asked.

"No. They're younger." He played with a strand of my hair that fell across his chest. "Born when I was away at the Gall Guild. I met them a few times when my mother had them visit her. Before she died. But not after. Not until I'd taken my father's throne and was looking for faithful allies."

"I understand your loyalty, but I didn't like how harsh Meck was with Dalya. I know what it's like to be a healer and unable to heal someone."

He tucked the strand of hair he'd been trailing through his fingers behind my ear. "You're thinking of your father and brother."

I nodded.

"We set off tomorrow for Solzkin's Heart," he said. "I've sent Morgolith ahead with Soryn and Pullo to meet a friend he has in the shadow fae clans. They'll meet us at Solzkin's heart tomorrow at sunset."

"We're that close that we can reach it in one day?"

"We'll take Drakmir. The rest of the Culled will follow." His mouth tipped up in a small smile. "And I'd like to take you somewhere tomorrow before we meet them."

"Where?"

"It's a surprise." He cupped my jaw and stroked the pad of his thumb across the apple of my cheek. "Now, get some sleep."

Sighing, I snuggled closer and tried to fall asleep, though my mind wandered, envisioning Meck's hard expression and Dalya's tear-filled eyes.

CHAPTER 37

Goll

It felt good to be on Drakmir's back, soaring through the clouds, holding Una close to me. The farther we'd ventured toward shadow fae territory, the stronger my fears grew. It wasn't the shadow fae I was frightened of. An unknown dread grew larger the farther we marched onward in this quest.

Finding the second text had been easier than I'd thought. Even while I'd nearly come out of my skin to protest Una drinking Grindolvek's blood. I knew she was right in following the gods' path, but it didn't make it any easier.

But even that wasn't what had my mood darkening these past few days. The attack by those hounds was only part of it. There was something I couldn't see ahead, some ominous portent in our future.

Before we left this morning, I'd checked on Ferryn to be assured he was well enough to travel with the rest of the camp toward Solzkin's Heart. Then I'd spoken with Dalya. I wanted to be certain she was all right as well after what Una had told me last night. I needed to assure Dalya that any falter in Ferryn's healing wasn't her fault, but the gods. She assured me that Meck was overly concerned for his brother and she was fine.

I also told her I'd want her to scry at base camp tonight. I hoped she could see what was coming for me. Something I apparently could not.

"This is wonderful." Una leaned against my chest and called back to me, "I missed Drakmir."

"You should tell him so."

"I already did." She laughed.

"You've connected telepathically again?"

She smiled over her shoulder. "He invited me in this time."

"What did he show you?"

"This, actually." She spread her arm to the sky. "He showed me the heavens and the earth below."

"That means he missed you, too. He wanted you to ride him." He'd done the same to me often enough.

It warmed my heart that she had a connection to Drak like I did. It was another sign that she was mine, and I was hers.

"Oh, look, Goll. A castle!"

"That's where I'm taking you."

Drakmir knew as well. I'd shown him mind-to-mind where we were going. He knew this place well enough. He glided lower and circled Windolek Castle, my mother's home and the one I grew up in away from my father at Näkt Mir.

Instantly, the sight of it filled me with both melancholy and joy. And then my reason for bringing her here brought on another emotion altogether—fear.

I held Una tightly around the waist as Drak circled the field then beat his wings to land inside the castle's courtyard. The bailey was large enough for a small army to gather but it had never housed one. It had, however, been filled with stables for horses, cows, and goats. There had even been a coop for chickens. My nursemaid used to yell at me for chasing them in the yard.

Once I'd climbed down, I reached up to help Una.

"I can get down easily enough in my new clothes," she told me. Scolded me, rather.

"I know, but I want to help." I didn't want her to fall in her condition.

Once down, she walked to the front of Drak. "Good boy," she cooed as she petted his snout.

He purred, his eyes closing at her attentions.

"You're spoiling him."

"He deserves it." She then turned and looked around. "It's abandoned?"

"For now."

"Who's is it?"

"Yours, actually."

She turned a startled expression toward me, her mouth dropping open.

"Come." With my heart in my throat, I held out my hand. "Let me show you something."

Without a word or a moment's hesitation, she took my hand, and I led her carefully up the stone steps to the walkway along the battlement that surrounded the entire castle. I guided her to the parapet that overlooked the open field to the northeast and the Solgavia Mountains in the far distance.

"This was my mother's home after she became pregnant with me. This is where I was born and where I was raised until it was time for me to learn to be a wraith warrior." I gazed down into the empty bailey that was once so full of life. "I know it appears empty now, but it could be beautiful and full of life again." I pointed behind us to the field filled with yellow grass at this time of year. "During summer, there's a purple wildflower that blooms here. Windolek means 'on the wildflowers' in my language."

Una watched me, listening intently. She probably sensed my tension in the tenor of my voice.

"This place is special to me because it reminds me of my mother, who I loved very much."

"And who loved you," she added.

"She did." I faced her. "Do you know that when I first laid eyes on you, bruised and terrified, standing on top of that ledge in the dungeon, I instantly thought of my mother. The abuse she endured from my father. He killed her after accusing her of fornicating with an Issosian ambassador. But I know my mother wouldn't have done that. She knew he was cruel and what he'd do to her. Seems he did it anyway."

My throat grew thick with emotion, thinking about the day I found out my father had murdered my mother in front of his entire court. Una lifted my hand in both of hers, holding tight.

"Do you know he sent one of his Culled to tell me? Erlik."

"I remember him," she said softly.

Yet again, I took a moment's satisfaction in having burned him to cinders right after I killed my father.

"I was in the middle of the training yard at the Gall Guild. Far from home in the wildlands. I was trying to learn the proper grappling technique to wrestle a weapon away from someone if I was unarmed. This all seemed futile to me since I could use feyfire to disarm anyone, but I was determined to make my Gall master proud."

I gulped, remembering vividly that day and the tormented feeling of despair and hopelessness.

"Then, suddenly, Erlik walked directly into the yard, stopped in front of me, and said, 'Your whore mother is dead. Your father commands that you never speak her name again.' He tossed her bloodied handkerchief at my feet, the one with the purple flower of Windolek embroidered on it, and then he walked away."

"Oh, Goll." She blinked back tears for me. "That's ungodly and horrifying." She pressed my hand to her mouth and kissed the top of it, a single tear slipping down her cheek when she closed her eyes.

My heart seized at the sweetness of her, at her pity for me, the boy who'd lost his mother. I never could mourn her. I could never even mention her name, or I'd have suffered the wrath of my father's fists.

"I come here sometimes to remember her."

Then I pulled the handkerchief from the flat pocket of my armor, where I often slid an extra blade. I'd been carrying something altogether different on this trip with this moment in mind.

"I thought perhaps"—I cleared my throat—"that you might like to have this." There were no blue stains on it now, no sign of my mother's brutal death. "It was precious to her. And has become so to me over time." I held her gaze, glassy with emotion. "As have you."

She took the handkerchief from me and admired the embroidered flower, tracing a finger over the delicate stitching my mother had done with her own hand. "I will cherish it, Goll," she said, her voice a rasp. "Always." Then she pressed it to her chest and wrapped one arm around my waist in a gentle embrace.

I exhaled a heavy sigh as if I'd been holding my breath for years and pressed a kiss to the crown of her soft hair. I'd often imagined giving her this small token of my mother's since the Rite of Servium. I hadn't expected this moment to mean so much to me, to transform my mother's memory into something beautiful rather than mournful. For the first time since I was a boy, I thought of my dear mother and no pain accompanied it.

"We should bring life back to this castle," she whispered. "The terrain is very lovely."

"It is. Do you see that high hill there?" I pointed toward the northeast.

"Yes."

"Not too far beyond it is Solzkin's Heart, and just beyond that are the foothills of the Solgavia Mountains, which you can see easily enough."

She faced me, her expression earnest. "Why did you say it was mine? The castle?"

Clearing my throat, I confessed, "I've always known I'd give this place to my mizrah. For I know it's a beautiful place to have a child and to raise one. Näkt Mir can be quite dreary to some…as I imagine it is to you."

"Goll, do you already know that I'm with child?"

Holding her violet gaze, realizing her eyes were the same shade as the wildflowers that will bloom here in the summer, I said, "Yes. You knew, too?"

She shook her head. "I suspected, but I wasn't sure. It hasn't been very long since my last bleeding." Then her face paled, and she licked her lips. "Are you saying you want me to leave Näkt Mir now and go away to have our child?"

"*No*," I answered sharply. "I do *not* want that. But I want you to be content while you are breeding."

"I'm content when I'm with you, Gollaya." The soft expression she wore with genuine love in her eyes nearly felled me on the parapet.

I cupped her face with both hands and pressed my forehead to hers. "I do not deserve you. But I will pay tribute to all the gods, even Lumera, for bringing you into my life."

She laughed, clutching the edges of my cloak. "I would love to see you pay tribute to Lumera."

"Una." I pressed a kiss to her forehead then another. "Una." I lifted her face and brushed a soft kiss against her sweet mouth.

"Though my heart has been blackened by all the blood I've spilled and all the dark thoughts I've kept and nourished over the many years, when you look at me like this, I believe there may be some good left in me yet."

She placed her hands over mine where they cupped her cheeks, the handkerchief still in one. "Your heart is not black from the battles you have fought or the murder of your father who didn't deserve the throne. If that were true then so would be mine from the bitterness I've kept of being tortured in your father's dungeon."

I shook my head. "You are filled with nothing but what is good and light, Una."

"That is a lie." She laughed, but then her expression sobered. "Our hearts are what we make of them. Like recognizes like. And mine knows yours." She pressed her palm to my chest over the organ beating hard for her. "As yours knows mine."

"Yes, my love." I brushed my lips against hers, but then pressed more firmly when my hunger for her taste urged me on.

The kiss was sweet but urgent, a soft melding with a tender intimacy weaving between us. I'd never known the like of it, this tantalizing connection with another fae. When I broke the kiss, I pressed my mouth to her temple then whispered, "You are so dear to me." A panicking fear gripped my heart at the thought of ever losing her.

After a brief time when we simply held one another, she said, "I accept your gift of this castle, but I will only come here when you come with me."

I smiled. "My mother would've loved you." I didn't know where that thought came from. Perhaps from my mother's spirit still lingering here in her favorite place in the world.

"I wish I'd had the chance to meet her." She pressed her cheek to my chest and hugged me tightly. "I'll cherish this handkerchief. Always. Thank you."

My heart soared.

We held one another in silence for a time before I stepped back and looked up at the sky. "Now, how about a tour of the castle? And Ogalvet packed a lunch for us."

She smiled brightly. "Did he make that buttery squash loaf bread I like?"

"Freshly baked this morning before we left."

"Yum. Let's have the tour. I want to see where you got into all kinds of trouble as a little wraithling." She stopped suddenly and pressed a palm to her belly, which was still very flat. She frowned.

"What is it?"

"The first day we spoke in my bedchamber, you told me that you didn't care if we had a boy or a girl first. Do you remember?"

He nodded with a solemn expression.

"Were you being truthful?" I asked.

"Una, I plan to have many children with you. I don't care what sex they are. But you should get used to the idea that they'll have horns, male or female."

Her eyes widened with the realization. "Oh, my."

I chuckled. "I hope that doesn't bother you."

"Not at all. I just never thought of it till now." She grinned. "He or she could have wings, too. Moon fae wings."

That gave me pause, trying to imagine a horned wraith male with light fae iridescent wings. That had Una laughing.

Then she grabbed my hand. "Come on. Let's get this tour going because I'm hungry."

So we spent the afternoon wandering one of my favorite places in the world, filling the halls with my old stories and Una's sweet laughter. It was one of the best days of my life.

CHAPTER 38

Una

The shadow fae male standing next to Morgolith was strikingly beautiful as well as unnervingly grave. His countenance was unreadable, though his red eyes were alert and watchful. Four smooth horns curled out of his head, adorned with decorative gold along the base and tips. His silver, gold, and black armor was fine but also scuffed in places from use. His dragon-like wings were folded at his back, the arched tips shooting tall toward the sky.

He held himself very still, his hands clasped at his back. But the blades at his waist told me he was always prepared for a fight, even if he appeared calm and docile at the moment.

"King Goll and Mizrah Una," Morgolith said formally, "please allow me to introduce Lord Vallon of House Hennowyn, high priest of Gadlizel."

My gaze flickered back to the decorative bands around his black horns. "Are you royal as well?"

His steady, red-eyed gaze skirted over my wings, then met mine with steely examination. "I am not."

Morgolith seemed to understand my confusion. "Shadow fae priests are very high ranking in their culture. They adorn their horns in gold as the royal family does."

Thinking of the fragile Elder Lelwyn, I could not help my blunt observation. "You do not look like a priest."

Goll stifled a chuckle at my side, clearing his throat. But he made no comment.

"You look like you're ready for battle, not the temple," I explained.

"The priesthood must always be ready. We honor the gods and keep their holy places well-guarded. We are protectors."

"What is it that you protect exactly?" I was trying to imagine there was some sacred temple with holy relics that these priests guarded, but from whom were they protecting it? If it was relics or a temple at all. And why would they need to? In Issos, and also as I saw in Silvantis, the locals revered and respected their gods' temples. They didn't need protection.

Vallon did not answer my question but asked one of his own. "What is it you are seeking in our lands, Mizrah?"

"Words," I told him. If he could be stoic and curt, so could I. I added, "Fortunately, I know exactly where to find them. The prophecy outlining where to find the third god-touched text I am seeking was specific enough that we are sure it's at or near Solzkin's Heart."

He kept his quiet examination for another moment, then said, "Then let us proceed. It is right through that grove of trees."

He walked ahead of us, which I found interesting that he trusted Goll and his warriors enough to leave them at his back. Or perhaps, he simply didn't see them as a threat, or he trusted Morgolith.

"He isn't friendly," I whispered up to Goll.

His mouth tipped up as he whispered back, "None of them are."

We followed the priest through a thin copse of thick-trunked oaks where orange leaves blanketed the ground. It wasn't even a woodland so much as a scattering of trees, like sentries on watch for Solzkin's Heart. I was excited to finally see it, a revered place to the shadow fae according to what Hava had told me one night on our journey. Apparently, the shadow fae held religious rituals there certain times of the year.

A giant boulder rose out of the ground into a triangular point, jutting upward like it was reaching for the sky. It was an odd-shaped stone twice as tall as the old oaks that surrounded it in sporadic display. It didn't seem to belong here as the stone was a darker shade than that of the foothill outcroppings of the Solgavia Mountains. Perhaps Solzkin himself had lifted it from somewhere else in the world and placed it here as an altar for the shadow fae, his devoted followers.

We were much closer to the vast mountain range where the shadow fae made their home, and we'd passed cliffs and caves as Drakmir had descended closer to the meeting point. Drak had taken back to the skies with an aggravated huff at the winged shadow fae in our presence.

A coiling burn began in my chest the closer we stepped toward the stone. Gods magick was present, radiating in tingling waves from the center point—Solzkin's Heart. Green lichen and vines grew along the sides of it, but the dark stone still showed through.

"I believe what you're looking for is on this side." Vallon stepped toward the center of the clearing where the stone faced south.

I wondered what riddle the Goddess Elska would show me now, or what form of text I might have to swallow. I shivered at the thought of words written in lichen where Vallon now stood looking up at the other side of the stone. Would I have to ingest mold of some kind? I pressed my palm to my belly, concerned for my babe and what effect the magick might have on him or her.

When I rounded to the far side, completely clear of vines and lichen, I wasn't prepared for what I found. Demon runes were chiseled into the stone, the same essence of the other god-touched texts emanating in waves of otherworldly energy. It prickled along my skin.

I stared up, dumbfounded and frustrated, then I turned to Goll. "How am I to swallow a boulder?"

The very stern shadow fae in our presence took a step forward, his expression finally having some emotion that resembled annoyance. "Mizrah, I am not certain what this quest of yours is about, but you cannot swallow Solzkin's Heart. It is sacred to my people."

I huffed out a breath, refraining from rolling my eyes. "I am well aware it's physically impossible. But I am sure this is where the Goddess Elska has been guiding me, and those are the words that I need." I looked around, wondering if perhaps I was wrong and there might be some other inscription or something else nearby. "I don't understand," I whispered more to myself.

Vallon's expression deepened into a scowl before he finally said, "As you said, it is impossible."

The thought of my people, my father, my brother suffering from the plague, dying even now, twisted my insides. Despair was beginning to sweep through me, for how could I have made it through the first two, only to have gotten to the third and not be able to accomplish the task? Why would the gods lead me here if only to be defeated now?

Goll had pressed a comforting hand to the small of my back, his deep, steady voice finally breaking the silence. "She doesn't need to swallow the stone. She only needs the words."

The way he spoke made me look at him in question. He was glaring at Vallon in a way that told me there was something I was missing.

Morgolith took a step closer to Vallon. "That is right. She only needs the words." Morgolith looked up at the stone, which had me then looking up at the engravings surrounded by thick branches of ivy but left uncovered. "Could he help us?"

Vallon's expression darkened further. "I do not see the possibility of him leaving Gadlizel to help a moon fae princess in her errand for the Goddess of the Wood," he spat rather cynically.

Morgolith said urgently, "Look at *her*. She isn't simply a moon fae." He gestured to my wings, the touch of darkness I wore. "She is more than that."

"Who could help us?" I asked.

Vallon's red-eyed gaze traveled back to me and to my wings. He did not answer. It was Morgolith who did.

"Prince Torvyn of Gadlizel has special abilities."

Vallon hissed at Morgolith, but I added quickly. "He can remove the words somehow?"

Vallon stared back at the stone, his irritated glare more prominent. "Again, it is not of our concern. What happens to the light fae is not of our concern." He said it with conviction, though there was a flicker of something in his eyes that resembled guilt.

A cracking sound from the stone made me jump. Then Goll had his arms around me, lifting me several feet back, all of us braced and staring at the sound coming from the stone.

But it wasn't the stone itself that was cracking. A vine as thick as my thigh that had climbed up the side of the inscribed words was lifting away from the surface of the stone.

I gasped when two emerald-green eyes opened from two leaves facing us. Trails of ivy dripped down around the eyes like hair.

"A dryad," I whispered, though I'd never heard of one like this before.

Goll stepped partially in front of me. Her mouth was carved from the bark of the vine. Spindly legs and arms made of other vines detached from the stone as she stepped down from where she seemed to have been attached for a very long time. Her dark-green vines of hair draped to the ground and around her thin, naked body, made entirely of bark.

No one said a word as she blinked at all of us then yawned, her leaves quivering, before settling those ethereal eyes on me. "I've been waiting for you." Her voice was strangely child-like, reminding me of Zu, Tikka, and Geta.

"You have?" I asked, stepping around Goll who kept a hand on my shoulder. "For how long?"

She blinked those leafy eyes, looking up as if to remember, then said, "Three thousand years. And one."

Soryn made a sound of surprise. Vallon shifted, but no one said a word.

"That's a long time," I said, my heart rate speeding wildly ahead.

She shrugged a shoulder as delicate as my wrist and flicked her ivy-leaf hair over her shoulder with long, twiggy fingers. "I waited a few hundred years then realized you might not be born yet. And might not be born for a long time to come. So I decided to sleep awhile."

"I see," I said. Then I thought of something and suddenly turned to Goll, "Can you understand what she's saying?" I wondered for a moment if I was speaking that old demon tongue he told me I did with the water sprites.

"Yes," answered Goll.

"They understand me," said the dryad, then she turned her head and looked at Vallon, her ivy hair floating unnaturally. "You are wrong, priest. What happens to the light fae *is* of your concern." She pointed one of those long fingers at me. "She has a part to play. As do you, priest."

While we'd all been thoroughly shocked by the sudden appearance of an ancient dryad, Vallon seemed cavalier and rather comfortable with the creature suddenly speaking directly to him.

"And what is mine?" Vallon asked her boldly.

She grinned, revealing a row of sharp, green teeth. "You shall see." Then she flipped her ivy hair over her shoulder again, reminding me of the court ladies at Issos when they were putting on airs, playing haughty to the fae of the court. "For now, you shall fetch your prince. He will give her the words." Then she turned a hardened gaze on him, her green eyes sparking brightly. "If you want to protect the mountain"—she glared and whispered eerily—"from *all* that dwell there, then you must do as I say."

I was confused for a moment because it seemed she should've said, "*and* all who dwell there," not "*from*." But I wasn't about to question her. She was obviously helping my cause.

Vallon dipped his head reverently to the dryad. "I will return with Prince Torvyn." Then without another word, he bent his legs, beat his wings, and shot up into the air, leaving a whoosh of wind in his wake.

The dryad turned her green-eyed gaze on me, blinking with childlike wonder.

"He may be gone awhile," I explained.

She shrugged her shoulder again and leaned back against the dark stone of Solzkin's Heart. Some of the ivy still growing upon the rock reached out and wove into her hair and around her limbs, tangling between her twiggy fingers.

"I'll wait." Then she leaned her head back and closed her eyes, blending and melding back into the lichen and green growth along the rock as if she were never there.

Goll didn't waste a moment. He urged me with a hand at my back. "The Culled will be arriving over that ridge any moment." We'd seen the line of them making their way north from Meerland when Drakmir flew us from Windolek. "I'd rather we wait near the stream. We can make camp there."

The stream wasn't far, so we walked. Morgolith, Soryn, and Pullo pulled their mounts behind them and walked at our sides.

"Morgolith, what is it the prince can do to help me?"

He looked ahead of us, sternness creasing his brow. "Prince Torvyn is a dubsheeva."

I started, darting my gaze at Morgolith. "I thought those were myths."

"They'd like everyone to believe so. There aren't many that I know of."

Turning to Goll, I raised my brows, "An actual shadow shaper? He's not just one of the novgala?" The novgala were illusionists. They could use glamour and shadows to create remarkable illusions.

Morgolith shook his head. "Vallon is a novgala. He has the capability of casting illusion to a high degree. But the prince"—he gusted out a heavy breath—"I've seen him do remarkable things. And terrible ones."

I now realized why the dryad thought the prince could help me. The demon runes were carved into the rock. They were basically made of shadow.

"Is it true they can manipulate anything made of shadow?"

"As far that I know. But Prince Torvyn is elusive and guarded. I've rarely seen him use the gift firsthand."

"More guarded than his high priest?"

Morgolith chuckled. "They're a sober lot. That's for sure."

"No wonder Hava left their city."

"Indeed," he agreed, nodding his head toward the hill on the horizon. "She's too jovial for the shadow fae at Gadlizel."

At the front of the caravan now drawing closer, I could see Hava on the back of my sweet mare, Laurielle, waving wildly.

I laughed. "That is for certain." Then I took Goll's hand, and we went to meet them and set up camp.

CHAPTER 39

Una

"**I** need to bathe some of this dirt off."

Goll glared at me from across our tent where I stood wearing my thickest chemise underneath a heavy winter cloak I was lacing at the top.

"You aren't going to bathe naked in the middle of camp," he declared firmly.

"First of all, I'm not getting naked at all. I'd freeze to death. Hava and I would simply like to wash off with fresh water. I realize you warriors can go weeks without a bath of any kind, but we cannot."

He tilted his head, his gaze taking on a seductive gleam. "What soap are you using?"

I bit back a smile. "The one made of night phlox and moon lily."

His deep, rumbling groan vibrated directly between my legs. "Come straight back to me. After I scry with Dalya, I'll be waiting for you."

After closing the distance between us, I wrapped my arms around his neck and pressed up against him. His hands slid beneath my cloak and around my hips, heating my skin beneath the chemise.

He pulled me close, dipping his head to my throat where he lapped at the skin with his tongue. His hands slid down to cup my buttocks. He squeezed, making that delicious sound in his throat again.

"If you keep that up, I'll never get my bath."

"You smell and taste divine to me." He kissed up my throat, scraping his fangs and giving me a tantalizing shiver. He squeezed my hips and pulled me against his hard frame meaningfully, nipping at the exposed skin of my neck.

He then lifted his head, his gaze trailing down the length of me. "Why does the sight of you in a thin shift and boots arouse me so intensely?"

I laughed and stood on my tip-toes with a hand at his nape to guide his lips to mine. He came easily, coaxing my mouth wider to slide his tongue along mine.

"I swear you're doing this on purpose," I murmured against his mouth. "Hava is waiting for me."

He kissed me one more time, his hands sliding up to my waist, then he eased me gently out of his arms. "Go. And hurry back."

"How long will it take to scry with Dalya?" I wasn't sure how long it took an oracle to peer into her king's future. Goll had told me he was concerned, sensing something he couldn't see, and wanted Dalya to scry to seek some answers.

"We'll be done before you get back. That I can promise."

With one more kiss pressed to his lips, I walked toward the exit.

"Watch for naiads. And bring Pullo and Soryn."

"Don't worry. Meck and Ferryn are coming."

"Ferryn is well enough?"

"Dalya did a wonderful job," I told him lightly, standing at the flap. "He's as good as new."

Then I ducked out toward the closest campfire. Hava quickly walked away from the firelight where Keffa was singing, the basket of soaps, oils, and cloths on one arm.

"It's about time," said Hava, sighing her impatience. "I thought you would never finish *whatever* it is you were doing."

"Hush, Hava," I shushed her.

Walking beside Hava, I looped my arm through hers, noting Meck and Ferryn stepping in front and behind us to escort us to the stream. I smiled at how well Ferryn looked, fully healed. He smiled back at me then focused on his task as our guardsman.

"You know, Hava," I said in a low voice, "I find it rather interesting how often I find you staring longingly at Keffa."

"Pish. Stop that," she shushed me.

I laughed. "You moon over Keffa like he's one of Ogalvet's sticky maragord puddings."

"I do not moon," she protested. "But he does have such a lovely voice."

Laughing, I said encouragingly, "Well, I think you should tell him."

"Why would I do that?" she asked.

"So he knows you admire him. You never know what could happen between you. If you really like him."

It warmed my heart to think of Keffa, who had lost his love so long ago and likely had not had much companionship since. Hava didn't seem to mind his scarred face, broken horn, and lack of one eye since it was quite true that Keffa had a beautiful voice and a lovely soul to match, too.

In the same way, Hava was a pretty dark fae, but she was a half-breed, which seemed off-putting to most of the wraith fae. At least, I hadn't seen any male wraith faes showing her any interest, and she was quite attractive with her bright red eyes and voluptuous figure. Not to mention she had a heart of gold and the kindest personality.

"No, no," Hava finally added. "He would not think of me like that. He likely thinks me only a child."

"But you are not a child, are you?" I nudged her with my elbow.

She grinned up at me. "No. I am not."

My spirit was light as we made it to the edge of the gurgling stream. Hava ignited a ball of feyfire in her palms then whispered a command in demon tongue. The orb of flame floated in the air, giving us enough light to see by.

"We will stand sentry from the edge of the brush, Mizrah," said Ferryn, pointing to the line of bushes that was not too far away but enough to give us privacy.

"Thank you," I told him, wondering if I was imagining things when his gaze roved down my body with interest.

I was still covered in my cloak, and Ferryn had never looked at me that way before. The way a male courtier at Issos might when I walked into the great hall in a sparkly formal gown. It unnerved me, but then he turned and joined Meck a good distance away, their backs to us.

Hava was jabbering away about how Keffa was also a good huntsman, not just a singer, while pulling out the soaps and oils.

"Here's a cloth for you." She passed me one and a bar of soap.

I lifted it to my nose and inhaled a deep whiff, noting the way Goll loved to smell this particular scent on my skin. Tugging on my cloak's lacings at the throat, I pulled it loose and set it over a fallen log next to the stream.

"Brrr!" Hava was now standing in the water, her short chemise revealing her shapely legs. "It's freezing."

I lifted the hem of my chemise, wishing that I'd worn a shorter one like Hava. My hem would trail in the water and be soaking wet before we were done.

"Gods, it *is* freezing," I trilled as I waded into the brook up to my shins.

We laughed and set to scrubbing our faces and necks then underneath our chemises. I glanced over at Meck and Ferryn whose silhouettes remained steadfastly facing away.

"So where did Goll take you on Drakmir yesterday?" asked Hava.

"How did you know he was taking me anywhere?"

"I had a suspicion."

I smiled at the memory of our day at the castle.

"He brought me to see Windolek, his mother's home when she was alive."

A bittersweet sting caught in my breast at remembering the look on Goll's face when he spoke of his mother. I'd folded the handkerchief he gave me and tucked it carefully in my satchel of clothes to keep it safe.

He had obviously loved his mother very much and lost her too young. And then his father locked him in a dungeon for years. It was remarkable that he'd grown to have such compassion. For though he liked to admonish himself for the blood he'd shed, there was such tenderness in his heart.

Perhaps it was his hardships that had forged a creature who longed for love. That was what I felt when he reached for me in the night and pulled me close, pressing his mouth tenderly to my skin.

Thinking of the wee babe now growing inside me, I rubbed the soapy cloth over my bare stomach, having lifted my chemise to my hips.

"What is that smile for?" asked Hava. "You have a secret."

I hadn't wanted to tell anyone yet. "I do."

"Tell me," Hava urged, running a cloth over one of her horns.

"Not yet. I want to—"

"Shh," she snapped suddenly, her gaze darting to our left where the stream disappeared into the shadow of trees.

I froze, staring where she did. I didn't hear anything.

"What is it?" I finally whispered. I didn't have the heightened sense of hearing that Hava did.

"I thought I heard—there it is again." Hava stepped backwards. "Get out of the water."

I didn't hesitate, sloshing through to the shallows and onto the soft bank.

"Meck!" I called.

My guards instantly turned and rushed over. Hava was still standing in the shallows, staring into the darkness. "I can't see anything, but I can hear it."

"What is it?" Ferryn demanded gruffly from beside me.

"Hava, get out of there," I urged, stepping toward the shore. I was about to yank her out if she didn't get to the bank.

"No." Ferryn gripped my shoulder and firmly pulled me back, then stepped in front of me toward the edge of the water.

Then I heard it. The soft sloshing of water. Something was coming toward us in the brook, slow and steady. Then more splashing. More than one of them, whatever it was. My blood froze, remembering the maddened Meer-wolves. But those beasts had come at a sprinting run and attacked fiercely. Whatever this was, it was moving methodically slowly.

"Hava!" I cried.

Ferryn reached forward and grabbed Hava by the arm and hauled her back. Meck stepped in front of me, facing whatever was coming.

And while instincts urged me to run, I couldn't move, frozen with both fear and frantic need to know what was coming for us. I could just barely make out movement in the shadows of the trees blocking the moonlight. Then they came into full view, marching up the stream in a staggered line, straight toward us.

"Gods save us." I stumbled a step back, dropped the rag and soap I still had clutched in my hands, watching my nightmare come to life.

Skeletal fae—half-rotten in trappings of their graves—lurched slowly forward. Some had the bones of their once flesh-covered wings spread behind them. They were the dead of the shadow fae. But the shadow fae didn't have the gift of neklia.

Meck jerked around but not to face me, his horrified and fear-stricken face on his brother. "How could you?" he ground out accusingly. Meck gripped his sword tight, pointing it toward Ferryn. "I won't let you."

My shocked gaze twisted behind me to see Hava on the ground beside Ferryn, unmoving. I gasped, disbelieving what was happening.

Ferryn glared at his brother, sword drawn as well. "You knew it would come to this."

"It is madness, Ferryn!" he cried, his voice cracking with terror and fury.

My gaze snapped back to the creatures emerging into the shallows, coming closer. Wights. More and more of the dead, hollow eyes and gaping mouths, their bones scraping and clicking together without flesh and tendon to soften their movements.

"No." I shook my head as Meck attacked his brother and swords clanged.

I dodged around them, running for the camp when a hand snatched my arm and jerked me into a hard body. Ferryn twisted my arm backwards behind my back, pressing me close.

"No, my mizrah." Black striations streaked like shards of black glass in his eyes, darkening his irises. "You're not going anywhere." Then he swiftly lifted the handle of his sword above me and swung down toward my head.

Sharp pain, then darkness.

CHAPTER 40

Goll

I sat staring into the blue-coal fire. I should've been thinking of my next move toward a proper alliance with Issos, or the trade routes that weren't settled, or the rebuilding of Lumeria, which wasn't moving as swiftly as expected. The people of Mevia and the surrounding villages rejected assistance of any kind, threatening the wraith fae I'd sent if they stepped foot on their land.

I'd expected some push-back from some Lumerians, but not such a rejection that was akin to denying the treaty. Of course, my soldiers still occupied Mevia and hadn't been hindered in any other way, but it was apparent there were still hostilities toward us. And likely would be for a while.

As much as I'd wanted to move into an era of peace between Lumeria and Northgall, I wasn't a fool. The hatred still simmered—on both sides. But try as I might to focus on what a king should be doing, my mind kept drifting back to Una. The soon-to-be mother of my child. Our child.

I grunted at the sweet sting of what lay ahead for her. The pain and danger of childbirth. The thought of it filled me with a dread I hadn't known before.

And yet, she still had her own quest to complete. The gods hadn't called her to Northgall at seventeen, where fate left her mutilated, only to regrow wings the color of our world, then send her on another hunt for the god-touched texts for nothing. If she was given the cure to help her people, *our* people, then our journey was just beginning.

The tent flap opened, and I glanced up expecting Dalya to step through, but it was Pullo. He appeared agitated.

I stood, unease curling in my gut. "What is it?"

"I can't find her."

I'd sent Pullo to fetch Dalya some time ago.

"What do you mean?" I asked, but I was already stalking past him and out of the tent.

He followed as I made my way swiftly toward the campfires. "I checked her tent, Sire, and the campfires at the back of camp, then I went to the tents of those who'd been injured in the wolf attack. She's with none of them."

"Did she go with Una and the ladies to bathe at the stream?"

"No, Sire. I saw Meck and Ferryn escorting them when I first went to Dalya's tent."

I stalked past the fire nearest my tent where Keffa was singing an old ballad. Dalya was nowhere in that circle. Soryn caught my expression, set his whetstone on the log he was sitting on, and walked toward me. "What's wrong?" he asked gruffly.

"Pullo can't find Dalya in the camp," I said in a low voice. "We need to do a full search."

By this point, Keffa had stopped entertaining the Culled and was wandering up to us as well. Before he even asked, I told him that Dalya was missing. Though there was no proof yet, I sensed something was wrong. I'd specifically told Dalya to be ready to scry after Olgavet served dinner. She hadn't come on her own, so I'd sent Pullo. Dalya never disobeyed a command, and there was no logical reason for her to leave the encampment at night.

"We need to search every tent and speak to every fae," I told them. "I'll fetch Una and—"

A cry pierced the night. One of my Culled. We all turned toward the sound.

For a brief moment, I couldn't believe what I was seeing. Wights stalked into camp, attacking the warriors at the fire at the front. One had grabbed one of my fae from behind and sank sharp fangs into his throat, blue blood streaming.

I sprinted into action as did those around me, a stone of dread sinking into my stomach. Dodging into my tent, I grabbed my sword I'd left at the bedside then ran across camp toward the stream.

Soryn, Keffa, and Pullo were right behind me, fighting wights as we went. The only way to kill them was to sever their heads or by burning them. I used feyfire to disintegrate the ones Keffa and Soryn hadn't decapitated and who stood in our way, coming from the direction of the stream.

"No," I prayed, running faster, fear bright and burning in my chest.

There were so many. They were winged, some with flesh and trappings of the grave clinging to their decaying corpses, some completely fleshless. Shadow fae didn't burn their dead in pyres as we did. They buried them in crypts in the mountains. And a wraith fae had summoned these wights back to life.

Who and why? None of my warriors were a nekliam. That I knew of.

A sinking realization awakened terrifying alarm. Dalya's vision over a year ago warned me of a traitor. I'd been overly cautious for so long, expecting the betrayal to come from inside my royal council or even from an old ally of my father in Silvantis. Not within my Kel Klyss, my devoted warriors. Fae that I considered brothers.

Panic gripped my entire being as we flew through the melee of savage wights using fangs and claws and horns. As I gripped the skull of an attacking wight, disintegrating it into dust, the dread multiplied.

This made no sense. Wights couldn't kill me. Why would a traitor use them to attack against me? There could be only two reasons—distraction or a delaying tactic. Perhaps both.

A thick wave of wights lumbered toward us from the stream. I growled, "*Etheline!*" They lit up into flames, still advancing on us. With a wave of my hand, they exploded into shards of smoking bone, crumbling to the ground. We never stopped, running faster past them.

A small body lay on the ground near the water. "No!"

I ran to Hava. Keffa knelt beside her. I checked for a pulse at her throat.

"Still alive," I told Keffa.

Frantically, I jolted up and waded into the water. "Una!" My own heart beat so hard, trying to tear out of my chest, needing to find her.

"My king!" shouted Pullo.

He knelt in the shadows next to a body that was half in the shallows.

"No." I couldn't even breathe as I hurried to him, realizing instantly it wasn't her. It was Meck.

Blue blood glistened on his armor under the moonlight, pooling at his chest. More blood streamed from his mouth. I fell on his other side, lifting his head to face me.

"What happened?" I demanded, even as I inspected his wound, realizing it had been done by a sword, not the claws or teeth of a wight.

"I'm sorry, my king," rasped Meck as a tear slipped from one eye. "I should've told you."

"Told me what, Meck?"

I sensed Soryn above us, but I couldn't look away.

"I tried to stop him."

Closing my eyes, I willed away the reality crashing inside me. I couldn't believe it, yet I knew it to be true before he said it.

"Ferryn is sick…in his head." He gasped, his face contorting with pain. "Dalya tried to heal him."

"Where is Una?" I asked, knowing the answer before he replied.

"He took her." Then he coughed, spattering blue blood onto his bottom lip. "It's my fault. I didn't think he would…should've told you, Sire."

I gripped Meck's hand in mine, seeing the shame and sorrow in his glassy gaze. His own brother had killed him. For without a healer, Meck would surely die of his wound.

"Where did he take her?" I squeezed his hand, bringing his attention back to me. He was drifting.

"Don't know…should've…"

Grief swallowed me at the loss, at the betrayal he suffered from his own brother, at the fact he never confided in me. I could've helped him. "Rest easy, my cousin."

His gaze shifted to mine. "No, Sire. Not cousin…my brother." Then his eyes lifted to the sky before going vacant, not seeing anything at all as his spirit left his body, another tear sliding down his face, pale gray under the moonlight.

I was aware that I was panting, panic tightening its iron fist on me.

My brother. My bastard brother.

It would have given my father appalling joy to seduce my mother's sister. Or worse, violate her and sire sons on her. Now I knew why Mother had appeared sad and anxious at the mention of her sister.

Dalya's vision echoed back to me.

Two sides of the same coin. Demon-fae. One true, one not. Beware the raven's back, for he seeks your place…in all things.

Meck, the true one. His brother—*my brother*—Ferryn sought my place. He'd taken my mizrah. My dear Una. My gods-given mate.

I lifted to my feet slowly, clenching my fists, claws digging into my skin. I relished the pain. Soryn stood in front of me, an expression of shock on his face. Keffa stood with an unconscious Hava in his arms. Pullo stared at me, horrified at what we'd all just realized.

"Kill the rest of the fucking wights." I breathed out a shaky breath, rage rattling through my frame as I reached out to my companion. "Then lead a party to search for her." I turned and marched toward the open field.

"Where will you be, Sire?" asked Pullo.

But I didn't answer. There was no need as a bellowing roar rumbled down from the night sky, the sweeping shadow of Drakmir circling downward. He felt my fury, my fear, and my urgency.

I had to find her. And then I was going to tear my brother to pieces.

CHAPTER 41

Una

I awoke to being jostled off a horse, my hands bound in front of me. My head pounded where Ferryn had struck it, nausea rolled in my belly. Some foul force enveloped me, tightening until I had to expel a breath from the pressure. It emanated from Ferryn.

It wasn't the same disgusting rot radiating from the wights. It was a palpable energy with fierce power and dark intentions. A sinister force independent of Ferryn's will, but also entwined with his.

I was in his arms being carried up a small hill. I caught sight of stars through the mostly bare trees overhead. Hazy, but aware, I took note of my surroundings.

Ahead of us, a rocky outcropping came into view against the backdrop of the half-moon. It looked like we were near the foothills I'd seen as Goll and I flew over Meerland toward Solzkin's Heart. So we were slightly southwest of the camp. How long had I been out? I couldn't tell since the half-moon still hung high, not seeming to have moved since the stream.

Mother of stars. Please let Hava be safe.

"Get your bag," Ferryn told someone, snapping my gaze to him. "You'll need it."

Had Meck helped him? No. They had been fighting right before Ferryn knocked me unconscious.

"Glad you're awake, my mizrah. I'll have you comfortable in a moment."

His voice was different. His inflection was too intimate, not the same as when I first met him and how he usually spoke to me. Had he been hiding his true intentions all along? Or had something changed?

That darkness I now sensed wasn't there before. Or was it? Since I'd ingested Grindolvek's blood, I'd been highly attuned to the wrongness inside those crazed wolves. I'd sensed dark magick when no one else did.

And afterwards, when I went to see Ferryn, I'd thought what I sensed was a lingering of the wolves. But now I realized that *this* was what I was sensing, this dark force living inside of him.

We were moving closer to the outcropping of mountainous rock. But that wasn't what held my attention. It was the clicking of bones and the groaning of the dead surrounding us. *So many.* As Ferryn stepped up toward a cave opening, I finally looked out.

Hundreds of them. Where had they all come from?

Their hollow eyes glowed white under the moonlight, a sinister sign that there was life there after all. A twisted, warped life intent to do their master's bidding.

"Why, Ferryn?"

He looked down at me, his expression somehow serene despite the insanity of what he was doing. "I should think that's obvious, my mizrah."

I hated the way he kept saying "my mizrah." Many had used the title before, but not with the possessive glee he held. That's when it truly hit me. He intended me to be *his*. I swallowed down the panic threatening to overwhelm me. I needed to keep focus and alert and find my way out of here.

But the wights. Terror wound its claws around me at the thought of those creatures taking hold of me. Flashes of them in that pit in the dungeon flickered in my mind.

No. Keep focused.

Ferryn carried me into a cave that was already outfitted with a blue-coal fire and a pallet on the floor. There was also the stump of a log on its side, like a table set next to the pallet, with a vial set on it. The liquid in the vial was deep purple, even by the light of the blue coal-fire. He had prepared this place to bring me here.

What in all the hells was he planning?

There was soft rustling in one top corner of the cave. A hive of bats clustered on the ceiling, some dangling upside down, others moving restlessly on a rocky ledge. Their eyes glittered silver-blue. Dozens blinked down at me, their ears and black wings tipped with yellow. Banshee bats. I'd heard of them but had never seen them.

Then I saw Dalya, her gray skin pale as the moon, walking not far behind with a satchel on her shoulder. It was the bag she had at Ferryn's tent when he was wounded. It would be filled with bandages, oils, and ointments to work with her healing magick. But none of us was injured. She met my gaze with overwhelming fear tightening her features, her mouth a grim line.

"What are you going to do?" I asked him, my voice a soft tremble.

He didn't answer as he laid me down on the pallet.

Dalya froze when she saw the vial on the log. "Ferryn. What is that tincture?"

I sat up, pushing my back to the cave wall that the thick covering of blankets was jutted up against. My feet were unbound, but I was also sluggish from being hit so hard in the head. Pain throbbed at my temple, and I could feel a slight wetness on my cheek. Blood.

"What do you think?" he snapped.

She shook her head. "You can't do that. It could kill her."

He grabbed her by the wrist and jerked her toward him. "Not the right amount, it won't. Just the child."

Horror unfurled with sharp claws sinking deep. Poison.

"*No.*" Dalya shook her head. "You can't do that."

Ferryn scoffed like her protests were annoying. "I'll hold her down, and you give her just enough to kill the babe." Then he let go of her arm and cupped her face like a lover. "I can't plant my heir in her with my brother's still inside her."

"Your brother?" The question slipped from my lips as my breathing became labored from cold panic taking hold of me.

He continued to stare at Dalya, who visibly trembled in his grip, but he spoke to me. "Half, actually. We shared the same father, which gives me the right to sit on the throne of Näkt Mir. I've always known I was meant to." With chilling tenderness, he wiped the tears streaming down Dalya's face with the pads of his thumbs. "On her deathbed, our mother forbade us to tell anyone who our father was. A good son keeps his promises. But that didn't mean I would ignore my destiny. Isn't that right, Dalya?"

She wrapped her hands around his wrists. "Please don't do this, Ferryn. I'll do anything you ask. Just not that."

"Oh, sweetness." He chuckled and pressed a kiss to her forehead. "I won't forget about you." Then he gazed into her eyes and said softly, "I'll still keep you. I know that you love me."

She sobbed, and I heard in that tender cry that she did, indeed, love him. Even while he spouted the most despicable things to her.

"You'll be my first concubine next to my mizrah. I promise." Then he dropped his hands from her face and turned to look at me.

A myriad of emotions tightened his hard gaze—determination, excitement, lust. "But she is marked by Gozriel."

His gaze shifted to my black wings. Unlike the times Goll had looked at them in a similar fashion, his attention repulsed me so much I wanted to hide them from him.

"She is marked as the divine mizrah, and so she must bear my heir."

I swallowed the lump of fear lodged in my throat, but I refused to cry. I refused to give in to any form of despair. There was no way I was going to allow him to murder the child growing inside me. I hadn't been certain this babe truly existed until very recently, and yet, I loved him or her with my whole heart. This was complete madness, and whatever was driving Ferryn reeked of evil.

"Oh, don't worry, my love," Ferryn told me with true sincerity as he knelt on the pallet, taking my bound hands in his. His eyes appeared near black now, those strange striations having splintered to swallow his irises almost entirely. "The pain will be little. And Dalya will ensure you heal quickly."

"She won't be able to travel." Dalya's voice shook.

"She'll have to. But we'll rest in a few days at my home in Belladum as planned."

"King Goll will be looking for her. He'll find you there."

"Good." He grinned at me, his fangs flashing menacingly. "My wights and I will be ready for him." He caressed his thumb over the back of my hand. "By then, his babe will be dead, and his mizrah will be officially mine."

I flinched, but he gentled his hold on my hands and his voice. "Don't worry, dear Una. I'll give you a new babe soon enough. You won't even miss this one." Then he flashed his fangs again and stood to face Dalya. "Set up whatever you need. We need to give her the hemlock now so it has time to work."

Dalya shook her head. "I can't, Ferryn."

He backhanded her so swiftly I screamed and pressed my bound hands to my mouth. She fell to the floor next to me.

"You'll do as I say, Dalya, or I'll feed you to the wights."

Bile crawled up my throat. "Ferryn!" I cried.

He snapped his head toward me, violence written in every taut line.

"There's something wrong"—I gentled my voice—"with you. I can see a darkness in your eyes. I can *feel* it inside you. It's not really you that wants this. Something is driving you to do these heinous things."

He chuckled, his mouth tilting up on one side. "No. The darkness has freed me. The Voice has shown me the truth. It's shown me visions of who I am to be, the *true* king of Northgall." His eyes flared with menace. "The *god* of Northgall."

Dalya pushed herself off the floor and shuffled on her knees to the stool. She uncorked the vial and smelled its contents, her sad gaze finding mine, a bruise already blooming on her cheek.

"I'm sorry," she whispered shakily. She set the vial back down and opened her satchel, pulling a thick rag from her bag, the kind we used to absorb blood during our monthly bleeding time.

I pushed the rising panic aside. I had to get out of here. A flash of Goll smiling down at me from atop Windolek pierced me hard. Then it hit me. *Drakmir.*

While Dalya rummaged in her satchel, I closed my eyes, trying to calm myself as I reached out to Drak. We'd connected telepathically several times now. Almost instantly, I felt him in my mind, then I could see through his eyes, searching from the night sky. Searching for me.

There was a nudge on his end, a palpable yearning question, his gaze still sweeping the tops of trees in the still darkness.

Then I realized he wanted me to show him where I was. I had no idea. Showing him the interior of a cave would give him nothing, but I did anyway. I had to get out of here and show him the land where I was being held.

"Come lay down," commanded Ferryn, now kneeling in front of me. As he said the words, he gripped me by the shoulders and maneuvered me flat on my back on the pallet. His touch amplified that nauseating energy inside him and spread through me.

"*No.*" I struggled and begged. "Please, no!"

"Calm down," Ferryn said soothingly, now leaning his face close to mine, those haunting black eyes sending a shiver of dread down my spine. "All will be well shortly and as it should be." He smiled again, his dark gaze dropping to my mouth. "You'll see."

Without warning, he pressed his lips to mine. I froze in shock till I felt the wetness of his tongue and jerked my head to the side, cutting my lip on a fang as I broke away from his appalling kiss.

He only chuckled against my ear. "You'll see." Then a sharp, "Hurry, Dalya."

I couldn't suppress the desperation speeding my heartbeat at an erratic pace. All the same, there was a well of fury swirling through my veins. It wasn't mine, though. It was Drak's…and Goll's. Of course. While he was connected to Drak, he could also see whatever I showed his dragon. His fury rolled like thunder through my body.

A squeak drew my attention to the ceiling again.

The bats.

Instantly, I snapped my eyes shut and severed the connection to Drak. A fierce roar vibrated through my mind, but I had to break the chain so I could connect with another.

I reached upward to the tiny creatures, trying to find one who'd let me in. Their energy was restless, high-intensity, and hard to grab hold of. Every time I tried to grip the tether of one of them, it slipped free. Then I realized my mistake. They were a hive mind. I couldn't grasp onto one. It had to be all of them. Even better.

I spread my magick outward like a net, feeling it pulse and build, seeking with a hundred tiny threads toward the squeaking and crawling creatures. It was almost instantaneous. The connection to dozens of them at once made me gasp, their thoughts a busy mess of movement and erratic energy.

I'd only ever opened myself up to other winged creatures and let them show me what they wanted. But I was as sure as I was of Lumera's guiding light that this new magick wasn't given to me for nothing. So rather than coast through the connection, I commanded them to act and do what I showed them.

Dalya lifted my head, which had me opening my eyes, my connection still strong, buzzing with all the tiny living heartbeats tethered to me, skittering in my mind. Not to get away, but to hear my purpose. They felt me speaking through the tether.

Ferryn held me down by my shoulders.

"Open, Mizrah." Tears trekked down Dalya's bruised face. "It will be over soon."

"No," I told her, my gaze flicking to the ceiling. *Now!* I shouted in my mind.

In one fell swoop, the bats dove from the ceiling with the high-pitched scream they were named for. It was enough to make both Ferryn and Dalya startle back. Dalya spilled half the vial, and Ferryn loosened his hold, turning his head to look up at the bats now diving straight for him.

I didn't hesitate. Bending my leg, I pressed it to Ferryn's chest and shoved with all my might. He went sprawling backwards onto the cave floor with a snarl right as the bats swarmed in a giant wave of wings and screeches around his head. He swatted the air with a snarling growl. Not even glancing at Dalya, I rolled up onto my knees and staggered to my feet, my hands still bound, then ran for the cave opening.

Standing on an outcropping of cliff, I peered down with helpless fear at the dozens upon dozens of wights. They'd been standing motionless, but now their hollow-eyed skulls tilted up toward me. They began to moan and move toward the cliff where I now stood not too far above them.

"Una!" bellowed Ferryn with fury.

I glanced back to see the bats still doing my bidding. I pulled at the bindings, trying to get free. I'd need my hands to climb down. How could I climb down with the wights right there waiting for me?

Then I shut my eyes and called the bats to me. I could only give them one command at a time as they were all intertwined, connected with the same will as one. Instantly, they shot toward me, winding around me in a tornado of beating wings, many attacking the bindings at once, the others whirling around my head, still squeaking and screeching.

A few nicked my skin with their sharp teeth, but I didn't care. I peered through the swarm at Ferryn coming toward me. But then Dalya was behind him with a rock raised above her. She slammed it hard against his head. He yelled and whirled around, lunging for Dalya.

The bindings were loose enough. "Go!" I shouted, sending the bats back after Ferryn, hoping it would save Dalya.

Then I turned and looked out in desperation at the treetops right in front of me. Lumera's moonlight glowed on the few leaves still grasping the trees, like glittering stars in the night, showing me the way.

"Una!" yelled Ferryn again from somewhere behind me, still in the cave.

Then I bent my knees and leaped off the cliff. Beating my wings wildly, I lifted right over the wights with their skeletal arms stretched toward the sky, reaching for me. But I was too high. This time, I had my wings, and they carried me away over the treetops, my boots touching branches, breaking a twig here and there.

I kept flying, realizing I was crying now. The cold wind struck me hard, freezing my skin, but I pushed on, flying just above the trees whose branches looked like arms reaching up to me. Tears poured from my eyes, not because of fear, but for the gratitude of my new wings. Ones I'd thought useless before the gods breathed new life into them. They carried me farther and farther until I began to grow tired.

Like any muscle in the body, wings needed exercise to grow strong, and I hadn't used mine long enough to carry me far. I hadn't known how high I could fly till now.

Beyond the thin line of trees, there was a rolling hill in the distance, the winter grass shining under the moonlight.

Windolek.

That was the hill I'd seen as we came into shadow fae territory, the one Goll pointed out to me from the parapet of the castle. Windolek wasn't that far.

"Thank you," I murmured to the gods.

Realizing I'd already lost the connection to the banshee bats when I'd leaped off the cliff, I now reached out to Drak, wanting to show him where I was going. If I could get to Windolek, I could summon Drak, and he'd know exactly where I was. I couldn't close my eyes, which always helped me concentrate and form a connection with another winged creature, so I tried with my eyes open as I flew over the treetops, my body growing heavy.

My booted feet scraped the tops of branches, breaking more thin branches. I'd have to go back to the ground soon. The thought of those wights lumbering after me had my heart racing even more.

Concentrating, I tried again to reach Drak, but I couldn't connect. I'd spent so much energy rallying the banshee bats to my aid that my magick felt almost completely drained. My leg hit a branch hard that had me spiraling through the air, down through the trees.

I cried out, fluttering my wings, but my momentum was lost, and my wings were too exhausted to pull me back up. I crashed through more branches on the way down, the limbs tearing at my chemise and scraping my bare legs and arms as I fell.

Landing roughly, I pushed out with my hands to brace my fall, not wanting to land hard on my belly.

My baby.

Something cracked in my wrist. I rolled into a ball on my side, cradling my wrist to my chest, my breath coming out in white puffs. The forest was quiet, only the sound of my soft whimper as I swallowed down the stinging pain in my wrist.

Then something moved beyond the tall oak in front of me. I lurched up into a sitting position, staring at the trunk where I had seen the movement. Two narrow yellow eyes glowed in the dark.

Slowly, I pushed up with my good hand, rising to my feet. The yellow eyes blinked, then a slender figure stepped out. A dryad with green skin covered in small, shiny golden leaves, like scales making a pattern over her body, crept around the trunk, one dainty hand still clinging to it.

She darted her gaze back into the forest, tilting her head, the leaves in her long green hair rustling. She heard something. Then those glowing yellow eyes found me again.

"You must hurry," she whispered. "They are coming." She tilted her head again. "They are coming fast." She crept back behind the tree, her eyes still on me. "Hurry, Mizrah."

I didn't need any more encouragement. I ran. The wights were coming after me. The thought of their gnashing teeth and bony fingers taking hold of me had me running faster as I cradled my wrist to my chest.

The end of the trees was up ahead, but before I reached them, I heard the distant clicking of bones and stomping of feet. I ran faster.

Coming out of the trees, I was at the base of the tall hill. I didn't stop, pumping my legs faster and faster, for I knew it wasn't my imagination that I'd heard something clomping through the woods not too far behind me. The dryad was right. The wights were coming fast.

Once at the top of the hill, I took a second to look back. The thin trees and bright moon allowed me to see movement in the forest. I sprinted forward again, running through the open field toward the dark silhouette of Windolek.

Rather than focus on the creatures making their way closer, and Ferryn most certainly with them, I thought of Gollaya. I remembered what he'd told me today at Windolek, on the parapet I could see from here. I remembered him giving me his mother's handkerchief, a gift of deep love even if he'd never said the words to me. His stories of playing in these very fields in the warm summers when the purple wildflowers bloomed.

That's when I felt it. A hard shove against my mind. I'd always been the one to do the shoving with my magick when trying to connect with another. But someone wanted in. And I knew who.

Still running, I closed my eyes and breathed deeply in, opening the psychic door for Drakmir—and for Goll. They both came flooding in with a violent snap and then tethered with a choking hold.

I wasn't upset at the violence of it. Goll's emotions flowed through the bond, feeding me his intense rage and deep worry and biting fear all at once. It pounded into me like a new heartbeat.

Opening my eyes, I showed both of them Windolek up ahead of me, looming closer. I'd have to fly up and over the closed gate. I was exhausted, but I had to do it. A tingling of power surged through me when I flapped my wings. Tired and sore, they beat hard and lifted me as I was running.

My feet left the ground, and my wings lifted me higher and higher, straight for the gate. I barely made it over, my boot hitting a spike at the top before I dropped heavily to the ground, but I kept on my feet this time. Protecting my wrist, I stared through the bars of the gate to the open field, swallowing the horror at what I saw.

There were more now. More than I'd realized. Hundreds of wights with wings marched across the fields toward Windolek. An army of them. And in the back, Ferryn was astride his horse, galloping down the center line of them. And running alongside him was a Meer-wolf. No. A Meer-wolf wight. It was mostly bone with tufts of fur clinging to its rotting corpse.

I whimpered. But it was a wave of rage that rolled through me again. Not my own. It was Goll's, still looking out through my eyes. His presence, even in a fury, comforted me. He and Drak were with me. They'd be here soon.

I had to hide. Turning from the gate, I ran through the bailey, trying the doors on one of the outbuildings. Each one was locked.

The stables. I hurried toward them, pushed open the heavy door, and then pulled it closed behind me. I rushed deep inside, down a side aisle of stalls and all the way to the back. The smell of old hay and leather and the subtle scent of horse still lingered here. I jerked open the second to last stall and huddled in the corner in a ball, panting heavily, trying to even my breaths.

Then I heard them, the distant sounds of Ferryn shouting commands and metal creaking. Were they bending the bars of the gate? I didn't know wights had otherworldly strength.

I closed my eyes and summoned my courage, calming my racing breaths. I needed to be silent as a mouse.

I waited, hearing nothing for so long I wondered if they'd gotten into the castle walls after all. Then the stable door opened with a loud bang.

I jumped and pressed my palms to my mouth. Something lumbered inside the stables. It was big, much bigger than a skeletal wight. It snuffed the air and wandered closer. The Meer-wolf. My entire body shivered.

Then I felt the presence of Ferryn. Whatever darkness had hold of him was practically pouring off him now. The energy of it made me tremble, but I kept statue still, deathly quiet.

"Unaaaa," he crooned sweetly. "I'm going to find you soon, darling."

My stomach rolled at the intimate tone of his voice and the endearment he had no right to call me.

"I promise I'll take good care of you, sweet Una." His voice seemed closer.

The other creature walked down another aisle, not the one I was in. I could hear his heavy steps. They were searching the right side. I was on the left.

"You hated Goll at first. I remember that day you cried and leaned on me. I was there for you. Do you remember?"

Nausea swirled at the thought I'd ever trusted him.

"But you changed your tune about him, didn't you?" His voice was laced with anger now. "I saw the way you fawned on him at the feast that night. Changed your mind about the king." I couldn't just hear it in his voice; I could feel it. An oppressive weight filled the air.

His emotion was affecting the elements around us. "I bet you let him fuck you every night, didn't you?"

I bit my lip to keep from whimpering at the shift in the air, a sharp whip of magick wrapping my ribcage and squeezing. His aggression and anger fueled both his fury and his magick. This was a new level of frightening. Was he aware he could affect the elements with his emotions?

Then he stopped talking. The creature with him was making its way back up the aisle. He'd be coming to search this aisle next, and he'd find me.

Slowly, I crept on all fours and peered out the slatted boards, seeing the back exit door. I knew the wights would be in the bailey yard, but I had no choice.

If I could muster enough strength, I could fly up and make my way to the parapet and wait for Goll. For I felt him drawing closer, there was no doubt of it. He knew exactly where I was, and he was coming.

Hope surged and gave me the courage to do what I must.

Without waiting another second, I shuffled slowly out of the stall and quietly stepped to the door. I'd have to fly the second I was outside.

Calming my breaths, I listened as the big beast snuffled the ground on my side of the stables. Then I opened the door and lunged outside, taking one step toward the castle wall, my wings extending.

But then I was snatched from behind. I screamed as big arms wrapped around me and pressed me roughly to a hard body. Ferryn.

His breath was on my ear, two strong arms banding my waist and chest, squeezing me close. "But it's my turn now, Una. I think I've waited long enough."

CHAPTER 42

Goll

Black. Black. Black.

My mind and body flooded with darkness. Wrath was no longer an emotion. It was a living, breathing spirit guide that had fully taken hold of me with an iron fist and scalding flame. It burned through my blood, filling me with grotesque, satisfying images of Ferryn being torn apart, limb by limb. There was no death good enough for him, no torture painful enough that would satisfy my all-consuming need to end him.

It wasn't simply that he'd betrayed me as his king or his kin, or that he'd killed his brother, or that he'd defied the gods by taking what was not his, for Una had been ordained by Vix himself as mine. She'd swam in the black lake, survived, and given herself to me. I'd chosen her before all of my people. Vix had blessed our union with a child. Ferryn had defied the gods by taking her from me.

And yet, it wasn't any of those things that stirred the deadly desire blazing through my entire being, my enflamed soul, to kill him. It was the fact that he'd caused her one moment of fear, one instance of pain.

It was unforgivable. For that, he would not live much longer in this world.

Drak soared close to the earth, speeding through the sky like a falling star. Windolek was within sight.

But it was the flashes of Una's mind, what was happening to her, that had me blinded with black rage. She'd managed to run and hide, but he'd caught her.

Another flash. He had her pressed to a wall, her cheek against rough stone, the outside of the stables, his hands trying to both hold her and pull up her chemise while she struggled.

I roared my fury. Drak felt my anguish and roared with me, beating his great wings to fly faster over the long field to the castle.

My mate screamed and reached back, clawing her nails across his face. He gripped her arm and jerked her around then slapped her cheek, knocking her to the ground. Then he was on her.

A guttural whimper escaped my throat, my entire body humming with malice and terror.

There was no redemption for Ferryn now. No words he could say that would prevent his death. Not even the gods could stop what was coming to my half-brother.

The shock of the reality that Meck and Ferryn weren't my cousins but my brothers had given me pause for only a moment as Meck confessed it to me with his dying breath. Guilt of what my father had undoubtedly done to sire them on my aunt—through coercion or brute force—was unforgivable.

They should've told me long ago. This entire night while I'd searched for Una and Ferryn, I'd tried to imagine what Ferryn was thinking, perhaps to right some wrong my father had done. But the *second* Ferryn put his hands on Una in violence, blood did not matter. Nothing mattered but her safety—and his death.

Wights surrounded the castle and filled the inner yard. Drak swooped down right outside the gate, landing and crushing several wights, the creatures screeching beneath his giant clawed feet. He flapped his wings, sending more spiraling backward. I leaped off his back, storming for the gates of Windolek.

More leaped toward Drak, but he reared up onto his hind legs, wings beating the air. As he came down, he spewed red-hot dragon fire, incinerating every wight in his radius as I rushed forward.

The corpses of shadow fae crowded toward me, gnashing their teeth and stretching out clawed hands. I raised my arms to my sides, the surge of feyfire filling my body, my flesh, my blood. It enveloped me entirely, flooding my soul with the burning fire of the gods. A righteous knowing invaded my mind; I was no longer a fae or a king, but an extension of their will, their wrath.

Ferryn had wronged them. Not as much as he'd wronged me. Still, they filled me with their power. Vix was here and present, walking with me, seeing through my eyes, guiding my fury. His power vibrated with strength and violence.

A wall of flames stretched out the sides of my body like giant wings, slicing outward like a blade, cutting across the land, speeding farther and farther until the fire extended beyond the walls of Windolek. As I marched forward, the flames moved with me, edging closer to the enemy, eating them and incinerating them with fire as hot as Solzkin's true heart.

Wights gibbered and screamed, igniting and burning to ash where they had stood seconds before. One lunged for me, claws swinging toward my face.

"No." The calm word left my lips, exploding him into cinders and dust.

I marched faster toward the gate, my wall of feyfire devouring creatures as I went. The bars of the gate were bent with scratches like teeth or claw marks. Regular wights didn't have that strength.

Ducking through, my wings of flame diminished to my sides, but lashed out like a whip to any wight who dared attack me. I didn't even need to give the command. The fire protected me as if it had a will of its own. The wights crept slowly, moving in a circle around me, hesitant.

They weren't completely mindless creatures. They wanted to survive like any other living thing. Though they had no souls, there was life in them. Until their master was dead. Which would be very soon.

I stalked through the bailey at a quick clip. "Ferryn!" I bellowed on a growl.

A Meer-wolf wight stepped out of the shadows of the stables with Ferryn at his side. He held Una in front of him, his arms holding her captive against him.

My heart left my body at the sight of her—the skin of her arms and legs scraped, her cheek bruised, her chemise torn down the middle to her waist, her eyes wild with fear and defiance and hope. The evidence of her claws streaked Ferryn's face where she'd fought him.

Wrath seized control again, wielding his burning desire for death and retribution as I walked forward, intent to pull her from his arms and rip him apart.

Una

"Stop!" Ferryn yelled, his command vibrating through his chest to my back.

Goll stopped, his expression that of a man possessed. He looked every inch the demon wraith king of Northgall with murder burning bright in his eyes. He wore only a loose white tunic unlaced at the neck and the doeskin pants he was wearing last I saw him in our tent, his cloak billowing off his shoulders.

But it was the flowing cape of flame that whipped around him, a glowing corona of demon fire, that had me hypnotized. He was Vix incarnate, his eyes luminous with bloodlust and rage.

He said nothing at all to Ferryn, simply stared with that terrifying expression, his eyes flashing brightly with otherworldly fire. His dragon ancestry seemed to be shining through them.

He was haloed by flames entirely that licked out and lashed any wight that came too close, bursting them into dust.

"If you use your fire on me," said Ferryn, "you'll kill her, too."

I heard it. The first tremble of fear in Ferryn's voice. He was afraid. He should be. My king wore nothing but death in every hard line of his face.

Goll began to take slow, steady steps forward again. His voice was low and eerily calm. "Do you honestly believe that any part of me could hurt my mate? *My* mizrah?" The flames haloing his body flared brighter, reaching outward along the ground, like a burning phalanx to take out his enemy.

The wights had stopped attacking him, but now circled with a wide berth. It didn't matter. Goll murmured some inaudible words and waved his arms outward. In a flash, the phalanx extended in all directions, finding every wight in the yard and incinerating them into sparks and charred dust, smoking the air with the echo of their screams and black ash.

Ferryn's arms tightened around my waist and chest where he'd bracketed me to him. The Meer-wolf wight behind us snuffled the air, a low growl rumbling.

"I'll kill her if you come closer!" Ferryn snapped, his hand finding my throat.

Goll froze, but his expression never wavered. His gaze found mine. For a brief moment, he blinked away the maelstrom of rage, wrath, and hard determination, letting a second's worth of adoration shine there. Then it was gone, his attention back on my captor.

"Ferryn," he said with chilling, dark certainty, "nothing is going to happen here that does not end with your dead body in my hands. It's best if you accept that now."

He scoffed. "You and your fucking arrogance."

"Is that why you wanted to be king? You thought me arrogant? Unworthy?" More steps closer.

Ferryn shuffled back. I stumbled with him, my hands on his forearms, his fingers tightening at my throat.

"You were doomed," Ferryn growled. "My mother told me you were likely dead already in that dungeon. She raised us on her own and told us over and over that I should be king, her firstborn." His breathing became ragged with anger. "One day, *my* time would come when I could slay our father and take his throne. It was her dying wish." He laughed with derision. "I was making plans to do just that when you appeared out of nowhere, killed him, and took *my* place."

Goll tilted his head, looking more animal than fae. "It was never your place."

"It is now," he growled and then shouted, "*Stygrim!*"

The wolf wight lunged toward Goll in a run. I screamed as the giant skeletal beast opened its jaws and launched through the air at him.

Goll caught the creature by its fangs, pushing back and keeping it from sinking its yellowed teeth into him. He whispered in demon tongue. *Etheline* didn't mean "fire" or "ignite" as I once had thought. It meant...

"Come alive," grated Goll, calling to his magick to live and breathe for him.

It did. Flames blazed up his arms and licked two lines across the undead wolf's back. The creature howled and snarled while Goll still held its jaws with unfathomable strength that I hadn't known he possessed.

Then I felt them. The presence of the gods surrounding us with their oppressive, almost painful, power. Yet it wasn't coming from the heavens or the earth. The power emanated from Gollaya himself. My king. My mate. My *love*.

A low groan slipped from Ferryn behind me before he started hauling me backward, his hand slipping free from my throat.

By now, the wolf wight was completely engulfed in flames. Goll pulled apart its jaws. The cracking of bones and snapping of rotten sinew rent the air, and then he shoved the burning carcass with both physical and magickal force so that it crashed into the castle wall.

He turned toward us, pulling his dagger from its sheath on his belt, and stalked our way with those bold, fearless steps, his expression nothing less than the embodiment of cold, merciless fury.

He was utterly beautiful. I couldn't look away if I tried.

Ferryn's hand found my throat again, but Goll whispered something and a snake of flame shot from his chest and wrapped around Ferryn's wrist.

Suddenly, I was free of Ferryn, falling roughly to the stone courtyard. Instantly, I scrambled backward, ignoring the biting of small pebbles under my palm and the pain in my wrist.

"You're safe, my mizrah," Goll said with a soothing, serene voice, his feral gaze still locked on Ferryn.

Ferryn was now held in place with four ropes of fire, his arms outspread, his feet held in place. His gray complexion had darkened with the exertion of trying to free himself. The flames weren't burning his skin, but simply keeping him still. Goll wanted to do the killing himself. He wanted it to be personal.

"I'm your brother!" screamed Ferryn.

"You were," said Goll, only a few steps from him now. "But then you touched my wife and dared to hurt her. Now, you're nothing. You're ash in the ether."

His wife? I swallowed thickly at the emotion swelling inside me at his cavalier admission. Like it was nothing for a wraith king to claim a wife.

"But I'm your blood," Ferryn protested. Then he scoffed, his bravado sounding pathetic, "She's just a concubine."

"No, Ferryn." He finally reached him and took one of Ferryn's horns with his free hand, bending his head closer. "She's my queen. She's everything."

I gulped at the earnest adoration in his voice.

"You should look away, my love," he told me in the calmest voice without looking in my direction.

"No," I said softly.

"Very well."

Then he proceeded to stab Ferryn in the throat over and over. Ferryn gurgled a dying groan, his lips moving, his eyes wide and shocked as Goll held him by the horn and continued his ghastly work. Ferryn's eyes glazed as his spirit left his body. I sensed when the dark essence swept away.

But Goll didn't notice. Or if he did, he didn't care. He moved to Ferryn's chest, even while the rope flames vanished and Goll held Ferryn's body upright with one hand, his dagger plunging deep in a nonstop rhythm of thrusts, blue blood spraying Goll's face and chest.

Nausea churned in my stomach, so I finally did look away. Curling into a ball, I pressed my face into my knees while still hearing the sounds of the blade sinking into flesh over and over. I wasn't sure how long it lasted, only that my mind took me away for a while.

I tuned into the magick surrounding us, the presence of the gods cocooning me in safety. I still shivered, but it was from the cold now, not fear any longer. My chemise was all I wore since I'd been taken, the cold wind nipping at my skin, and my wrist throbbing where I'd fallen on it.

But my babe was safe. I was safe. Gollaya had come for me as I knew he would. As I knew he always would. He'd called me his wife. His queen. I sniffled.

A heavy cloak fell around my shoulders as I was lifted into Goll's lap where he'd sat on the ground in front of me.

"Shh," he murmured, hauling me against his chest, rocking me in his arms. "You're safe now, my precious mizrah." His body was warm and welcoming. "My beautiful mate. I'm so sorry. You're safe now," he ground out against the crown of my head. "I promise I'll never let anything happen to you again."

I uncurled and slid my arms around his neck, peering up into the fierce face of Goll, spattered in the blue blood of my captor. I thought it was me still trembling, but it was him.

"I know you won't."

"Are you hurt?" He swallowed hard, his throat working as his arms held me fiercely. "Did he…harm you?"

"Except for my wrist, I'm not injured. In any way." He needed to hear those words, so I assured him.

"I'm so sorry. It never should've happened."

"You didn't know. You couldn't have known."

"It doesn't matter," he said gruffly, his voice rough and shaking. "It's my place to protect my mizrah. I'll never forgive myself."

I reached up, pressing my palm to his cheek so he'd look at me. His eyes were wild and full of guilt and misery, the flare of gold around his slit pupil bright in the pool of blue.

"Your mizrah?" I asked gently. "Or your wife?" My own voice finally broke, a tear slipping down my face.

"Gods, Una." He pressed his forehead to mine. "You're my *everything*."

I didn't care that he was covered in blood or that the smoking remains of hundreds of wights filled the air with a putrid sulfuric smell. I held him close, needing the sensation of his warm embrace. He seemed to need mine, too. We remained there for quite a long time, my husband holding me and me holding my husband.

Sometime later, he lifted me into his arms, keeping his cloak tucked around me as he carried me out of the bailey and into the field where Drak waited, chomping on the bones of one of the fresher wights.

I sniffed. "So King Goll is going to change the laws again. He's going to have a wife, not a mizrah or a concubine."

He looked down at me as he carried me closer to Drak, who rumbled a pleasant growl at our approach. The gray light of early morning lit his face.

"Something I've come to understand about Vix and Mizrah. They may not have been bound in the formal sense—as husband and wife." He stopped before Drak, still holding me tight, his fierce gaze on mine. "But she was his world." Those dragon eyes flicked between my own, holding me captive. "As you are mine," he added, voice gravelly and rough. "There will never be any concubines. But the title Mizrah means more than mother to my children. She was the most precious treasure Vix ever held in his arms." He squeezed me tighter, reminding me I was still in his. "I understand that now."

We climbed up onto Drakmir's back. I sat sideways on Goll's lap. He wrapped me tight against him, cocooning me in his cloak and his protective warmth, his possessive arms.

When I pressed my hand against his chest, wanting to feel the strong beat of his heart beneath, I noticed the threads of our moon-binding shimmering brighter along my hand and wrist. As Drakmir lifted us up and up into the clouds, the kiss of dawn brightening the sky, the threads glowed.

Goll took my hand from his chest and laced our fingers together, aligning our bare forearms, the sleeve of his tunic having risen. The threads of our union actually moved and entwined like they had when we stood in the Moon Temple with Elder Lelwyn. He marveled at them as did I, then he marveled at me as I did him.

"I love you, Una," he said with such sincerity and certainty that my heart beat harder, a knowing sinking into my soul.

I smiled and tucked my head in the crook of his neck. "As I love you," I whispered as Drak carried us through the golden morning sky.

CHAPTER 43

Goll

Three days later, we stood beside Solzkin's Heart, staring across the small circle at the two shadow fae. I kept Una close to me. Perhaps too close. She kept glaring over her shoulder since I hadn't removed my hand from her waist and allowed her to greet Prince Torvyn and his priest properly.

I knew I was being overbearing since the shadow fae hadn't demonstrated any threat, but my will was no longer my own when it came to Una. My need to keep her close and safe defied rational thought. And I didn't quite fucking care what anyone thought about it.

Much to her protest, Hava had remained behind at the encampment with a few Culled and Morgolith, who was nursing a wounded leg from the wight attack. I wanted no distractions with this encounter, and as much as my Una loved her handmaiden, her friend, Hava rarely kept quiet or still.

It had been a somber few days. We'd had many funeral pyres to burn. The wights had killed four of my Kel Klyss. Then there was

Meck. When they were preparing his body for his pyre, I'd inspected his back and found exactly what I thought I would.

His demon runes had traced over his shoulder to his back as some often did. One of the marks was the sign of the raven wing, given to him by Gozriel, and the sign of one with the gift of neklia. His brother surely bore it as well. I'd incinerated Ferryn's body after I was done with him, not thinking of anything else but wiping him from this world.

It still galled me I'd never known they were nekliam. It was a rare gift and one that could've helped their king. But it seemed Ferryn had ulterior motives from the moment he and Meck presented themselves to be considered for my Kel Klyss. And Meck was more loyal to his brother than his king. I could understand that. Still, if Meck had confided in me, he might still be alive.

And finally, there was Dalya. We'd found her in the cave where Ferryn had taken Una, strangled. It broke my heart that she'd come to such an end.

Even knowing she'd betrayed me, for what Una had told me of the conversations in that cave, she must've been Ferryn's lover. She'd betrayed her king in not telling me about the plot against me and my mizrah, but she'd betrayed her vows to Vix as my soul-seer. I'd never know what led her astray, but I could imagine.

Like me, she'd been born into a role. Her magickal gift had marked her by the gods for a life as an oracle, a priestess of Vix's Order. That also meant forsaking a life of family and embracing one of isolation, no mate or children to come.

Then Ferryn, appearing to be a strong, honorable warrior devoted to me as she was, appeared in her life. I could guess he had seduced her rather than the other way around. Una had said he was sick with some kind of black magick madness. He could've entranced Dalya against her will. I didn't know when or how it all had happened exactly, and those who had the answers were now all dead. It didn't matter now.

So I let it go as my mate had advised. No good could come from dwelling on my mistakes or the betrayal of those close to me. And I refused to let my heart fill with bitterness when there was so many more reasons to fill it with joy.

As we'd watched Dalya's pyre burn high, I forgave her for any wrongdoing. I did the same for Meck, a devoted brother who'd tried to correct Ferryn. And failed.

Una had sworn there was dark magick inside Ferryn, guiding him to do its bidding. I berated myself for never having seen or sensed it. Never noticed anything at all. Their expedition to the Solgavia Mountains had brought us the gold we needed. But apparently, Ferryn had brought something else back with him.

I leaned down and whispered to Una, "Do you sense anything?"

We'd discussed the fact that Ferryn most likely encountered this infection of darkness when he was on this expedition. I was more than a little paranoid of the shadow fae. I didn't question why the gods had touched Una with the sight to sense this darkness when I hadn't been. The gods did as they chose, and I accepted that.

"No," she answered quietly. "Nothing at all."

I wondered what it was and where Ferryn had encountered the dark essence. But now wasn't the time for that discussion. There was a far more pressing matter.

Prince Torvyn stood the same height as his priest, Vallon. However, his black wings arched higher, and they shimmered in the afternoon sun with a red sheen. His golden hair was braided in tight plaits along the sides, falling to the wild mass of wind-whipped hair that fell past his shoulders. Four smooth horns curved back in a regal swoop over his head.

But it was his eyes that set him apart more than anything. They were a vibrant orange-gold, as if his magick was eternally ignited by Solzkin's fire. He was surely touched by the sun god, an anointed of the royal line of shadow fae.

"And what do I get for aiding you in desecrating our sacred altar of Solzkin by removing the words and giving them to your mizrah?"

He did not ask why. Nor did he protest that we wanted something that by all rights belonged to the shadow fae. They were a grave people. But this was beyond the usual sober or disinterested mannerism. There was resignation and below that, a layer of sadness, reeking from this young prince.

"What is it you want?" I asked, holding his fiery gaze.

At that moment, I wondered at the fact that none of his kind held the gift of zephilim. Vix had not bestowed the ability to use feyfire upon their kind. Their magick came from the bloodline of their ancestral mother, Mizrah, the daughter of Näkt, the gifts of night. And I would give this prince whatever he wanted, within reason, to use his manipulation of shadow to give my Una the last of the god-touched texts.

The prince walked forward to stand alone within our circle, made almost entirely of my Culled. Vallon remained in place at the perimeter.

Torvyn lifted his chin, his deep voice in earnest when he said, "I want to know how you managed to break your father's wards in the dungeons of Näkt Mir so that you could kill him."

My pulse quickened in surprise at his demand. "You want to know how I broke my father's wards?"

Did his father, the one that was rumored to be mad, keep him in some sort of prison with wards? He was obviously free to go where he wanted. This was a strange request, especially for what we would get in exchange.

"Tell me how you broke his magickal chains. He held the power of Vix as the wraith king. Yet you managed to defy that power, the gods' will, and take his throne."

I thought back, trying to remember exactly what it was. Vayla and I had been imprisoned on the same day. I saw her in the cell, beaten and bruised, as my father's bone guards had dragged me in shackles to my own cell near the wight pit.

"There was an oracle—a very special one." Keffa stiffened and straightened at the mention of her. "She had prophesied I would usurp him, so I always knew it would happen. I simply didn't know when."

I shifted closer to Una, glancing down at her. She stared across the shadow fae.

"But days before I broke free, I felt a strengthening in my magick. I didn't know then, but it was because my gods-ordained mizrah was near. In that very same dungeon."

Una looked up over her right shoulder at me, a small smile teasing her lips.

"I wouldn't know for a long time where that strength had come from." I looked back at the prince whose hard expression hadn't wavered at all. "All I knew was that when the guards had tied her to a hook to be fed to my father's wights, I would die before I allowed that to happen. My magick was suddenly more powerful than my father's. I broke free and helped my future mizrah to safety. Later, when Una's life was endangered yet again by my father, I went to his throne room and took off his head. And nothing has felt more right."

Except for killing Ferryn.

Prince Torvyn remained very still, his jaw setting sharply. "So the gods decided. They changed their favor."

"I suppose you're right. The gods changed their mind about his worthiness to be our king. And so I was free and able to take his throne."

His expression shifted to something other than stone. He appeared disheartened as he muttered, "Hopeless."

"Is that all you want?" I asked.

His golden eyes narrowed. "And a boon. From you and your mizrah."

"What and when?"

"You'll know when I tell you. And whenever I ask for it."

I clenched my jaws but nodded in agreement.

That was when the dryad decided to wake again from her slumber. She detached her spidery limbs from Solzkin's Heart, blinked her leafy eyes, her ivy hair floating around her head. She stepped to the side of the stone and pointed to Torvyn. "You think of the right things but at the wrong time."

If Torvyn was surprised by the sudden appearance of the dryad, he made no show of it.

"When will that time be then?" he asked her aggressively.

"Your priest will tell you."

Torvyn rounded on Vallon, whose eyes widened with surprise. "I know nothing, Sire."

"You will," said the dryad. "Now give her the words, Prince. They belong to her."

His gaze shifted to Una. As always, it made me stiffen with unease when a male looked at her with scrutiny. I had already been protective before the nightmare with Ferryn. Now, I wanted to cocoon her in our bedchamber at Näkt Mir and never let her leave. But I knew she had much to do on the quest given to her by the gods.

Tor made no protest of any kind. He stalked toward the stone, his giant wings flaring out behind him.

It was late afternoon, the sun falling behind us, the tall trees nearby casting light shadows on Solzkin's Heart and the circle where we stood. There were no clouds in the sky even though the day was cold and crisp.

And yet, with a soft murmur of inaudible words from Torvyn, the light shifted as if it wanted to get away from the prince. The shadows moved, gathering toward the winged fae holding his palms up and facing the stone as he whispered softly.

The darkness shaded him from any light, a dome of shadow covering him entirely until we couldn't see him at all, only an impenetrable black space where he once stood.

But above him, the engraved words on the wall shivered. The words were embedded deep in the stone, the letters themselves made of shadow. They trembled as a pulse of magick reverberated from the stone. All at once, the letters fell, sliding down the boulder.

The dryad had her hands cupped beneath the lines of runes. When there were no letters left upon Solzkin's Heart, the stone smooth and devoid of any engravings, she stepped back and nodded to where Torvyn stood in the well of shadows.

Suddenly, the darkness surrounding the prince fled from him, the normal shadows fleeing to their normal places beneath the trees. The pressure of fae magick vanished, and a calm breeze rustled the trees.

When the prince turned, his eyes glowed even brighter than before, a piercing gold. He glanced at Vallon, who flared open his wings, before the prince turned to face me again.

"Take the words," he said, voice devoid of any emotion. "They mean nothing to us now anyway. I suggest you take your mizrah and leave our lands quickly."

He did not say it like a warning, but more like sage advice. Then he beat his giant wings, spanning so wide they nearly reached my Culled circling the clearing. With a slight bend of his knees, he lifted off, leaving a rush of wind in his wake.

Vallon nodded toward me. "We wish you well, King Gollaya. And your mizrah." Then he lifted off, leaving only a gust of air that stirred the orange leaves on the ground as the shadow fae flew over the treetops toward the Solgavia Mountains.

Una stepped toward the dryad. On instinct, I followed but kept my distance. The dryad's business wasn't with me, and these handmaidens of the gods—for that was what these odd fae creatures were—were testy when it came to their missions.

I thought back to the sprites at Dragul Falls, remembering how they almost refused to let me go with Una. But then my attention was immediately back on the wispy dryad, her bark-like limbs moving toward Una.

She stretched out her cupped hands, a wide smile on her face, flashing her sharp, serrated teeth.

"See. I have them for you. My goddess will be so proud."

Una peered down in the dryad's cupped palms. The letters had pooled into swirling black smoke, their markings indecipherable as they had melded into one vaporous mass.

"Why did Elska give this task to me?" Una, who'd been quieter since I brought her back from Windolek, asked softly. "Why *me?*"

The dryad shrugged her slender wing-like shoulder. "She did not tell me." Blinking her gem-green eyes, she then craned her viny neck down and whispered, "but I can guess."

"Tell me," pleaded Una.

"My goddess was very sad for a long time."

"Why?"

"The light fae killed the dark. The dark fae killed the light. So much hatred. So much sorrow. My goddess's heart was broken." She widened her eyes, the leaves attached to her barky skin shivering with excitement. "I saw her whisper magick words and divide them into threes."

"But why do that? Why hide them?"

"Because my goddess is gone. She had to go to sleep. Her heart was too broken to stay awake and deliver the spell. She gave that job to me and to others you have met. So she hid her spell till the time was right."

For thousands of years.

"Why me?" Una asked yet again. "It could have been anyone."

"Yes," the dryad agreed with a nod of her head and rustle of her leaves. "It could have been anyone. But one night, a brave young girl flew away from her home with only goodness in her heart to cure her people from a foul sickness. Her courage and goodness were repaid with pain and torture and the theft of her god-given gifts. A tragedy. A blasphemy against the gods."

Tears streamed down Una's face as she looked up at the dryad and listened to her own story very quietly.

"And so," continued the dryad, "the female born into the light was remade in the darkness. The dark fae lady." The dryad smiled, tendrils of her ivy hair reaching out to caress Una's cheek softly. "You are deserving of her healing gift. And far more than that."

Una whimpered, her knees buckling. I rushed forward and caught her by the shoulders from behind.

"Are you all right?"

She glanced up at me and stood straight again. "Very." Her eyes shimmered with glassy tears. "I was right. I will have the healing gift again. Greater than before."

"So much greater," agreed the dryad, holding out her cupped palms. "Now you must drink. And take the gifts the Goddess of the Wood has prepared for you."

I noted she said the word "gifts" in the plural sense, but I didn't question. There was a rightness to this moment I couldn't explain.

Una patted my hand on her left shoulder then stepped out of my embrace. Locking my limbs to hold me in place, I refrained from going to her, always wanting to protect her. The last two times she'd ingested the god-touched texts, she'd experienced pain with the swallowing of power. She'd fallen into an otherworldly sleep after she'd drank Grindolvek's blood. One that had lasted almost two days.

But this was what the goddess Elska wanted. It was what Una wanted, what she was destined for. So I kept myself still as she dipped her head and cupped her hands beneath the dryad's, lifting them toward her mouth.

Rather than drink, she opened her mouth and inhaled deeply. The black swirling smoke twisted into a funnel, pouring into her mouth and down her throat. She gulped it all down, making a small grunt of distress before she crumpled to the ground.

She fell too fast for me to catch her. I lunged for her but a blast of wind knocked me back, lifting me off my feet and dropping me farther away. Keffa and Soryn and the rest of my Culled were on the ground as well. The dryad had not moved, now smiling down at Una's crumpled form.

I was on my feet again, sprinting across the clearing, but Una's body was lifted off the ground by invisible hands. I froze. Her legs, arms, and white cloak hung limp toward the earth while her hair floated wide, a beam of green light shining from inside her. It blazed through her dark blue trousers, tunic, and her skin.

"Gods above and below," murmured Keffa close behind me.

Beams of green light shot from the tips of her fingers and the strands of her hair, piercing the darkening clearing where we stood. I shivered as a thin shaft of light traced across my chest, leaving a palpable sensation of deep comfort and serenity in its wake.

"Do you feel that?" asked Soryn.

I snapped my head to the side to find my second in command grinning like a babe, his hands pressed to his chest where several rays of green light crisscrossed there.

"Feels like heaven," he said dumbly, his eyes almost drunk with the sensation.

I glanced around to see all of my Culled wide-eyed in wonder.

"She is ascending," said the dryad.

My attention shot to Una, my heart stopping when I thought for a moment the dryad told me she would continue to fly upward, right into the clouds with the gods of the heavens. Vix knew she deserved it. But she belonged here with me. She was mine.

Then her wrists lifted, a rope of golden light encircling them. Una gasped out in pain.

"Una!"

I stormed forward again, preparing to use a whip of feyfire to drag her back down, but then her body began floating back toward the earth, the Goddess Elska's light beginning to dim.

When she was within reach, I grabbed her around the waist and pulled her back down to me. That powerful force drenched me in tranquil ecstasy. Not the kind I experienced when our bodies joined but the kind that could soothe the soul of any ill at all—a disease of the body or a sickness of the heart.

"Una," I whispered down to her, hoping she had not fallen unconscious like before.

Her eyes fluttered open, glittering a vibrant purple with the new magick inside her. She smiled. "You can put me down."

I set her on her feet. She lifted the sleeves of her blouse where her wrists were now completely encircled with runes. There was a finger-width cuff of gold—the size we wore on the base of our horns—wrapping her wrists above her bracelet of ancient markings.

"What is this?" she asked, voice quivering as she marveled at them.

I took the backs of her hands gently in mine and studied the rune sign first. The last ones to complete the circle made my pulse trip faster.

"The runes mean *mother of all fae kind.* But this sign that means *mother* with the slight tail at the tip can also mean something else."

Her brow pursed. "What?"

Staring down, I brushed the pads of my fingers over the gold cuffs encircling her wrists.

"What is it, Goll?" she persisted.

I leaned down and pressed a soft kiss to her lips. "It means something I've known for some time."

I took one of her hands in mine and turned toward my Culled, all of them staring with wide, wondering eyes.

"Kel Klyss," I bellowed across the clearing. Then I raised her arm, her cloak falling behind her, her sleeve sliding up to reveal her slender arm and the gold cuff the gods had placed there. "I present to you Tiarrialuna Hartstone Verbane! My mizrah, my wife"—I turned to her, my heart in my throat as I declared before all—"and my *queen.*"

Her breath hitched, but she kept her chin up and her face forward.

"The gods have declared it so, and I affirm it. I welcome it. Queen of Northgall!"

She squeezed my hand, a single tear sliding down her milk-pale cheek, but she kept her eyes forward.

Soryn was the first to break from the shock of the first wife and queen to ever be claimed by a wraith king. He thumped his fist to his chest and fell to one knee. "Queen Una!"

Keffa, Pullo, Morgolith, and the others fell instantly to one knee, loudly thumping their chests. All horns bowed. "Queen Una!"

They didn't say it once but began to chant her new name, her rightful role as my partner in this world and hopefully the afterworld when this life was done. For I could not bear to ever part from her.

When their chant grew louder, smiles on their faces and joy in their voices as they lifted them in praise, she finally turned her head to me.

Her face shone bright, glistening with tears. She was too overwhelmed to say a word, it seemed. She did not need to.

As the Culled continued to chant her name, I pulled her into my arms and pressed my lips to her ear. "My beautiful queen."

I held her close as the Culled echoed her new name to the sky, the sun dipping slowly and kissing the horizon with gold.

CHAPTER 44

Una

"Your father is dead." Athelyn faced me with a concerned and surprised expression. "You did not receive my message?"

I'd known this already. Somehow, I'd known. "When?" I asked. Gollaya pressed his palm to the middle of my back beneath my wings in comfort.

"Not long after I left Northgall, actually. I sent word, but we heard nothing back."

Goll rubbed his palm up my spine and back down in a soothing stroke but said nothing.

Exhaling a deep breath, I said, "We've been traveling since your visit to Näkt Mir."

A lump thickened my throat, but the tears didn't come right away. Perhaps it was because I'd been mourning his imminent death for years, or perhaps because it had been so long since I'd actually spoken to the father I knew as a young girl. The one who'd do anything for me. Even rage a war against an entire realm of dark fae.

For whatever reason, I didn't crumble at this news. Father was dead, and I needed to mourn him. I needed to see his tomb, but I must see Baelynn first. "Where's my brother?"

"In his bedchamber." Athelyn clamped his jaw and whirled. He led us through the palace, what was once my home.

Soryn and Keffa followed close but at a respectful distance behind us. We'd left the majority of the Culled in the great hall where Hava had set about organizing the servants to bring drink and refreshment.

At first, everyone simply stared in awe and shock, for the last time the wraith fae had entered was to demand their war prize and take me away as their prisoner. However, it didn't take long before the servants quickly set about doing her bidding.

I felt the eyes of the Issosian guards and servants as we passed, all of them stopping where they were, staring in wonder, and dipping their heads in respect. I knew what they were thinking. Why would the Wraith King of Northgall let his concubine return to her former home to visit her brother? Why wasn't she bound in chains, high in the palace of black glass?

They did not know him. They did not know me either. Not anymore. But soon, the world would hear of us, the King and Queen of Northgall and Lumeria. Our union would change everything. I felt it in my soul. Just as I sensed this new magick coursing through my blood.

I'd been able to sense the black essence in Ferryn because the gods had been feeding me the opposite through the two god-touched texts I'd ingested. They'd given me a different kind of sight, one that now, with the power of all three inside me, allowed me to easily weigh what and who was good and evil.

I was no longer a moon fae. I was both light *and* dark, a creature somewhere in between the two. And I loved it. Our child would be, too. I pressed a palm to my belly as we walked the final few steps to my brother's bedchamber. Two Issosian guards stood at the door, one of them opening the door as soon as Athelyn nodded.

I was suddenly glad Gael had abandoned my brother. Athelyn had taken his role as steward with honor. Gael would not have done. I was sure of that.

Once inside, I rushed past Athelyn to my brother's bedside. The nursemaid dipped in a curtsy then hurried away. It was strange to see him laying so still in his bed. My brother had always been a male of action, of movement.

His eyes were closed. I sat on the edge of his bed and placed a hand on his arm. "Baelynn. Can you hear me?"

His face was a sickly pale, his beautiful white hair slick with sweat around his forehead and pointed ears. When he opened his eyes, I bit my lip to keep from making a sound. They were no longer a vibrant violet like mine but swallowed almost entirely with white. The plague had worked quickly on him.

"Una?" His brow furrowed. "I must be dreaming again."

"You are not," I assured him, taking his hand in mine and pressing a kiss to it before holding it to my cheek. "I'm here, brother."

His frown deepened in concern and confusion before his gaze slid over my shoulder where I could feel Goll standing. Soryn and Keffa had remained outside the bedchamber.

"You are truly here?" His face broke into a weak smile. "He allowed you to come say goodbye?"

My heart lurched at the thought of Baelynn being on death's doorstep. The disease had progressed so quickly through him, not like it had with our father. It seemed the mutation of the virus had increased in its aggression. Thank the gods, I now had the power to cure all those afflicted.

Baelynn's gaze returned to Goll. "Thank you for allowing her to come."

"I allowed nothing." Goll brushed my shoulder gently before letting his hand fall away. "As Queen of Northgall, she can do whatever she wants."

Baelynn was frowning again, his gaze flicking between us. "What is he talking about?" he asked me. "Queen?"

I nodded and sniffed to delay the tears coming. "It is true, brother."

Then he did something I didn't expect at all. He laughed. "Now I know I'm not dreaming. Only my headstrong sister could walk into Northgall a prisoner and make herself a queen."

I laughed with him, for he'd always said I was too headstrong for my own good, and my stubbornness would get me into trouble one day.

"I've come to help you, Baelynn."

"How?"

I gusted out a breath on a laugh. "That story is too long to tell right now. I simply need you to lie still."

"I can hardly do anything else, sister."

His sarcasm didn't suit him. He had always been the hopeful one, the one determined to find a way out of any situation. He had been sure we'd somehow win the war up until the moment they were in Issos and at our gates. Even then, he tried to convince me not to sign the treaty.

Smiling at him, I pressed both my palms to the linen shirt covering his chest. I didn't need to say any words of magick to summon it forward. It was always there now, brimming to the surface. I was bursting with healing magick.

Without a word, it flowed down my arms, through my fingers, and into Baelynn. He gasped, his mouth opening wide as he arched his neck, his eyes sliding closed. He pressed a hand over one of mine. An ethereal glow of green flowed from my fingertips into his body.

When I knew it was enough—I don't know how I knew, but I did—I removed my hands. He opened his eyes, both shining bright like purple gems.

"By the gods, Una. You can make miracles happen."

"No, brother. It is the gods' work, but I can heal all those sick with the plague."

I knew that was my purpose. And as the new Queen of Northgall, it would be the wife of the wraith king who healed both the light and the dark fae. Not the Princess of Issos. Somehow, I knew that was what Goddess Elska wanted. A fae in between light and dark to heal the sick, to wipe the lands clean of this plague. To start anew.

He struggled to sit up and get out of bed, not because he seemed weak but because the nurse had tucked him so thoroughly beneath the covers. I stood quickly, and Goll helped him to stand.

"Thank you," he said gratefully, then opened his arms to me.

I fell into his embrace, sighing with relief. We hugged for a moment, and then I heard him say again, "Thank you."

I pulled out of his hold, prepared to tell him there was no need to thank me. It was why I'd come and why I'd be journeying across Lumeria and then through Northgall to heal everyone of this terrible sickness. But he wasn't looking at me. He wasn't thanking me. He was staring at my husband.

Goll dipped his head in reply and then said, "I'll give you time alone and wait outside." He brushed his hand on my back, then left quietly.

"Baelynn?"

My brother turned back to me, having watched Goll leave with that frown on his face.

"How was father in the end?" I asked.

His expression softened with sadness. "The night he died, he did say your name."

"Oh, Baelynn." My heart plummeted that I hadn't been there to say my own goodbye.

"I lied to him," he said with a quirk of his lips. "I told him you were well married to a fine house and living happily away from Issos."

I smiled. "That wasn't a lie."

He blinked quickly, worry wrinkling his brow. "It wasn't?"

I shook my head. "I am very happy."

"Thank the gods." He embraced me again. "I'm sorry you weren't here in the end. But he went peacefully."

For a moment, I wondered if I could've helped him since he'd been so far gone from the disease. It had robbed him almost entirely of his speech and his ability to even walk long ago. I suppose I'd find out how well my healing magick worked as I sought out other victims.

But then I had the sad feeling that the gods didn't want my father to live, didn't want me to heal him. My father had loved me, but he had also sent Vaylamorganalyn away when she'd only told him the truth in her vision. She'd been sent to her death in the dungeons when another king had rejected her vision as well.

Vayla had been touched by the gods to deliver her message. For that, she'd been outcast and killed. And now both of those kings were dead. I couldn't help but know—and sadly agree—that there was justice in that.

My husband and king would not ignore the gods. Just as I would not. We would embrace their guidance as we stepped onto this new path together.

I gripped my brother on his upper arms so I could look at him and wrinkled my nose. "You need a bath."

"Pardon me for being so unkempt, sister, but I thought I was on my deathbed up until a few moments ago." He smiled, some color returning to his face.

I gave his shoulders a squeeze and then walked toward the door. "I'll call up a bath for you."

"Then I'll take you to see Father."

I stopped at the door and turned to look at him, his expression having returned to the austere one I was so accustomed to.

"I'm sorry, Una. If you suffered anything because of me, because of my failures."

He still didn't understand or fully believe that I was right where I was supposed to be.

"I suffered nothing at the hands of King Goll. You can put your mind to rest."

He finally smiled, and I let him dress so I could say my final goodbye to Father.

I'd placed a cluster of primrose on my father's tomb and had been standing outside the family crypt behind the palace for quite some time. Goll stood behind me, silently waiting. Silently supporting.

I'd cried all my tears for my Papa and wiped them all with the handkerchief that was once Goll's mother's. My father was the one who started a war he shouldn't have but he'd done it out of love for his daughter. And perhaps some selfishness and prejudice of his own. He wasn't perfect. But he was my father, and I loved him.

Dusk had settled. The moon was full and bright, glistening off the high towers of the palace. It always seemed brighter here at Valla Lokkyr. Perhaps because this was where Lumera's most devoted worshipers lived.

The familiar sounds of evening in Issos surrounded me. A night lark called to its mate with a whirling cry. The chirp and buzz of the seekie flies echoed in the garden, their glowing blue lights blinking prettily. And in the near distance, the sounds of Issos itself—laughter outside a tavern, the neighing of a horse, the rattle of a cart on the cobblestone street.

"I'm sorry we didn't make it in time for your father," Goll said softly, stepping up beside me and taking my hand.

"I am, too. But I've accepted it." I looked up at him. "But that's not what I was thinking about."

He pulled me to face him, cupping my jaw gently. "Tell me."

I slid my hands beneath his heavy cloak and around his waist, pressing my body against his. "I was thinking how familiar everything is here at Valla Lokkyr, but also so foreign."

He brushed the pad of his thumb across my cheekbone. "You haven't been away that long."

"But everything has changed." I smiled, noting the intensity of his gaze. Always, those dragon eyes watched me with such care. Not with only the hunger of a mate but with tenderness, too. "I miss Näkt Mir," I admitted. "I'm ready to go home."

His mouth slid into a smile. My heart raced faster as he dipped his mouth toward mine.

"Home," he whispered against my lips. "I like hearing you call Näkt Mir 'home.'"

"It is my home now," I confessed. "It reminds me of you. And wherever you are is my home."

At that, I held him tighter, pressing my body against his. He brushed his lips against the sliver of skin exposed above my cloak. "I can't imagine what I did to ever deserve you, but the gods better beware if they try to take you from me."

"Hush, Goll. They'll hear you and do something terrible."

He chuckled against my skin, tickling me. I laughed, too, then hummed with pleasure when his lips brushed softly, hotly up the column of my neck.

"One more day to visit with your brother, then we'll leave."

"Now you're concerned about me having quality time with my brother?" I pulled back to quirk a brow at him.

"Once I get you tucked away at home, you won't be leaving for quite some time."

The baby.

"And besides," he added soberly, "you still have some work to do before then."

"I do," I agreed, knowing we had a long road ahead before we'd be back in the comforts of Näkt Mir. The thought both invigorated and exhausted me.

But we still had tonight.

"Come," I told him, taking his hand and leading him back toward the palace. "I'd like to sleep with you in my old bedchamber."

"Will we be sleeping?"

I peered over my shoulder at him. "Not much."

He swept me up into his arms. "Point the way, my mizrah."

I loved it the most when he called me his mizrah now. A term I'd once thought equaled my enslavement was not that at all. Vix's Mizrah had been his most precious partner in life. That was what I was to Goll, and me to him.

I wrapped my arms around his neck. "I'd like to forget about everyone and everything else for a little while."

"I can help you forget," he rumbled in that lusciously dark voice of his, sending a tendril of heat straight to my core.

I lay my head on his chest, content that for tonight, we could tuck ourselves away from the world—from all that had happened and from all the responsibilities awaiting us. Tonight, it would be just us.

EPILOGUE
Goll

I couldn't take my eyes off him. After two full months, I was still helplessly enamored with our newborn son. His complexion was a paler gray than mine, and he had no wings. I could see the tiny nubs of his first two horns beneath the skin and cap of black hair.

But his eyes. They came from his mother—a bright indigo, like the color of twilight at the edge of night. His pupils were slit vertically like mine and a tiny core of gold encircled them. There was also a lock of silver-white hair streaking through the black on one side.

He gurgled, reaching his chubby hand up. I let him grab my finger. When he squeezed, I felt it all the way to my heart.

"Strong little grip, Malcus."

He cooed as if he understood me. Rising from the window seat of our bedchamber at Windolek, I told him, "Let's go find your mother." Though I was sure I knew where she was.

Taking the spiral staircase in the corridor, I climbed up to the battlement, and there she was, overlooking the eastern field of wildflowers now in full bloom. Malcus had been born at the height of spring, and now the wildflowers bloomed in bright profusion around the entirety of Windolek.

Pullo and Stanos stood nearby at attention. Stanos was one of the newest members of the Kel Klyss. We'd needed to recruit following our return and after our losses on our journey. Stanos was haughty and young. I'd put Pullo in charge of teaching him the ropes of the Culled in the hope that a new purpose might help him after the loss of Tierzel. Apparently, I'd been right since the two of them had been seen carousing in Belladum every night they had off.

While I wasn't sure Pullo drowning his sorrows in wenches and ale was the best solution, it was better than him moping in guilt all alone every night. For that was what Keffa had told me he'd been doing after we returned to Näkt Mir. He'd thought it was his fault for not seeing the traitor amongst us.

I'd told him that the fault was all mine. But he rejected my words and refused to accept my apology, saying it wasn't my fault that evil had rooted itself in what should have been my loyal guard. I'd told him it was not his either. Shortly after, the new recruits joined us, and Pullo had finally begun to break out of his deep mourning.

I gave them a nod as I passed where they stood guard, close enough to handle a threat, but far enough for privacy.

When we left Valla Lokkyr on our journey to heal the fae afflicted with the plague, Pullo had fallen into the role of guardian to the new Queen of Northgall. He hadn't asked, but simply took ownership of her safety. Then he roped in his newest friend, Stanos. I'd simply given him a nod of approval. The Kel Klyss were all as devoted to their queen as they were to me. Their allegiance and loyalty warmed my soul.

"I knew I'd find you here," I said, standing beside her.

Her gaze instantly went to her son, a smile curling her mouth. "Let me have him."

He thrashed his arms at the sight of his mother, trying to get to her. I smiled, knowing that feeling very well. I handed him over and then wrapped my arm around her waist, pulling them both close.

She wrapped the blanket more tightly and tucked him close, his mouth opening like it was feeding time. "He can't be hungry already."

"I believe he can. He eats like a little monster."

"Like a dragon," she corrected.

But Malcus seemed content at the moment, staring up at his beautiful mother with nothing but adoration in his dark violet eyes. I glanced out at the blooming field, the wind gusting the tall wildflowers in a soft breeze.

"I'm happy you wanted to come here," I told her. "I wasn't sure you'd ever want to return here again."

"I didn't want *that* to be my last memory of this place."

She cradled Malcus while he wrapped a tight fist around her finger. He seemed to always be grabbing for things. I'd have to watch him carefully as he grew.

"I didn't either," I agreed softly, pressing my lips to her hair.

"This was your mother's sanctuary and home. I wanted that spirit to remain here."

I'd ensured that any trace of the wights or of Ferryn had been well-cleaned before we arrived. I'd also hired new servants, and they'd put the castle back to rights, cleaning and dusting the halls until they were sparkling like new. New linens, drapes, bedding, and rugs had restored it to its early glory.

But even so, there might have been a lingering of the evil energy of what had happened here before. When Drak had delivered us here that first day, I'd waited to see if Una felt it still living here. But she'd only looked up at me with joy before she greeted her smiling housekeeper, a wood fae who'd been living in the Borderlands and leaped at the opportunity to run the house for the moon fae queen.

My wife had ensured there was a mixture of both dark and light fae working in harmony at Windolek. She'd told me she wanted to show the world that we could all live in happiness together. And so far, she'd been right.

We realized quickly she wouldn't be able to heal every person with the plague one by one, but she'd infused the moon vessels—those expensive healing instruments created in Issos—with her healing energy. Then we sent the Culled out to every village across Lumeria, delivering the healing orbs.

That alone had taken much of her energy, but she was able to rest and replenish at Näkt Mir. She'd spent her days filling vessels, and we'd spent our evenings taking walks in Esher Wood. Until one night, she looked up at me beneath the moonlight, her hand on her full, rounded belly and said, "It's time to go to Windolek. Our child is coming."

Malcus gurgled again when I peered over his mother's shoulder at him. "He's a happy child."

"Of course, he is." She kissed him between the two horn nubs on his forehead. "He is well loved, and he knows it."

"He'll be ridiculously spoiled. Keffa, and even Soryn, can't seem to stop wanting to hold him."

"None of the Culled can." Una laughed. "Not to mention Hava."

"Hava," I repeated with a sigh. "Gods save us. I believe she's obsessed."

She laughed again. "Look at him. Can you blame her? He's so handsome. Aren't you?" she asked the little bundle. "I think she may want one of her own."

"Hava?" I tried to imagine it. "She doesn't even have a mate."

Una arched a brow up at me. "She has her eye on someone, though."

"Who?" I asked, trying to remember if I'd seen her with anyone.

"Keffa." Una grinned.

"No." I laughed. "That can't be."

"Look at the way she watches him. And I've seen Keffa give her a few lingering looks as well."

Keffa had doted on Hava ever since Ferryn had knocked her out. I thought it was simply his natural inclination to protect. Perhaps I was wrong.

"It would be good for him," I admitted.

"And her," added Una. "I think the fields below would make a beautiful site for a ceremony," said Una, pointing with a finger now that Malcus had let it go, his eyes blinking sleepily. "Right down there at sunset would be perfect. Oh, look at that little blue bird teasing Drakmir." She laughed.

Drak had taken up permanent residence in the purple fields, seeming to not want to leave Una's side since the incident with Ferryn. I smiled down at the bird flitting around his head. He huffed a breath, and the tiny creature dodged and dove sharply, pecking him on the snout. He rumbled a growl in warning.

I squinted at the creature. "I don't think that's a bird."

"It's coming this way."

On instinct, I stepped in front of Una and Malcus, deeming anything a threat until I was sure it was not. The tiny blue creature zipped straight up for us and only slowed when I raised my palm, ready to shoot it down with feyfire if it attacked.

It flapped its wings to float in place in front of us. It was a wood sprite. Her miniature feminine form was covered in downy feathers up over her breasts, her feet ending in sharp black talons. Instead of arms, she had bird-like wings, tipped black, and her feather-capped head had wispy feathers that curled at the neck. Her round black eyes shone with bright intelligence.

"Hello," said Una.

She had a sense for things now since she'd swallowed the gods' magick. She could feel when a creature was good or evil. I relaxed since she seemed at ease.

"Greetings, pretty queen," the sprite said in common demon tongue, "and deadly king." She blinked those round, black eyes at me. "I am Gwendazelle."

"What business do you have here, sprite?"

She dipped a curtsy midair, reminding me of those water sprites at Dragul Falls. Thank the gods, she was much more even-tempered.

"My master bid me come to you."

"And who is your master?" I asked sharply, needing to know who had sent this strange messenger rather than an emissary.

"Lord Vallon of House Hennowyn."

The shadow fae priest.

"What message does your master send?" asked Una.

"He would like permission to visit you here at Windolek Castle. He knows you are protective of your queen and the wee one, so he sends me ahead."

"He could've come himself and presented at the gate," I told her.

She squeaked and blinked her dark eyes. "No, no. He has a hostage with him. He must be certain. And..." She flew closer and whispered, "He wants you to keep it a secret."

"From whom?" I asked.

"From Prince Torvyn, of course."

Very strange. He was entirely devoted to his prince. Or, at least, he had been.

"And who is this hostage?" asked Una, concern in her voice.

The wood sprite blinked those dark eyes, as if wondering if she should tell us. Then she finally answered, "I cannot say. But she's very, very pretty. And nice, too," she added as an afterthought.

"Tell them to come right away," Una said before I could.

Gwendazelle chirped then zipped away in a southeasterly direction, away from the Solgavia Mountains. He must not be in Gadlizel with his hostage then.

"What in all the world could that be about?" asked Una. "And the loyal Vallon hiding a hostage from the shadow fae prince? A female?"

"Indeed." I looked toward the peaks of the Solgavia Mountains where a storm gathered, black clouds billowing. "Let's get you both inside. And prepare for our visitor."

"Visitors, plural, you mean," Una added. "I wonder what Vallon is up to."

"I suppose we'll know soon enough."

A foreboding washed over me as I wrapped an arm around Una and guided her along the battlement. Pullo and Stanos followed behind us. Right as we took our first steps down the stairwell, a rumble of thunder followed us, warning of the coming storm.

Thank you for reading book one in THE RISE OF NORTHGALL.
An enchanting novella following the shadow fae Vallon and
the seer Murgha is available now in KINGS AND BONES.
Book two, THE BEAST LORD, will be released this fall, 2025.